HEARTLESS

Kaye

Heartless (Previously Titled "Heartbreaker: Luvin' a Savage 1-3") © 2020. By Kirsten D. Bailey (DBA Kaye)

Acknowledgments

As always, I thank God for giving me the talent and ability to write these crazy stories. Always remember people, that anything is possible if you believe and trust in Him.

To my family, I thank you for your continued support. No matter where you are in the world, I love you. To the love of my life, thank you for always pushing me and holding me accountable. To my children, I do this for you.

Last but not least, the readers. I deeply appreciate every last one of you. It goes without saying that you all are the reason that I am able to do this.

Thank you all for your continued support, enjoy the book, and as always, I wish you lots of Kitty Kisses!!!

Author's Note:

This is a new and revised version of the previously published works, "Heartbreaker: Luvin' a Savage 1-3". Due to prior publishing issues, all rights to publish have been released to that of the original author, Kaye. Although previously published, please note that there are revisions, new scenes, and additions for you the reader to enjoy.

Preface

“9-1-1, what's your emergency?”

“Help me, please! Help!” the girl screamed.

“Okay, I want to help. I need you to calm down,” she said. “What's your name?”

“Miracle. But—it’s—it’s my daddy. Please, you have to send an ambulance now!” she urged.

Tears blurred her vision and the operator could barely make out the words of the young girl, her cries were so strong.

“Okay, Miracle. Now, sweetie, I need you to calm down. Can you tell me the address?”

“Yes. It's 1821 Thomas Place,” she recited slowly.

“Okay, good sweetheart. You’re doing good. An ambulance is in route to you right now,” the operator assured her, rapidly inputting the information. “But I need you to tell me what happened.”

“I don't know,” the girl sobbed hysterically. “Everything happened so fast. There's blood everywhere. It’s…people are…it’s people dead on the ground. I just heard gunshots and…my…my… my daddy jumped on me and the next thing I know, he's laying here bleeding to death. Daddy! Please stay awake! Please, somebody help me!” The girl continued to scream.

“Ok, Miracle, I promise you, somebody is coming honey. Just hold on a little bit longer. What's your daddy's name?” the operator inquired.

Her heart was breaking hearing the young girl crying for her daddy. She prayed that the ambulance made it in time to save the girls father.

“Miracle, can you tell me how old you are?” she continued, typing the information into the system.

“I'm seventeen. I turned seventeen today,” the girl managed, her eyes on her father.

“Okay, honey. I’m here with you. Help is on the way,” she paused, already knowing the answer to her next question. “Can you tell me if anyone else is hurt?”

“It’s people on the ground not moving,” the girl responded looking around her at the bodies. “Somebody just…they just started shooting. My daddy’s bleeding. It won’t stop.”

“Do you know where he was shot?”

“He has two holes in his chest!” the girl looked. “Oh God. Daddy, please! Please stay with me. Daddy, please don't leave me. Please hurry!” the girl continued to scream.

“Help is on the way, honey. Help is on the way,” the operator assured her. “Stay with me sweetheart.”

She could hear the girl crying and praying as she tried to hold it together to do her job. She was used to taking calls like the one she had, and could get through them with ease but, it was something about the pain and fear in the girl’s voice that was different.

The operator breathed easy hearing the sirens in the distance, but the sound of the girls screams pierced her to the core.

“Daddy? Daddy? No!”

Chapter One

"DJ Mob on the ones and twos! Everybody turn up! Y'all, the party is live! The birthday girl, Miracle, is in the building! Let me hear y'all scream happy seventeenth birthday!"

"Happy seventeenth birthday!" the room erupted in screams.

I stood in the middle of the room and everybody around me was screaming and shouting "happy birthday". I looked up to see my father standing at the top of the stairs looking down, and grinning from ear to ear. The party was poppin'! I couldn't believe how many people showed up. Almost everyone in the school was there and I was loving it. Daddy had hired one of the hottest DJs from one of the biggest night clubs in Dallas, and of course he made sure that the birthday girl was looking fly. Everybody expected me, Miracle Davis, to be the baddest chic in the room, so I definitely wasn't going to disappoint.

I had the Remi Indian weave in and my hair was snatched. And even though Daddy didn't like it, my face was beat to the gawds, complementing my sexy mocha skin! My outfit was Gucci from head to toe, with some bad ass red bottoms on my feet. Needless to say, I was the shit! I was so happy. If he did all of this for me on my seventeenth birthday, there was no telling what he would do on my next birthday.

I looked over to see my best friend, Myesha, dancing with one of the niggas from my class. Her ex-boyfriend, Wood, was standing to the side muggin' the shit out of him. Myesha was over there poppin' her ass with a banging ass outfit on and her hair flowing down her back. She looked like a younger Black Chyna to me. I don't even think she noticed that Wood was staring at her. I will give it to her though. She knew how to get attention. She was working on the dance floor like she was in a Lil Wayne video. The boy that she was dancing with looked like he was ready to bust a nut right there on the dance floor. I laughed and turned my attention back to the friends that were closer to me.

I mingled with everybody, while the DJ continued to mix it up. He started to play Beyonce's "Get Me Bodied", and every girl in the room lost her mind. I moved to the center of the floor with Myesha running to catch up with me, and everybody cleared the way so that me and my girls could get it on the dance floor. Me and Myesha both were on the dance team in school and we always gave a show.

Ladies on the floor, all my ladies on the floor,

if you ready, get it ready, let's get it and drop it.

Drop down low and sweep the floor wit it

Drop, drop down low and sweep the floor wit it,

Drop down low and sweep the floor wit it

Drop, drop down low and sweep the floor wit it.

I looked to my right and my girl, Myesha, was right there with me, swinging her weave. All the guys stood to the side and watched us take control of the dance floor. My father had disappeared from watching, so I figured he was probably running around the house to make sure everything was good.

The speakers blared as we all strutted on the floor like we were on the runway. I smiled when I saw Lamar gazing at me. I gave him a little wink and a pose for the camera like I was featured in a magazine. The song ended and everybody cheered.

"Give it up for the birthday girl!" the DJ yelled in the microphone.

Everybody hollered and clapped, and I was beaming. I walked over to Lamar and gave him a hug.

"Hey. I didn't know if I was going to see you here," I said.

"Why'd you think that, boo? You know I had to come see you on your special day," he told me. "Happy birthday," he said as he kissed my lips.

My mocha face flushed and I moved away quick in case my daddy was watching. Lamar was fine and all, but my daddy didn't play. Looking at Lamar up close, I felt something that I never felt before. Almost everything in my body was screaming. For a second, I thought I had peed myself because I was so wet down there. This boy was fine as hell!

Something told me that I was being watched so I backed away from him.

"You good?" he asked, looking confused.

"Yeah, I'm good," I answered, playing it cool. "But you know my pops probably lurking around here somewhere. And last time he saw you, remember, he damn near killed you."

"True," he said. "But I'm saying though, your daddy ain't here now, is he?" he asked.

"Oh, he's here, but he's probably upstairs with my godfather," I told him.

"Okay then, cool," he smiled. "So, why don't you walk with me outside really quick."

"What's up?" I asked him, a little cautious.

"Just come on. I got something for you," he told me.

I took his hand and followed his lead. Everything in me was praying that my father didn't see me at that moment.

"I see you, girl," Myesha cooed.

I looked over at her and gave her the "bitch be quiet" look. She smirked and turned her attention back to J.B., the same guy that she was dancing with earlier, who was practically stuck to her like a second layer of skin. I walked outside with Lamar and he led me over to the side of the house.

"Ummm...what the hell are we doing over here? Why are we on the side of the house?" I asked, confused.

He looked down and gripped my hand tighter.

"Check this out, yo," he started. "I know that you probably ain't really feeling me like that, but I wanted you to know that I've been feeling you for a while. Like, I want you to be my girl. I know I ain't living like this or nothing," he said, pointing to the large five-bedroom house with a three-car garage. "And, I mean, I know you got a lot of niggas tryna' get at you, but I'm feeling you," he confessed.

That damn wet feeling returned in my panties, and quick.

"I'm feeling you too, Lamar. But you know what the deal is. My daddy ain't really tryna hear about me having no boyfriend," I told him. "He wants me focused on getting ready for college next year."

"Well, we don't have to tell him," he hinted. "I mean, it's not like we going to be doing anything that can get you in trouble." I smiled at his suggestive tone. "I just want you to be my girl. You're fine as hell, you're smart, and you're not like the other girls out here."

"What do you mean?" I asked.

"Well, I mean, some of these other hoes, all they're out here trying to do is have all these boyfriends, and see who can give them what. Like your home girl, Myesha. Every time I turn around, she got different niggas she fucking with and she getting these niggas for all they got. But you're not like that. Like, you are real cool. So, I'm saying," he told me.

I wanted to cuss his ass out for tryna play my best friend, but I felt so dizzy and my stomach was doing jumping jacks. I couldn't even think straight.

"Soooo, what does me being your girl mean? You saying you not tryna do nothing, but I heard about you. So, what's the deal? What do you want?" I asked.

Word around school was that Lamar liked fucking the baddest bitches for sport. He would date a chick and then once he got the pussy, he would dump them. But him standing here in front of me, he didn't seem that way.

"Whatever you want," he answered. "I mean hell, just calling you my girl, I'm good."

Shit. I damn sure wanted to. But, I didn't want him to think I was some easy fuck. If he did try something, I could break up with him. And he already knew my daddy was crazy. He saw that first hand when we had a party at the crib when my daddy came home early and saw me sitting in Lamar's lap. He damn near broke his neck. I'm seventeen. Daddy can't always keep me on a leash.

"Okay," I agreed. "But, we just have to be careful 'cause if my Daddy finds out, then I'm in trouble," I warned him.

"I feel you. So, can a boyfriend get a kiss from his girlfriend?" he asked in a whisper.

My heart started pounding and my face once again flushed.

"I guess," I answered, tryna play it cool.

He pulled me to him and put his lips on mine. His kisses tasted like grape Now & Laters. I never really kissed anybody before, so I let him do everything and tried to mimic what he was doing. A few seconds later, I felt his hand on my butt and I heard someone giggle. I jumped to see Myesha standing there smirking like she was my mama or something.

"Excuse me," she interrupted. "But, Miracle, your daddy is looking for you. So you better hurry up and get your ass in that house before he sees you over here kissing this nigga and flip the hell out," she joked.

"Oh shit!" I shrieked, breaking Lamar's hold and running towards the door.

I licked my lips instinctively and she laughed.

"I see you," she said.

"What?" I asked, trying to maintain composure.

"Girl, if I had come any later, you probably would have ended up pregnant," she joked, laughing hard.

"Shut up, Myesha," I said.

My insides were fluttery as I thought about Lamar's delicious kiss. I walked inside and saw my father and godfather, Goody, standing in the middle of the floor, holding a huge box, while everyone stood around talking and watching.

"Well, there's the birthday girl," he announced. "Where did you disappear to?"

"Oh. I just went outside for a second," I told him.

Lamar walked in and my dad frowned.

"Uh huh," he said, eyeballing him.

He gave me a look that let me know I was going to hear about it later, but because my friends were there, he let it go.

"So, what's in the box?" I asked, trying to change the subject and get his mind off of Lamar.

"Well, birthday girl," he said smiling. "Your godfather got you a little something for your birthday."

“What?” I inquired.

I was racking my brain trying to figure out what it could be. He and my dad had already thrown me this party, and me and my friends had tickets to go see Beyoncé in concert as a gift from the two of them, so I didn't know what else could top that. I giggled as I ran over to the box and opened it up. Everyone in the room had grown quiet as they waited for me to pull out the gift to display.

I reached inside the box and pulled out a very gorgeous Louis Vuitton bag and make-up caboodle. My face showed confusion as I examined it and set it down.

“A bag?” I asked.

“Yes, a bag,” he repeated. “Don't sound so ungrateful.”

My godfather laughed

“I'm not,” I argued. “I’m sorry. Thank you. I was just trying to figure out why you got me this. I have some like it upstairs,” I said.

He laughed again.

“Why don't you open up the bag? I think that there's something in there that you might like,” my daddy suggested.

I giggled, knowing that my father was up to something. I opened up the bag as he requested and found a small envelope on the inside with a car key sticking out.

To my baby girl, Miracle, from your father.

I looked at my father who stood next to my godfather, both smiling a mile wide.

“Thank you, Daddy!” I squealed. “Oh my God, a car!”

He laughed and nodded his head.

“Well, you know I wasn't about to give you this big party and not have a grand gift, baby girl,” he smiled. “But the car has rules. You have to keep your grades up and no boys,” he stressed, looking right at Lamar.

“Okay. I won’t. Where is it?” I screamed.

He pointed to the back door and I took off towards it. I opened the door to see a brand new, white 2013 Mercedes C300, parked with a large red bow.

I ran over to my father and gave him the biggest hug. I looked over at Myesha and she was excited. She already knew she was going to be shotgun so she didn’t have any worries. All of my other friends were looking at me, some with happiness and some with envy. I was so excited I thought I was going to burst.

“Thank you so much, Daddy!” I repeated, squeezing him tight.

“You’re welcome, baby girl. Now, it’s used and got a little over 15,000 miles on it, but it’s yours. Just don’t forget what I said, okay?” he warned.

I giggled at his idea of me actually dropping my grades. I had a 4.0 practically my whole life and was going to Howard University. He wanted me to go to an Ivy League school, but I was determined.

“Yes, sir,” I agreed.

“Alright now. Let’s get back to the party,” my father ordered. All of my friends walked back inside and my father spoke into the wireless mic that was in his hand. “DJ, go ahead and get the music going,” he yelled.

The DJ started spinning again and everyone went back to dancing. Myesha ran up and hugged me.

“Girl! Your daddy is too much,” she laughed.

“This is the best birthday ever,” I sighed. “I can't believe my dad did all of this.”

I wanted to go find my father so that I could thank him for making my birthday special. I looked around and once again, he had disappeared out of sight. I figured he disappeared to his office so I headed in that direction, only to find he wasn’t there either. I stood by his desk for a few minutes and could hear talking outside. I looked out the window and he and my god father were discussing something. I don't know what it was, but the look that he had on his face was saying that it was something serious.

Everything in me was saying to go back to the party, but there was a strange feeling in my gut. I went downstairs and I told Myesha that I would be right back and headed to the front door.

“Hey, Daddy,” I smiled, walking up on him.

He and my godfather Goody immediately stopped talking when they saw me.

“Hey, baby girl,” he said, changing his tone.

“Is everything okay?” I asked with an uneasy feeling, once again.

“Why wouldn’t it be?” he answered. When he saw I wasn’t satisfied, he gave me a warm smile. “Of course. Everything is fine.”

“Daddy. No, it's not. I saw you a minute ago and you looked mad. What's going on?” I pressed.

“Nothing for you to worry about, baby girl,” he promised. “All I want you to worry about is having fun on your birthday.”

I smiled, still a little worried, but I let it go for the time being. I knew he was lying, but as long as he was there, I was fine.

"And I am. Thank you, Daddy, so much for this party. I love you," I said hugging him.

He squeezed me back.

"I love you too, baby girl," he whispered.

"What? A godfather can't get no love?" Goody spoke up.

I laughed and went to give him a hug. I didn't notice the black delivery truck that had parked until I heard someone else's voice.

"Hey, uh... I have a delivery," the young boy said. He couldn't have been more than seventeen or eighteen.

My father looked at him and frowned.

"What delivery? And how'd you get past the front gate?" he questioned.

"Um, the uh…the guard let me in. And it's a delivery for a… Miracle Davis," he answered, looking down at a paper.

My father looked at him strangely like he didn't believe him.

"My guard just doesn't let anybody in without calling me. And, I'm looking at my phone and I don't see any calls," he said, looking at his cell. "And, I know I ain't order no flowers."

"Aye, look, man. I don't know about all that, I just know I got the delivery here. I'm just tryna' do my job," the boy responded.

Goody pushed me towards the door.

"Miracle, go inside," he said.

I looked at Goody's face and back at my father. They both looked very angry. I opened my mouth to say something but Goody pushed me towards the door again.

I walked back towards the door with a very scared feeling.

"Did you order flowers?" I heard my father ask my godfather.

I turned to see him reaching for the back of his pants as if he already knew the answer. Goody moved closer to the boy.

"Nope. Didn't order any," he answered.

My father, realizing I was still watching, looked at me and his eyes were the darkest I had ever seen them.

"Go inside. Now," he ordered.

Before I knew what was happening, the door opened to the side of the truck. While my father was looking at me, a man jumped out and started shooting. I screamed and ran towards him.

"Daddy!" I yelled.

I watched my father run towards me as the bullets ripped holes through his body. He kept running even though the shots continued.

"Daddy!" I screamed again.

Goody pulled out his gun and began shooting. I screamed over and over as I heard the bullets flying around me. My father reached for me and threw himself on top of me, knocking me to the ground. I could hear the kids inside the party screaming and looked to see them hitting the floor. I would have given anything to be inside. I looked over to see my father struggling to breathe. Goody shot the young boy that had spoke to my father and the truck sped off, still shooting bullets at any and everything. I was scared to move after the truck left.

"Miracle!" I heard Goody calling out to me. "You okay?" He asked as he rushed to me.

I tried to move from underneath my father.

"Daddy!" I kept screaming. "Somebody shot my daddy!"

Goody grabbed my father, who was gasping for air, and pulled him off me.

"Come on, man. Come on, not like this," he groaned. "Come on, bro."

Once I got feeling back in my legs, I jumped up, running inside and grabbing my phone. Kids were on the floor crying as I dialed 911. I ran back outside to be next to my father. I could see him slipping away and I was losing it.

"Daddy, please don't leave me," I begged, listening to the automated voice. "Please, Daddy. Please stay with me."

I grabbed his hand and squeezed, praying to God that He wouldn't take the one parent I had left from me.

"9-1-1, what's your emergency?"

"Help me, please! Help!" I screamed into the phone.

"Okay. Calm down," she said. "What's your name?"

"Miracle Davis. It's my daddy. Please, you have to send an ambulance quickly!" I begged.

The operator could barely make out what I was saying. I sounded so flustered.

"Okay, sweetie, I need you to calm down. Now, can you tell me your address?"

"Yes. It's 1821 Thomas Place," I replied.

"Okay, good. I'm sending an ambulance in route to you right now," the operator responded. "Now can you tell me what happened?"

"I don't know," I cried. "Everything happened so fast. There's blood everywhere. People are lying on the ground and bleeding and…my…my… my daddy jumped on me and the next thing I know, he's laying here bleeding to death. Daddy, please don't leave me! Please, somebody help me!" I continued to scream.

I could see my father leaving me as his grip on my hand became weak. Goody was trying to pull me away but I was fighting him.

"Ok. Miracle, I need you to focus, honey. What's your daddy's name?" the operator inquired.

I just kept blubbering uncontrollably.

"Miracle, can you tell me how old you are?" The operator asked.

"I'm seventeen. I turned seventeen today," I sobbed.

"Okay, honey. It's okay. Help is on the way," the operator paused. "Can you tell me if anyone else is hurt?"

"Everyone is laying down," I told her what I was seeing. "My daddy is bleeding. I think…I mean… he was shot," I answered.

"Okay. How do you know he was shot?" the operator asked.

What the fuck did she mean how did I know he was shot?

"He has two holes in his chest!" I yelled into the phone. "Oh God. Daddy, please! Please stay with me. Daddy, please don't leave me. Somebody help!" I cried, as I heard the sirens in the distance.

"Help is on the way, honey. Help is on the way," the operator assured me.

I looked down and my daddy's eyes were blank and lifeless.

"Daddy! Daddy, no!" I bawled, as the world went dark.

*****

I could hear the police officer talking to me, but it seemed like such a bad dream. He was looking at me and I could see his mouth moving, but I couldn't focus. Did he say what I think he said? Is my father really dead? I tried to rationalize what I was hearing as the officer tried to talk to me.

"I'm really sorry," I heard.

I just couldn't wrap my head around my father being dead.

"I was just talking to him," I whispered. "He was right here."

The officer looked at me in my clothes covered in my father's blood and shook his head. He looked so sympathetic. He called one of his partners over and they tried to speak to me.

"Can you tell me what happened?" the officer asked.

I looked up in a daze.

"They shot my daddy," I answered meekly.

Everything around me was a blur. I watched parents coming to pick their kids up and all of them looking at me as if I were an exhibit at a museum.

"I'm so sorry, Miracle," I kept hearing over and over.

"I told y'all that her daddy was dangerous. I figured it would happen sooner or later," I heard one of the parents say.

"Let's take her inside," the officer suggested.

I watched as the coroner covered my father up with a sheet. We walked inside of the house and I tried to make sense of everything.

"Now, we know that you just experienced something very traumatic," the officer stated. "But, I really need you to try to remember everything that happened. Can you do that for me?" he asked.

I fought back tears as I nodded my head.

"Okay, good. Now, can you tell me what you remember?" he asked.

"I went up to my daddy's office and I saw him and my godfather were talking from the window. I don't know why, but something told me to go down there. So, when I went outside, him and my godfather were talking and then they just stopped," I told him.

"Okay," the officer soothed. "You're doing good. What else?"

"We were talking about the birthday party and this truck pulled up. They said that they had a flower delivery for me. I thought my dad had gotten me flowers because he bought me all of this other stuff for my birthday," I said.

"Uh huh," the officer mumbled, jotting down some notes. "What did the truck look like?"

"It was dark," I told him, not remembering much. "I think it was a dark blue, but it could have been black. It was an Expedition."

"Were there any signs or anything on the truck?" he inquired.

"No," I answered. "Which I thought was weird because if it was a delivery truck, you would think he would have a sign or something," I murmured.

"You're absolutely right," the officer agreed. "What else did you see?"

I swallowed hard as I relived one of the most traumatic experiences of my life.

"This boy got out. He looked like he was a teenager. He said that he had a delivery for me. That was when my father said that he didn't order any flowers. My daddy asked my godfather did he order any and Goody said no. The next thing I know…" I trailed off.

"Miracle?" the officer said, looking up from his notes.

"They shot him," I choked. "They shot my daddy. Oh God, they shot my daddy! My daddy's dead!" I wailed.

Goody came from outside and swooped me in his arms.

"It's okay, baby," he said. "I'm here. It's okay."

"Why did they kill my daddy, Goody?" I cried. "Why'd they shoot my daddy?"

"I don't know," he answered as he held onto me. "But I'm going to find out."

"Sir, we understand the stress that is on you right now," the officer interjected. "But I am going to need to ask you some questions as well."

"Can't it wait?" Goody asked. "Right now, I need to get my goddaughter out of here," he told them.

"Of course," the officer agreed. "But, I need you to contact us ASAP. We have four dead bodies," he pushed.

"Four?" Goody asked, and we both looked at the officer. "I thought it was three."

The only bodies I knew were my daddy and the boy.

"No," the officer disputed. "We got a guard at the front gate that's dead as well. So, right now we have four. I understand that right now may not be the best time considering… but we really need to speak with you," he said, handing him his card.

"All right," Goody agreed, taking the card and putting it in his pocket.

He and I left out of the house and walked to the car. I got inside the passenger seat and looked out the window at the array of officers and crime scene investigators all over what I have known as my home for so many years.

"Miracle, look at me," Goody said. "I'm gonna find out who did this, okay?" he vowed. "I promise you I will."

I looked at him with an empty feeling, hearing the words coming out of his mouth but not processing.

"I want my daddy," I whispered.

"I know," he said. "I know. You can't stay in the house. You're going to come stay with me for a couple of days. Okay, kiddo?" he told me.

I nodded my head and lay back against the headrest, too tired to say anything else. I watched as the man put my father on a stretcher and wheeled him to the coroner's van. Tears silently fell down my face as we pulled away and I left my father.

*****

Chapter Two

"Here you go, baby," Aunt Tori said, handing me a plate. "How are you feeling this morning?" she asked.

I hated it when people asked dumb ass questions like that. *How the fuck do you think I feel?* I wanted to scream. *My daddy was just murdered in cold blood, in front of me. How am I supposed to feel about that?* Instead, I just chose to remain silent. I sat in the kitchen of my godfather's house with his wife, my aunt Tori.

"Look, Miracle, I know this is hard for you right now," Goody started. "I don't know what happened yesterday. I don't know how they got in. I don't know who those niggas are, but best believe, I'm gonna find out if it's the last thing I do. Best believe that, baby girl. I…baby girl, I am so sorry," he apologized.

I looked up at him with fresh tears in my eyes and saw the pain in his.

"I should have been there to protect your father," he said.

It was then that I remembered the conversation that my father and uncle were having before I came out there.

"What were you and Daddy talking about before I came outside?" I asked.

Goody looked confused, as if he was unsure of what I was talking about. Goody had damn near an eidetic memory, so I knew he knew the conversation that I was talking about. He was playing stupid and I wasn't feeling that shit at all.

"You shouldn't be worried about that right now," he told me after a few minutes, and walked to the refrigerator.

"You can't just tell me something like that, Goody. My daddy was shot right there in front of me at my birthday party,

MINUTES after you and him were having some heated conversation. And I'm just supposed to act like nothing's going on? He wasn't shot for nothing," I cried out, my voice raising a little. "Now, what were y'all talking about?"

He walked around and sat down next to me, grabbing my hand.

"Look, Miracle, I promise you that this is all going to make sense at some point. Your dad didn't want you to be involved in certain stuff that was going on," he tried to reason.

"What do you mean this is gonna make sense at some point?" I snapped, pulling my hand away. "Ain't nothing gonna make sense! It's never going to make sense why my father died. He was taken from me! One minute y'all are standing outside talking and then the next minute, somebody just starts shooting at my father and kills him. That is NEVER going to make sense. I really wish you would stop talking to me like I'm some kid. I'm seventeen years old. I know more than you think I do. You don't think I knew that my father was dealing with more than just the restaurant? Huh?" I demanded. "I'm not stupid. I know that all those times he would be gone and handling business, he wasn't just going to the restaurant. I already know that he was still dealing drugs. I already know that he still has a few warehouses. So, what's going on?" I asked him again.

"Miracle, listen to me," he said sternly. "Your dad was taking care of you. That's what matters."

I was getting really tired of people trying to protect my feelings. I had been hidden from the truth for as long as I could remember. My father was the only stable parent that I had since I was three years old. I had literally been around drugs my whole life. My mother died of an overdose when I was three years old and my father had been taking care of me ever since. He would always tell me how much my mother loved me and how she just had too many demons that she was dealing with, but no matter how far he took me out the hood, the streets still talked. I learned a lot about him without him even knowing.

My father claimed to have gotten out the game after my mama died, but I wasn't stupid. I knew that he was still dealing. The way we were living, he had to be. He was just smarter with it because he and my godfather had started to invest money in other ventures. They had a few restaurants, a recording studio, and even a nightclub in Richardson.

I saw a lot of things and I never questioned them. But, now that my father was dead, the gloves were off and I didn't care. I needed to know.

"Obviously, it didn't matter enough because somebody killed him. And you're going to sit here and tell me that nothing was going on?" I barked.

I was angry and tears were welling in my eyes but I wasn't going to cry. I wanted answers.

"He was still dealing, wasn't he?" I asked.

"What?" he replied.

"You heard me," I answered slowly. "I know daddy used to be heavy in the game. And I know you still in it, which means he is...was, too. He was still in the game. Hell, people still talk about him all the time. And, I know that the night club ain't doing that good for us to be living like we were, I just never said anything. I knew he was still in that lifestyle. I know he didn't want me to know about it, but I did. I remembered a lot more than he thought I would," I babbled.

"Miracle, honey," Tori spoke up. "Your godfather, he…he just wants to protect you."

"I'm not the one that needs protecting!" I screamed, feeling as if I was losing touch with reality. "If anything, my daddy was the one that needed protecting. But you let him die!" I pointed at my godfather in a rage. "I hate you!"

All of my anger and frustration came spilling out and I became a blubbering mess. Goody just grabbed me, held me tight and let me cry. Tori wrapped her arms around me from the other side.

“My daddy's gone,” I cried over and over.

“I know, baby,” Tori said. “Let it out. It’s okay. Just let it out.”

“I... want…my...daddy!” I wept.

A knock at the door interrupted my cries. Tori broke her grasp and walked to the door to see who could be stopping by so early.

“It’s the police,” she said, as she opened the door and the two officers entered.

I wiped my tears as they walked in, thinking that they were going to tell me what happened with my father.

“What's going on?” Goody asked.

“Mr. Goodwin, can you step outside?” one of the officers asked him.

I was confused as to what was going on. Why were they asking him to step outside? My aunt Tori had the same facial expression that I did.

“What's the matter?” She asked.

“Ma’am, please,” the officer addressed her. “I need you to stay put. Sir, can you please step outside?” he repeated.

“For what?” Goody answered, his voice sounding agitated. “I told y’all last night that I would call when I got the chance. It ain’t even been twelve hours.”

“Sir, I really don't want this to get ugly,” the officer told him. “But we need you to step outside. Now, do you really want to do this in front of them?" the officer asked, gesturing towards me and Tori.

Tori looked as if she was ready to break down in tears. Goody looked disgusted.

"Man, fuck," he mumbled.

"Goody, what's going on?" I asked.

"Nothing, baby," he said with a weak smile. "The officers just came by to ask a couple of questions."

He looked at the officers, his eyes pleading for them to ease up, but the hardened officer in the front didn't care.

"Sir, can you please turn around put your hands behind your back?" the officer requested.

Goody looked as if he wanted to protest but he did as he was told.

"Marques Goodwin," the officer started. "You're under arrest for drug trafficking, money laundering, murder, and murder in the second degree," the officer said.

The officer turned Goody around and slapped the cuffs on him.

Drugs? I thought to myself. *Money laundering? What the hell was going on? What else didn't I know?*

*****

My aunt looked at my godfather with worry written all across her face.

"Goody, what's going on?" she asked.

We were sitting across the table from him at the Dallas County Jail.

"What the hell were they talking about laundering money and everything?" she asked.

"They got charges on me for drug possession and all of that," Goody explained. "When Eddie got shot yesterday, an anonymous phone call was made to the police and they were told that there were drugs and a lot of cash in the restaurant."

"Well, was there?" she whispered.

Goody looked at her as if she already knew the answer to the question.

"Never mind," she said with an attitude.

He turned his attention to me.

"I know this has been a rough time for you, huh, big head?" he asked.

I just sat quiet. I knew he was trying to make me feel better, but I really didn't have anything to say. What good would it do? My father was dead and now, my godfather is in jail for drugs, murder, and God knows what else.

"Once I have my court date, and the judge gives me an amount for bail, you post it. I can handle some things and try to figure some stuff out," he continued. "There should be more than enough in the accounts…"

"Baby, they took everything." Tori interrupted.

"What are you talking about?" he asked.

"Just what I said. They took everything," she stated. "I tried to use my bank card and it didn't work. When I called the bank, they said everything was frozen."

"What the fuck? It ain't been but like…a day," he grunted. He paused and I could see he was thinking. "Alright. Well, it should be some cash in the house."

"No," she said. "You're not hearing me, baby. They took everything. They took the cars, the cash from your office, safe deposit boxes, everything. They're talking about going to the restaurant. What have you gotten us into?" she asked.

He looked at me and a look of something I had never seen overcame him. I almost thought it was fear.

“Look. It's too many ears around for us to be talking right now. But, I'll figure out a way to handle this,” he promised.

“How, Goody?” Tori whined. “I don't know how I can deal with this. We got the kids, and your baby mama been blowing up my damn phone, talking all this shit. She’s talking about how she's going to take the girls,” she rambled.

“You tell that bitch that she better not even think about taking my kids,” he threatened.

“And what are you going to do?” she asked. “Huh? Goody, you are in jail. They have you on some serious shit!”

A few people, including the guards, looked in her direction and she calmed down. She looked around and leaned into the table so that no one else could hear.

“I knew that you were out there hustlin’, baby, but what the fuck!” she said. “Money laundering? What the fuck were you and Eddie doing?”

When I heard my father’s name, my eyes perked up.

“Time's up,” the guard yelled.

Two guards walked over to the table.

“Goodwin, time to go back,” they ordered.

We all stood up and I looked at my godfather, not sure what to think. He had this sadness in his eyes.

“This isn’t fair,” I told him. “Now, I got to lose you, too?”

The guards began to tug at him to lead him back to the cell. He looked back at me with sincerity.

“It’s okay, baby girl. It'll all work out. I promise. I’m gonna fix this,” he promised.

Somehow, I doubted it.

*****

The next few weeks were a blur. Tori tried to take care of me the best that she could, but with little income and five other kids to take care of, it was getting harder for her. Plus, I had been missing school and had to do a lot of work to catch up from my time out. Next thing we knew, Goody’s attorney had informed my aunt that he was going to take a plea deal and do seven years to avoid trial and risking a larger sentence. Because of the fact that Goody shot the boy in self-defense, they took that into consideration on the murder charge, but the evidence they had on him was heavy for all the other charges. The Feds wanted to lock him away for life, but what saved him was my father’s death. Because he was shot, they couldn't pin everything on him, and because he only had one charge on his record from when he was a teenager, pushing dime bags. So, he agreed to the deal and to serve the seven years.

Things couldn't get any worse for me, so I thought. That is, until the city of Dallas told me that I was a ward of the state and would have to be placed in foster care until I turned eighteen. I literally had nothing or no one. I was seventeen years old, and everything that I once knew was now a thing of the past. I was a ward of the state.

*****

“Miracle, I know this is hard for you, sweetie. I’m sure that this is a major transition from your normal lifestyle, so we're going to be checking in on you frequently. And if you ever have any problems, you know you can call me.”

I looked at this woman, April, that was talking to me. She was a child care social worker that had been assigned to me since I was being placed in a foster care home. She was a little, itty bitty white girl that looked like she had never had dick before. Her nose reminded me of a fish and she smelled like mayonnaise. I just nodded my head because I didn't even care to speak. I was tired of saying "okay" to everything when I knew I wasn't.

It had been a few weeks since my father had passed, and everything had happened so quickly. Everyone at the funeral was crying and saying how much they missed him. Then there were all of these nobodies screaming, like they were best friends with him, begging God to bring him back. I was numb the entire time while people walked up to me and hugged me, telling me how great of a man my father was. All I could imagine was the look on his face before he died, as the bullets ripped through him while he tried to protect me. I wanted to kill the nigga that killed him. The way I saw it, this was his fault that my life was snatched from me. I vowed the day of that funeral that I would hunt the man down that did this and make him suffer.

I promised myself that I would never give up looking for his killer. My heart was so heavy and all I could think about was someone taking my father away from me. My aunt helped me pack up a lot of my clothes from the house before the federal agents came in and took everything else. The way they ransacked the house, you could tell they got enjoyment out of it. I could see the smirks on their faces as I tried to gather my belongings. They were like vultures the way that they snatched everything. My entire life was now in two suitcases. And because Goody had his assets frozen, Tori could no longer take care of me. So, she was forced to give me to the system. She tried to keep me as long as she could, but because we weren't blood, and because of her association to Goody, the state was more than happy to take me away.

Supposedly, the state received an anonymous phone call warning them that I was in an unsafe living environment. And because Tori couldn't prove her income and had no way of showing ways for immediate care, they removed me and his twin girls by his crazy baby mama, Lisa. Everyone knew that Lisa was probably behind it and was being petty, but what could Goody do? He was doing time in Texas State Penitentiary in Huntsville.

I hadn't talked to Goody since he took the plea deal, but I knew he was probably already game to the shit that Lisa had pulled with the kids. I felt just as helpless, if not more so, as everyone else in this situation. Now, here I was sitting in this car with this white woman as she was dropping me off with someone that was getting paid just for me living with them.

"Are you ready?" she asked me.

"Yeah. I guess," I answered.

We got out of the car and she helped me with my bags as we walked to the front door. She knocked and we waited a few seconds before a heavyset black woman opened the door.

"Hey, baby, how are you doing?" she greeted us.

"Hi," I mumbled.

"Well, y'all come on in the house. I know it's hot out there," she fussed.

She had the raspiest voice I had ever heard and I just knew she was a chain smoker.

We stepped inside of the house and stood by the front door. I looked around and saw pictures everywhere of lots of kids and wondered how many she had in the house.

"It's good to see you again, Ms. Johnson," April spoke, as she shook the woman's hand.

"It's good to see you too, baby. But I told you, call me Patricia," the woman fussed and smiled.

"I'm sorry, Patricia," April laughed. "Well, this here is Miracle Davis. This is the young lady that I was telling you about."

Patricia looked at me with a warm smile and wrapped me up in an unexpected bear hug.

"Well, hey, baby. Everybody calls me Ms. Pat in this house," she beamed.

"Hi, Ms. Pat," I responded, still trying to recover from the hug.

"Well, bless your heart, baby. You look like you're just skin and bones," she laughed. "How old are you, sugar?" she asked.

"Seventeen," I answered, still looking at the ground.

I guess she noticed how I wasn't really into having a conversation so she just laughed it off.

"Well, I guess at that age you know us adults really don't matter much, huh?" she joked towards April.

April smiled and set my suitcase down.

"Well," April started. "I'm going to leave you two ladies to get acquainted. Ms. Patricia, I should be back in about a week or so to check on the progress and see how things are going with you and Miracle. And, Miracle, you have my card. So, if you need anything, give me a call, okay?" she said, looking down at me.

"Okay," I answered.

She gave me a quick pat on the shoulder as if she was trying to comfort me, and headed to the door.

"Ms. Patricia, I'll be in touch," she said, looking over her shoulder.

"Alright, baby," Patricia responded. "Now, you be careful out there. Miracle, why don't you take your things into the kitchen. My daughter Whitney should be in there. She'll show you where you'll be sleeping," she instructed.

"Ok," I said, as I picked up my belongings and headed towards the kitchen.

Whatever she was cooking definitely had my stomach's attention. The last couple of days I had eaten nothing but fast food, if I had eaten anything at all. So the aromas were taunting me. I walked into the kitchen to see a girl about my age at the stove. She was very pretty and she looked as if she could be a leading girl on one of the videos.

"Miracle, this is my daughter Whitney," Ms. Patricia introduced from behind me.

"Hi," I said with a slight smile.

"Hey," she returned, as she put the spoon down from the pot that she was stirring. "It's nice to meet you, Miracle. I've heard so much about you. Well, like my mama told you, I'm Whitney," she told me. "You'll meet everybody else in a minute. We're about to have dinner. But, if you want to, I can go ahead and take you to the room and show you where you will be putting your things and sleeping?" she asked.

"Okay," I answered shrugging my shoulders.

"Follow me," she said, walking away from the stove.

I followed her towards the back of the house as she led me to the first bedroom.

"So, how old are you again, Miracle?" she questioned.

"I just turned seventeen a few weeks ago," I answered.

"Oh, okay," she huffed. "I'm about to be eighteen in a few days, but because of my birthday, I won't graduate until right before I'm nineteen."

She looked me up and down as we entered into the room.

"Damn, girl, you got a nice body for a seventeen-year-old," she laughed. "I'm jealous as hell."

“Thanks,” I answered nervously.

I looked around the room and the walls were bare on one side.

“I'm assuming this is where I'm sleeping?” I asked.

“Yeah. I didn't want to decorate it or anything ‘cause I didn't know what you like,” she replied.

“It's cool,” I shrugged.

I put my suitcases on the bed and opened them so I could put away my things.

“So, what put you here?” she asked.

“My father was killed a few weeks ago and my godfather got locked up,” I told her. “Since I’m not eighteen yet, here I am.”

“Damn,” she sighed. “That’s messed up. What happened?”

I really didn't feel like explaining the story anymore, especially since I had been explaining it so many times to my family, friends, and every nosey person. But, I figured since I was going to be living there, I would have to at least one more time.

“I still don't know the whole story, but I know my dad and godfather were involved in drugs or something and somebody just up and shot my dad. It was at my birthday party and we were outside. The next thing I know, somebody just ran up and shot him,” I said.

“Well damn. That’s some crazy, movie type shit,” she gawked.

I just stood there listening to her babble. Clearly, she was free to talk however she liked in the house because this girl was popping off about how “fucked up the shit was” and how she was “fuckin’ blown”.

“Well, why don't you go ahead and get your stuff put up and shit, then come into the kitchen. Mama is cooking some chicken, macaroni and cheese, and greens,” she said.

My stomach started growling just thinking about the food.

“Okay,” I agreed. “So, that's actually your mother? Not like your foster mother or anything?”

“Yeah,” she answered. “I'm the only child that she had biologically. But, we got three other kids that live here. You'll meet them at dinner.”

“Oh. Okay. Are any of them our age?” I inquired.

“Yea, two of them. Christopher, he's seventeen, same as you and me. Nikki, she’s fifteen. She really doesn't talk much. Like, I don’t know if her head is fucked up or what. That bitch done been through some shit. Kim is six, so she just mostly plays with her dolls and shit,” she informed me.

“Wow,” I replied.

I noticed Whitney eyeballing my things and I put them away in the drawer.

“You got a lot of nice stuff,” she admired.

“Yeah,” I told her. “My dad always made sure that I had the best. This was all that was left that the Feds didn’t take though.”

“Do you miss it?” she asked.

“Miss what?” I asked, confused.

“The lifestyle,” she laughed. “I mean, you said your daddy was a drug dealer, right? So, I'm pretty sure you had everything. I know he kept you laced, right?”

“I mean, yeah. I guess,” I answered. I really hated to think about him as just some drug dealer. He was my daddy.

To the outsiders, he was a dope boy, but to me, he was my everything. "He always bought me new stuff. We always went places together but it was him that I miss most. Me and my daddy were close. Especially since I really didn't have a mom. She died when I was younger of a drug overdose," I told her.

"Wow," she swooned. "I would give anything to have all of that stuff."

"Well," I offered. "If you can fit it, you're more than welcome to borrow it, I guess," I said.

She was looking at me funny which made me a little nervous, so I continued to put my things away as she watched. After a few seconds, I spoke up.

"Um. I'm almost done. Is there a place where I can wash my hands?" I asked.

"If you go through that door on the other side, it'll take you to the bathroom," she told me, pointing to her side of the room.

"Ok, cool. Thanks."

I went into the bathroom and closed the door, locking it behind me. I looked into the mirror and turned the water on to drown out my tears that I could no longer contain.

"Daddy, I miss you," I whispered.

I took my time washing my hands and dried them on the rack. I went into the kitchen and sat down at the table. Ms. Patricia was at the stove fixing everyone's plate.

"Well, Miracle," she started. "How are you liking it here so far?"

"It's okay," I answered. "Just going to take a little bit to get adjusted I guess.

She put the plate down in front of me and put her hand on my shoulder, gripping it tightly to the point where it was a little painful.

“Well, eat up. You're going to need your strength,” she told me.

What the hell did that mean?

As I was about to dig into my food, I heard the front door open and slam shut.

“Y’all get right on in here and eat,” Patricia yelled.

I watched two kids that looked to be my age walk into the kitchen and throw their things down.

“Before you sit down, Chris, go upstairs and get Kim and tell her that it's time to eat,” she ordered.

“Yes, ma’am,” the boy said.

He ran out of the kitchen to do as he was told. A few minutes later, he came back with a very small and quiet child with a doll in her hand and sat at the table.

“Now, before we all eat, I want y’all to meet Miracle. She's going to be staying with us for a while,” she said.

The children just looked at me. I smiled and nodded briefly before looking down at my food.

“Hi,” I mustered up.

“Hey. What's up?” Christopher said.

It was an awkward scene as we all sat at the table, not really sure what to say. I decided to eat my food and remain silent.

“Miracle, when you finish eating, we're going to go over the house rules,” Ms. Patricia told me.

“Ok,” I answered.

“Yes, ma'am,” Whitney spoke up.

“Huh?” I asked, looking at her confused.

“We say yes ma'am,” she said, still eating her food not looking at me.

If I didn’t know any better, I could’ve sworn that she was agitated.

“Oh. I'm sorry. I apologize,” I mumbled.

“Thank you,” Patricia said.

What was that about? I thought.

I just met these people and already they're telling me how to talk to them. I ate my food and stood up.

“You ask to be excused from the table,” Whitney pointed out, again, not looking at me.

I sighed and sat back down.

“May I please be excused?” I asked.

“Of course, sugar,” Patricia answered.

Whitney snorted as I went to take my things to the kitchen sink. I looked to see Chris chewing slowly and looking nervous, but I didn’t know about what. Was this bitch bipolar or something?

“Is it ok if I go to bed?” I asked. “I'm really tired. I haven’t really slept much over the last couple days,” I told her.

Ms. Patricia chewed the rest of her food before answering.

“Go ahead. We'll talk in the morning,” she answered.

I walked to the room and changed clothes to get ready for bed. I took the picture of me and my dad out of the pocket of my jeans and got under the covers. I looked at the picture and smiled. In the photo, my daddy and I were standing outside of the club on opening night. Goody had taken the picture of us. I laid it next to me and just looked at it, thinking about how happy I was that day. With the memories of my father dancing in my head, I let my tears drift me to sleep.

*****

Chapter Three

I woke up to the dark room, sweating and confused. It took me a few minutes to remember that I was no longer in my own bed at my house, but rather in some bed of some foster family. I turned over to see Whitney lying in her bed, her head wrapped and her breasts protruding from her sports bra. She reminded me of Myesha the way that she was built. I got up and tiptoed to the door on her side of the room so that I could use the bathroom. I closed the doors as quietly as I could and sat down on the toilet. I looked around for toilet paper so that I could pee and I saw something familiar in the trash. I picked up pieces of fabric that looked like one of my shirts.

"I know this girl didn't take my stuff and throw it in the damn trash!" I hissed.

I flushed the toilet and walked back towards the room confused. I got in the bed and told myself to ask her about it in the morning when everyone was awake. Just as I closed my eyes, I heard her speak.

"You better not say shit," she muttered.

I turned over to face her and stared right into her cold, dark eyes. My mouth opened slightly but no sound came out.

"Don't make it hard for yourself while you're here," she warned.

She turned over with her back to me and went to sleep. The rest of the night I sat wide awake, afraid to close my eyes. What the hell was wrong with this girl? What did I do to her? The better question was, what was I going to do? Before I knew it, it was time to get up and get ready for school. I was supposed to start my new school that day. Since my father died, there was no way for me to get to school all the way on the other side of town anymore. So, I was now going to be attending South Oak Cliff High School. I knew I would have to call Myesha soon because she hadn't heard from me since the funeral. And since all of my godfather's accounts were frozen, he couldn't afford to pay my phone bill. I had some cash stashed, so one of the first things I planned to do was get a phone. Even if I had to get a Metro PCS phone, I needed something.

I got up feeling sluggish from lack of sleep, and went into the bathroom to take a shower. While in the shower, Whitney walked in and began to do her hair. I peeked out of the shower curtain and saw that she was wearing my Seven jeans. I could tell they were mine because they had the star that I had decorated on the back pocket. The jeans looked like they were practically painted on her. She grinned at me, noticing I was looking at her.

"You don't mind if I borrow your clothes do you?" she asked.

The way she smiled at me, I could tell she was being sarcastic.

"Naw. It's straight," I said, rolling my eyes and closing the curtain back.

"Well, hurry up because mama wants to talk to you. And if you utter a fucking word, I promise you, I'm going to make your fucking life miserable," she sang.

This bitch is crazy. I don't know what it was that she was on, but I damn sure wasn't going to be staying in the room with her. I was going to put a stop to it right then and there. I got out of the shower and grabbed the towel, wrapping it tightly around my body. I walked into the room and quickly began to get dressed so that I could go into the kitchen and let Ms. Patricia know what was going on with her crazy-ass daughter.

I wasn't no punk or no shit like that, but I had never actually been in a fight in my life. The most I had ever done was pop off at the mouth. No one ever really tried me because everyone liked me. I walked into the kitchen and sat down at the table as she sat watching television.

"Ms. Patricia, can I talk to you about something?" I whispered.

"What is it?" she answered, not looking at me.

"Um...I'm not sure what I did, but Whitney has been acting real funny towards me. She took some of my clothes and like, cut 'em up and put them in the trash. Then, she told me that if I said anything, she was going to give me trouble," I told her.

She continued to look at the television as if she didn't hear me.

"I mean...I don't mind her borrowing my stuff, but she can at least ask. And I don't have that many clothes, so I don't wanna be having nobody cut up my stuff," I continued.

I looked at her to see if she heard what I said. She was so into the TV, I don't think she heard anything.

"Ms. Patricia? Did you hear me?" I called out louder, slightly agitated.

She turned the television down with the remote control and slammed it down on the table. I jumped as she startled me, catching me off guard.

"You listen to me you little bitch," she growled. "Don't come in my muthafuckin' house telling me what the fuck my daughter is doing to your little stuck-up ass. You're in my house, understand?"

Words couldn't describe the feeling I had at that moment. I swear, I thought I was in the Twilight Zone or some shit. All I could do was open my mouth in shock, listening to the words come out of this woman's mouth. This is the same woman that sat in the kitchen the night before and smiled at me as if I was welcomed. Now, this bitch was acting like Cruella Deville.

"Now, in this house, you do what the hell I say. And I don't want to hear shit about what Whitney is doing. That's my muthafuckin' daughter, not yours. You ought to be glad that I'm letting you stay here. Walking around this muthafucka like you better than everybody else, with your disrespectful ass. But I'm gone fix that. I'll be damned if I let some little bitch like you come in here and run shit just 'cause you think that you're entitled. If it's one thing that I don't tolerate in this household, it's disrespect," she spat. "Your daddy may have let you run around and do whatever the hell you wanna do, but it damn sure ain't gon' go down in this muthafucka! So pay attention 'cause you gonna learn the goddamn rules today."

I stood flustered, my eyes wide, listening to someone that I thought was a sweet woman completely switch. No wonder Whitney was so fuckin' crazy! Her mama was Cybil!

"And, let me tell you something else," she kept going. "What goes on in this house stays in this house. So don't be taking your ass to school telling everybody what the fuck is going on in here." She walked towards me and put her finger in my face. "You take your ass to school in the morning and then you bring your ass home. Don't bring trouble in this house. And, your ass is gonna pitch in and take care of this house just like everybody else, if not more. A little, rich bitch like you probably never did anything for your damn self. Always had other people doing shit for you. Walking around here like you the shit. But now, you're in my house. Your damn daddy can't save you now. You're mine," she growled.

I frowned and was ready to pop off. Nobody was going to disrespect my father. I stood up and got ready to tell her about her damn self. But before I could say anything, she reached up and slapped me hard, completely catching me off guard.

"Sit your black ass down, bitch!" she snapped. "Oh. You mad? Guess what? Don't nobody give a fuck if you mad. I said it. Your daddy can't save you. His ass ain't fuckin here. He's dead because his ass was out there selling dope," she taunted. "I wish you would stand up on me like that again. Girl, I will fucking kill you." She leaned down to me and spoke through gritted teeth and all I could smell was the nicotine. "You don't pay a bill in this muthafucka and you going to do what the hell I say, understand?"

My hand was still stuck to the side of my face, grasping the stinging cheek.

"Do you understand?" She repeated.

"Yeah," I whispered.

"What did you say?" she asked, still standing over me.

"Yes, ma'am," I said louder.

"Good," she smirked. "You do what I say and it makes things a whole lot easier. But if you cross me, little girl, I promise you. I'm gonna make it hard for you to do anything, let alone breathe for the next year you're here. And don't think running back to that little white bitch is going to help you. She may say that she's going to call and check in, but they never do. And ain't nobody else gon' want you," she sneered.

She looked at me and my fearful expression and actually laughed!

"Just like I thought. Some little uppity, bourgeois, brat that thinks she's supposed to get everything in life that she wants. Well, you got another thing coming," she fussed. "Now, get the hell out my face. Chris! Nikki! Get your asses down here so y'all can walk to school!" she yelled.

They came flying down the stairs as soon as she said their names. I walked into the room to get my backpack that I left on the bed. Whitney sat on the bed painting her nails.

“Told you not to cross me,” she said. “I thought we could be friends…guess I was wrong.” She looked up at me with those evil eyes.

I grabbed my bag and headed for the door.

“Catch you later,” she chimed.

I rushed out of the front door and followed Chris and Nikki to school. I couldn't even say anything. I was still in shock over what happened.

“Just try to stay out of her way,” Nikki said to me after a few minutes of walking.

“Huh?” I asked, snapping out of my thoughts.

“Just try to stay out of her way,” she repeated. “If you stay out of her way, she won't bother you as much. Just do what you're told and keep your head down. Time goes by quick.”

“You make it seem like this is something that she does on the regular,” I observed.

“Well, yea,” Chris said.

“So, you mean she's like this all the time?” I inquired.

Both of them shook their heads in agreement as we walked the few blocks to the school.

“Why hasn't anybody said anything?” I prodded.

“Because it's hard to prove,” Nikki explained. “Last time somebody said something about Ms. Patricia, it was hell to pay afterwards. It was this girl, Reese. She had only been there for like two weeks but Ms. Patricia and Whitney tortured her.”

“But why?” I pushed.

“She was pretty. Like you,” she told me, looking at me with sad eyes. “Reese was gorgeous and Whitney was jealous of her. So, she did any and everything to that girl. When Reese told the social worker and they asked Ms. P. about it, she made it seem like Reese was just being trouble. And it was easy to believe because Reese had a record. The minute that the caseworker left, Whitney beat her bad. And Ms. P locked her in the room,” she recalled. “So you know… you just kind of learn to just not say anything, especially if you can't prove it.”

“But that's crazy!” I exclaimed. “It’s more of us than it is of her.”

“Yeah. But on the real, Whitney is the one that you have to watch out for,” Chris told me. “Compared to Whitney, Ms. Patricia is a walk in the park. Like, Whitney has issues. That bitch is bona-fide psycho. She burned Reese while she was asleep and cut off all of her fuckin’ hair. It's something wrong with that girl,” he stressed.

And I got to sleep in the room with this crazy bitch, I thought to myself.

“Well, I guess now she's coming for me,” I told them. “She was talking about how she liked my clothes and I told her she could borrow them. But this morning, I found some of my stuff in the trash, cut up.”

“Yeah,” Nikki nodded. “If she feels like you may be a threat to her, she's going to try to break you.”

“But I'm not a threat to anybody,” I argued. “I'm just here.”

The rest of the walk, they told me about their time in the house. Hearing them tell me about their experiences, I was scared to go back into the room with this girl. Maybe I could sleep on the couch or something. But wherever it was, Whitney damn sure couldn’t be in the room.

We got to the school and I went to the principal's office to get my schedule as I was told to do. Nikki went with me and Chris went on to class.

“Alright. I'll see y'all at 3:30. We got to be home by four because the caseworker is coming by today to check on things,” he informed us.

“Okay,” Nikki answered. “We’ll be here.”

She waved at him as he walked off, then she turned her attention back to me.

“He has it the easiest and the hardest in the house,” she sighed.

“What you mean?” I asked her, confused.

“Nothing,” she quickly dismissed. “Come on. I’ll help you find your classes.”

She took my schedule and looked to see where I was.

“Ok. Your homeroom is right across from mine. Looks like we have the same lunch together, too, so that's good,” she smiled brightly.

I couldn’t get my mind off of Ms. Patricia and her crazy ass daughter.

“So, has she ever hurt you?” I questioned her.

I saw the sadness return in her eyes as the smile faded.

“Once,” she mumbled. “Whitney had brought some boy into the house and Ms. Patricia came home early. The boy tried to run but got caught, and Whitney told her that I was in the house being a hoe. I tried to deny it, but it didn’t matter. She hit me so hard, I couldn't see for almost a week.”

I couldn’t believe what she was telling me. I never actually saw this stuff actually happen. The most abuse that I saw was on TV, like *Law and Order SVU.* I never thought I would actually be living it.

"She can't honestly think that her daughter is a damn angel," I blurted.

"I know," she agreed. "She knew Whitney was the one that had a boy over, but she just didn't want to admit it. I tried to explain to her that it wasn't me, but of course she's going to take her daughter's side. So, I make sure that unless it's important, I stay in my room. The minute I turn eighteen, I'm moving. I'm going to go to a four-year college in DC. I want to go to Howard. Everybody's talking about how live it is up there. And they have a good medical program," she beamed.

"Wow!" I smiled for the first time. "I wanna go to Howard, too. I wanna major in criminal law. So, going away is definitely not a bad idea right now."

"Yea," she giggled. "Shoot, anything to get out of that house."

"I feel you," I agreed.

We stood in front of my homeroom in the hall and chatted until the bell rang.

"Alright. I'll see you in a little bit," she said. "If you need anything, I'm right across the hall."

Whitney was right about one thing. Nikki seemed to have her stuff together. She was really sweet and I hated that she was involved in the same mess that I was. I wondered how she got into the house with her in the first place. What happened to her parents? I walked into the classroom and the teacher acknowledged me.

"Are you supposed to be in here?" she asked.

"Yeah, uh… my name is Miracle Davis and I'm new," I told her.

"Okay," she sighed. She looked like she had already had a hard day even though it was just starting. "Let me see your schedule."

I handed it to her and she looked it over.

"Alright. Well, find a seat. Everyone, this is Miracle Davis and she's joining us from…" she trailed off.

"Oh. Sorry. Arlington Heights," I answered quickly.

Her face formed a surprised look.

"Arlington Heights?" she repeated. "How did you end up here?"

"Oh. Um, just some family stuff," I told her.

I didn't feel like explaining to another person what happened to my father, so I quickly found a seat, damn near at the back of the class and sat down, trying not to draw any more attention to myself.

"Well, welcome to South Oak Cliff High," she smiled. "Class, try to settle down, please."

I don't think any of the students were paying her any attention. From the back of the classroom, I looked around at the students. There were girls that were popping their gum and texting on their phones, flipping their long, cheap weaves. Some of the boys were bent over the desks trying to spit game at the girls, and some were even asleep. I looked at my schedule and scanned what my day would consist of.

"Aye. What's good, yo?" I heard someone say to me.

I looked up to see this charcoal black boy sitting in front of me with a toothpick in his mouth. I frowned up my nose and spoke.

"Hey," I answered.

"So, you're new here, huh?" he asked.

Why in the hell was this trout-mouthed boy talking to me? I know he just heard this damn teacher say that I was new. Did he not have anything else better than that?

"Yeah," I told him dryly.

"So, I'm saying, you're kind of cute, yo," he said. "Let me get your number."

"Um…no thank you," I refused quickly.

"Oh. What, you think you're too good or something?" he barked.

My eyes grew large.

"Excuse me?" I asked.

I was trying to be nice but I wasn't in the mood.

"You heard me. I'm saying, what you trying to be all stuck up and shit for?" he asked.

"No. It's nothing like that. I just I'm not allowed to talk to boys," I lied.

After hearing what Ms. Patricia did to Nikki for allegedly having a boy over at the house, I would be glad to lie and say that I couldn't talk to any boys.

"Alright then. Fuck you, bourgeois bitch," he dismissed, turning back around in his desk.

I could see a few of the girls looking out the corner of their eyes and talking shit.

"This bitch thinks she's cute," I heard one of them say. "She ain't nothing but a skinny, black hoe."

The bell rang and I hightailed it out of there. I didn't even wait for Nikki like she told me to. I just ran to my next class, handed the teacher my schedule, and headed to the back to find a seat. Every class, I had to introduce myself over and over. I was ready for lunch and starving. I met Nikki in the cafeteria and we both went to the line to get something to eat. The food looked horrendous but I didn't care because I was starving. I hadn't eaten but a few bites of breakfast that morning at the house because I was scared to stay in the kitchen with Ms. Patricia's crazy ass.

We got our food trays and headed to find a place to sit.

"I'll be right back," I told her. "I need to go to the bathroom."

"Okay," she said, beginning to eat.

I headed to the restroom to pee. When I came out of the stall, I was face to face with Whitney, along with two other girls.

"I told you that I'd see you soon," she smirked.

I tried to walk around her but one of the girls stepped towards me.

"What's the matter? I know you see me standing here," she egged.

"Look, Whitney, I don't know what I did but I'm not tryna have beef with you, ok?" I said, trying not to get frustrated.

Whitney grabbed my hair and yanked me to the ground. I was in no means a punk, and I can handle my own. My daddy had me in boxing classes since I was ten and we used to scrap fight with each other. He taught me how to use my hands. But I had never fought three girls at one time, especially when one of them was significantly bigger. I knew I had a few seconds to try to come out on top, so I swung hard on the bigger girl, figuring if I could knock her down then it would be easier to handle the other two.

My hit barely connected as she punched me and sat on me, preventing me from me from getting up off the ground. I hated when bitches did shit like that. It was never a fair fight. She held me down while Whitney kicked and punched me over and over. I tried to fight back but it was pointless. The other girl stood at the door, making sure I couldn't get out and no one else could get in. After what seemed like an eternity, the girl stood up and I was able to breathe.

"You open your mouth, and I promise you it'll be a lot worse," Whitney threatened. "I told you don't fuck with me and you didn't listen. Tamika, grab her," she ordered.

Her fat friend grabbed me and snatched me to my feet as I struggled to break free. Whitney pulled a blade out of her pocket and grabbed me by my hair. She pressed the blade on the side of my face, making a small cut.

"You don't want it to get worse," she warned.

She put the blade back in her pocket and the girl holding me threw my small frame to the ground. They left the restroom and I was left alone with my tears. I looked in the mirror to see how deep the wound was and cringed at how messed up I was. I tried to straighten myself up, but I couldn't stop shaking. Why was all of this happening? What the hell did I do to her that was so wrong? The blood that was seeping from my cheek was now dripping onto my shirt.

I hurried out of the bathroom to quickly find the nurse's station, leaving Nikki to wonder about me in the cafeteria. I ran inside the room before anyone else could see me. The nurse looked up from her reading to see me and gasped.

"Are you okay, child?" she asked.

She stood up and walked towards me as I was holding my face.

"I had an accident," I told her.

"Lord, who did this to you?" she questioned.

“Nobody,” I lied. “I cut my face on a loose nail that was on the bathroom door.”

She looked at me as if she didn’t believe me, but didn’t argue.

“Mm hmm,” she said. “A pretty little child like you don’t need to be doing any fighting. Now, come on. Let's get you cleaned up,” she instructed. “I'm going to need to call your folks.”

“Why?” I asked nervously.

I did not want to give Ms. Patricia anymore ammo.

“Because, any time you have an accident like this, we have to notify the parents to avoid any disciplinary action,” she explained. “It’s procedure. Now, what's your mom's name?”

“I just started here today, so they may not have my stuff in the system yet,” I told her, praying that they didn’t.

“Well, baby, you gonna have to call somebody,” she fussed. “You can’t just be standing in here bleeding on the floor all day. You gonna at least need someone to bring you some clean clothes. I know you have somebody that you can call.”

I thought about those that were once close to me. Anyone that I could think to call wouldn’t dare come this far out to help. I would call Myesha, but what could she do except tell her mom, who would call child welfare and put me right back at square one? I had no choice but to call that evil ass foster mother of mine.

“Um… you have to call my foster mom,” I said, my heart racing.

I couldn't tell her that her daughter was the one that did this to me. She wouldn't believe me anyway.

She picked up the phone and handed it to me.

“Do I really have to call her?” I pleaded.

The nurse looked at me and could tell that something was wrong.

“Okay. I can look at you and tell that something is going on. So what is it? Is it your parents? Your foster mother?” she asked.

“No!” I answered quickly.

I smiled a little to try to make myself less obvious.

“I just didn't want to bother her because I know she's got a lot that she's doing today and she’s not trying to be behind schedule,” I lied.

“Well, be that as it may, I really have to call her,” she pushed. “Do you have her number?”

I wanted to keep lying and say that I didn't, but I knew more than likely, she would just go to the principal's office to get it. I gave her the phone number and she dialed.

“What's her name?” she asked.

“Patricia Johnson,” I answered.

She waited for a few seconds before speaking.

“Hi, Ms. Johnson. This is Ms. Brooks from the nurse’s office at South Oak Cliff High School. I've got a Miracle Davis here with me. It looks like she had some type of incident and cut her face. She said it was an accident, but we have to notify the parents any time this happens and have them come to pick the child up,” she informed her. She paused for a moment and smiled. “Sure, not a problem.” She handed me the phone. “She wants to talk to you really quick, hun, to make sure you're okay. She sounds worried,” she added.

I took the phone from her and placed it to my ear.

“Hello?” I answered, hiding my fear from the nurse.

“Wait ‘til I get you to the house,” Ms. Patricia whispered. “You just had to be fuckin’ hardheaded. Just wait til I get there,” she said.

She hung up the phone and I heard the dial tone. All I could do in that moment was pray that if she saw my face, she would finally understand how psycho her daughter was. But something told me that I was just playing myself.

*****

Chapter Four

"Get your ass in that damn room," Ms. Patricia ordered, as we walked into the house.

The entire car ride, I was nervous as hell. She never even looked in my direction. When the school nurse explained to her that I was hurt and suggested that she take me to the hospital, it was as if I was with Mommy Dearest. She was hugging on me and clutching me as a normal, worried mother would. It took everything in me not to scream to the nurse that her daughter was the one that was responsible for cutting my damn face.

We walked down the hallway and she held a tight grip on my arm as we headed to the car door. When we got in, I jumped in the back seat, hoping that she wouldn't be able to hurt me while she was driving. As quiet as she was, I actually thought that for a moment, she was going to take me to the hospital. But instead, we drove straight to the house. I prayed that my punishment wouldn't be too severe.

We walked into the house and I immediately began to apologize.

"Ms. Patricia, I'm sorry. I wasn't trying to get in trouble, I swear. It was just…it was just a big misunderstanding. I'm sorry," I repeated over and over.

I braced myself, wondering if she would hit me.

"Get your ass in that damn room."

She took a cigarette out of her purse and lit it.

"Yes ma'am," I complied, rushing to the room to avoid any further physical torture.

I got into the room and sat down on the bed, throwing my backpack on the floor and closing the door behind me. I was telling myself that maybe Ms. Patricia knew what her daughter did and took pity on me. Maybe she realized the pain that I suffered was enough punishment and decided that I didn't need to endure anything more. My face was swollen and I wanted nothing more than to go to sleep, especially since Whitney was still at school. I felt safe for the moment. I was going to enjoy my nap and when I woke up, I was going to try to find a way to call Myesha to get her help. I know she was probably going crazy since she hadn't talked to me in almost a month. I laid down and within minutes, I had fallen asleep.

I woke up several hours later and the room was significantly dark. I stood up, stretched, and straightened out my clothes so that I could go freshen up. I turned the knob and panicked because I couldn't open the door.

"What the hell?" I mumbled.

I pulled and yanked harder and of course, nothing happened. I walked over to the connecting door on Whitney's side of the room but got the same result. My heart began to race and I started to panic because I couldn't get out. I flipped the light switch and I cried out when no lights came on. The window above my bed was the only source of light in the room. I walked over to the bed, standing on it so that I could get a better access to the window.

Pulling the blinds up, I attempted to open the window so that I could try to get out. There were nails in the window! I got dizzy and my head started to swim. What the hell were they doing to me? I went and knocked on the door, pleading to be let out.

"Hello?" I screamed. "Is somebody out there? Hello!" I banged on the door.

I knocked for several minutes but no one ever came. I had been jumped at school and now I was being punished. Was Whitney behind this? Ms. Patricia? No wonder she didn't say anything to me. She had this planned all along.

"Can someone let me out? Please!"

I knocked on the door for what seemed like forever and my cries continued to go unheard. I fell to the floor in defeat. I didn't have any energy left. All I wanted to do was to be with my daddy. But instead, I was stuck here in hell. Sitting with my thoughts, I thought I heard someone laughing outside of the room. I didn't know how much more I could take. I hoped that my caseworker would come and check on me soon. I wanted her to take me away from here. I crawled over to the bed, eyes swollen from the abuse that I had endured earlier, mixed with the tears that I had shed, and I started praying. My stomach began to growl. I looked out of the window to distract myself and keep my mind from hunger.

"Daddy, please come save me," I whispered as I let sleep overcome me, hoping that by some small miracle, my father would come walking through the door and this would all be one horrible nightmare.

*****

I stood outside of my house at my birthday party, looking at a delivery guy with a bouquet of flowers. I looked to my father and to my godfather and it seemed as if they were moving in slow motion. *Why do I feel like I've been here before?* I turned to my father and called out to him.

"Daddy, what's going on?" I asked.

My father looked in my direction but didn't say anything.

"Daddy, answer me!" I cried. "Why aren't you talking to me?"

He looked at me and he appeared sad. He began to cry, but strangely, blood was pouring from his eyes. I tried again to reach out to him but failed. He and Goody pulled their guns out and started shooting. I stood there in the center, unable to move, frozen by fear. Bullets flew around my body and my father just stood as holes were ripped into his body.

"Daddy, no!" I screamed.

I started to run to him but when I looked down, my legs weren't moving.

"Get down, Miracle," he yelled, as it seemed to take forever to him to get to me.

Goody stood watching as I screamed.

"Help me!" I cried.

He looked at me and a grin formed on his face.

"Goody, please!" I begged. "Help me."

He walked over towards my father who was lying on the ground. I tried to bend down to him but I was still paralyzed from the waist down. Goody pulled out his gun and stood over him as I cried in shock.

"What are you doing!" I screamed. "Why are you just standing there? Help him!"

Why couldn't I move? My daddy was just lying there and I couldn't do anything. I could see the bullets and hear the screams. Why couldn't I stop this? I felt a sharp pain and my entire body started to tingle. I looked to find the source of the pain and saw blood forming on my shirt and a hole the size of a dime.

"Who shot me? No!" I cried.

I fell to the ground as I felt myself slipping into the abyss.

*****

"Wake yo' ass the fuck up!"

I heard someone yelling as I felt a sharp stinging pain on my face.

Where's Daddy?

I opened my eyes and quickly realized that I was just dreaming.

“Stop all that damn screaming and crying.” Ms. Patricia stood over me with a frown on her face and a cigarette in her mouth. “What the fuck is wrong with you?” she snapped, slapping me in my head again.

I sat up and tried to block her heavy hands.

“I'm sorry,” I sniffed. “I guess I was having a bad dream.”

“This ain't no fucking story book,” she said, rolling her eyes. “I don't give a fuck what the fuck you were dreaming about, just shut the fuck up before I lock your ass in here again and you never get out.”

I looked around the room, hoping to see if there was any way of knowing what time it was or even what day it was for that matter.

“Ms. Patricia, I'm sorry,” I repeated.

“Yeah. You're sorry alright,” she hissed. “Next time you pull some bullshit like that at school and I have to come pick your muthafuckin' ass up, I'm a lock you in here for more than just a damn day. Now, get your ass up, go wash your ass and go into the kitchen and eat that damn food. When you finish eating, you wash all the fucking dishes and then you go clean the bathrooms. And don't half ass clean them shits either ‘cause I'll have your ass up all fucking night, you hear me?” she barked, damn near nose to nose.

“Yes, ma'am,” I mumbled.

“Speak up!” she spat.

“Yes, ma'am,” I answered louder.

She walked out of the room, slamming the door behind her. I walked over to the dresser and opened it to get out some clothes. Once again, Whitney had taken it upon herself to go through my things, but I decided not to say anything for fear of what she would do. Instead, I just grabbed an oversized t-shirt and some shorts and headed to the bathroom. I almost threw up at the bathroom sink. It was so horrendously nasty. I rushed to take a shower. My stomach growled so loudly that I thought someone else was in the room for a minute. I finished with my shower and rushed to get dressed.

I walked into the kitchen and my plate sat on the table. I will give it to her. She was a good cook. She had made pork chops, mashed potatoes, and corn bread. I scarfed it down so fast, I don't even remember tasting it. I hadn't eaten lunch the day before because of Whitney and her friend, and I had barely eaten anything for breakfast that morning, so the food was welcomed.

I got up to see if there was anything more, but couldn't find anything. I walked to the pantry and could not open it. Looking at the refrigerator, I noticed that all of the cabinets and doors were locked. I shook my head in disgust as I carried my plate over to the sink full of dirty dishes. Stacking everything, I begin to organize so that I could clean. I had just emptied the sink when I heard the footsteps and turned around to see Nikki.

“Are you okay?” she whispered.

“Not really,” I answered.

She peeked around the corner to make sure that the coast was clear.

“Don't worry,” she said. “I got some snacks upstairs in my backpack that I got at school I can sneak you. I know you’re hungry after being locked up all day,” she offered.

"No. It's ok. I don't want to get you in trouble," I whispered back.

"What happened?" she asked. "I waited for you yesterday and you never came back."

"I know," I grimaced. "Whitney happened. I went to the bathroom and the next thing I know, her and two of her fat ass friends were punching me and kicking me. Like, what the hell is with this bitch? I swear, the next time that bitch even thinks about putting her hands on me, that's that ass. The only reason I didn't fuck her ass up was because they fucking jumped me."

"She's coming at you because she sees you as a threat," she whispered.

"But a threat to what?" I stressed, confused with her statement. "I don't even know that girl. I've been here all but what, four days, and she's cut up my clothes. I've been slapped in the face by her crazy ass mama, and got jumped in the damn school bathroom. So I don't understand how I'm a threat to her," I said.

I know that it wasn't because of the way that I looked or no dumb shit like that because she was bad as hell. So, I still didn't know what the fuck this bitch's issue was with me.

"You gotta try to understand, Miracle," Nikki explained. "Whitney's always been this way."

"What way?" I pressed. "Crazy?"

"She's the type of girl that feels like she has to have the spotlight. Like always wanting all eyes on her. When she has competition around, then she knows the attention is no longer on her and she will do anything to get it back on her. If you act like you worship her, things go by much easier," she continued. "I remember a while back, there was this boy that lived here…Darrell. I had just gotten here and he was a few months from turning eighteen. Whitney had a crush on him but there was another girl that lived here that he was liking or whatever.

Next thing we knew, the girl was in the hospital and ever since then, Whitney has gone out of her way to get rid of anything or anyone that she sees as competition."

"But, I don't understand. Who is she thinking I'm tryna compete with her for?" I inquired.

"Oh. You ain't figured that out yet?" Nikki asked, surprised.

"Nikki, what the hell are you talking about?" I pushed.

"Chris," she answered, looking me in my eye.

What the hell was this girl talking about?

"I don't get it."

"Whitney and Chris," she said.

"Huh?"

This girl was talking in riddles.

"Just be careful," she warned. "I can't get into it right now but just please, be careful. Whitney doesn't like when someone gets in her way. And right now, you're a target."

She handed me a plate to dry off and I changed the subject.

"So, what about you?" I asked. "How long have you been here?"

"About a year and a half," she replied sadly.

"What happened to your parents?" I prodded.

"Well," she started. "My father was killed in a drive by. And after that, my mother started messing with these bums that were just using her. She was with this one guy that was a total jerk and he um…he started molesting me. I went to school and I told my teacher, then child services came and took me away and gave me to my grandmother. But every time they took me to her, she would give me back to my mom after a couple of weeks because my mom would say that I was just making things up, or that she had gotten rid of her boyfriend and stuff, and my grandma believed it. So after a while, they ended up going to the courthouse and getting married. One day he told her that he didn't want to deal with kids anymore. So she gave me $50 and she dropped me off on the door steps of the fire department," she recalled. "They had one of those safe zone signs or whatever. They called the state and next thing I know, I ended up here. But, it's not so bad most of the time," she shrugged. "As long as you do what you're told, then Ms. P is okay," she told me. She paused and put the dishes in the cabinet. "But, I will admit, I'm ready to graduate so that I can go as far away to college as possible. Just two more years."

"Well, I'm sure you'll be great," I smiled.

We stood in silence for a few moments as we finished drying and putting away the dishes.

"So, your father was a drug dealer, huh?" she asked quietly. I shook my head slowly.

"Yeah. I guess. I knew he was back in the day but he said he was out. I'm still finding stuff out. Can't really ask him now 'cause he's not here," I shrugged.

"I'm sorry. I didn't mean to…bring up bad memories," she apologized.

"No. It's ok," I answered. "I need to get it out of my system."

"Well, at least you had a father that loved you," she said sadly.

I noticed a sadness in Nikki's voice. I hated that she had been here so long and dealing with this crazy shit. She was a sweet girl.

"Yeah, but sometimes, it was like I was fatherless too," I mumbled.

"So, what was your life like before you got here?" she asked. "Was it like the stuff you see in the TV and videos?"

"What do you mean?" I asked, laughing.

"Well, you know, all the money and stuff. The lavish lifestyle."

I shrugged my shoulders.

"I mean, I honestly didn't really pay attention to all that kind of stuff. It was just what I was used to. I knew that he was heavy in the game when I was younger. He doesn't think that I remember much but I do." I leaned against the counter and dropped my head. "When I was little, I would hear people talking about how amazing he was because nobody could touch him. Him and my godfather Goody were unstoppable. Like, Goody and him were down since day one. He wouldn't let anyone near my daddy," I remembered. "But, to the outside world, my father was just a businessman. He had some really good restaurants and he owned one of the hottest nightclubs in town."

"Oh really? Where?" she inquired.

"In Richardson. Limelight," I smiled proud.

Her mouth dropped open in surprise.

"Are you serious?" she squealed.

Realizing how loud she was, we both turned towards the steps to see if Ms. Patricia had heard us.

"Wow. So you were like ballin' and shit," she whispered, giggling.

"Not really," I disagreed. "I mean, I got stuff that I asked for, but his thing was just making sure that I went to school."

"But, I don't get it," she pushed. "If he was making all that money from the restaurant, why was he still selling drugs?"

"I don't know. But I'm going to find out," I said after thinking for a moment.

We heard the door open upstairs.

"Damn. She still up. Be careful," she warned. "Don't tell her I helped you."

"Thanks, Nikki," I told her sincerely.

We could hear Ms. Patricia coming down the steps, so Nikki rushed to the bathroom. A few seconds later, her face appeared as she observed the clean kitchen.

"So you cleaned all this up?" she asked.

"Yes, ma'am," I mumbled.

"Speak up when I'm talking to you!" she snapped.

"Yes, ma'am," I spoke louder.

"Ain't no fuckin' way you cleaned all this shit up by yourself," she hissed. "Who helped you?"

"Nobody," I answered.

She picked up one of the glasses I had set to dry and threw it at me. Thank God for reflexes because I ducked before it could hit me and watched it shatter against the wall. This bitch is crazy!

"Stop fuckin lying to me, bitch! Who the fuck helped you?" she yelled.

I stood there, my eyes large and not knowing what to say.

"I…I…." I stuttered.

"I did."

I turned around and Nikki was standing there looking just as scared as I was.

"Uh huh. That's what I thought," she dragged, pulling a cigarette out of her bra. "I knew you didn't do this shit by yourself."

She walked over to Nikki, grabbing her by her hair and slapped her in her face. She winced in pain but she didn't cry.

"Did I give you permission to help this bitch?" she snapped.

"No, ma'am," Nikki answered.

"So why the fuck did you do it? I told you to stay in your room," Ms. Patricia growled.

"Yes, ma'am. I'm sorry," Nikki tried to apologize. "I was just trying to —"

"You were just trying to get your ass beat!" she yelled, cutting her off. "If I wanted you to help her, I would have told you to help her."

I stood there and watched this girl getting in trouble for doing the dishes. Hell, I know Myesha wouldn't do the dishes if you paid her, so for Nikki to be getting in trouble for it had me dazed.

"Ms. Patricia, please," I tried to reason with her. "She was just helping me out because I was still a little tired. I'm sorry. It will never happen again. Just please don't punish her," I begged.

She turned to look at me with the most deranged look I had ever seen.

"You shut the hell up and go to that fucking room, girl. I'll deal with you in a minute," she ordered. "As for you," she said, turning back to Nikki. "Since you like cleaning so much, yo' ass is gon' clean every room in this house, starting with the basement," she said. "And it better be done before you go to school tomorrow."

"But that'll take me all night!" Nikki whined.

Ms. Patricia pulled her hair tighter and brought her face to hers.

"I don't give a damn! You should have thought about that before you decided to get in this shit!"

She pushed Nikki hard enough to make her fall. When she saw that I was still in the kitchen, she began walking to me.

"I said get to that fucking room!" she said, picking up a bottle and throwing it at me.

I ducked and hurried back to the room, not sure what was going to happen to me. But, I knew I had to do something and quick. I wasn't going to keep dealing with this shit. This was going to stop and soon.

*****

I pulled my notebook out of my backpack and started writing. I needed to let somebody know what was going on and get the hell out of here.

Dear Goody,

I don't even know where to begin with this letter. I'm still trying to figure out if I'm living in some bad dream. So much has changed since Daddy died. This has been one big nightmare and all I want to do is wake up. To wake up and be back in my old bed, or with you and Daddy. I really wish it was that easy. They have me living with this woman and her crazy ass daughter. Goody, I'm trying to be strong but stuff is really bad. I just don't know what to think anymore. Daddy's dead, you're in jail, and they put me in foster care with a woman that is beyond abusive.

I hope you're not mad at Aunt Tori. She tried to take care of me for as long as she could, but when you got locked up and the Feds took everything, she lost everything just as fast. And I feel so bad for her because she's alone. I wanted to stay with her. Anything would have been better than this. Instead, I'm living in a foster home with a woman that has it out for me.

The kids here are okay for the most part, but this one chic, she is so hateful. I don't understand why. The stuff that is going on in this house, Goody, is only stuff that you would see in the movies. It's crazy here. She has this daughter named Whitney. I swear something is seriously wrong with this chic. She has had it out for me since day one and I haven't done anything to her. She jumped me on my first day of school with some of her friends, and I don't know why. I'm not getting any sleep from constantly looking over my shoulder. I haven't heard from anyone from school, and now I'm stuck at South Oak Cliff High instead of back home with my friends.

Throughout all of this, I have made a friend here. There's three other kids in the house. It's only a few besides Whitney that's close to my age. Chris is the only boy in the house and he doesn't really seem to get in trouble as much as everyone else. He's real quiet but I think there's more to it. There's also a little girl named Kim. She doesn't really talk much and I don't blame her. I think something may be wrong with her mentally. And then there's Nikki. She's really sweet. She doesn't deserve what is happening to her. None of us do. Since I've been here, I've had a black eye, been slapped, I've been locked in my room, and gone without food.

I wish things could go back to the way they used to be. I miss you and Daddy so much. I can't imagine what you're going through in there either. You and Daddy were all I had. I don't know what's going to happen here, but I know I can't keep living like this. I can't keep living in fear. I'd much rather live on the streets. That's why I'm writing you. Because if I don't say anything, I have a feeling it's only going to get worse.

But, Goody, there's something else that's really been eating at me. I know you told me not to worry about it, and that I'm too young, but I'm not as naïve as you think I am. I need to know what's going on. I need to know why suddenly my entire world was turned upside down. I need to know why my father was taken from me and why my godfather was locked up. Don't you think I deserve that much? You promised my father that you would always look after me. And now you're behind bars. By the time you get out, God knows where I'll be.

Please write back to let me know you got this. Send it to Myesha's address because I don't want to risk it coming here and upsetting the evilness that I call a foster mother. I will write you again soon. I love you.

Miracle

I quickly folded the paper and put it inside my notebook between some pages. I slid the notebook back in my backpack and got ready for school. I had pretended to go to the bathroom the night before and snuck down to the basement to check on Nikki. I wanted to apologize to her for getting her in trouble because of me. I told her my plan of sending the letter off and getting outside help and she agreed to help me. So, as far as Ms. Patricia knew, I was going to school, but I had to get help somehow. Nikki thought that I was taking a risk but I didn't know how much more I could endure from this house. She may be comfortable living this life, but I wasn't.

I finished getting dressed and hurried to head out. I knew Nikki and Chris would be leaving soon and I didn't want to make her suspicious.

"Y'all make sure y'all bring y'all tails straight home," Ms. Patricia warned as we headed towards the door.

"Yes, ma'am," we said in unison.

We began to walk and I actually felt excitement for the first time since I had been there. Chris looked at me confused.

"What the hell are you over here smiling about?" he asked.

"Nothing," I answered.

Even though I knew he was in the same predicament that we were, I also knew that Whitney looked out for him so I didn't want to say too much. At least until I knew the whole story. He shrugged his shoulders and walked further ahead.

"Aren't you going to tell him so he knows what's going on?" Nikki asked.

"No. For what?" I whispered.

"Well, maybe he can help us," she suggested.

"Help us do what? Didn't you say that Whitney and Ms. P. take it easy on him?" I pushed. "What's to stop him from telling them to get out of trouble or something?"

"Well, yeah, but trust me, it's not like you think," she said.

"What you mean?"

"Just trust me. It's not like you think," she repeated.

I stopped walking and Nikki kept going. She turned around when she noticed I was no longer in pace with her.

"What's the matter with you?" she asked.

"What is it that you're not telling me? 'Cause I'm not about to risk putting myself on the line if it's something I need to know," I stressed.

Chris was so into his headphones that he hadn't even noticed that we were no longer near him.

"Look, I can't say too much because I don't want him mad at me," she said, looking towards him. "But trust me. Chris is on our side."

"How?" I questioned. "I never see him getting yelled at or getting hit."

"That's because he gets it the worst," Nikki said with sad eyes.

"What do you mean?"

"The reason why they favor him is because Ms. Patricia turns the other way. Whitney has been fucking Chris for as long as he's been here," she blurted out.

I damn near choked hearing her say that.

"What?" I asked in shock. "So, they're dating or something?"

"No," she shook her head. "You're not hearing me. Whitney is fucking him." I still looked dazed so she kept going. "Okay. It's like this. When Chris got here, Whitney decided that she was going to be with him. So, pretty much, in order for him not to get hit or beat, or threatened to be punished, he has to do whatever Whitney says, including fucking her."

She had just rocked my entire morning by what she said.

"So you mean, like, she's like raping him or something?" I asked slightly confused.

"Exactly," she responded. "But who is going to believe that he's being raped? All they're gonna see is a boy fucking a girl in the house. They're not gonna listen."

"Damn," I murmured.

I wasn't even sure how to respond to what was just said.

"But, he doesn't even act like anything bothers him though," I said.

"Can you blame him?" she sniffed. "It's his way of dealing with it. When he first got here and everything started happening, he tried to stay away. But, then, I guess it became too much for him to deal with. For him, it was either get beat and risk getting put out, or do what Whitney wanted." She paused for a moment before she finished. "I asked him about it one time, and all he said was that he would be turning eighteen soon and able to leave."

Chris looked up from his headphones and saw that we were no longer close to him.

"Hey, man. Y'all need to come on. I ain't got time to be waiting on y'all," he barked.

We ended the conversation quickly and followed.

"Remember," Nikki reminded me. "You gotta make sure that you're back before that bell rings."

"I got you," I promised her.

The plan we came up with was for me to leave after homeroom. Once the first bell rang, I was going to head out of one of the side doors. Nikki helped me with figuring out which buses I needed to take to get to my old neighborhood. I was going to drop the letter in the outgoing mail and then go see Myesha to figure out my next move.

We walked into the school building and I rushed to homeroom. Finally, the bell rang and I ran as quickly as I could to hide in the bathroom. Once I couldn't hear the students anymore, I peeked out the door. Satisfied that no one was there, I hauled ass towards the side door of the school. I ran like I had a pit bull on my ass. I had to pass by the house which was the scariest feeling in the world. I knew that Ms. Patricia would be inside watching TV, smoking her cigarettes. But with my luck, she would be outside or something for some unknown reason, and I would get caught.

I cringed when I got close to the house, putting the pedal to the metal, and ran as quickly as I could, praying that she was nowhere near the windows or doors. When I got to the bus stop, I started breathing, not even realizing that I had been holding my breath. I pulled my hood over my head and kept my head down so as not to be recognized. About ten minutes later, the bus pulled up and I got on, paid my fare with the money Nikki had snuck me, and sat down in a seat. I kept my head down and once I was out of the neighborhood, I was able to relax.

I looked out the window at the neighborhood. It was such a drastic change from what I was used to. I went from a posh neighborhood and big houses, to living in the hood and I felt so out of place. I couldn't wait to see my girl because even though it had only been a month, it seemed like it had been years. We arrived at the bus depot and I got off to catch the bus to my old school. The ride took almost thirty minutes but I made it.

Getting off the bus, I smiled as I walked the last few blocks. I felt completely different because I knew that I was back home. I saw a few familiar girls walking ahead of me. I called out to one of them, happy to see a familiar face.

"Hey, Sierra!" I called out.

She turned around and her eyes grew large when she saw me standing there.

"Miracle?" she said. "Oh my gosh. Hey, girl!" she grinned. "How have you been? Where have you been? The last time I saw you was at your birthday party…" She trailed off, remembering the events that took place. A look of embarrassment overcame her. "Miracle, I am so sorry. I didn't mean to—"

“It's okay,” I cut her off, not wanting to spoil my mood. “It's been hard to deal with but I'm making it,” I told her.

“I feel you,” she responded. “So….” she said, changing the subject. “What's up? Where you been at?”

“For lack of better words, hell,” I told her.

“Huh?” she frowned.

“Just dealing with some stuff right now,” I murmured.

I looked at my watch and saw that I only had an hour and a half before I had to get back on the bus.

“Hey, do you have your cell phone with you?” I asked.

“Yea, sure,” she answered, handing it to me.

“I just need to send Myesha a message really quick to let her know I'm here,” I said as I texted her.

“What are y'all doing out here so late? Classes started like two hours ago.”

“I know,” she told me. “But I had to run back home to get a change of clothes for gym class.”

“Oh. Okay,” I answered.

I hit the send button to let Myesha know that I was on the campus and to meet me at our spot. Back in the day, we would skip class sometimes and hang out at the pit, at the back of the school. So I knew she would know exactly where to go.

“Alright, girl, I got to get out of here. I need to go meet Myesha really quick,” I told her so that I could get away.

“Well, call me,” she added. “We can all go hang out or something.”

“Sure,” I agreed, knowing that the probability of that happening was slim to none.

I gave her a quick hug and thanked her for letting me use her cell phone. I ran to the back of the school, hoping that no one would see me, and waited at the pit. I didn't wait too long and soon saw Myesha running in the distance. I jumped up from my spot in the grass and hugged my best friend.

"Girl!" she squealed. "Where in the hell have you been? Ain't nobody heard from you. Last thing we heard was that your aunt Tori had put you out. What the hell is going on?" she asked.

Everything came over me at one time and I broke down in tears.

"Myesha, everything has been going wrong. Daddy gets murdered in cold blood and Goody gets locked up. I don't know what the hell is going on, but the next thing I know, I'm being put in foster care. And, I got the fuckin' foster mother from hell! Her daughter is a total bitch and I feel like I'm in some fuckin' twilight zone or some shit!" I cried out.

"Wait. What the hell are you talking about, Miracle?" she asked.

I tried to catch my breath as I told her everything.

"Ever… ever since I got into the house, this girl and her mother have been torturing me," I sniffed.

"Who?" my best friend grilled. "And why the hell is she messing with you?"

I could see anger all over Myesha's face.

"Some girl...Ms. Patricia's daughter, Whitney. She's a total psycho. The first day she was all nice and everything but then she takes my clothes and cuts them up. She takes my stuff without asking and I never get it back. Then, her and her friends jump me in the fuckin' bathroom at school. When I get home and try to tell her mother what's going on, she makes shit even worse. They locked me in the room a couple of nights ago, and I didn't eat for a whole day. Then, she had me scrubbing and cleaning everything in the house like I was her own personal slave," I wept.

At this point, tears streamed down my face as I cried hysterically.

"What the fuck?" Myesha gulped.

She was trying not to cry but I could see her eyes watering. For as long I had known her, Myesha has never cried.

"That's not even the worst part," I told her. "It's other kids in the house. One of them is this dude named Chris and I just found out he's getting it the worst."

"What do you mean?" she prodded. "What could be any worse than getting beat and locked in a room?"

"Chris, um…Whitney is using him as her own little fuck buddy," I spoke up.

"What?"

"Yeah. You heard me. The only way that he can avoid getting beat or put out is for him to do whatever Whitney wants, including giving her the dick," I explained.

"I don't get this shit," she sighed. "Like, this bitch needs her ass whooped. You should've been beat this hoe by now!"

"I know," I agreed. "But Myesha, I can't take her by myself! I ain't saying I can't handle myself but these bitches play dirty. And I damn sure can't take on her mama. Her mama is crazy and I have nowhere to go, so what other choice do I have?"

"You can come and stay with me, you know that," she fussed. "You know Mama wont care."

"Yeah, but your mama would have to go through all that legal stuff. And that shit can take forever. I would still have to deal with the bitch, and by the time it goes through, hell, I'll be eighteen," I said. "Your mom can't keep me. It's like she gets a kick out of it or something. Like, I don't even really see her torturing anybody but me. It's been less than a week and all this shit is happening," I complained.

"Well, can't you tell somebody or something?" she asked.

"The last time that happened, the girl in the house that told ended up being beaten severely," I told her.

"Well, damn, boo. What are you going to do?" she sighed.

"I don't know," I told her. "But, I had to come and see you and let you know what was going on."

I looked down at my watch and saw I had a little under an hour.

"Like I said, I don't know what I'm going to do. But this is home for me, Myesha," I pointed around me. "This is all I know. I can't deal with that lifestyle. I can't be around people like that. In that world, Nikki is my only friend. Chris is cool, but he doesn't really like being bothered by anyone. And Kim, she's so young. All she does is play with her dolls and stays in her room," I said.

"Well, we gotta figure out something." Myesha fussed. "Because this shit ain't cool."

I could tell she was trying not to cry, as mad as she was. Myesha was a thug by nature and I always teased her for that. So, seeing her cry, I knew she was really hurting.

"Thanks, boo," I told her. "I love you, girl. I miss you like crazy."

"Love you too, sis," she said.

"So, what's been going on here?" I inquired, trying to get her mind off of the mess I was in.

"Girl, the same ole, same ole," she shrugged.

"You still talking to Wood?" I asked.

"Girl, bye," she laughed. "I stopped fucking with that nigga long before you left."

I laughed because I knew Myesha had more niggas tryna get at her every day.

"So who are you talking to now?" I asked laughing.

"Oh…" she stalled. "Nobody special. I mean, we haven't really made it official or anything so I don't really want to get into it right now."

"Okay," I conceded.

I noticed how her mood changed when she said that. Normally, she would be bragging about every boy that she had talked to, so for her to not want to tell me who it was had me puzzled.

"Miracle, I think I have an idea," she blurted.

"What?" I asked.

"Well, I was just thinking. You're almost done with your junior year. We only have our senior year left," she said. "And, from what it sounds like, she's gonna put you out the minute that you turn eighteen. So, if you still tryna go to college and all that, or hell, just survive, you know you're gonna need money. And I know a way I can hook you up with some," she smiled.

"How?" I asked, intrigued.

Myesha is sneaky, so whatever she had planned had to be something that, more than likely, would get one of us in trouble.

"Well, I mean, you know I never really said anything about it, but I got some money stashed to the side. Whenever my daddy comes to visit, he always gives me large stacks of cash and makes me promise not to tell my mama," she explained.

"Okay. I already knew that, Myesha," I observed. "But, what exactly does that gotta do with me?"

"I can hook you up with some money, girl!" she strained.

"Okay, Myesha, but what am I going to do with it?" I stressed. "Even if I could take your money, where would I put it? I mean you heard me say that this girl goes through my stuff and takes my shit without asking. Bringing money in that house ain't gonna do shit but raise questions. I don't need any unwanted attention."

"Well," she thought aloud. "We could go to the bank and open up an account. And then you can make deposits into it whenever you get money."

"I don't know, Myesha," I told her. "I don't want to be taking money from you."

"Girl, please," she laughed. "I'd much rather give it to you then to just let it sit there," she said. "And, I think I may have another way for you to make some quick money, but I gotta look into that."

I looked at my best friend and a smile crossed my face.

"Why are you smiling like that?" she frowned.

"Cause you being all soft and shit," I joked.

She sucked her teeth and rolled her eyes.

"Whatever."

"Oh," I snapped my fingers, remembering what else I needed. "Before I forget, I wrote a letter to Goody. I told him to respond to your address and put your name on it. So I need you to send it off for me and if he writes back, make sure that your mom doesn't get it and open it," I told her.

"Alright. Cool," she said. "I hate that you're going through this shit, Miracle."

"Me too. Hopefully, it'll be over soon," I whispered.

I changed the subject and we talked about the good old days until it was time for me to leave. Twelve o'clock came, and I felt like Cinderella as she prepared to go back to her wicked stepmother.

*****

Chapter Five

"Are you waiting on the bus?"

I looked around to see where the voice came from. I saw a young boy sitting across the street, leaning against a black SUV, looking in my direction.

"Yea," I yelled out.

"Ay. Yo, that bus came about ten minutes ago," he hollered.

Shit!

I looked at my watch and realized that I would have to wait another forty-five minutes for another bus.

"You need a ride?" he called out to me.

"Nah. I'm good," I said as he began jogging towards me.

My mind was racing as I began to wonder how I was going to get back to school without getting caught. I thought about going back to the school and asking Myesha to call her mother to take me back. I knew I would be risking a lot, but I didn't know what else to do. The boy was now a few feet away from me.

"Ay, that bus always comes extra early," he told me, catching his breath.

"Yeah. I see that," I responded, not really wanting to hear him.

Looking up close at him, I knew him from somewhere but I couldn't figure out where.

"Where you trying to go?" he asked.

"I gotta head back to school," I told him.

"Ain't your school like right around the corner, though?" he laughed.

I looked at him again trying to figure out how he knew that.

"You go to Arlington Heights, right?" he inquired.

"Yea," I answered slowly. "Why?"

"You look familiar." He stared for a few moments longer and snapped his fingers. "Oh. I know. My little brother used to talk to your home girl, Myleta, or some shit like that, right?"

I relaxed a little bit.

"Who is your little brother?" I asked.

"Wood," he told me.

"Oh yeah," I smiled. "And her name is Myesha."

"Oh. Damn. My bad," he apologized. "Yo, I can give you a ride if you need it," he offered again.

What did I have to lose? I looked at his ride and figured what the hell.

"I have to go to the other side of town though," I told him.

"It's cool. I got a little bit of time. Just let me make a stop really quick and I can run you over there," he told me.

"Are you sure?" I asked.

"Yeah. You straight. Come on," he told me.

I followed him towards his car.

"What's your name again?" I asked.

I figured I should at least know his name since I was getting into the car with him.

"Trevon. But everybody calls me Black," he said.

Looking at him, I can understand why. He had the darkest skin I'd ever seen but it was so pretty.

"Okay, Trevon. Well, I appreciate the ride," I thanked him.

"No problem," he smiled. "But call me Black."

"I think I like Trevon better," I told him.

We got in his car and immediately, the sound of Future blared through the speakers.

I wear Gucci, I wear Bally at the same damn time!

He turned the music down when he saw me jump from how loud it was.

"My bad," he apologized sheepishly. "Usually, it's just me or one of my boys riding."

"No. You're fine," I told him. "I like his new one that he has out with his baby mama, Ciara, 'Anytime'."

"Yea. That joint is hot. That nigga got bars for days," he grinned. "So, why you don't go to the Heights anymore?"

"Wow. I've been asked that question like a million times," I said not really wanting to get into it. "But, long story short, my father was killed and my godfather was put in prison, so I got put into foster care and can't go to Arlington anymore," I told him.

"Damn. That's messed up," he snorted.

I shrugged my shoulders and looked out the window.

"It's cool."

"Yeah. I had seen you a few times before when Wood was talking to your home girl," he told me. "Your pops name was Eddie, right? Now I remember."

Well, if you remember, why the fuck would you ask me?

"So, what you doing over here right now aside from cutting class?" he asked.

"I needed to see my best friend," I told him. "We needed to handle some stuff."

"Oh word?" he asked. "Well, you're too cute to be taking the bus and shit. I'm going to give you my number. You don't need to be out here by yourself. Niggas are crazy, even out here at the Heights," he smirked. "If you ever need help or anything, let me know."

"I'll keep that in mind," I smiled. "Right now, I just gotta make sure that I get back before the bell rings," I reminded him.

"Alright. Cool. I'm about to make a stop really quick and I'll take you straight there," he told me as he pulled into an apartment complex and pulled out his cell phone. "Hey, yo. I'm outside."

A few seconds later, a boy about the same age as Black came outside and approached the truck.

"Yo, I need you to drop this off for me," he told him, reaching behind the seat to grab a bag.

"Aight, my nigga. I got you," the boy answered.

"Make sure that he checks it before you leave," he told him.

"Fa sho," the boy responded.

He looked in the car and saw me sitting in the passenger seat.

“Who’s that?” he asked.

“Don’t worry ‘bout all that. Nobody you know,” Black snapped. “Just go ahead and get that handled.”

The two dapped each other up and the boy went back inside the building.

“Alright. Let's get you back to school. Don't want you to get the detention,” he laughed.

I smiled a little. I looked at him, trying not to make it obvious, and noticed his handsome features. He had smooth, pretty skin and his body was definitely in shape.

“So, you slang, huh?” I asked him.

He continued to drive, looking at the road ahead.

“Why do you say that?” he asked after a few moments of silence.

“I know the deal,” I told him. “Let's just say I've seen it before.”

“Well,” he answered, “don't worry your pretty little head ‘bout it. I do what I do.”

“Hey. No judgment here,” I said, throwing up my hands in mock surrender.

“What do you know about that life anyway?” he asked.

“You forgot who my daddy was. Back in the day, he was that nigga. Him and my godfather, Goody, were the ones that everybody talked about and everybody respected,” I told him.

“Word?” he asked.

“Yep,” I told him. “I think that's what got him killed.”

I looked Black in the eyes.

"Damn," he replied. "I heard rumors about the two but never knew it to be true. That's deep."

"Don't I know it," I mumbled.

Thinking about it angered me and I remembered my vow to find the person responsible and make them pay.

He took the exit off the highway.

"So, how you liking your new spot?" he questioned.

"I don't," I answered almost immediately with a change in my tone.

"Damn. My bad. Chill with the attitude," he responded.

"I don't have an attitude with you," I told him. "It's just the situation. I'm not trying to be there and they don't want me there. I'm just...I'm just ready to get out," I sighed, frustrated.

Quite honestly I was trying to get as far away from him as possible. This nigga is fine as hell and he was making me nervous as hell.

"And go where?" he asked. "How old are you?"

"I just turned seventeen. I wish I hadn't," I answered sadly.

"Damn, yo. Why you say that?"

"Because everything changed when I turned seventeen. My whole world changed for the worst," I concluded.

"Damn," he sighed, trying to be sympathetic. "I don't even know what to say on that."

"Ain't nothing that can be said. Just as soon as I get the opportunity, I'm out," I promised.

"So, what are you going to do?" he asked.

“I'm gonna stack up my money however I can, and then I'm gone,” I told him.

“That's what's up,” he nodded. “Well, while you out stackin’ money, make sure you holla at your boy and don't forget about me.”

I looked at his grinning face and couldn’t help but to smile.

“Make a right up here,” I told him once we got close to the neighborhood, trying to ignore how fine he was. I could see the school ahead so I was grateful for the distraction. “You can pull up over here,” I instructed him, pointing a few yards ahead.

He slowed down and pulled over to the side.

“I really appreciate it,” I thanked him.

“No problem. Yo, give me a call when you can,” he said. “We can chop it up or something. Go kick it or some shit.”

“All right. It might be a little while but I'll see what I can do,” I said.

I don't know what it was, but it was something about him that made me like him. Despite the fact that his chocolate ass was fine as hell. I knew he was the type of nigga that my father wouldn’t even want me talking to, but he had me smiling. I rushed back to the side door of the building and walked back in. I went to the library to wait for the final bell to ring. I should have gone to my last class, but I really didn't feel like being around other people. So, I sat at a table in a corner, pulled out my notebook and started writing. One thing that I loved doing was writing because I knew it was a way for me to release all my emotions. I had considered a career as a writer for a while, but law was something I was more passionate about. I let my fingers take over and got out all my frustrations.

The bell rang and I packed up all of my things so that I could meet Nikki at her class. She came out and we went to the front to wait for Chris.

"So what happened?" she asked, eager.

"Everything is good I think," I told her. "I gave the letter to my best friend for her to mail off. She's going to help. I'm going to go back in a few days and we're going to go to the bank and open up an account," I filled her in. "She's going to loan me some money and I'm going to use that to save until I can figure out what to do next."

"Well, do you think that your godfather will be able to do anything?" she asked. "I mean he's in prison so it might not be much that he can do," she pointed out.

"I know," I said. "But I gotta at least try. If I don't, she wins, and I'm stuck."

"So, what do you think your godfather can do?" she pushed.

"Hell if I know," I admitted. "But, I do know that Goody is a very resourceful person."

"Well, I'm glad you made it back before it was time to go," she smiled.

"Girl, I almost didn't," I told her, thinking about Trevon.

"What?" she said, looking horrified. "What happened?"

"I missed the bus coming back," I told her. "But, girl, thank gawd. A niggga that I used to go to school with offered me a ride."

"Girl, you got lucky!" she sighed.

"I know," I laughed.

Chris came walking out at that moment and we both got quiet.

"We'll talk later," I whispered. "Dang. It took you long enough," I said to him.

He frowned at me and kept walking.

"Whatever. Let's go," he mumbled.

"What's wrong with you?" Nikki asked him.

"Nothing. Let's go," he snapped.

Nikki and I looked at each other and she shrugged.

"What the hell is eating him?" I hissed.

"My money is on Whitney," she guessed.

"So, what, is he like at her beck and call or something?" I inquired.

"Pretty much," she answered. "If she wants it, she's going to get it, and nobody's going to stop her. Not even her own mother."

"Well, that's all about to change," I stated matter of a fact. "I don't know how, but both of them are going to be stopped."

She laughed at my words.

"Look at you over here sounding like you in the mob or something," she teased me.

I rolled my eyes. I know it sounded silly but I was serious about putting a stop to their bullshit.

"You think I'm joking but I'm so serious," I told her. "I might have to endure this for a little bit longer, but I'm getting us up out of here."

"Ok, girl," she laughed.

She looked at me and saw how serious I was, so she left it alone.

"Well, we should have an easy night. Ms. P is going to see her boyfriend," she filled me in, which shocked the shit out of me.

"She has a man?" I asked, surprised.

"Yeah. He's a truck driver. I think he's married, though. When he comes to town, she's a whole different person. Only thing is, Whitney's still here," she said.

"And so is Chris," I finished her sentence.

"But, at least we don't have to worry about getting in trouble for anything," she cheered up.

"Yea. I guess," I replied, thinking about the shit Chris had to endure.

We walked home and to my surprise, Ms. Patricia was dressed up with her hair done and makeup on. She still had her nasty attitude.

"I'm going out for a while," she told us. "I'll be home later on tonight. Y'all better act like you got some damn sense," she ordered. "You eat and then you take your asses in your rooms."

"Yes, ma'am," we replied.

I hoped that Whitney wasn't in the room as I walked towards the door. Chris headed straight for his room.

"Um…Ms. Patricia, is it okay if we watch TV for a little bit?" Nikki asked.

I braced myself because I knew that she was going to pop off on Nikki for asking that question. But she shocked me with her response. After hesitating, she responded with a "yes" as she rushed to the door.

"But, you better not watch it for more than an hour," she warned.

I got excited and hoped that she would stay in this mood for a while. She left and soon it was just Nikki and myself in the living room watching television. Whitney walked in the house about ten minutes later.

"What y'all doing watching TV?" she asked.

"Ms. Patricia said that we could," Nikki told her. "She went out for a little bit."

"Okay," she answered. I glanced at her and noticed that she was smiling. "Alright. Well, y'all stay down here and don't bother me," she told us.

I wanted to take my chance and slap the hell out of her, but I remained quiet. I saw her walk upstairs instead of going to her room.

I nudged Nikki to see if she noticed, but she stared straight ahead at the television. As soon as Whitney disappeared up the steps and I heard a door close, I turned and looked at Nikki.

"I know she's not about to do this while we're in the house?" I whispered.

"Just act like you don't hear it," she told me.

"You're just gonna ignore the shit?" I asked, surprised.

"Yes," Nikki said, finally looking at me. "Because I'm used to it. After a while, you will be too."

"No," I said. "I could never get used to anything like this," I mumbled.

We sat and watched TV and then went into the kitchen to eat our dinner while we did our homework. I tried my hardest not to think about what was going on upstairs, but it tormented me all night.

I went to bed close to eleven o'clock and Whitney still had not come down. Lying down, I started thinking about what Chris was doing to her. I thought about how he may have touched her, or how she may have touched him. I thought about him on top of her, and somehow, my mind wandered to Black. I wondered what it would feel like to have him touch me like that. I started to get that feeling in my panties again. Myesha laughed at me and said that I was getting wet. I had never been with a boy before, so I didn't know what to expect.

I woke up a few hours later to Whitney climbing into her bed. She smelled like sex. This nasty bitch didn't even get up to wash her ass. I closed my eyes back and pretended that I was asleep. She hadn't messed with me in a couple of days, but I never let my guard down with her. No sooner than I began to doze back to sleep, I heard the front door open and Ms. Patricia came stomping in.

"Shhh," she whispered, laughing.

Hers and another voice grew louder in the kitchen.

"Be careful, baby," she fussed, still laughing.

They continued laughing and joking for a few more minutes before I heard her take him upstairs. This shit was just too much. I closed my eyes yet again and tried to get a few hours of sleep.

When I woke up the next morning, I got ready for school. The smell of breakfast drew me to the kitchen. I walked in to find some man in his fifties sitting at the table. He was heavyset and damn near bald. He reminded me of a larger version of Sherman Helmsley. He looked up when he saw me come in and the look that he gave me, gave me a strange feeling.

"You must be one of Pat's kids," he grunted.

"Yes," I mumbled, looking around trying to see where everyone else was.

"Well, come on in here and get you something to eat, girl," he grinned, staring me up and down.

Nervous, I stayed where I was. Lucky for me, Nikki came in and I relaxed a little.

"Morning, Nikki," I said rushing to her side.

"Hey," she greeted, a little taken back by my demeanor.

We both fixed our plates and sat down at the table to eat. I avoided eye contact. Ms. Patricia came in, hair wild and her robe on.

"Girls, did you say good morning to Mr. Earl?" she asked.

"Good morning," we both mumbled through our mouths full of food.

We looked over in his direction and he winked at me. I put my head back down quickly and focused on my plate.

"Yeah. Hurry up and finish eating. Then go upstairs and get Kim and Chris and tell them that we're leaving in fifteen minutes. I gotta take Kim to that damn therapist of hers. Tell Chris he'd better hurry up too," she instructed us.

"Yes, ma'am," we said, rushing to finish our food.

I could practically feel Mr. Earl's eyes watching Nikki. I finished my food and ran upstairs to knock on Chris's door. I opened it, ready to get out of the house.

"Chris! Ms. Patricia said come on 'cause we gotta leave in fifteen minutes," I told him.

"I'll be there in a minute," he mumbled.

"What's wrong with you?" I asked, noticing how grouchy he was.

"What did I just say?" he snapped, looking at me.

I almost snapped back at him but then I remembered what happened the night before.

“I'm not the one you should be mad at. At least you only have two more months,” I said, walking out and closing the door behind me.

Walking back down the steps, I thought about everything that Chris was going through. Rape was harder to prove with men than women, and for the last several months, Chris’s mentality had been messed up. I grabbed my bag and waited outside with Nikki.

“Is he coming?” she asked.

“He said he was,” I told her.

We waited for a few more minutes before Ms. Patricia popped her head out the front door.

“Y'all go ahead and get to school,” she told us.

“Okay,” I replied, standing up from the step we were sitting on.

“You don't want us to wait for Chris?” Nikki asked.

“No. He'll catch up to y'all. You just go ahead and go,” she rushed us.

We didn't ask any other questions and headed to school. Nicki was yapping about some guy in her class and I just stayed quiet, listening to her. I couldn't get my mind off of Chris and what he was dealing with.

“Hello?” Nikki said, interrupting my thoughts.

“My bad,” I apologized. “What's up?”

“Did you hear anything I just said?” she laughed.

“Yeah,” I told her. “You were talking about the boy in class.”

“Girl, I stopped talking about that like five minutes ago,” she said, laughing. “Where were you just now?”

I shook my head.

“I don't know. It's just something nagging at me,” I told her.

“Well, try not to think about it whatever it is,” she soothed. “Trust me. The next few days will be good. Ms. P's boyfriend is here so she's going to be like a whole different person. He doesn’t know how she really is or the shady shit she be doing.”

The question is does she know how he really is? I asked myself, thinking about the way that he was looking at me and Nikki at breakfast.

We walked into the school and agreed to meet up for lunch as we always did. I went to homeroom and started writing in my notebook. I wrote how angry I was that I had to go through the same routine day in and day out. I wrote about how pissed off I was at the person that shot my father in cold blood. I wanted them to suffer. I wanted them to die. I wasn't a killer, but every time I thought about my father lying there bleeding to death, evil thoughts possessed me. The first chance I got, I was going to visit my godfather and get some answers. The police wouldn't tell me anything because I was a minor, and because I was directly involved with my father. So, I knew I had to find out another way.

My mind drifted to Black, and I wondered if he was someone that I could be with. If he was as resourceful as he seemed. Something told me he kept his ear in the streets and could find out anything for me. All I had to do was get in touch with him again. I hoped that when I went to see Myesha, he would still be interested.

The bell rang and I got ready to head to my next class. I was almost to my locker when I felt someone tap me on the back. I turned around to see Chris standing looking anxious.

“Hey. What's up?” I smiled.

“Meet me outside,” he said, walking towards the side door.

“Okay,” I nodded, putting my things away and closing the locker back.

He walked off and I followed behind as instructed, and he paced back and forth.

“What's up? I asked, a little nervous.

“Look,” he started. “I know that I don't really talk to you like that. And, I don't really want to get into it, but I need you to look out for Nikki,” he advised.

“Okay, Chris, I know you got stuff going on but you're making me nervous,” I confessed. “What are you talking about? What's going on?”

“Look, man, like I said, I can't get into it, but I gotta go. Just make sure you look after Nikki and Kim,” he told me. “Mainly Nikki. They don't really mess with Kim like that because she's a little slow and she stays away, but you gotta make sure that Nikki don't end up getting hurt,” he pleaded.

“Chris, talk to me,” I begged. “Why are you telling me all of this? What are you about to do?”

“I'm out,” he announced. “I'm not about to be dealing with this anymore. I have two months until I turn eighteen. All I was waiting on was to graduate. I already went and took the test for my GED so I'm good.” He looked around to make sure no one could see us. “Don't tell nobody that you saw me today,” he warned.

As shocked as I was, I understood. I shook my head and agreed.

"I won't," I promised him. "But, where are you going to go?" I asked him.

"I don't know. I'm a stay with one of my boys for a couple of days over in Houston. I got some money to get a bus ticket. After that, I don't know. But, I ain't gonna be nowhere near here. Just make sure that you do what you promised. Look after Nikki and Kim," he repeated.

"I got you," I told him.

For the first time since I met him, I looked at him through different eyes. I always thought that he was just being rude, but now I understood him a lot more.

"Now, go get back inside before the bell rings," he ordered.

"Alright," I whispered. "Be careful."

"No doubt," he answered.

He turned and began to walk off.

"Wait!" I called out. "What do you want me to tell Nikki? Don't you think she deserves to know?"

He stood for a few seconds.

"No. Just act like you don't know anything. The less she knows, the less chance she has of dealing with that bitch," he sneered.

I assumed he was referring to Ms. Patricia. Next thing I know, he turned and started running. I watched him for a few seconds and was interrupted by the bell ringing. I rushed inside so that I could get to class and not be marked late.

*****

The rest of the day went by pretty quickly and the final bell rang. I stood outside the front of the building waiting on Nikki so that we could walk home together and I could tell her about Chris. After a few minutes, she didn't show and I got nervous. I went inside the building and checked her classroom but she wasn't there. I checked the cafeteria, her locker, and a few other areas where we hung out and still nothing. Looking at my watch, I saw how late it was and decided to head to the house. I only hoped that Nikki could catch up.

I ran the whole way home and burst through the front door. Immediately, my senses were up as Ms. Patricia was extremely jumpy.

"What took you so long to get home?" she questioned me.

"I'm sorry. I was waiting on Nikki but I couldn't find her," I explained.

"Well, she's not gonna be living here anymore," she mumbled.

Her boyfriend Earl sat in a chair looking uncomfortable. Alarms were ringing in my head. Where the hell was Nikki and what did they do? I had a feeling that he did something the way he was acting and she trying to act all calm when I could see she was rattled.

"What…where, where did she go?" I asked.

"Don't worry about all that," Ms. Patricia answered quickly giving me a daring look. "She ain't here. You seen Chris?"

"No ma'am," I lied, not wanting to tell her what I knew. "Last time I saw him, he was still in his room this morning before school."

"Well, apparently he done run off. All of his stuff is gone out of his room and none of his teachers saw him today," she rushed, lighting a cigarette. “I don’t need this today. State can come in here at any moment and I got a runaway and another that’s….well, she had to go.”

“He ran away?” I whispered, pretending like this was news.

Inside I was smiling seeing how shook she was. It’s exactly what the fuck she got.

“That's what the hell I just said!” Patricia snapped. She tried to fix herself when she saw Earl staring at her. “Look, just… go in the kitchen and do your homework. Go on in there,” she demanded.

I did as I was told and went into the kitchen and pulled out my notebook to do my homework. With Chris running away and Nikki suddenly disappearing, something was telling me that my time was limited. I didn't realize I was crying until the ink on my paper became smeared from my tears. It wasn’t like Nikki to just leave and not say anything, and the way that they were acting, I had a feeling that they had done something to her. She was just in school happy and talking about some boy and now, it was like she had vanished into thin air.

Nikki was the only thing that I had that mattered. She was the only person that mattered to me now, since everything had been taken from me. If they did something to her, I would lose it. It was like anything that I loved, God was taking away. I wanted Nikki here with me where I could look out for her, but a part of me was hoping that she was safe wherever she was. Maybe Ms. Patricia gave her back to the state and she was in a better home.

As for Chris, watching him walk away was a ball of mixed emotions. I hadn’t really had the opportunity to get to know him like that. Although he was always in a funky mood, he took so much more than any of us. He deserved happiness. He deserved to live a normal life. Hell. We all did. He got away and he would be able to start over. I was happy that he was finally free, but a part of me was jealous because I wished that I had the same courage. I only hoped that my daddy was watching over me from heaven. Because I was going to get a way out, and it was going to be hell to pay.

*****

Chapter Six

It had been six months since I had been in the house with Ms. Patricia and things were still crazy as hell. Even though Chris had run away and Nikki had disappeared into thin air, they had actually placed another child into her care, but thankfully, she was nice. NaTasha had been placed about three months before when she lost her parents in a car crash. She was a year younger than me but you would never know it the way she behaved. I don't know what she did, but she actually kept Whitney in her place, which I was grateful for. Ever since Chris and Nikki left, Patricia was worse than before and her boyfriend Earl hadn't come around as much, so every little thing was setting her off. If we made one wrong move, it was a slap, punch or an object flying at our head.

Whitney had moved into Chris's old room and NaTasha had moved into the room with me. Kim was still there as well, but not much had changed with her. Natasha and I had grown really close and both of us were counting down the days before we could leave Patricia's house for good.

I had still been sneaking off twice a month to see Myesha, and as she promised, she had been helping me with money. Goody had responded to my letter and promised me that he would help me. I had gotten a cell phone and had been talking to Black through text messages. He was really sweet and nothing like I thought he would be. He had been trying to get with me and had started helping me out by having me sell dime bags in the school. I would sell it and then give him the money, but over time, he trusted me enough to just pay a percentage and I kept majority of the profit. At first, I was against it, but I knew it was a quick way to get money. I never flaunted my money and kept my stuff hidden at school. I was making a lot of deposits and stacking up my money steadily.

I was particularly excited to head to school that day because Myesha had texted me and said my godfather had sent another letter. I had let NaTasha in on my ventures to my old high school and she was cool with it. We rushed out the door to head to school and I had no idea how that day would change my life.

*****

"Damn, baby, how you doing?"

I was walking down the street with NaTasha, rushing to get to school. It was only forty-five degrees outside which was rare in Dallas. I hadn't brought a jacket, so the weather was motivation for me to hurry up and get inside and not stop to talk.

I tried to ignore him, but of course, NaTasha insisted on slowing her ass down to talk to him.

"What's up, baby. You can't speak?" the guy asked, following behind.

I slowed my walking some and NaTasha smiled. All I wanted to do was get inside because I was starting to get cold, but after being in Oak Cliff for the last six months, I knew better than to ignore a nigga. Niggas were crazy and known for popping off at the slightest thing. I had a friend, Andrea, that was in my class. She had tried to ignore this nigga that was tryna holla at her from a car and she had to get ten stitches on the side of her face from him throwing a beer bottle at her. I didn't want them thinking that I was stuck up, so I stopped and turned so that I could get a good look at who was preventing me from the warm school.

"What's up?" I asked in a hurry.

"You, baby," he answered with a grin.

Seriously? I stopped for this? I swear these niggas are so fucking corny.

"So, you stopped me to say what's up?" I asked.

“Nah. I stopped you because you’re thick as hell,” he said, eyeballing the fuck out of me.

His friends huddled around him, watching to see what would happen. This shit was starting to get old so I sucked my teeth, annoyed.

“Seriously?” I answered. “Well, thank you, but I gotta go.”

Me and NaTasha started walking and of course, they had to say something.

“Girl,” she fussed. “Don't you know who that is?”

“Who?” I asked annoyed.

“That’s Chief,” she told me.

“Okay, and?” I pushed. “Am I supposed to be impressed or something? Like you’re not going to stop me and tell me that you want to talk to me cuz I'm thick,” I told her. “Like for real, that’s some dumb ass shit to say. That nigga sounds stupid as hell.”

NaTasha looked at me like I was some retard and just shook her head.

“Girl, you crazy as hell,” she laughed. “Everybody and they mama want that nigga. He is one of the finest muthafuckas I have ever seen. The baddest nigga out of Highland Hills. Shit. If you don't want him, I'll damn sure take him,” she grinned.

“Knock yourself out,” I told her, unimpressed, walking into the school.

I had to listen to her admiration of some fuck nigga all the way down the hall to my locker. She talked about this nigga Chief as if he was some God. He didn’t have shit on Black. Black didn’t have whack ass lines like that and I was glad.

"Girl, you should be happy he said something to you," NaTasha fussed. "Chief usually messes with older chicks and shit. But he likes you!"

"So what?" I replied, annoyed.

"So, you are gonna be dumb as hell if you don't talk to him, Miracle. I mean, damn. I know you like Black and all but…. damn!" she groaned.

It was moments like this that I had to remember that she was younger than me and hadn't been in the house as long as me either. I was focused on making money. And even though I was feeling Black, the only thing I was gonna be to that nigga was a friend.

"Look. I ain't got time for some bum ass nigga whose only way of talking to me is by telling me that he tryna holla at me 'cause I'm thick. That nigga probably got like six or seven kids and don't pay child support or some shit like that."

The way NaTasha looked at me, you would have thought I insulted her personally.

"Kids? Chief ain't got no kids. Don't you know who he is?" she asked.

"No. Should I?" I asked, rolling my eyes, wishing she would just tell me already.

"Girl!" NaTasha screamed. "Chief is like one of the baddest niggas in Dallas. Not just Highland Hills. Shit, probably all of Texas. He got the blocks on lock. Hell. He's like the nigga everybody tryna be. Everybody works for that nigga including your little boyfriend and every bitch wanna fuck him. I damn sure do," she cheesed.

I couldn't help but to laugh. This girl was so damn shallow it made no sense.

"Girl, come on," I strained. "I ain't got time for that. I'm tryna get the hell out of here. Besides, you know damn well I done had enough of folks and drugs. I lost my father to that shit and I ain't tryna be around it," I reminded her.

But, that did remind me to look into him later. If he was that known, then he probably knew about my father and I could try to get some answers.

"Yea. You're right," she laughed. "Your godfather would probably kill you anyway."

"Anyways…" I said, deciding to change the subject. "Aight. So, you haven't forgotten, right? As soon as the bell rings, I'm going to take the bus to see Myesha," I told her.

"Yeah. I know," she huffed, her whole demeanor changing.

I detected a little attitude but I didn't mention it. Besides, it was important for me to do this to make things happen. I didn't want to have to worry about anybody else for at least this day. I tried to be extra nice to her to cheer her up.

"Thanks for covering for me, Tash," I grinned, squeezing her. "I may not say it all the time but I really appreciate you looking out for me," I thanked her.

She smiled and shrugged her shoulders.

"No biggie," she said. "Just make sure your ass is back before we gotta go back to Cruella."

I laughed at the nickname that she had given Ms. Patricia.

"Oh, don't worry. I got you," I promised as we walked into the building.

I went to homeroom, which was now next door to the bathroom, and waited anxiously for the first bell. As soon as it rang, I snuck out the side door and ran like hell to the bus stop. I knew the bus system better, so I knew exactly when to leave to make sure that I didn't have time to be waiting around and risk getting caught.

I fixed my hair and stood waiting no more than a minute for the bus to arrive. An hour later, I got to the school, heading straight to the pit. And sure enough, Myesha was already there waiting for me.

"Hey, girl!" she squealed.

"Hey!" I said, giving her a big hug.

We hugged each other and for a while, I felt like my old self. Myesha had really been a big help the last six months. I'd only seen her twice a month, and every time, she always came through. When I came back after our initial talk, we went and opened up a bank account and put it in her name since she had just turned eighteen. Last time we talked, she had $1,300 sitting in the account. I felt bad at first taking her money from her that her father was giving her, but she assured me several times that it was okay. As soon as I could, I planned on paying her back.

"Okay. So, where's the letter?" I asked.

"Oh, yea. I almost forgot," she replied.

She reached into her backpack and handed me an envelope. I looked at the left-hand corner and saw that it came from the Texas State Correctional Facility. I got excited and ripped the letter open and ten one-hundred-dollar bills fell into my lap. I stuffed them into my bag and returned my attention back to the letter and began to read.

Dear Miracle,

I know you're probably mad that it took me so long to respond, but they had your godfather in solitary confinement for a while as a "precautionary measure." I don't even know what to say other than I'm sorry. You're right. I should have been there to protect your father. And trust me, when I get out, we're going to find out who the fuck did this shit and make them pay. But, like I said before, Miracle, some things I don't think you understand. But just know that your father was my best friend, you are my goddaughter, and I love just as one of my own.

Tori did tell me everything that happened, so no, I'm not mad at her. Hell. The Feds will do anything they can to pin something on the black man, especially one that is doing good for himself. They're trying to say that I was caught up in some drug trafficking, but the only reason that I am in here is because of stuff that me and your daddy did back in the day. Miracle, I hope you know that your daddy loved you and was doing everything he could for you. I hope that you are continuing to be the beautiful, young lady that your father raised you to be.

Enjoy the gift. It's not much, but I hope that you can do something with it. I hope that the letters have been getting to Myesha's okay. I got the memo to send them to the PO Box, too. I got an attorney that says that I have a strong chance of getting out early due to something with the evidence. I'm waiting to see what happens and waiting on a new trial date. Don't worry, baby girl. Soon, I'll be out and things will be different. Hold your head up, and stay strong. Your godfather will be home soon.

Love, Goody

I sniffed, folding the letter up and putting it back in the envelope.

"So, what did he say?" she asked.

"Well, he told me that he was sorry and that he would explain things at another time, and that he is supposed to get a new trial," I told her.

"Well, it's better than nothing," she reasoned.

"Yeah. I guess," I told her.

I needed to put the money that my godfather had sent me in the bank account so that no one would steal it. Thinking about it, I knew Black would probably run me to the bank if it meant that he would get the opportunity to see me. I hit him up and asked him to come and pick me up to take me home. He responded back within a few minutes telling me that it was no problem.

Myesha opened up her purse and pulled out a small bag.

"What's that?" I asked.

"Oh. I was about to smoke something," she told me. "You want to hit?"

"Naw. I'm good," I told her.

I didn't want to risk having anything on me smelling like weed and Ms. Patricia finding out. It was bad enough I was already hustling the stuff at school. I had a good system going though, I had to admit. Whenever I saw Black, I would buy a few hundred in dime bags and sell them for almost double. Niggas was on that loud hard as hell. I was gonna have ten grand in no time. But, I didn't want to smoke it.

I started playing with my phone and decided to text Tori to check on her. I had only spoken with her twice since Goody was arrested and I knew she had also been going through it. His baby mama, Lisa, threw it in her face every chance she got that she was no longer living it up in some penthouse, but was back living in Bora Bora in the projects. With two kids and no steady money supply from Goody, who was only able to send chump change, she had resorted to getting a job at Dallas Cabaret North.

Myesha finished smoking her blunt and her eyes were low as she talked to me.

"So, what's going on with you and Ms. Bitch?" she asked.

"Ain't nothing going on. I ain't even thinking about that right now," I told her. "Right now, I just gotta figure out what to do."

"Shit. You could always kill her ass," she joked.

I laughed at my friend's crazy ass suggestion.

"You need to quit smoking that shit," I told her. "When did you start smoking anyway?" I asked.

"I ain't smoking like that," she answered. "Just every now and then I might take a hit."

"Uh huh," I replied, not believing her. "But seriously, what am I going to do?"

"Damn. You live in some old soap opera, Little Orphan Annie type shit," she joked.

I couldn't help but to laugh. My phone buzzed and I looked down to see that I had another text message from Black letting me know that he was on the way.

"I gotta leave a lil' early because I need to go to the bank and make a deposit with the money Goody sent. Plus, I need to talk to Black about something," I said.

She smiled and shook her head at me.

"Oh. So, you're finally going to give him some, huh?" she laughed.

"Myesha, if you don't shut your loud ass up," I demanded, laughing as well. "I'm not like you!"

"And what's that supposed to mean?" she returned, frowning up her nose. "Don't knock it til you try it!"

"Uh uh. I'll pass," I giggled. "I ain't even trying to go there right now."

"Girl, you don't know what you're missing! Ain't nothing like getting some good dick," she grinned.

"You're just so damn nasty!" I laughed. "So who was it? Wood? I know you back fuckin' with him again," I questioned her, trying to be nosey.

"What? Girl, bye!" she said. "Wood is nowhere near ready for me. He's so damn weak. He's just a hook up for some loud."

"Well damn. Tell 'em how you really feel," I laughed.

"Well, it ain't like I can get it from you."

"What you talking about?" I asked, caught off guard.

"Girl, bye. I know you slanging for that nigga, Black. Wood tells me everything," she laughed, her eyes barely open. "Relax. I ain't tripping. Just be careful, bitch."

I wasn't sure what to say so I just nodded my head.

"On the real, Myesha, I really appreciate you for being there for me," I told her. "I swear it seems like I'm living in a hell hole and the only thing that keeps me sane is knowing that I can get away. I know I'm lucky because some of them in that house, Myesha…they don't get that."

"Girl, you're good," she said, smiling. "You know I'm gonna be there. You ain't getting rid of me."

I laughed at her silliness.

We both joked with each other for a few more moments and I thanked her again for her help.

"Well, since you leaving early to go be with that nigga, let me go ahead and get back to class. I know they done probably called my mama by now anyway," she complained.

"I wonder why, slut," I teased.

"Whatever, heffa!" she said over her shoulder, walking back to the building. "One more semester and I'm out this bitch!"

I texted Black to let him know I was headed to the bus stop where we usually met up. I didn't have to wait long because no sooner had I got there, he pulled up.

"What's good, sexy?" he greeted me.

"Hey," I replied, jumping in the car.

"Okay. So, you're gonna tell me why I only hear from you every now and then, when you need some work?" he questioned.

"Can you run me by the bank really quick first?" I asked.

"Yea. Aight," he answered, shaking his head.

We drove a few more minutes to the bank and I ran in to make the deposit. The teller made sure to give me my receipt and I saw that I had almost $5,000. I gawked when I saw the amount and knew that Myesha was the reason.

I had over an hour left and it only took thirty minutes for him to get me across town.

"Why don't I get us some food really quick and you can tell me why you are using me?" he suggested.

I wanted to snap at him but he was helping me out.

He pulled into the drive thru spot of this popular soul food restaurant and we both ordered. For a minute, I thought I was having an orgasm, the food was so good.

"Damn. I take it it's good, huh?" he laughed.

"Huh?" I said, looking confused.

"You're over there going to town on that chicken, moaning and shit," he pointed out.

I flipped him the finger since my mouth was full and I couldn't say what I wanted.

"So… talk," he said, taking what little smile I had off my face.

"Well," I started in between bites. "It's not that I'm using you. And, I'm sorry if you think I'm trying to. It's just…"

I stopped because I felt myself getting tearful and I didn't want him looking at me crazy.

"Basically, after my pops died and Goody got locked up, I ended up going to this foster home. I've been staying with this chick, Patricia, that is pretty much hell on Earth since day one."

I bit into the chicken and chewed.

"Like, my nigga, my first week of being in the house I got all my stuff stolen. And then, on top of that, her daughter is fucking psycho. I told her so-called mama about her and me having a problem, and the next thing I know, I get jumped in the bathroom. It's been all kinds of crazy shit happening since I've been there," I heaved.

"Damn. You ain't fight back?" he asked.

"Hell yea," I said. "But shit, I can't fight all them hoes by myself."

He shook his head.

"Damn. I feel you. So, why you ain't said nothing to nobody?" he pushed.

I sighed in frustration.

“I mean, I've tried to contact my caseworker a couple of times. There was a dude, Chris, that was there with us for a little bit and he gave me her number ‘cause she was his caseworker too. From what I was told, they’re supposed to do monthly visits, but I ain’t seen her ass after the first month. But, for all I know, she could have come and visit and Patricia told her everything was fine. But I know I'm tired of feeling like I gotta sleep with one eye open,” I huffed. “Like, for real, her daughter is fucking mental. This bitch was fucking one of the niggas, and then fucking Nikki just up and disappeared.”

“Damn, yo. That's some fuckin’ crazy shit,” he said.

“Yeah,” I agreed. “So, now it’s me and two other kids, and one of them is too small to really fend for themselves. I don't even know what to do. I'm trying to just go day to day, but I'm not built like that. Like, I can't just let somebody keep hurting people.”

“Aight. Well, I'm probably sure this gonna sound stupid, but why don't you just leave?” he asked.

“And go where?” I pressed. “I mean, I got money stashed up and everything, but it's only going to last for so long. I'm seventeen. I don't have a job and I'm still in school. The only people that could have helped me was my father, who’s dead, and my godfather is in prison. If they find me, ain’t no telling what would happen.”

“Shit. You can come and stay with me,” he offered.

I smirked at his suggestion. I didn’t know shit about him, aside from the fact that he was a dope boy, so there was no way in fuck I was gonna go live with his ass.

“As nice as the offer is, I would have to pass. For one, I don't know you like that. And two, I damn sure ain't ‘bout to be shacked up with no nigga. No offense,” I said.

“None taken, yo,” he shrugged. “But, it’s only going to keep getting worse if you don't do anything about it. Just take the paper you done stacked up and dip. Get you a spot and just lay low 'til you turn eighteen. After that, they can't do shit."

I knew he was right but I didn't want to say it. We rode in silence for a few more minutes and before I knew it, he was driving up to the school. I looked down at my watch and saw that we still had close to fifteen minutes before I had to get back inside.

"Damn. It didn't even seem like we were riding long," I said.

He turned off the ignition and faced me.

"So, since you saying you don't know me and shit, why don't you get to know me?" he winked.

I looked at him and laughed.

"Why you sound like you coming out of some romance movie or something?" I questioned him.

"Cause I'm Mr. Romance, baby," he grinned, showing me his gorgeous smile.

I rolled my eyes into my head.

"Okay," I said.

"Nah, but I'm serious though," he said. "You cool. I'm just saying. I could use a chick like you rockin' with me."

I shot my eyebrows up in surprise.

"A chick like me?" I said. "And what does that mean?"

"I mean you're a good girl. You ain't been out here with all these niggas and you're smart. Man, it's so many chicks out here that I meet that ain't doing nothing but trying to get paper from niggas and opening they legs to the highest paying nigga and shit," he explained.

I nodded my head in agreement to what he was saying.

“That's true,” I agreed. “But, I mean, you barely know me, Black. How can you tell all of these things? We text each other, but like, you’ve only seen me maybe seven or eight times in the last six months,” I told him.

“I know,” he admitted. “But I know things about you. I hear things.”

“And what have you heard?” I asked, a bit curious.

“Well, I know for a fact that ain’t no nigga got with you,” he pressed. “I know you ain’t been touched yet.”

This nigga had to have been talking to Myesha. I'm going to kick her ass for running her damn mouth so much.

“So, how do you know all this? Myesha?” I inquired.

“Nah, baby girl. I just do my research. Plus, because of your daddy, I know damn well ain't no niggas gon’ step to you like that. No street nigga anyway,” he added.

I smiled a bit. No one had called me baby girl since my daddy.

“And yet, here you are trying to get at me and uh... you’re definitely a street nigga,” I said sarcastically.

He laughed at my response. I was trying not to stare, but his smile and his eyes were making me feel some type of way.

“Baby, I ain't the average street nigga.”

I rolled my eyes.

“Oh. I'm sure about that.” I smiled. “But— “

“Look, baby girl,” he said cutting me off. “I'm going to be 100 with you. I'm feeling you and I want you to rock with me.”

He pushed some strands of hair from my face and his finger grazed mine. His touch was so electric that I thought I was going to combust.

"I know you got a situation right now, but trust me. I can get you out of it. Just rock with me," he pushed.

I looked at him and just shook my head.

"Well," I answered slowly. "Thank you for the ride and for my gift."

"So, when am I gonna get to see you again?" he asked, grabbing my hand as I grabbed the door handle.

Another bolt of electricity ran through my entire body. I pulled my hand away quickly and smiled sweetly.

"I don't know. We'll see," I rattled off. "I'll hit you."

"You make sure you do that."

He grabbed me and kissed me before I could stop him. Every fiber of my being was screaming. *Damn. This shit feels good!*

He finally pulled away from me looking at me as I closed the door, flashing me that sexy ass smile.

I rushed back to the school trying to calm down the butterflies in my stomach.

*****

"Wassup, stranger?"

I turned around and I almost passed out when I saw Chris standing in front of me.

"Chris?" I whispered. "Oh my God. Where you been? Look at you!"

I rushed to hug him.

"What's been going on with ya?" he asked.

"I should be asking you that," I said. "Your ass just disappeared."

"Man, I had to," he said. "Shit was getting too crazy. You know it."

I nodded because I knew that he was telling the truth.

"So, what are you doing roaming the halls?" he asked. "Looks like you were just getting in."

"Well...yea," I hesitated. "I had to go handle some business."

"Well, why don't you come outside and holla at me for a minute?" he said.

I agreed since it was no one else in the hallway at the time, and I had already been missing from class anyway. We walked out of the school and I followed him to the park down the street.

"So, what's up?" I asked him once I was settled on the bench. "What have you been up to?"

"Surviving," he said. "It's hard as hell out here but I'm making it."

"I feel you. At least you got away," I told him.

"I guess. How's Nikki? I know she's probably pissed at me," he said.

I looked away because I had forgotten that he didn't know that Nikki had left.

"She left the same day that you did," I told him after a few more seconds of silence.

His face grew angry and he looked at me harsh.

"What are you talking about?" he inquired. "Where'd they take her?"

"I don't know," I answered. "I came home and she was gone. I had been waiting on her after school and then when I got home, Ms. Patricia said that she wasn't there anymore. She was acting all funny and I never got an answer. I just figured they came and took her or something. Then she flipped out 'cause you were gone. After that, she didn't say anything else," I explained.

I studied him and he looked like he wanted to say something. I took a good look at him and he looked almost the same. He had lost a little weight from what I was assuming him living on the streets, but other than that, he was still very much like his old self. But, the look on his face had me worried and I began to wonder if I was missing something.

"Something ain't sitting right," he said. "It's not like Nikki to just disappear, and if Pat and that bitch did get rid of her, then I'm sure the caseworker would have said something by now."

"Well, there's a caseworker that's been by a few times but it was to check on Kim, and then we had a different caseworker when NaTasha was brought into the house," I explained.

"Who's NaTasha?" he asked.

"She's cool. Sixteen. Came a few months ago. But she's cool. She covered for me so I could go do what I needed to do," I told him.

"And what's that?" he inquired.

"I'm saving up to be out," I confessed. "My best friend has been helping me out and I've been saving my money. The day that I turn eighteen, I'm out. I got a little bit of money stacked up and my godfather helps me out when he can. Myesha's been a really big help and she's been putting money in my account. So, I go over there like twice a month and make sure everything is good. I got a cell phone that I keep here in my locker so that Ms. Patricia or Whitney can't find it, and I text her when I need something."

I left out the part about Black because I didn't want him to know just yet.

"Damn. Sounds like you got your plans together," he admitted. "I tried to hold out as long as I could, but I just couldn't take the shit no more. Those bitches are fucking crazy. And Whitney's ass walked around there like she was the shit. Bitch had to threaten me for some dick. That bitch burnt me before too," he growled. "But, I got something for that ass."

He looked away and had a hint of hatred in his tone when he said that.

"What do you mean?" I pushed.

He looked at me with this stressed expression and pulled his shirt up revealing a gun. I got a little nervous but he held his hand out letting me know he wasn't tryna hurt me.

"Look. I know you haven't been in that house long, but those two bitches are evil. They ain't gonna be happy until they kill somebody. The fucking child welfare services keeps putting these kids in that house and I plan to stop that," he told me with a cold expression.

"Okay, but how?" I prodded. "You just gonna kill 'em?"

"You'll know soon enough," he said.

I didn't push because I didn't know if I wanted to know the answer quite honestly.

I glanced at my watch and saw that it was ten minutes left before school let out.

"Look. I gotta get back in there and meet with Tash before it's time to go home. Can you come back?" I asked him.

"Here. Give me your phone."

I handed him my phone like he requested and he programmed his number into it.

"Just hit me up," he told me. "If anything happens and you can't deal, or if you hear anything about Nikki, I got you."

I put the phone back in my pocket and stood to hug him again, feeling the hard metal from his gun in his waist.

"Be careful," I said.

He hugged me back and smirked.

"I should be telling you that," he replied.

I turned and headed back towards the school so that I could meet up with NaTasha and head back home. There was so much to tell her about that day that I honestly didn't know where to begin. But, I knew Tasha would be in disbelief.

*****

Chapter Seven

It was three o'clock in the morning and I was lying in the bed texting on my phone. It was the safest time that I could talk when I knew everyone would be asleep. I was talking to Chris about how I was ready to leave after another Ms. Patricia episode.

Chris and I talked on the phone almost every day since we ran into each other for several weeks. At first, it was hard because I had to hide everything from Whitney, but after a while, she got off my back and I didn't have to hide my phone at school anymore. She must have found someone else to mess with because she left me alone completely. But I still had Ms. Patricia on my ass. She liked hitting us for the pleasure of it. Every time we thought stuff was good, she would remind us that it could be bad, just like that. Chris kept saying that he was going to teach Ms. Patricia and Whitney a lesson, but I never questioned him. I wanted to teach them a lesson too, especially Ms. Patricia.

On top of that, Black and I were talking a lot more too. We messaged each other every morning and every afternoon just to talk. He was really starting to show me another side of him that I liked. I had gotten to the point where I was skipping classes and meeting him down the street for him to pick me up instead of Arlington Heights. And every time we got up, we were all over each other. We still hadn't fucked, but he was making it hard for me to keep saying no. He would kiss me and my panties would get wet quick.

He and I had gotten really close and he had even met Chris. He had taken me to meet some of his friends and I even got to see Myesha a lot more. She had started talking to Lamar, who was my man all of five minutes at the birthday party. I figured it was her big secret, but I wasn't mad at her. Hell. I had Black. And even though we hadn't put a title on anything, and he had this whole dope boy thing going about him, he was sweet to me.

He helped me stack up my money even more, and even put Chris on so that he could make money, too. Chris got put on and was out there working the corners, but he was still sketchy around Black. I didn't say anything about it because I figured he was just that way because he didn't really know him.

I was a month away from my eighteenth birthday and two months from graduating. I couldn't believe that I had been in this house for damn near a year, but I had, and I was damn sure itching to get out. Every day, I wished something would happen to them and my hatred for that fat ass evil bitch grew.

I was counting down the days until my birthday, and Black had promised me this big surprise. We kicked it so much that everyone thought we were together, including him. It was getting harder to make Natasha cover for me over time. She would always catch an attitude whenever I mentioned spending time with Black. I knew that I had been neglecting her in a sense because I was always gone, but I felt like the way she acted, she couldn't stand him. The one time I introduced her to him when we both managed to sneak out, she barely said anything and ignored him, even though he was taking us out. I tried to find out why she hated him so much but every time I asked, she would just tell me I was tripping. But I knew she was lying. I figured she would tell me when she was ready.

I needed to go to sleep but for some reason, I was wired. I had checked my bank account earlier that day and I had a little over $25,000. Every time I saw that number, a warm feeling came over me. I was ready to get out of here. I could leave right now but the only thing holding me back was NaTasha and Kim. I figured I would be able to take care of them if I needed to take them with me, mainly Kim since NaTasha was older. I knew Natasha could hold her own and work, but I didn't want to expose Kim to the lifestyle that we were in. I knew I would need to start over and push my work somewhere else. It's not like I could just go back to the school.

I thought about what Chris did with getting his GED. I really wanted to go to Howard and get a degree and make my father proud, but with everything that had happened in the last year, it would be harder for me to do that. If I went and got my GED, even though I could apply and pray for acceptance, I would still need to have good test scores to get in. I wouldn't qualify for any scholarships since I was barely passing my classes. I was skipping school so much to either handle business or spend time with Black that I had gone from skipping school twice a month to pretty much skipping school twice a week. I knew which teachers would take attendance so the ones that did and I missed their classes, I would have to race home to erase the automated message on the machine. The good thing was that Ms. Patricia wasn't home when I came home from school. She would be down the street playing cards and running her mouth, which gave me plenty of time to delete them.

I knew that I needed to catch up on my work and do what my father wanted. He wanted me to graduate, but I needed to make this money because once I turned eighteen, nobody cared about my situation. Hell. Nobody cares now but the few people that were in my life. And even though they weren't blood, I wanted to make sure that my foster sisters were taken care of. They didn't deserve the abuse any more than I did. Somebody had to take Patricia down for the hell that she had brought on me and so many other children. It was time.

The idea came to me so quickly it was almost scary. But I needed Chris's help. I texted him to let him know that we needed to meet up immediately.

Miracle: Hey I need 2 talk 2 u about something. Can u meet me like ASAP?

I knew he would still be awake since I had just messaged him, and I knew he did a lot of hustling late and slept, like all day.

Chris: Like right now? At 3 o'clock in the morning? U good? What's wrong?

Miracle:

Nothing's wrong. But I just really need to talk to u. Can't do it over the phone. Meet me at the Glendale Park in twenty minutes.

I was too excited about this plan. I was going to wake up Natasha and let her go with me but, she was sleeping. And the more I thought about it, the less that she knew, the better.

I jumped up and threw on some sweats and stuffed some pillows underneath the bed to make it look like I was still there. It was doubtful she would even wake up because she was such a heavy sleeper, and no one had ever come into the room in the middle of the night before, so I didn't I think it would be too much of a problem.

I tiptoed to the kitchen and peeked up the stairs to see if there was any noise that would implicate them being awake. But at three o'clock in the morning, I could hear Patricia snoring hard. I got mad at the thought of her even breathing. I hurried to the front door and opened it and ran as fast as I could to Glendale Park. I hoped that Chris was on time because I didn't want to risk staying out too late and Patricia or Whitney waking up and finding me gone, especially since I left the front door unlocked.

I sat on the bench waiting on him to show, looking around. I felt a hand on my shoulder and damn near peed myself. I screamed and jumped from the bench only to see Chris standing in an all-black hoodie and jeans.

"Chill out," he said, trying to calm my nerves. "It's just me."

“Damn it, Chris!” I fussed. “You could have called me and said that you were here or something. Shit. You just scared the fuck out of me!”

“My bad,” he mumbled an apology. “So, what's up? You got me out here at three o'clock in the morning.”

“I know. I uh…I need to get out of here,” I told him. “I got enough money sitting in the bank and I turn eighteen next month. I know graduation is a couple of months away but I can’t wait any longer. Like, I can do what you did and just go get my GED.”

Chris shook his head in disappointment.

“Come on now, Miracle. You only gotta hang in there two more months until you graduate. One really ‘cause you can walk the hell out the house when you turn eighteen and it ain’t nothing that them folks can do,” he tried to reason.

“That’s one more month too long, Chris,” I argued. “I’ve spent close to a year going day to day, wondering if one of them would do something crazy. Or if they would hurt the kids. No,” I told him. “I need to get out. And they need to pay for what the hell they been doing. Especially, Patricia.” He stood not, really seeming to care, which was pissing me off. “Have you forgotten what that bitch Whitney did to you? You want her doing that to another boy?”

“Hell no,” he finally said.

“Okay. So, help me.” He pulled a blunt out of his pocket and lit it. “They're bringing another kid into the house next week. And what the hell you think is going to happen to them, huh? Me and Natasha got each other to look out for. But, every time I turn around, Patricia and Whitney are picking on Kim. Kim can’t fend for herself, Chris. She’s…slow. Patricia calls her every name in the book from stupid to a retard and then getting all this money off of her. She hits her for not responding or when she’s in one of her moods. She doesn’t deserve that. And…Whitney's walking around here acting like she owns the damn place, still setting people up to take the fall for shit that she's doing. Tasha took the fall last month for some bullshit that Whitney did. Patricia knocked her unconscious and taunted her with a damn cigarette. These damn social workers haven't come by in so long. Hell. The last time we saw April was like a month after I came. So even if we tell them, it could be too late."

"So, what you tryna do?" he asked.

I sighed and told him my plan.

"I definitely wanna get the kids out of there before this new kid comes in," I started. "God only knows how old they are or what kind of torture they're going to have to put up with if they get in that house. We gotta stop this shit like right now."

"Okay, but you still not telling me what the hell you tryna do," he stressed.

"Well, we both want to make them suffer, right?" I asked.

He nodded his head.

"You still got your gun?"

"Always," he smiled.

"Alright, so this is what I'm thinking. I'm going to get Natasha and Kim out of the house at some point later on today," I paused. "I know. I'll tell her, Natasha, that we're taking Kim to the park since we usually take her anyway. That's one of the few things that we can do on our own. Patricia ain't going to care because we getting out the house and out of her way. So, while we here at the park…"

"I can handle those two broads," he finished. A weird smile appeared on his face. In the dark, he looked creepy. "Shit. I can catch that bitch Whitney at school. Put a bullet right through her fucking head the minute she steps out the door."

"Nah. That's too risky," I told him. "Somebody could walk up or something. Too many eyes would be around to see it. It's better to do it at the house. Like I said, I can get Natasha to take Kim to the park, and I'll make up an excuse to come back to the house or something. You can handle them at the same time and we can all be out. Tasha can put in work if she wants to, and I'll take care of Kim. Anything is better than living in that house, Chris. Anything," I reiterated.

He paced the bench for a minute and I could tell his wheels were turning.

"Alright, cool. Say no more," he agreed.

"Alright. So, when we get home, once everything kind of calms down for the night, I'll tell Natasha that we need to take her to the park. I'll leave the back door unlocked for you to get in. Once you are close to the house, just text me and I'll pretend that I need to go to the house for something," I told him.

He pulled his gun out of his waist and I froze.

"What are you doing?"

"About to show you something. Come here," he said.

"What?" I said, getting close to him.

"Here. Take this."

"Chris, I don't know how to shoot your gun!" I whined.

"I know," he smirked. "That's why I'm about to show you."

He put the gun in my hand and I raised it.

"Alright. I want you to aim for that tree," he said, pointing to the tree that was about twenty feet away.

"You want me to shoot this thing now?" I asked. "Somebody's going to hear it."

He laughed at the fearful look that I had on my face.

"Miracle, we're in Oak Cliff," he pointed out. "It's gunshots going off all the time."

"But what if I miss?"

"Don't," he stated. "Focus and point. Make sure that you keep your pointer on the trigger and don't squeeze until I tell you to."

"Okay."

"Okay. Now, keep your hand steady and plant your feet firm," he warned.

I did exactly what he said.

"Now, focus on something on the tree. Pick a spot and aim."

I nodded my head in understanding. I looked at the tree and saw a red circle near one of the branches and aimed for it.

"Alright. You got your mark?" he asked.

"Yeah," I told him.

"Alright. Count to three and shoot."

I counted to three and fired. The loud noise from the bullet scared me and I almost dropped the gun. Chris held his finger to his lips for me to be quiet. I stood as still as a mouse and waited to see if anyone would pop up. It was doubtful since we were in the middle of the park, but still.

"What did you aim for?" he asked.

"Um…there was a red circle on the tree that I saw."

He jogged towards the tree and looked to see where the bullet struck. He nodded his head and jogged back over.

"You were close," he told me. "You didn't hit it dead-on but you were within a couple of inches." He smiled at me and gave me a playful pop on the arm. "I'm not expecting you to get this right in the matter of a day. But…you doing good."

"Thanks." I smiled.

"You good. Keep it on you," he told me. "Don't take it to school though. Put it somewhere where you know they won't be able to find it. I may need you to back me up."

"But I'm not no killer," I argued.

"Neither am I," he looked down at his feet. "But… it's a first time for everything."

That look that he gave me told me that he was dead serious.

"So, we really about to do this?" I asked.

"Yep."

I thought about the severity of what was about to happen. Not only were we going to get out, but the two people that were the cause of all of this were going to die.

"Time to put the plan into action."

I sat back down on the bench and looked at the dark grassy area in front of me. Chris sat next to me and put his hood back on his head and we both sat in silence for several minutes.

"Don't say anything to your little boyfriend," he finally spoke.

"Huh?" I asked, kind of taken aback by his random request. "Why would I say anything to him?"

“I don't know,” he shrugged. “But you can't trust everybody.”

“Yea, but Black ain’t never done anything. Hell. He’s on my side.”

“Still,” he argued. “With some shit like this, you don’t want anything coming back to you. Trust.”

He looked at me and something in his eyes said that he wasn’t telling me everything. But I knew that even if I asked him, he wouldn't tell me.

“Chris, I know how to keep my mouth shut, okay?” I said. “You don't have to worry.”

I patted him on the knee and stood up to get ready to head back for the house.

“Soon, this will all be over and we can all break out. With the money that we’re making, we’ll be fine. Myesha’s already eighteen, so I can get her to put an apartment in her name for me. That way, I don’t have to even say anything to Black,” I explained. “And I don’t have to, really, tell her the whole story either. I can just tell her that it’s time for me for when I graduate. She ain’t gonna question it. And, with the money that I got saved up? Hell, I can pay the rent up for the year. At least that'll give me time to figure out what I’m going to do from there. And I know my godfather was saying that there was a possibility that he was going to be getting out early. So if he does, I know he got me. And if he got me, then he got you.”

“I got a friend of mine,” Chris mumbled. “She works at the Red Roof Inn out in Plano. I can get her to hold a room for you and Natasha. But you can't bring Kim.”

“What?” I asked confused. “Chris, I can't leave her in that house!”

“I'm not saying leave her in the house, Miracle. But if you take her with you, folks are gonna be watching. Dallas ain’t that damn big. Eventually, somebody gonna come find you,” he reasoned. “You gonna have a better chance of getting away without her being with you. She’s too young to keep up, and you know it.”

I sat quietly, knowing that he was right, but not wanting to say it out loud.

“Besides, she needs her therapist and all of that,” he added. “So you have to let social services take her. She’ll have a better chance.”

I was trying not to get choked up at the thought of leaving Kim. I knew that Chris was right, but Kim was so sweet. What if she ended up in another home like ours? What if it was worse? I would never forgive myself if something happened to her.

“If you want to do this, then you have to do this right,” Chris stressed. “I need you to trust me. I know what I’m doing.”

I just wanted to protect her, but Chris was right. If we took her with us, then everybody would be looking for me. Chris saw how upset I was and grabbed my hand.

“Yo, you gonna be good,” he assured me. “I put that on my life, for real, that this is all going to work out, okay? I know it's a lot right now, but just look at it like this. They ain’t gonna be able to hurt nobody else.”

I nodded my head and tried to blink away the tears that were forming. It had been a while since I had cried. The last time I truly cried was when I told Black about my father being killed.

“You good?” he asked, studying me.

I nodded my head again. We looked at each other and I think both of us were overwhelmed by the amount of pain that we had dealt with. I was lucky enough that I had only endured my pain for a year, but Chris's was more damaging. As much as losing my father hurt and having to deal with the craziness for the last year, I'm surprised that Chris hadn't gone crazy.

I felt a tear fall from my eye and he instinctively reached up to wipe it away. He kissed my lips softly, and I felt him part them. His tongue wrestled with mine so quick that I got lost. Before I knew it, his hands were gripping my ass and he was squeezing me. I could feel his dick getting hard pressing against my clothes. It was damn near four o'clock in the morning, and I'm sitting on a park bench, making out with my foster brother. After a few seconds, I realized what was happening and pulled away.

"Chris, we can't…we can't do this."

"Why not?" he asked confused.

"Chris, you're my foster brother," I sniffed.

He groaned in frustration.

"Miracle, come on. We're not…we're not related. You know that," he argued.

"Yeah, but, even still, we lived in the same house," I reminded him. "And besides, you know I'm talking to— "

"Oh. Yeah, your little boyfriend," he snorted. "I forgot."

"Come on, Chris." I tried to get him to understand. "We're all messed up in this. I just want us to be able to live a normal life. Just get us the hell out and then go from there."

"Yea. Aight," he gritted. He stood up off the bench and cleared his throat. "Well, it's late. I gotta go. Just hit me when you're ready."

I wanted to say something but I had no words, so I watched him walk off. Once he was gone, I put the gun in my jacket and headed back to the house. I snuck in the front door, locking it behind me and ran to my room. I moved as quickly and as quietly as I could to get undressed, and climbed into my bed. I knew the minute that I fell asleep, it would be time to get up and get ready for school, but for the first time in a while, I couldn't wait.

*****

Chapter Eight

As I predicted, the minute that I felt like my eyes drifted off to sleep, the alarm clock went off, waking me up. I jumped up to shower and saw that Natasha was still in the bed. I shook her awake to let her know that it was time to get up and get ready for school. I really needed her to get up because I had things I needed to do and she played an important part of my cover.

"Come on, girl," I said, shaking her.

She groaned and slowly got out of the bed. She looked at the clock and whined.

"Damn, Miracle," she complained. "You could have let me sleep for like ten more minutes."

"Girl, get your ass up!" I fussed.

I was way too excited. I reminded myself that I had to make sure that I hid my emotions from Patricia and Whitney so that they wouldn't get suspicious. I was ready to leave for school so that I could meet up with Black and Myesha to do what I needed to do. I'm sure that Natasha would cover for me one more time so I wasn't too worried about that. Hopefully, this would be the last time she ever had to cover for me again, if my and Chris's plan went accordingly.

Thinking about Chris, I thought about the kiss that he planted on me last night. I really hoped that he was just acting in the moment, and that he didn't actually have feelings for me. It was too weird. Plus, I was really feeling Black and wanted to see what was going to happen with that.

I went into the bathroom to take a shower. A few minutes later, I heard Natasha come in, turning on the faucet to wash her face. I stuck my head out of the shower curtain to make sure that it was her.

"I need a favor," I whispered.

She rolled her eyes, brushing her teeth.

"Tash, for real. I need you to cover for me one more time," I told her. "After today, I won't ask you anymore."

She spit out the mouthwash into the sink and wiped her mouth.

"What? You're going to see your bestie?" she asked sarcastically.

I heard Ms. Patricia in the kitchen making a bunch of noise and I ended the conversation.

"Tell you later. Can't talk about it right now. Wait 'til we leave for school."

She must have heard Ms. Patricia, too, because she nodded quick.

"Okay."

I finished taking my shower and jumped out so that she could get some of the hot water. I went back into the room, getting dressed, and rushed to go to the breakfast table. When I walked into the kitchen, Kim was already sitting at the table, finishing her breakfast, as usual.

"Hey, Kimmie boo," I smiled, patting her on her head.

She smiled but didn't say anything, eating her food and holding her Barbie doll in her hand. She took that thing with her everywhere she went.

"You okay?" I asked.

She nodded her head. Ms. Patricia was sitting in the den, yelling at the TV.

"Hurry up and eat the damn food so y'all can go to school!" she yelled. Kim flinched but I gave her a smile, letting her know that it was going to be okay. "Y'all gotta come home and clean this house from top to bottom. My new man is coming over tonight and he ain't gone be thinkin' I keep a dirty house!"

"Yes, ma'am," I answered, trying to remain calm. I looked at Kim and she was still eating her food. "Tell you what, little munchkin. If you eat all your food and have a good day at school today, once we finish cleaning up and Ms. Patricia's friend comes over, I'll take you to the park. You want to go to the park?" I asked, already knowing that she would. I smiled at her innocent face as she nodded her head and cooed. "Okay. But remember, you have to be good, okay?" I reminded her.

She nodded her head and Ms. Patricia started screaming.

"You bitches ain't going no goddamn where if this muthafuckin' house ain't clean. So you better tell her little, stupid ass that she gonna clean up, too," she ordered. "I should put that little dumb bitch out. Shit. She better be glad that money is coming in from her ass. Hurry up and get this little retard the fuck out my house."

I wanted to kill that bitch right then, but I had to play it cool. Kim grew sad and I reminded myself that soon that bitch, Patricia, would be done.

I sat down at the table and scarfed my food down quickly. Natasha came in and noticed how quickly I was eating.

"Why are you rushing?" she asked.

I could feel Ms. Patricia's eyes on me.

"I'm not," I quickly recovered. "I was just trying to hurry up 'cause Ms. Patricia wanted us to hurry."

"About fuckin' time you listened," Ms. Patricia snapped.

I guess Natasha remembered that I had just asked her to cover for me because she closed her mouth, quickly.

"Y'all have five minutes, so hurry the hell up!" Ms. Patricia yelled. "If I gotta get up, somebody is getting fucked up."

We knew what that meant, so we both finished our food quickly and I helped Kim clean herself up. I quickly washed the dishes in the sink. We grabbed our backpacks and rushed past Ms. Patricia to the door.

"Don't forget what I said," she warned. "Y'all come straight home so that y'all can get this damn house straight."

"Yes, ma'am," we both replied.

I practically flew out the front door, ready to get to the school. We walked Kim to her bus stop and waited on the bus with her. A few minutes later it arrived, and I watched as she got on the bus.

"Okay. What the hell is going on?" Natasha asked once the bus pulled off and we were walking to school.

"Nothing," I lied. Thinking about it, I didn't want to tell her because I didn't know if she would back me. "I just need you to cover for me."

"So, you want me to cover for you but you don't want to tell me what's going on?"

She had a point. I guess I could tell her what was necessary without risking too much. I really didn't want to tell her everything, but I knew I had to tell her something. Otherwise, she might not cover for me and that would mess up everything. I didn't think she would be shady like that, but I wasn't going to chance it.

"Okay. Look," I said. "I'm going to meet up with Myesha and Black today. I can't really get into it right now, but it's about what I'm going to do when I graduate."

Technically I was telling the truth, but I just wasn't telling her that I was speeding the process up.

"Oh," she answered. "So, you were already planning on how you were going to get out of here?"

"I mean, it's not really like that," I tried to explain. "Myesha was just wanting to help since she's already eighteen and can help without anybody watching."

I noticed that her attitude changed quick. I decided to stop ignoring whatever the hell was bugging her and find out for myself.

"Okay, Natasha. I tried to let this shit rock, but what the hell is going on with you? Because every time I mention Myesha, you all of a sudden get this funky ass attitude. So what's going on?" I questioned.

"Nothing," she snapped, stomping off faster.

"Clearly that's bullshit and you know it," I replied. "Now, are you gonna tell me what the hell is up?"

She turned to me and her eyes were filled with tears.

"I mean… Damn, Miracle!" she yelled. "You act like this girl is the best thing ever."

"What?" I asked. I didn't know where this was coming from. "Seriously? She's my best friend, Natasha," I explained.

"So!" she cried. "Where was your best friend for the last year, huh? It's been me and you in that house, not her. She doesn't understand what we're going through. She's not getting her ass beat. You go cry to her for a few hours and then guess what? You're right back in that same fuckin' house with me. You get to go and kick it in your old neighborhood and I'm stuck in this hell hole. You run off and you see your best friend and then you tell me about it. And I'm sitting here like some little puppy waiting on you to come back," she wept, stopping her steps and wiping her face angrily. "At least you have someone to go to! The only person that I have is always rubbing it in my face about how she has the best friend in the world that ain't me!"

I stopped in my tracks and looked at Natasha. I never understood until now, how she really felt. I wasn't trying to intentionally throw my friendship with Myesha in her face, but she was right. At least I did have Myesha to go to. Natasha didn't have to cover for me all of those times so that I could see my friend. She did it because she cared about me. I hated that I hurt my friend so bad.

She stood in front of me bawling in tears and I wrapped her up in a hug.

"I'm sorry, Natasha," I apologized. "I am so sorry."

"I just want this to be over," she cried. "I'm tired of going in that house. I'm tired of living like this."

Seeing her break down made me choke up myself.

"I know," I said. "I know it's hard. I'm going to figure out something, Natasha. I promise. I just need you to hang on a little bit longer for me, but I will figure out something."

I broke away from her embrace and looked at her. I wanted to tell her more than ever, but the less she knew, the better.

"Just know that I would never intentionally throw her in your face. You know that, right?" I said. "I look at Myesha the way you look at me," I told her. "If anything, you two are alike."

She sniffed and wiped her eyes.

"Really?" she asked.

"Yea," I smiled. "I'll tell you what. I really gotta handle some stuff today but the next time I go, you can go with me. I know last time, y'all didn't have a lot of opportunity to get to know each other but I think once y'all hang around each other more, that'll change."

We were close to the school so I helped Natasha fix herself up.

"Now, I gotta go handle some business but I will be back soon," I told her. "I'm gonna leave after first period, but I will be back before the final bell. Now you know what to do. If we get called to the office early, just tell her I had a feminine emergency and that'll buy me some time to get back."

Natasha nodded her head as we walked to our homerooms.

"Well, be careful," she mumbled.

I smiled at her sincerely.

"You know I will."

I watched her walk into her class and walked into mine. I pulled my phone out and texted Black. I told him that I needed him and Myesha to pick me up down the block from the school in an hour. He responded back with a smile and let me know he would do it. I texted Myesha to let her know to hop in the car with Black and head my way.

First period dragged by but finally, an hour later, the bell rang and I darted out the side door like I always did to get to Black. He was down the block just as I had asked, and I smiled looking at his sexy face.

I got in the car and he planted one on me.

"Wassup, sexy?" he greeted.

"Hey, baby," I answered, closing the door and turning to see Myesha in the back seat. "What's up, chic?"

"What up, girl?" she responded.

Black headed to the highway and I dove right into telling them what I needed.

"Okay. So, I'm leaving the house of horrors but I need y'all help," I announced.

"It's about time!" Myesha screeched from the back seat.

She pulled a blunt out of her bag and lit it, rolling down the window, and started smoking. Immediately, the loud hit my noise.

"Damn, Myesha," I complained. "We ain't even on the damn highway yet and your ass is blazing. Like, it ain't even ten o'clock yet."

"Damn, Miracle. What the fuck is this, a 'just say no' commercial?" she snapped. "You that bothered 'bout what the fuck I do?"

I turned around and looked at her concerned.

"What the fuck is your problem?" I asked. "Why you acting all funny?"

"Ain't shit wrong as long as you ain't all up my ass about what the fuck I'm smoking," she said.

"I ain't trippin' like that," I told her. "I just said it was early, damn. Calm the fuck down."

"Yea. Okay," she mumbled.

I turned back around and Black squeezed my thigh.

"So, what do you need, baby?" he inquired.

"Well," I sighed. "I need to get an apartment since I'm leaving for me and Natasha. But I need it like fast."

"How fast?" he asked.

"Like, today," I told him. "I'm tryna leave tonight."

"Well, baby, you know it ain't gonna be that easy to get a spot like that. Like, if you get an apartment, you have to do the application and all that. They have to do credit checks and shit," he told me. "And one main thing is, you have to be eighteen."

"I know," I agreed. "That's why I was gonna ask Myesha if she could get the apartment in her name so that nobody would think twice about it."

I turned back to Myesha as she blew the smoke out.

"You think you can do that for me?"

She coughed and nodded.

"Yea. I got you," she strained.

"I appreciate it."

"Yea, but you not hearing me, baby girl," Black said. "You still gotta wait. They not gonna approve you the same day. And even if they do, you don't have shit."

"It ain't like I can't get it," I told him. "I got some money sitting in the bank. Why are you acting like this is a bad idea or something?"

I wasn't feeling the way that he was acting, like he wasn't with it.

"Nah, baby girl, I got you. I know you wanna do this and I got you. I was just being real though."

"Well, I can hit my pops up and see if he knows anybody that have some spots that you can rent," Myesha offered.

"That's wassup!" I answered happily. "I'll be eighteen on next month, so I just need to lay low for like the next month, until then."

"Okay. So why not come stay with me until then?" Black asked. "It would make more sense than you going through all of that. Especially if it's just for a month."

"Cause I ain't bout to be living with a nigga I don't know like that," I answered simply.

"So, you ain't been getting to know me for the last ten months? But you know me enough to let me pick you up and buy you shit all the time, or give you work to push."

"Wow. Really?" I asked, amazed. "That's how you do? This is why I want my own shit. I was just waiting on you to throw it in my face."

"Aye. That's not what I'm saying," he argued.

"Okay," I said, not wanting to talk to him anymore.

He had pissed me off and if I didn't need to handle my business, I would have left.

"Girl, don't trip," Myesha said. "I got you. Black, quit being mean 'cause you ain't getting any," she laughed.

I snickered and Black's jawline tensed.

"I'm good on that, trust," I heard him mumble.

I wanted to call him out but I changed my mind.

"So, where you need to go?" he asked.

"I was thinking about going to look at apartments in Richardson, maybe. Myesha, how fast do you think you can hear something from your dad?" I asked her.

"I texted him so he'll probably hit me up later on today," she replied.

"Cool. Well, I still wanna look, just in case," I said.

"Aight," he answered. "Any particular ones?"

"Um. I was thinking Cutters Point and City Limits," I told him.

"Ewww," Myesha groaned in the back seat. "Girl, them shits is in the hood."

"Well, Myesha, I only have $25,000," I explained. "I ain't tryna spend all my money on an apartment. I still have to get stuff for the apartment. And, I gotta help Natasha 'cause she's not eighteen yet."

"So, she going with you?" she asked. "How is she gonna go to school and all that shit if she's with you?"

"I'll figure it out, Myesha, okay? But we ain't staying in that damn house another day."

"I mean, I'm just saying."

"Well, I'll take care of it," I said.

"So, what you gonna do once you get your spot? You gonna keep hustling?" Black asked.

"That's the plan," I told him. "Only thing is, I ain't gonna be able to hustle at the school anymore. So, I just gotta figure something out."

"Well, I may have something for you to do but we'll talk about that later," he said, looking in the rearview mirror at Myesha who was on her phone.

"Cool."

Black got off the exit and we pulled into the parking lot of the bank. Myesha hopped out and went inside to get the money that I needed. The minute she closed the door, I turned to Black.

"Look. I don't want you helping me if all you're gonna do is throw it back in my face later on. I didn't ask for your help, and I definitely don't appreciate you pulling that shit in front of my friend," I snapped.

"My bad, yo," he apologized. "You know I ain't mean for that shit to come out like that."

"I just don't want to be one of those chicks that you think you can help and get something from," I confessed.

"C'mon, baby girl, you know it's nothing like that," he said. "Hell. I must be feeling you 'cause you got me driving across town all the time to come and see you when I'm supposed to be putting in work."

"So, why you helping me then?" I asked.

He was right. He was always out hustling, but the minute I said that I needed him, he was there. And he had never asked me for anything.

"To be real, I know what you going through," he said.

"What do you mean?" I asked.

"I know what it's like to want to get away. You remember I told you that I had an older brother, right?" he said.

When we were getting to know each other, he told me about his older brother and how he had died when he was eleven.

"Yea. I remember," I answered.

"Well, when my moms was killed, they put us in a foster home for a while. My brother went to a separate home and they used to beat on him really bad. Well, one time, they beat him to death." He looked out the window and I could see that he was trying to hold it together. "The police found his body in a dumpster and the foster home was shut down."

I didn't know what to say. I leaned over and kissed his lips.

"What? I'm getting sympathy kisses now?" he asked.

"No," I said. "I just…wanted to do that."

He returned the kiss and a few seconds later, I pulled away to catch my breath.

Myesha was walking down the sidewalk towards the car and hopped in, handing me an envelope.

"Okay. There's $5,000," she said.

"Cool," I thanked her, putting it in my bag. "Hey, can you run me past the post office really quick before we go look at the apartments?"

He agreed and drove to the post office around the corner. I hopped out and went to open the box that had my mail. Goody had been writing me more so I was getting letters from him weekly just about. I opened the box and pulled out two envelopes, both from Goody, and headed back towards the car.

I felt my phone vibrating in my back pocket and pulled it out to see that someone was calling me private. I answered knowing that it was probably Natasha.

"Hello?" I answered.

"Miracle, you gotta get back to the school now!" I heard her crying.

I started running back to the car.

"What's going on? What's wrong?"

"There's been a shooting! They started evacuating the building. Get here fast! Hurry up!" she screamed.

I hung up my phone and jumped in the car, scaring Myesha.

"We gotta go back now!" I told them. "Somebody got shot at the school and I gotta get back before anybody notices I'm gone."

Black nodded his head and headed to the highway and I prayed that I could still pull this off.

*****

Chapter Nine

Black pulled up down the block and I hopped out.

"I'll hit you later," I told him, slamming the door and running.

I heard him pull off and ran towards the school. I was close when I heard someone call my name.

"Miracle!"

I turned to see Chris, standing behind a tree. I turned around and ran back towards him.

"Chris?" I asked. "What the hell are you doing?"

"Listen, Miracle, I fucked up," he said. "I fucked up bad, and I gotta get the hell out of here."

"Okay. Slow down," I suggested. "What happened? What did you do?"

"I killed her."

I felt the breath leave my body. What the hell was he talking about?

"You killed her? Killed who?" I asked slowly.

"I killed her, Miracle."

He looked like he had seen a ghost and I needed to find out what the hell he was talking about.

"Okay. Chris, you're scaring me. Tell me what happened."

He looked at me and his eyes were full of tears.

"I saw her, Whitney, and everything just came flooding back," he whispered. "All I remembered was the shit that she did and I got mad. The way that she forced me to do that shit. Her burning me with cigarettes or making me do shit to her that I didn't want to do. And…and…when she saw me, she just acted like she wasn't fazed. Like she didn't give a fuck. And I had the gun in my pocket and…she was there…"

I started to piece together what he was saying and knew that the reason the school was evacuated was because of him.

"Is she dead?" I asked.

He nodded his head slowly.

I was in shock and wasn't sure what to say. Honestly, I was glad that she was dead but, I didn't want him in trouble for it. He was supposed to get away.

"Give me your gun," I demanded.

"What?"

"Give me your gun. Now," I repeated.

He stared at me and I explained my reason.

"I don't know if anybody saw you shoot her. But, if they did and the police catch you without the gun on you, you have a better chance of getting off. So, give me the gun."

He hesitated but handed it to me. I threw it in my backpack and closed it quickly.

"Okay. Now, listen to me. You gotta get out of here," I said. "You gotta get as far outta Dallas as possible. That's the only chance you have of getting away with this. How much money do you have saved up?"

"A couple of grand," he answered.

I opened my bag and pulled out the envelope that Myesha had given me with the money and shoved it in his hands.

"It's $5,000. Take it and get out of here. You call me when you get somewhere safe."

"But I can't…"

"Just take it," I urged. "Get out of here. NOW!"

He stood for a second and hugged me tight.

"You be careful," he warned.

"You too," I said.

We locked eyes and then he ran off until I couldn't see him anymore. I wiped the tears from my eyes that I hadn't realized had formed, and ran to the school. My phone buzzed again and I answered.

"Hello?" I answered.

"Where are you?" Natasha whispered into the phone.

"I'm walking up now."

"Okay. Well, meet me by the side door."

"Aight. Cool," I said.

I hung up and walked among the crowd of students, faculty and police. An officer stopped me and asked me where I was supposed to be and I told him I was looking for my sister. I spotted Natasha and ran over to her.

"Oh, thank God!" she sighed. "Miracle, it was crazy. We were sitting in the cafeteria and the next thing I know, you heard someone scream and then gunshots. Everybody started running and screaming. It was crazy."

I didn't want to tell her what Chris told me, so I just played dumb.

“Did anybody see anything?” I asked.

“I don’t know,” she said. “One minute everyone was running and then the next we were out here.”

“Sooo, they don’t even know who got shot?” I pressed.

“No,” she answered.

I wondered how long it would take before Whitney was identified and they called Ms. Patricia.

We were being led into the cafeteria to wait on our parents as the police continued their investigations and questioning. I looked to see parents pulling up outside, crying, trying to find out if their child was okay.

We were in the cafeteria for over an hour before our names were called over the bullhorn. We gathered our things and headed towards the door where we saw a deranged and upset Ms. Patricia. You could see that she had been crying her eyes out and she was screaming at the officers and faculty that were standing near her.

“Who did this? Who killed my baby?” she screamed.

Folks stood watching, not knowing what to say as she continued to cry.

“Natasha Jackson? Miracle Davis?”

An officer was standing watch as we left the cafeteria. Natasha looked nervous once she realized what was going on.

“You’re her foster kids, right?” he asked.

“Yes,” I answered.

“You guys come with me. We’re uh…gonna take you guys home since your foster mom is still trying to take the news in,” he said.

I could tell that he wasn't sure what to say with us so we followed quietly. I watched as they led Ms. Patricia to a car and we got into the back of the officer's car. They drove us back to the house and I studied Natasha to see how she was processing everything. She had this blank expression that I had never seen.

"You're okay?" I whispered. She didn't answer and I nudged her, snapping her out of her trance.

"Huh?" she said.

"Yo, you aight?"

"I don't know," she said. "I didn't know it was Whitney. Damn…"

"Yea. Me either," I lied.

We pulled up to the house and the officer let us out of the car. We walked inside the house and sat in the kitchen while the officers were in the living room with Ms. Patricia. I could hear bits and pieces of their conversation. A small part of me felt bad for Ms. Patricia, especially as hard as she was crying.

"Somebody killed my baby," she cried. "Lord, why did they take my baby?"

One of the officers came in to ask us questions, but since we were in class, we couldn't give them much information. We were talking for so long that I barely noticed that it was time to go and get Kim from the bus. Whitney normally did it, but now that she was dead, I knew I would need to.

"Um, excuse me, officer, but I need to go get our younger sister from the bus stop," I told him.

"Younger sister?" he asked.

"Yes. We have a little sister as well. She's in elementary school. Her bus should be here in about five minutes. Um…normally, Whitney would get her from the bus stop but she—"

The officer held his hand up and stopped me.

"I understand," he said. "I'll go along."

He walked with me as I headed towards the bus stop. Ms. Patricia was so distraught that I don't think she noticed I left. I honestly don't think that she noticed we were even in the house.

"So, were you and Whitney close?" he asked.

"Not really," I told him. "I mean, we were cool but it wasn't like we were besties or anything."

"So, do you know anybody that would want to do this to her?"

Me, I thought.

"No," I told him. "I mean, I never saw her having beef with anybody, so I don't know."

He nodded as we waited for the bus to pull up.

"So, you said that she was your foster mother? How long have you been here?"

"About ten months," I answered. "My dad died last year and I was placed here."

"Oh. Ok," he answered. "Sorry to hear about your dad."

The bus pulled up and Kim hopped off. She smiled when she saw me and ran over, hugging me tight.

"Hey, munchkin!" I greeted her.

She grinned and hummed as I took her hand. She saw the officer and waved.

"Well, hello there," he said.

"She doesn't speak," I told him.

"Oh."

"So, Kim, I know I told you that I was gonna take you to the park today if you were good at school, but we may not be able to go," I explained.

She looked at me and pouted. I tried to explain to her what was going on without telling her too much.

"I'm sorry, munchkin," I apologized. "Right now, it's some stuff going on at the house and well, we gotta wait a while, okay?"

Kim slumped her shoulders and dropped her hand from mine.

"I'm sorry, munchkin. But I promise I will take you soon, okay?"

She nodded her head and kept walking.

We got to the house a few minutes later and I took Kim into her room so that she wouldn't have to be around all the chaos downstairs.

"Okay. Now you sit up here and read one of your books. I will be up here in a few minutes, okay?" I instructed her.

"Color," she said.

I looked around the room and found her crayons and handed them to her. I couldn't find any paper but I knew I had some in my backpack.

"I'm gonna get you some paper. Hold on, okay?"

She nodded her head and I ran downstairs to grab my backpack off the table. I jogged back upstairs and opened the backpack, grabbing my notebook out. I zipped it up, put it in the chair and helped her get situated.

"Okay. I'm right downstairs if you need me, okay?"

She nodded her head and began to draw in the book.

I left her to coloring and went downstairs to finish talking with the police. Ms. Patricia was calm and was answering the police's questions. She saw me and rolled her eyes, reaching for her cigarettes.

I decided to go do my homework to avoid any problems. I had to rethink my plan since everything had gone bad with Chris. I was still leaving, especially now that Whitney was dead. Ms. Patricia was liable to take her pain out on anybody. I ran back upstairs and grabbed my backpack off the chair in Kim's room. I saw she was happily coloring in her own world. I smiled and closed the door softly, going back downstairs. I heard a knock at the door and opened it, shocked to see April standing at the door.

"Hello, Miracle. How are you?" she asked, stepping inside of the house.

"I'm ok," I answered.

I was really surprised to see her. I hadn't seen this bitch in over six months. I wanted to ask her where the hell she'd been especially since they were supposed to show up at least once a month for a check-up and hadn't.

"You look good," she observed. "How are you holding up through all of this?"

"How'd you know?" I asked.

"Procedure," she answered. "Anytime an incident occurs with a foster home we have to come and do a home visit."

"Oh."

"So, how are you holding up?" she repeated.

I could feel Ms. Patricia's eyes on me from the chair.

"I don't know," I told her. "It's just hard to deal with."

It's hard to deal with knowing her fuckin' mama is still alive, I thought.

"I'm gonna go finish my homework," I said, excusing myself out of the living room.

I went into the kitchen as April approached Ms. Patricia.

"Ms. Johnson, I am so sorry to hear about your daughter," she apologized.

"Thank you," Ms. Patricia sniffed. "Sorry that you have to be here in this craziness. I didn't know we had a visit scheduled today."

"Oh no, ma'am, you didn't," April explained. "As I was telling Miracle, anytime there's an incident with a foster family, we have to do a home visit to rule out any abuse from the children. I promise, I won't take up too much of your time as I'm sure you want to grieve in peace. I see Miracle is looking healthy. And what about…Natasha?" she asked, looking at her folder.

"She's in the kitchen," Ms. Patricia told her.

"Okay, and…Kim?"

"Oh, hell. She's probably still at that bus stop," she fussed.

I stood up and popped my head in the living room.

"No, ma'am. She's upstairs. I went and got her from the bus stop," I told her.

Ms. Patricia gave me an evil look but said nothing.

"Well, let me just go speak with her really quick and see how she's doing," April smiled as she started up the stairs.

BANG!

"Oh my God!" she screamed.

Several of the officers jumped up and ran towards the stairs where the shot had come from.

One of the officers ran in and my heart was beating a mile a minute.

"We need a medic! Get a medic in here. Now!"

*

Natasha and I sat at the kitchen table crying as the ambulance took Kim to Parkland Hospital. I prayed so hard that she was going to be okay. She had shot herself with the gun that I had left in my backpack. The cops were up in her room searching for it so I knew that it was only a matter of time before they found it and then linked mine and Chris's prints.

"Where the hell did she get a gun from?" Ms. Patricia fussed.

April was on her phone and was ending her call, while Natasha and I sat holding hands. This entire day had gone to shit. Everything that I had planned was now down the drain. I prayed to God that Kim was okay. How the hell did she find the gun anyway? Why did she go in the backpack? Why in the hell didn't I put that shit in my room first? It was then that I remembered the gun that Chris had already given me. I had to get that shit out of the house. And I had to go too. Because if I didn't, they would see my prints on the gun and even though they weren't in the system, it would only be but so long before they questioned me and I would be tried as an adult. My life would be over.

April walked over to us and Ms. Patricia followed behind her.

"Ms. Johnson, a gun being in your home is a very serious problem, especially when it is so easy for a six-year-old to get ahold of it," she accused.

"I don't know where the hell that girl got that damn gun from!" Ms. Patricia snapped.

"Well, that doesn't help the situation, Ms. Johnson," April continued. "Now, while I am sympathetic to the events that took place today, I also have to think about the welfare of the other two children. We were already hesitant after you informed us that your last placement ran away; however, we were sympathetic to the fact that Nikki had caused so many problems."

My head popped up when I heard Nikki's name.

"What problems did Nikki cause?" I asked.

"You mind your business, little girl," Ms. Patricia hissed.

April noticed her tone and Ms. Patricia tried to correct herself.

"I'm sorry. I'm just so frustrated with everything that's going on," she tried to smooth over.

"Nikki didn't cause any trouble," I spoke up. "Where's Nikki?"

April turned to me curious.

"You were close with Nikki?" she asked.

"Yes," I answered. "We talked every day. She never did anything wrong, except be in her way," I said motioning towards Patricia.

Everyone in the room, except April, was looking at me like I was crazy, but I didn't care anymore. April looked confused at what I said, and Patricia stood frozen like the ugly gargoyle statue that she was. And then, the flood gates opened.

"It's horrible here!" I blurted out. "We get punished for stuff we don't even do. It's been times that we've gotten beatings because we didn't come home on time or we didn't clean up the kitchen. I've been burned with cigarettes and slapped in the face by her. Her dead daughter jumped me in the bathroom with her friends. She punches Kim in the head and everything."

April's mouth dropped open in shock. I told everything that I could think of while Natasha sat next to me shaking.

"Patricia is lying about everything," I added. "Her daughter, over here, was sleeping with Chris, the foster kid that you said ran away. She was forcing him to have sex with her and abusing him too. Since I've been here, I've been locked in my room with no food, jumped, beaten, and anything wrong you could think of."

"And you don't care because it's been over six months since you came to check on us and we have to keep dealing with this," Natasha accused her.

I wanted to smile when I heard her say that.

"I hate it here! We hate it here! If this is what being in foster care is like and having a family then I'd much rather die," she said, starting to cry.

I grabbed Natasha's hand and held it tight. April was so shocked and turned her attention to Patricia. I could see the anger written all on their face.

"Is this true?" she asked her. "Can you explain this?"

"Now, you know that these kids nowadays have overactive imaginations," Patricia tried to reason.

“There's nothing overactive about it,” April answered with an attitude. “Either it’s true or it’s not. And I’m starting to believe by what’s going on here, that it’s true.”

“You lying bitch!” Ms. Patricia screamed, charging towards me.

I jumped up as well as Natasha. One of the officers grabbed her. The caseworker jumped in between us and tried to protect us.

“Girls, please. Get back!” she ordered.

The officer placed cuffs on her and I smirked.

“Patricia, I'm sorry, but after hearing these accusations, I'm going to have to remove the children immediately until the investigation is complete. You'll get a phone call with an appointment to speak with the supervisor,” she informed her. “Girls, go get your things and hurry.”

She pulled out her cell phone and made a phone call.

“Yes. Supervisor Searcy, please. This is April Green. I'm at 1125 Lincoln Street now. I was in the process of doing an incident investigation and unfortunately, abuse has been reported in the home. I'm requesting immediate response,” she rushed.

“Now, wait a damn minute!” Patricia yelled. “I did everything for those girls! I gave them a home when nobody else wanted their asses! I should whoop y’all asses!”

Although small, April was not scared.

“Ms. Johnson, need I remind you that I work for the county. If you so much as lay a hand on me, I will have you locked up before you can blink. I am also armed. Now I would suggest that you calm down and allow the girls to gather their belongings. You are not under arrest but you will be, should you continue with your behavior. It is in your best interest that you do not interfere." She turned back to us. "Girls, please. Go grab your things."

Natasha and I hurried to the room to grab our things and packed as quickly as we could. I knew that if I was going to get away, this would be the time. I wasn't going to another home. I remembered that I had to grab the other gun I had hidden.

"I'm so glad we're getting the hell out of here," Natasha sighed. "Let's hurry up and get our stuff."

We grabbed as much as we could and threw it in the suitcases and I grabbed Natasha and hugged her tight.

"I am so sorry, Tash," I said.

I couldn't tell her that I was leaving her behind, but without a solid plan, she would only slow me down. And, she deserved a normal life. She looked at me strange and went back to her suitcase. I ran into the bathroom and grabbed the other gun from under the sink and put it in my purse wrapping it around my body.

We headed to the kitchen where April stood still on her phone. I watched the crime scene investigators walking out of the house and one of the officers talking to another one in uniform, who I assumed was the one in charge.

"We can't find the gun, sir," they said.

I sighed, slightly relieved.

"Well find it," the officer snapped. "The kid didn't shoot herself with an invisible gun."

His phone rang and he waved the young one away. He nodded his head and after a few more seconds, hung up the phone. He walked up to April and whispered something to her and April's eyes immediately became glossy.

"What is it?" I asked, already fearing the worst.

"Um…it's Kim. She uh…she didn't make it," she whispered.

I felt my knees buckle and I began to cry uncontrollably. It was like losing my dad all over again. Only this time, it was my fault. I shouldn't have left that backpack in the room. I was so busy trying to see what was going on that I didn't think about the gun at all.

"I'm so sorry, girls," April apologized. "I know you guys loved her."

"She was only six, man," I sobbed. "She didn't deserve this. She was only six!"

April tried to comfort me but I just snatched away.

"Okay. Um…girls, I don't think you all need to be here any longer than necessary. Why don't you go wait in the car with the officer while we wait for my supervisor?" April suggested.

One of the officers took us over to his car so that we could wait inside and get away from Patricia.

"Oh my God. I can't believe that just happened," Natasha panicked. "What are we going to do? You think they're gonna separate us? I can't believe Kim is gone. I'm sorry, Miracle," she apologized.

"I know," I sniffed. "But, ain't no need for you to apologize. You ain't do shit."

It was dark outside and I knew it was time. I contemplated telling her but I knew she would want to go with me and if I told her no, she might ruin my getaway. So I made up a lie. Everything I needed was in my backpack and I could get new clothes so all I needed was Black. I grabbed my phone out my back pocket and texted him, letting him know it was an emergency and to come get me.

I looked out the window and saw that the officer was standing on the porch talking and not even looking in my direction. It was go time. My purse was still wrapped around me and I was ready.

"I forgot my dad's picture. It's still in the room. I ain't leaving without it. I'll be right back," I told Natasha.

"Okay," she said.

I got out the car and walked towards the house moving quickly and quietly so as not to get the attention of the officer. I looked over my shoulder to see Natasha's head down and took my chance. I ran hard as I could until I couldn't see the house anymore. I ran all the way to the bus stop and checked my phone to see how long it would take before the bus showed. I had to wait almost five minutes so I called Black to let him know the deal.

"Yo, I'm on the way," he answered.

"Okay. Well, meet me at the Illinois station," I told him.

That was the closest depot from where I was and I wouldn't have to wait as long.

"Aight. I got you. Yo, you good?" he asked.

The bus pulled up and I hopped on quickly as it pulled off. I paid my fare and sat down in the seat.

"Miracle? You good?" he repeated.

I finally relaxed and sighed knowing that I had finally gotten free.

"I am now."

*****

Chapter Ten

"Yo. You need to try and get you some sleep," Black said to me.

I was at The Embassy Suites in one of the rooms trying to calm my nerves. Black had gotten a room for me because I didn't feel comfortable staying with him just yet. Lucky for me, he had an oversized tee shirt in his car because I didn't realize, until after I showered, that I had no clothes since I had left my suitcase there.

I was thinking about how I left and the guilt was killing me. I knew I hurt Natasha when I left and I wanted to go back for her, but I was sure that April had taken her to another home.

I had to admit that a part of me was happy that Patricia was sitting in that house miserable. I wanted that bitch to suffer for everything that she had done to us. She deserved to feel some pain for once. Maybe, she'd see how the fuck the shit felt for once.

"I'm not tired," I told him. "Too much shit has happened today."

"Aight. So, what's up?" he asked.

"I don't know if I should tell you."

"Come on now. You know you can tell me. With the shit I do, who am I to judge?" he laughed.

I laughed a little bit.

"I guess," I sighed. "Well, last night I met up with Chris and I told him that I wanted to leave and get out of the house. I don't know. I guess I just finally had enough. So we came up with a plan to leave. He was going to come and take care of

Patricia and her daughter, Whitney. But while we were gone today, I guess he couldn't take it, and he killed Whitney. But…I saw him before I went to the school. I told him to give me his gun so that way if the cops caught him, they wouldn't be able to charge him. So, I put it in my backpack and went back to the house. And um...while the cops were downstairs talking to Ms. Patricia, Kim…she…sh…she shot herself." I started to cry and tried to keep it together to tell him the rest. "I had the gun in my backpack and…and I took the backpack upstairs so she could use my notebook to color with. I didn't know that she would find the gun, Black. I didn't know!"

I broke down and he grabbed me, holding me tight while I cried.

"Black, this shit is so fucked up. Why the fuck does all this bad shit keep happening? Why can't anything good happen to me? Instead, every person that I care about is taken from me. They're either killed, they run away, disappear, or they are fuckin' put in prison. My dad, Goody, Nikki, Chris, Kim and Natasha. I don't have anybody left," I wept.

He continued to hold me and kissed my forehead.

"Calm down, baby girl. You got plenty of people still here that care about you. I'm here. You got Myesha and Goody. Even though bruh is locked up, I know he's still holding it down for you. So don't trip. I ain't going nowhere," he promised.

"Yea. But, Black, I have nothing," I sniffed. "I left the house with nothing. I mean, I packed my stuff but I left it in the car and I ran. The only thing I got is what's in my backpack. I gave Chris the money Myesha withdrew today. I gotta watch my money. I gotta get a new hustle…"

"And I got you," Black swore. "I'll get you some new clothes. It ain't nothing. You my baby so I'ma take care of you. And hell, I can help you get a little whip too. That way you can drive yourself around and I can stop being your chauffeur," he teased.

I gave him a playful shove.

"Shut up," I giggled. "I know that I never thanked you for everything that you've done. I know that you don't have to and you probably got a lot of girls tryna get at you."

"Nah…"

"Nigga, please. You know Myesha tells me everything," I told him. "I know you got a lot of hoes on you…"

"Yea, but I told you I ain't tryna wife no hoe," he said. "I can smash any hoe out there. I don't need a hoe on my arm that everybody and they mama done been with. My girl is gonna be the one everybody wants."

"Oh, really?"

"Yea. And I'm looking at her," he smiled, cupping my chin.

He kissed my lips and I, once again, lost myself. I don't know what he was doing to me because it was so crazy but, whenever his lips touched mine, I would lose control and couldn't even think straight.

I felt him pushing me back onto the bed and he began to trail his hand up my bare legs until I felt his hand in my extremely wet panties. I moaned and he smiled in between kisses as he began to explore the origin of the wetness. My head was spinning when I felt his fingers playing with me and I moaned again from it feeling so good. My brain was saying stop, but my body was on fire and my pussy was screaming.

He continued to caress my clit with his fingers. I tilted my head back and closed my eyes as he began to kiss my neck. Everything was feeling so good. I was practically dripping all over him. My body started to feel something that I wasn't sure of and I felt all warm and tingly all over. I felt like I was ready to burst and he stopped.

I opened my eyes and looked at him with a wild expression, not even realizing that I was panting.

"Why'd you stop?" I asked.

He gave me a wicked grin and I didn't know what to think.

"Open your mouth," he said.

"H-huh?" I asked.

"Open…your…mouth."

I did as he asked and he took his hand and stuck his pointer finger in my mouth. I closed my lips around it and sucked the juices off of it, slow. I had never tasted any type of bodily fluid before aside from spit, let alone my own.

He grabbed me by the back of my neck and began to kiss me again, trailing his tongue along my neck while I tried to maintain my sanity. I wanted him. Bad.

I pulled him on top of me and fell back on the bed as our lips connected again. His hands began to caress and massage my body, kneading the inside of my thighs and teasing my area that wanted him the most. He pulled away from me and stared at me with those dark eyes, that in the light, looked like pools of ink.

"You sure you want this?" he asked. "I know you've never been with anyone. Don't do nothing like this if you're not ready."

I smiled warmly at him. Even though the streets knew him as this thug nigga, he never showed me that side of him. He showed me him and I loved it.

"I do want it," I whispered.

He kissed me again and pulled away.

"I want you to be mine and mine only," he whispered.

I nodded my head and smiled again.

"I want to hear you say it," he said, nipping at my neck.

"I'm…I'm all yours," I moaned.

"Are you sure?"

"Yes!" I promised.

He plunged his tongue into my mouth and I wanted nothing more than for him to take me right then. He grabbed at the shirt I was wearing and pulled it over my head. Then he pulled my panties off, exposing my now, completely naked body.

"I just want to look at how beautiful you are," he murmured.

The way he stared at me made me nervous and I instinctively tried to cover myself.

"No," he said. "I want to see all of you. I want to see all of my baby. You're mine and I want to admire it."

He took his hands and ran them all over my body. It drove me crazy. He grabbed his shirt and pulled it over his head, revealing his amazing six pack. The boy's chest was perfection. I took my hand and placed it on his pecks and trailed it down, slowly, to his belt buckle. I looked at him and he smiled, standing to take his pants off and exposing his equally fit bottom. He had on briefs that hugged his body just right and I swallowed hard at the massive bulge that sat in the middle.

"Um…do you have an uh…"

“I got you, baby,” he promised, reaching into his pocket, pulling out a gold wrapped condom. “I’m gonna always protect you.”

He walked over to me and grabbed my legs, spreading them. I was breathing heavy in anticipation as he started planting soft kisses up my legs and thighs.

“You’re so beautiful, baby girl,” he whispered.

He kissed my inner thigh so close to my pussy that I thought I would explode. I felt his tongue licking my inner essence and I gasped loudly. Every part of my body was on fire.

He continued exploring my walls with his tongue, faster, and flicked it on my clit. I felt the room spinning and I couldn’t stop my legs from shaking.

“Let it go,” he demanded as I tried to contain the feeling.

“I…I…I don’t wanna cum yet,” I stuttered.

“Baby, don’t worry. We got all night for me to make you cum,” he promised.

I couldn’t hold it in any longer and I felt myself convulsing. I moaned so loud that I almost scared myself.

He sat up satisfied and wiped his mouth as I tried to stop my legs from shaking. He smiled and we began to tongue wrestle once more.

“I’m gonna go slow, okay?” he said.

I nodded my head and watched him stand up and take his briefs off, looking at his beautifully hard dick. He rolled the condom on and climbed on top of me as I braced myself.

“Relax, baby,” he said. “I’ll be gentle.”

I did as he said and he did as he promised. I felt him entering me slowly and it felt as if my insides were tearing for a few minutes. He kept his eyes on me the entire time and moved slow.

"Are you okay?" he asked.

"Uh huh," I answered.

He pushed a little further and began a steady rhythm. Things started to feel good. My pussy gripped his dick like it was a suction valve and I felt the same feeling that I had a few minutes ago. I couldn't get enough of him. His movements, his kisses, everything had me in a whirlwind. This nigga was a savage! I was loving it though. I didn't want it to end.

"I think I'm…I think…" I tried to speak.

"It's okay, baby," he groaned. "That's what I want you to do. I want you to cum all over until you can't no more."

"Oh God!" I screamed. "Oh God! I'm cummin', baby!"

Once again, my body felt the convulsions and exploded as I felt all of my juices dripping onto him.

I whimpered for a few seconds as he kept stroking. I thought about us making love all night long. He pleased my body so much, I lost count of the number of times I came. And for the first time, I fell asleep peacefully.

*

I woke up to pee and looked at the clock on the nightstand to see that it was four in the morning. I looked over to see Black lying next to me, snoring softly. I smiled at how sexy he looked and got up quietly to go to the bathroom.

I sat down and peed. I looked to see my book bag in the corner. I reached to grab it, remembering the letters that my godfather had sent. I checked the date on the stamp to see which one to open first and read.

Miracle,

Hey, baby girl. I got good news for you. My lawyer got me a new trial date to see about the case being thrown out. Remember, I told you that he was arguing that the evidence wasn't strong enough? Well there was a judge that agreed with that, so in two weeks I'll be going to court.

I'm praying that I can get out and start to fix everything that has gone bad. I know it's been hard for you. I can't believe you're almost 18! When I do get out, we're going to have to do a lot of celebrating to catch up.

I know your father would be proud of you, Miracle. I hope you're hitting those books. You know your daddy definitely wanted you to go to college.

Baby girl, I want you to know how sorry I am for everything that has happened. When I get out, we'll take care of the situation that you are in. You can come live with me and we will find out who killed your daddy. I can promise you that.

I gotta cut this letter short though. I gotta get ready for visitation, but I'll write you soon to tell you what happens.

Be good, baby girl.

Love,

Goody

I smiled at the thought of Goody being released early. I opened the other letter to see what it read.

Baby Girl,

Your godfather is a free man! The attorney got my case thrown out due to lack of substantial evidence. Although the prosecution was pissed, it wasn't a damn thing they could do about it, so I will be coming home soon!

I can't wait to see all of y'all. I miss my kids, Tori, and of course, you. Soon, baby girl, you wont have to worry about that crazy woman or her daughter. I gotta make sure I'm on my best behavior because you know they will try any and everything to pin something on me.

You just hang tight because your godfather is coming home and we will be a family again.

Love,

Goody

I folded the letter up, put it back in the envelope and placed the letters back in my backpack. Finally, things were going to get better. My godfather was coming home and I would be one step closer to finding out who killed my father. I couldn't wait to tell him about everything that had gone down with Patricia and her fucked up daughter. I was so glad that she was dead. Her mother deserved to die right with her.

I wondered if the cops had found the other gun. I wanted to go back and see for myself. My mind was made up. Besides, I had the other gun so if Patricia even thought about trying it, she would get what was coming to her.

I flushed the toilet, grabbed my clothes that I had tossed in the corner, and threw them on. I grabbed the gun out of the bag and walked back out into the room. I grabbed Black's hoodie and car keys, scribbling a note to tell him that I was running to the store for some clean panties, just in case he woke up. I put it on the nightstand and headed to his car.

I drove the twenty-five minutes to South Oak Cliff and killed the lights once I turned on her street. I parked about a hundred yards away, pulled the hood over my head to hide my face, and got out, heading towards the house. I went to the back door and opened it where I had left a key. I used it to let myself in. Tiptoeing inside, I headed for the stairs to Kim's room.

I could hear Patricia snoring as I passed her room and fought the urge not to empty the clip in my gun. I opened Kim's door and froze when it creaked. I waited to see if Patricia would awake, but after several seconds of hearing her continued snoring, I figured it was safe.

I walked in Kim's room and began looking, trying to see if I could find the gun. I looked underneath the bed and her dresser. I checked her closet and everywhere imaginable but couldn't find it. I was trying to move as quiet as possible so that she wouldn't wake up. I stood in the middle of the room, staring, trying to figure out where it could be. I leaned against the wall and stared up at the ceiling when I noticed something black sticking off the side.

I grabbed a chair and stood up on it to see the small handgun sitting there. I grabbed it and climbed down off the chair, putting it back against the desk.

"What the fuck are you doing in my house?"

I jumped hard and turned to see Ms. Patricia standing there looking a hot mess in her bathrobe. She looked and saw the gun in my hand and her mouth flew open.

"You shot my baby, didn't you?" she whispered.

"No," I swore. "I didn't."

"But, you know who did," she said. "Otherwise, that gun wouldn't have made its way in this house."

"I don't know who shot Whitney," I lied. "I was just coming to see if I could find the gun and turn it over to the police."

"You lying, little bitch," she snapped, walking towards me. "Your ass wasn't taking shit to the police. That dumb ass little girl got the gun because of you and you know it. And, I know you had something to do with my daughter being killed."

I was starting to get nervous so I did what I instinctively thought to do. I held the gun up and aimed at her, stopping her in her tracks.

"Oh, so you know what you doing, huh?" she pressed. "So, you're gonna use the same gun you killed my daughter with, the same gun that Kim killed herself, to shoot me?"

"I didn't kill your daughter!" I growled.

"But you killed Kim," she sneered. "Otherwise, how else did she get the gun?"

The guilt of seeing them rush Kim on the stretcher tore at me and she laughed.

"I knew I was right. Your little dumb ass," she taunted. "You should've killed your damn self. Would have been less stress for me. Ungrateful ass."

"Ungrateful?" I hissed. "How was I ungrateful? What? I was ungrateful because your bitch of a daughter and her friends jumped on me for no fucking reason? Was I ungrateful when you popped me across my face for not getting out of bed fast enough? Was I ungrateful when you took Nikki away from me? Was I ungrateful when you locked me in a dark room like I was some lab rat?"

I wiped angry tears from my face while I kept my aim on her.

"You should be thankful that I took your ass in," she said. "You was a worthless piece of shit that thought she was supposed to have everything handed to her by your drug dealing ass daddy. Well, you got what you deserve."

"You deserve so much worse." I sniffed. "You tortured and tormented us for so long. You and your daughter. You covered for the shit that your daughter did to us. She raped Chris. She forced him to have sex with her and you let her do it. You let her come up to his room. You didn't stop her. And Chris wasn't the first one." I could see the anger in her eyes but I didn't care. She was gonna hear what I had to say. "Your daughter was a hoe. Your daughter walked around here and did whatever the hell she wanted to do and you let her. You let her torture us and now she's probably burning in hell, where you should be."

She suddenly charged towards me.

"You little bit— "

I pulled the trigger and watched as the hole formed in her chest. She dropped to her knees and then fell to her side, gasping for air. She stared at me and I watched as she struggled to breath.

I stood over her and tried to steady my breathing. I couldn't believe that I had pulled the trigger. I was scared shitless. I bent down to try to help her and she grabbed my arm.

"You gonna have the most miserable life, you bitch," she strained.

I jumped back and stood in shock. Even dying, the bitch was still evil. I watched her as the life finally left her body.

"Well, now your miserable life is over, bitch," I whispered.

I looked at her lifeless body and I wondered how in the hell I was going to explain this. What if the cops came looking for me? What if someone saw me? How long would it take before they found her body?

I stuffed the gun in my pocket and ran downstairs. I was walking through the kitchen when I passed by her liquor bottles. That was when the idea came to me. I grabbed one of the towels and a few bottles and ran back up the stairs to Kim's room where her body still lay. I poured the liquor on and around her and doused the rag in it as well. Searching through her pockets, I grabbed her lighter and pack of cigarettes and lit one and placed it in her mouth. I put the empty bottle in her hand using the rag and watched and waited for the ashes to spark.

Within minutes, her body was on fire and I ran. I didn't stop until I got to the car. I hopped inside and calmed my breathing as I just stared at the house. I don't know how long I sat there until I began to see smoke coming from the house and the flames engulfing the windows.

I cranked the car and sped off, turning on the lights once I got away. I drove back to the hotel and stopped at the Walmart nearby, remembering that I told Black I was going to get panties. I ran in, grabbed a pack, a few pair of pants and shirts, and checked out. I barely made it back to the room before the sun came up.

Putting the bags down in the chair of the suite, I peeked to see that Black was still asleep. So, I tiptoed into the bathroom and stripped out of the clothes, throwing them back on the floor. I almost choked when I saw the blood on my hand.

"Shit," I whispered.

I turned the water on and scrubbed my hands until it came off. I picked up my clothes to see if it was there as well and saw a small spot on Black's sweatshirt.

"Fuck!"

A knock at the door almost made me piss myself.

"Yo. You good?" I heard Black ask.

“Yea,” I answered.

“Aight. I’m just making sure,” he said.

I hurried up and threw the oversized tee shirt back on and opened the door.

“My bad, baby,” I smiled. “I had to run to Walmart and get some stuff.”

“Yea. I saw. Why you didn’t just wake me up?”

“Cause you were over there snoring your ass off like you ain’t slept in weeks,” I teased.

He grabbed me by my waist and pulled me back down to the bed as I burst out laughing.

“That’s because you had me putting in all that work,” he growled in my ear. “And, it’s ‘bout time for me to put in some overtime.”

I laughed and held my nose with my fingers.

“Yea, but you need to go brush your teeth first,” I teased.

He tickled me and stood up, walking across the room to the bathroom.

“Aight, but your breath ain’t spring time fresh either,” he laughed.

He closed the door and I heard the faucet turn on. I checked my phone and saw that Chris texted me while I was in the house.

Chris:

I’m in Houston. Have the police said anything?

Miracle:

No. No suspects yet. Will call later.

I put the phone back on the nightstand and heard the water turn off. The door opened and Black stood with his sweatshirt in his hand.

"Why is there blood on my sweatshirt?" he asked.

"I…uh…" My heart began to beat a mile a minute and I was at a loss for words.

He came over and sat down next to me on the bed.

"Just tell me what happened," he said.

I sighed and I explained to him of how I went back to the house to find the gun that Kim had used to kill herself and how everything spiraled out of control.

"Do you have the gun with you now?" he asked once I finished.

"Yea," I told him. "Both of them. The one Chris gave me the first time is in my backpack. But the gun that he used to kill Whitney, I told him to give it to me and well…you know the rest."

He sat quiet for a few minutes.

"Aight. Say no more. I'll take care of it," he told me. "But, you can't go and do no shit like that again."

"I won't. Trust me," I promised.

"Aight. I know that shit was fucked up, but that life is behind you now. From now on, I got you."

He kissed me again, and I smiled at his minty tasting lips.

"And I got you."

*****

Six Months Later… (Yea everything doesn't happen In a week!)

Chapter Eleven

Black was fussing at me about the furniture that they were putting into my apartment. I had planned on getting basic furniture, but he insisted on taking me shopping for my getting accepted into school, so now he was having to deal with it.

I laughed as he helped the movers arrange the furniture in the apartment and jumped on top of the couch that they were carrying in.

“I will drop you on this floor,” he teased.

I laughed and hopped off and gave them directions on where to put everything.

Things were great with me and Black. Ever since I decided to be his girl six months ago, he treated me like a queen. I never had to worry about anything and he kept his hustling separate. He wanted me to stay in school, but because of both Whitney and Patricia being killed and the police still not having any leads, I decided to go ahead and get my GED. I had gone to social services once I turned eighteen and confess to running away the night that Kim died. Of course, I didn’t confess to any of the other shit that I did, but I didn’t want to leave anything to chance. Of course, as I suspected, their paperwork was so far behind that by the time they got to my file, I was already legal. So there was nothing that they could do but give me references to shelters and halfway houses, which I damn sure didn’t need, so I walked out the office happy.

I had enrolled in courses online and was getting my Bachelor’s in social services. I didn’t know what exactly I wanted to do when I graduated, but I knew that I wanted it to be working with needy kids somehow.

I was able to breathe a little bit because the police had not had any luck in finding Whitney's killer. Patricia's death had been ruled an accident so I was happy. I don't know what Black did, but I trusted him and was happy that I got to start over.

Myesha and I were still cool, but she was becoming extremely distant from me, although I didn't know why. She and Lamar were still together, but she didn't really come around as much but I didn't want to push.

Goody was getting the run around with his release date since the prosecution kept throwing appeals, but he made sure to keep me updated on everything. His lawyer was optimistic, so as long as he was getting out, I was happy.

I was the happiest that I had ever been. I know my father may not have been a hundred percent happy with the way my life was going, but I knew that me getting out of the mess that I was in was definitely something he'd be smiling about.

I looked at Black going back and forth with the movers and smiled. Life was good.

"Baby, can you go down to the truck and grab those two floor lamps?" Black asked.

"Yea, I got you, babe," I said, walking downstairs to get the lamps out the truck.

I walked down the sidewalk heading to the truck and noticed a girl who looked younger than me arguing with an older man. He slapped her and she fell to the ground.

"Hey! Get the hell away from her!" I yelled.

Black, who was coming out the building, heard me yelling and came running.

"What's wrong?" he asked.

"That guy just slapped that girl," I said, pointing across the street.

The girl was trying to stand up while the guy was grabbing a fist full of her hair.

Black walked across the street and I followed. The guy saw us coming and rushed her up.

"Hurry up!" he yelled.

The girl stood dazed and walked towards the passenger seat of a black Nissan. We locked eyes and my mouth dropped open. I couldn't believe what I was seeing.

"Nikki?"

She tried to turn her head, but it was too late. I had already recognized her. I reached out to grab her as she tried to get in the car. I looked over and Black was handling the guy that had hit her. Apparently, he must have recognized Black because he backed off.

"Nikki, what the hell are you doing out here? Where have you been? Are you okay?"

"Don't expect another dime from me, bitch!" the man yelled out, getting into his car and screeching off.

I grabbed Nikki's arm and led her off the street.

"Nikki, are you okay?"

"I'm fine, Miracle," she mumbled. "Just leave me alone."

"What you mean leave you alone? Nikki, that nigga just smacked you upside your damn head. You disappear on me and you want me to leave you alone? Hell no!"

People were staring at us as we stood on the sidewalk. Black looked around and urged us to go in the house while he finished up with the movers who were watching us like hawks.

"Take her to the apartment," he told me.

"Come on, Nikki," I told her, grabbing her hand.

"I'm fine, Miracle, damn!" She snatched away from me.

I was not about to have this. I grabbed her and yanked hard as I could.

"You don't have a choice. You ain't eighteen, so you either come with me or I'll call the cops on your ass. Don't think I won't."

I knew that I wouldn't actually call the cops on her, but I was desperate and I would have said anything to get her inside. She frowned at me, but she followed. I took her up the stairs and walked her into my new apartment, taking her straight to my room and closing the door. She flopped down on the new bed and looked around avoiding eye contact.

"Nikki, what the hell is going on? You out here hoein'?" I asked her.

"No. That was my boyfriend."

I knew she was lying. Ain't no way in hell that was her man.

"Nikki, it's me, Miracle. C'mon you can tell me."

"Look, you don't know what the hell you talking about, okay?" she snapped.

She stood up to leave and I ran after her.

"Nikki, please! I missed you. You just disappeared on me and…I'm just tryna make sure that you're okay," I pleaded.

She turned slowly and sat back down on the bed.

"I'm not really hooking like that," she said after a few minutes. "Sometimes, I gotta go work to help pay bills, but I'm not out there all the time."

"Pay bills? Nikki, what's going on? Tell me."

She sighed and tried to fight the tears that were forming.

"Miracle, shit got really bad when they took me up out of there. That bitch, Patricia....she came to pick me up from school early one day to go for a meeting with the social worker, and when I got home, she had to run to the store. Her punk ass boyfriend decided he was going to make me a woman while she was gone. She walked in on it, and I told her that I didn't do anything wrong and that he came after me. He hurt me! I didn't do anything. She grabbed me, threw me in the car, and then told social services that I was a problem child and threatening to kill myself. They put me in a psychiatric home and it was even worse there. The nurses were mean and would beat us on the low. Some of the guards would stick their hand in me and make me do stuff to them that I didn't wanna do. One day this guard took me into the laundry room for me to give him head. I bit as hard as I could, and I grabbed his keys and ran. I got out of there as fast as I could."

She stopped to sniff and to wipe her eyes and I sat there in shock at her confession.

"I slept on a few park benches for a couple of nights because I couldn't risk going to a shelter and somebody calling social services. Then I met Rakim and he told me that he could help me get my stuff together. He took me home and gave me new clothes and food and stuff. He didn't try to touch me or anything. I thought everything was good. I was starting to feel comfortable, and then the next thing I know, I came in the house one day and there was this guy sitting there. Rakim told me that the guy wanted to take me out. I was confused because the guy was old enough to be my daddy, but I didn't want to make him mad because he had helped me and everything. So I said okay. I got dressed and went with the guy and he took me back to his apartment. He started kissing on me and stuff and he told me that he would make me feel good. So I let him. And then when I got back to Rakim, he treated me like a princess. He told me that he wasn't gonna let me do that all the time and only when stuff got tight. But then, he started bringing in other girls, and I guess stuff got tight because, after a few months, he had me doing it more and more. I just…I couldn't tell him no. He saved me from the streets. Sometimes it just…it just gets hard because I just wanna be a normal teenager and I can't. I gotta make his money or otherwise I get in trouble."

"What do you mean you get in trouble?" I probed.

"If I don't make my share, Rakim, well, he hits me. Sometimes he kicks and punches me. He says that he doesn't like doing it but that he has to lay down the law. So I have to be good and do what he says."

I couldn't believe my ears. Who was this nigga, Rakim? I couldn't let her go back to him. Maybe Black knew something. But I couldn't let her go back to him.

"Nikki, I'm so sorry. I should have been there to protect you."

"It's not your fault," she shrugged. "You wouldn't have been able to stop it. That woman was just evil. Like she was the bane of my existence."

"Well, you got me now. You don't have to worry about going back. We gonna get you straight."

"I can't just leave Rakim. If I don't come home, he will find me. I've never had to deal with him like that, but I know the last girl that didn't come home ended up in the hospital for a few days and couldn't see out her eye for like two weeks. I don't need that."

"But you can't just keep doing this!"

I couldn't understand why she didn't want me to help her. Why was she tryna go back to this nigga?

"Miracle, you don't just up and leave. Not after everything that he's done for me. I can't. He will kill me."

Black knocked on the door and came in.

"Everything good?" he asked.

"Baby, do you know of a nigga named Rakim?" I asked him.

Judging by the slow exhale he gave, that was a yes.

"Yea. Nigga live out there in Ag-Town. That's who she works for?" he asked, gesturing to Nikki.

"Yea," I answered. "But she can't go back there, baby."

"It ain't that easy, Miracle," he said. "I mean I ain't in the pimp game and shit, but I know that nigga handles his business. So if she working for that nigga, I'm sure she can't just walk up out of there. If she does, she'll have niggas looking for her."

"But she's not eighteen!"

"And? Don't nobody fuck with Rakim like that, bae. I know you wanna help but if she saying she can't dip, you gotta chill."

I was so mad. I had just found Nikki and now I was about to lose her again.

"I gotta go," she said, getting up.

"Nikki, wait!" I stood up and hugged her tight until she returned the hug. "Just promise me you won't disappear again. You call me if you need me for ANYTHING. You hear me?" I wrote my number down on a piece of paper since I didn't see a phone in her hand and gave it to her. "I'm serious, Nikki. You call me any time of day. I don't care, I got you."

I hugged her again and she left. Black wrapped his arms around me and I tried to hold it together. I didn't know how I was going to do it, but I had to save Nikki.

*****

Chapter Twelve

I was so excited because today was the day that my godfather, Goody, was coming home. He got locked up right after my seventeenth birthday, but even though the courts found him guilty, his attorney filed an appeal and the judge had no choice but to dismiss the charges. He should have been out, but right before he was to be released, he got locked down in solitary confinement for a fight that they claimed that he started, even though he was stabbed. But he survived it and now he was coming home.

I jumped out of bed that morning and hurried to get myself ready. Black had gone back to his apartment to handle some business and to give me and Goody time to catch up. I told him I would bring him by later so that they could meet. I had my own car that Black had bought me so I could drive myself. Goody was the one that had taught me how to drive, so I know he would be shocked to see me a year later on my own.

I had talked to Tori, Goody's wife, and told her that I was going to ride with her to the prison to pick him up. I knew he would be so happy to see us once he got out from behind those bars. I had so much to tell him. Plus, with him being out, I knew that I would be that much closer to finding out who killed my daddy. I didn't have to worry about answering to anybody or looking over my shoulder. Black held me down, I helped him with his weight, and we were making money. I knew my godfather wouldn't be too happy with it, but I was eighteen now, and after everything that I had been through over the past year and dealt with, it wasn't much he could tell me.

I checked myself out in the mirror and smiled. I had on a cute sundress with matching sandals and a small heart shaped pendant that Black had bought me as part of my gift for getting into college. I tugged at it and kissed it like I did every morning, put my hair in a messy but cute bun, and headed out the door.

Getting in my car, I headed to my aunt's, who was already waiting for me outside. I parked and hopped out rushing to get in her car.

"Hey, girlie! Look at you! You look cute!"

"Thank you," I smiled, putting on my seatbelt. "I can't wait to see him! I know he is gonna be blown."

"I'm just happy that he doesn't have to be behind them bars no more," she sighed. "That attorney worked magic. Now he can be home where he belongs and be with his kids. Now, how are you holding up? I know you got your own place and everything now."

I nodded my head. Since I had been on my own, Tori and I talked a little more than what I was able to before. She knew certain things about what I had done to get away, but of course, I left some shit out; like me killing that bitch, Patricia.

"I'm good. I'm supposed to start my next class in about a week."

"Well, that's good. What you trying to get your degree in?"

"Social Services."

"Well, that's a good major."

"Yea," I agreed. "I figured after everything that I've been through in the past year and dealing with these shitty foster homes, and the way some of the kids are treated, I wanna be able to help."

"Well, I know you are gonna be great at it. And I know your daddy would be proud."

I got quiet for a second and wondered if she was right. I tried to stick to what my father wanted. Even though I dropped out of high school shortly before graduation, I did get my GED, and I enrolled in classes online. Although I wasn't on an actual college campus, I was still getting my education. I took care of myself for the most part, but Black did help me out. I had a job, but I just couldn't file taxes on it. I knew eventually I would have to tell Goody, but being in the drug game, I was learning names and faces. Black always took me with him unless he thought it would be too dangerous. I needed to get as close as possible to know who was my target and who was my ally.

"You alright over there?" she asked, pulling me out my thoughts.

"Huh? Yea, I'm good."

"Miracle, you know your daddy is proud of you right? You have been through a lot, but you still got your head on straight. Be proud of that. He's looking down at you right now, beaming," she said.

I looked up at the sky and thought about what I was doing. I knew the shit was gonna get bad, but I had to get to the bottom of it.

Daddy, forgive me for what I'm gonna do, I prayed. *But there's gonna be bloodshed.*

*****

"Baby!"

I watched as Tori ran to Goody and jumped in his arms. He held her tight and kissed her for damn near five minutes straight. You would've thought they were in one of those cheesy Black romance movies the way they were going at it. But I couldn't knock it. I would be that way too if I hadn't seen Black in over a year.

I looked at my godfather, and although he was a little bit skinnier, not much had changed. He was still the same for the most part, though, so I was happy. The two finally broke their grasp from each other and he looked over to see me still leaning against the car.

"Baby girl?"

I smiled and let the tears that had formed at that point to fall freely. I ran over to him, and he embraced me in a hug, letting me cry.

"I'm so glad you're here," I told him through muffled sobs.

"It's okay, baby girl. I'm home now."

I just let him hold me for a few more seconds and cried my eyes out. Goody knew everything that I had been through, and it felt good to finally be able to get that shit all out.

"Ain't shit else gone happen you hear me?"

I nodded my head because I was still sobbing. I had waited on this day for so long. Goody was the only thing that I had left of my father. I couldn't lose him too.

"It's okay, baby girl. Let it out. I promise, ain't nothing else gonna happen to you, ya hear?"

"Okay," I sniffed.

I pulled away from him and wiped my eyes. What little makeup I had on was smeared on my face.

"Alright, let's get out of here," Tori suggested. "I don't want you to be here any longer than you have to be."

We all got into the car and headed back to Dallas. I was excited for my godfather because I knew how happy he would be when he saw his kids, and I knew that he and Tori would be tied up for a while. We drove the whole way home catching up and letting him know what had been going on. I told him about how I was enrolled in school and had gotten my GED and that I was living on my own and had a boyfriend. I couldn't help but to laugh when I told him that and watched his face frowned up.

"You know I'm gonna have to meet this little boyfriend of yours," he said.

"Yes, I know. And he is eager to meet you. I told him all about you. And don't worry, he's a good guy."

He just happens to sell drugs just like you and pops.

"Uh huh. Well, I'll be the judge of that."

"Hush up, Goody," Tori fussed. "Miracle, baby, you wanna join us for dinner?"

"Nah," I told her. "I think I'll wait for another day. I know what they say about coming out the joint and whatever," I joked.

"You better not know about that," Goody laughed.

We rode, clowning, and I felt so much at ease. This was the life that I was used to. This is what I missed. I was happy that things were finally going to get back to normal. Now that Goody was home, everything was going to be straight and I would finally get justice; my way.

*****

"Black, stop now, come on. We can't be doing that right now. We gotta meet my goddaddy in like forty-five minutes."

Black was behind me grinding his dick against my ass. I was trying to focus on getting ready, but he was not making it easy. He started rubbing on my thighs, and underneath my thin dress, my pussy was screaming. He kissed me on the back of my neck and a bitch went crazy.

"Baby, please....you know I gotta finish getting ready now come on."

"Just give me like five minutes," he said, biting me.

That nigga knew just how to get me ready. I was fighting it, too, but fuck it, a bitch was about to get a quickie. I turned around and leaned back against the sink, lifting my dress up. The panties I did have on he snatched off so fast I was surprised that he didn't tear them. I grabbed him, wrapped my legs around his waist, and he slid in me with ease. That shit felt crazy! It ain't nothing like the feel of a nigga fucking you raw! Don't get it twisted though my ass damn sure was on the pill, and I had his ass go to get tested. More folks in Dallas was popping up with AIDS than niggas in third world countries. If I would have caught something, I knew it would have come from him and I would've killed his ass. But my baby came back clean, so I was good.

The strokes he was giving me made me remind him that we didn't have all night to play and that we had to meet up with my godfather soon. Otherwise, I would have let him carry me to that bed and give him the business for real. But the way that he was pounding me, I doubt I would have made it another five seconds.

"Shit, baby!" I moaned.

Black knew how to make me cum in every possible way. I don't know if he was on something or what, but once he got in there, I had to beg his ass to stop. I hated it for all these bitches that talk about how they get a nigga that bust after a few minutes cause Black's ass wasn't gonna stop until he knew that I had cum at least three times.

I pushed him off me and turned around gripping the sink so he could fuck me from the back.

"Hurry up, baby, put it in."

He did just what I asked and I gripped the shit out the handles on that sink! My legs started shaking, and I thought I was gonna fall to the floor. Black pulled a Lil' Wayne on that ass and put his leg on the tub and steadied me while he was still pumping. Damn, his dick was good! It wasn't like I had any other dick other than his, but I didn't want anybody's but his. I swear this felt too damn good. Black was going to keep fuckin' around and we were gonna be late to Goody's.

"Here lean against the tub and bend that ass over," he told me.

"Yes, baby," I moaned.

I grabbed ahold of the tub and held on for dear life as he fucked the hell out of me.

"You love this dick, baby?" he smiled.

"Yes, baby!" I screamed. "Yes, daddy, I love his dick!"

"Shit…and I love this pussy," he groaned, which sounded like he was about to cum.

He grabbed my hair, which he knew drove me crazy, and put his hand around my throat. The first time he did it, I thought he was trying to kill me, but then I realized how much I liked it. He was turning me into an all-out freak.

"Oh God don't stop!" I screamed.

"Nah, baby, I ain't stopping."

"I'm cummin', Black!"

He gripped me tighter and quickened his pace. I felt myself exploding all over his dick. My body was shaking so hard you would have thought I was having convulsions. I knew he came, too, 'cause he plowed me so damn hard I almost fell into the tub. He kissed my back and pulled out as he playfully slapped me on my ass and sighed.

"We gonna finish this up when we get back home tonight. So don't be trying to take your ass to sleep."

He was always talking shit.

“Whatever, boy,” I laughed, turning on the shower trying to hurry up so that we could still leave somewhat on time to head to Goody and Tori’s house.

“You just don't be trying to kill me. I got shit to do.”

“I hear you talking.”

“You want me to leave the water running for you when I finish?” I asked.

“I’d much rather be in there with you,” he smiled.

“Black, get your ass in the room and get yourself together,” I giggled. “Come on now, ‘cause we gotta hurry up and go. That's why we late now ‘cause your ass always wanna start some shit and get me all horny.”

“Can you blame me?” he laughed. “Look at what I got. Shit, I’m tryna get that pussy every day.”

“Damn right,” I said, closing the shower curtain and rushing to wash my body.

Even though he didn't say anything, I was going to leave the water running just in case. I finished my shower a few minutes later and stepped out and sure enough Black was stripping out of his clothes walking into the bathroom. He tried to take off my towel, but I pushed him out of the way and closed the door behind me. After a few minutes, I was dressed and waiting on Black. His phone started buzzing, and I picked it up, assuming it was one of his boys. I looked at the caller ID to see that it was Myesha sending him a text message.

Myesha: Hey, can you talk?

What the hell was she messaging him for? I really didn't think much of it because I knew that she got her weed from him if she didn't get it from me. The shower turned off in the bathroom, and I put his phone back down. I didn't want to be one of those girlfriends that was snooping through their man's phone. He hadn't given me a reason not to trust him, so I wasn't going to go create one from thin air. Plus, Myesha was my best friend. She wouldn't try any shit like that. We'd been friends for too long.

He came out of the bathroom, drying off and putting on his clothes that I had laid out on the bed.

“Hey, babe, Myesha just messaged you a minute ago. You might want to holler at her later.”

“Alright cool,” he said still getting dressed. “She probably just tryna get back in touch with my brother. They been playing games and shit lately. I think they fucking around again.”

I just shrugged and finished prepping myself in the mirror.

“So are you nervous?” I asked him.

“Nervous about what?”

“Meeting my godfather.”

“Man, as much as you talk about him, I pretty much feel like I know the nigga,” he laughed. “But, nah, I'm not nervous. This is somebody that's important to you, so yea I want to meet him. I know he's like your family or whatever, so I'm glad to be meeting him. I feel like I’m meeting your pops or something,” he said, smiling. “Look at ya, got me meeting the folks and shit.”

“Whatever.” I rolled my eyes.

Black gets on my nerves with his goofy ass. But I love him.

“I just really want y'all to get along,” I said.

“Like he's literally the only family I got left. And you're all I got,” I told him. “So of course I want the two most important people in my life to meet and be cool. Plus, I think that he can really help us try to figure out who killed my dad," I added.

"Look, babe, you got to be careful with that," he told me, walking over to me and grabbing my hand. "I know you want to find out who killed your dad, and you know I'm all for it. I got you one hundred. But you can't just go poking around and asking questions. You might get an answer you ain't ready for, or somebody gonna wanna keep you away and do anything to keep you from finding out."

"I know that Black. That's why I want you to meet Goody because he and my dad have been best friends for years. He was there when my father was killed. He's been a part of the game for years, so he's gotta know something. And whatever information he can give me, I'm going to take that and I'm going to find out who did this shit. And when I do, I'm going to watch them bleed slowly."

Black stood looking at me and saw how adamant I was about it and nodded his head.

"Alright I got you," he surrendered. "Well, let's ride then."

I grabbed my purse and we headed out. I couldn't wait for the two to meet. I just hoped that Goody liked him. Cause if he didn't, it would make things real hard.

*****

We pulled into the apartment complex after spending the last couple few hours at Goody's house. We decided to go to Black's apartment since his house was closer to Goody's than mine, and he had some of his boys coming to get some work for the next day.

I don't know what the hell was going on, but Black had been real quiet most of the night. He didn't say anything the entire ride home. I had asked him was everything okay, and he told me it was fine but ever since we got to Goody's house, it was like he froze up. I don't know if he was nervous about meeting him or what. Goody was his same old self, but Black just completely shut down. Like he was acting like he was scared or something. He didn't talk unless somebody said something to him, and he rushed me the entire time to get out of there.

Getting out of the car we walked into the apartment, and I turned on the light.

"Okay, Black, you gonna tell me what's going on?" I asked. "Obviously, something's up."

"Nah, it's nothing like that," he assured me. "I'm good."

"No. I can tell just by looking at you. The minute that we got to my godfather's house you started acting funny. What's going on?"

"It's nothing, Miracle, okay?"

"So we lying now?" I pressed. "Is that what we doing now? I thought we kept it one hundred?"

I was starting to get irritated because clearly his ass was lying to me and I knew something was up.

"I just don't want to say anything until I know for sure."

"Know what for sure?" I questioned. "You sitting here talking in circles right now. Nigga, what the fuck is up?"

He sighed and walked to the refrigerator, grabbing him a beer. He pulled a blunt out of his pocket and lit it. Taking a few hits, he finally sat down and spoke.

"Like I said, I'm not a hundred percent sure, but I think I've seen Goody somewhere before like…recently," he said.

"Okay?" I responded not understanding.

"Like the minute I saw him, I just got this weird vibe like tryna figure out where the hell it was. Like it fucked a nigga's head up."

"Okay, well, like I said, Goody and my pops were known everywhere. A lot of people knew who he was. So maybe that's it?" I asked. "I mean they had a restaurant and everything, so maybe you saw him there."

"I don't know. But it was just a little weird that's all."

"Care to elaborate?" I asked.

"Like I said, I don't know," he answered. "But I'm never wrong when it comes to my gut. If something tells me not to do something, I don't do it. And if something tells me that that nigga is shady, then nine times out of ten he is. And that's what my gut was telling me tonight. Like the minute that I saw that nigga, I just felt like he was being shady."

"Being shady how? You barely said anything to him or anybody else for that matter," I spat.

I was past pissed off now. How the hell was he just gonna come in here and talk about how he don't trust my godfather? I brought him to meet him and he acts like Goody ain't shit.

"Miracle, just calm down," he said. "Like I said I gotta look into some stuff."

"Look into what though?" I pressed. "He's been gone for over a year. The last time I saw him, the cops were carting him off to jail over a bunch of trumped-up charges. He's a dope boy. Just like you. Only, he was bigger than you."

He looked at me and blew the smoke out.

"So what you trying to say? What, I'm just some fuck boy?"

“That's not what I'm trying to say, Black. You know what I mean when I say bigger. Him and my dad did dirt for years. And they did a lot of moving around. They were like running the drug game. So if you got a bad feeling maybe that was it.”

He drug the blunt a few more times before he put it out.

“Look, man, I tripping or nothing like that, but all I’m saying is, I just want you to be careful. I know that’s your godfather and everything, and you said he family, but you need to be careful. If I'm not around you really need to be careful around him,” he warned.

“He hasn't done anything though, baby,” I told him. “He's barely been out a week. All he’s doing is spending time with his family. And he’s my GODFATHER.”

“Yeah, but niggas like that, when you been in the game for so long you ain't going to just walk away from that shit. And I guarantee you his ass is still in the game right now,” he said. “Which means that I got to get ready.”

“For what?” I asked confused.

“Miracle, you can't be that blind.”

I gave him a blank expression like I still didn't know what the hell he was talking about.

“Now that Goody’s out, he's going to go back to hustling. And if he goes back to hustling, then that's going to fuck with my work. It's already enough niggas in Dallas, hell in Texas for that matter, trying to be at the top. I ain’t tryna be noticed like that ‘cause it brings unwanted attention, but I got a good set up and pulling in good money. Goody? He can take that easy. Niggas like that take any and everything and make niggas they bitches,” he expressed.

"Well, I'm sure that I can go talk to him, and if he is planning on getting back into hustling, I'll just let him know not to fuck with your operation," I suggested.

He smirked and downed his beer.

"Yeah. How does that look for my girl going to another nigga to fight another battle? Going to your godfather asking him not to fuck with her boyfriend's business." He sat back and a weird smile formed on his face. "Actually, yea that may not be a bad idea."

"Okay, what the hell are you talking about now?" I sighed, getting tired of the conversation. "You are really starting to bug me right now dude. If this is what happens when you smoke weed, you need to let that shit go."

"Nah, you said that you want to find out what happened to your pops, right?" he asked.

"Yeah..."

"So what better way for me to find out than for me to get close to Goody? He may not tell you because he may be trying to protect you from something, but niggas in the streets talk," he explained.

"Yeah, but niggas in the streets been talking all this time and ain't nobody said shit about my daddy being killed," I pointed out.

"Not necessarily," he said, looking away. "You just gotta know how to ask. A street nigga ain't gonna trust a chick like you. But another street nigga—"

"I mean the streets is talking, but don't nobody really know nothing. So what the hell are people saying happened?"

I never thought to ask that because I was there and saw everything happen in front of me. But maybe he knew something I didn't.

“Far as I know, what little I heard about it before I knew that it was your pops, apparently he did some type of deal or something, and the niggas wasn’t too happy with it. They wanted him to fall back and give up his product and he didn't. They tried to take over some of his territories, but he wasn’t having it. Niggas were talking about how they set up a hitter to come through.”

“Hitters?” I asked. “What you mean like a professional hit man or something?”

“Yea pretty much,” he answered. “It's some niggas out there that you can hit up when they need to murk a muthafucka real quick. I ain’t never had a need for ‘em, but I know I can get a way to call.”

“So that day at the party when that truck pulled up, those were hood hit men,” I recalled. “That wasn’t just some accident?”

“Probably not,” he told me. “They rolled up in a truck?”

“Yea,” I told him. “I was in my daddy’s office and I looked out the window at Goody and my daddy, and they looked like they had been arguing. So, I went out there to thank them for my birthday party, and the next thing I know this truck pulls up and this guy got out talking about he had a flower delivery or something. I think my dad knew what was going on because him and Goody got suspicious real quick. The boy was like nervous or whatever now that I think about it, and he started stuttering talking about how he had to drop it off, and he didn't know anything about it but he was just told to drop the flowers off. And then the next thing I know gunshots started coming from the truck.”

Black listened and was frowning up. I knew something was wracking his brain.

“What? What are you not telling me?” I asked.

"I think I may know the nigga that was in the truck." My eyebrows shot up in surprise. "You said it was a flower delivery truck?"

"Yeah," I answered. My heart was racing at this point. Did he know who killed my father?

"I don't know. But I know one of the homies got a cousin that delivers flowers and shit. It's part of his release from the joint that he works like a part time job or some shit like that."

"Okay. So…you think this guy was going to kill my daddy?" I asked.

"Baby, I don't know. But you said it was a young nigga that was doing the delivery it made me think about the lil' nigga, Loco."

"Loco," I repeated. "Yo, who the fuck names these kids?"

He laughed at my reaction and nodded his head.

"Yeah. I think the kid's name is like Lorenzo or some shit like that. But I can find out."

"Good. Find out if it was him."

"I got you," he promised. "But I still want you to be careful around your godfather. 'Cause if they came after your pops and he's gone, now that Goody's out, it's only going to be a matter of time before the niggas that did it find out. And it's only a matter of time before he wanna get back into the game. And if they know that you out there, and you with him, that's a wrap. I'm already risking you doing shit with me. I don't think niggas will come for you, but I know damn sure they'll come for him, and if you happen to be there, they ain't gone give a damn."

"I promise," I told him. "Ain't shit going to happen. I'll be careful."

“You better be,” he warned.

“Or what?” I asked, teasing him. I got up, walked over, and stood directly over him, looking down. “What you going to do?”

He grabbed me, making me squeal, and straddled me on top of him.

“You don't want to know what I can do,” he smiled, kissing me.

Before I could say anything, he was taking off my dress, and we were getting it in right there at his kitchen table. And just that quickly, I completely forgot about everything.

*****

Chapter Thirteen

My phone was going off at four o'clock in the morning. I was damn near in a coma and my phone ringing woke me up out of a very good sleep. I don't know who the hell was calling me this early in the morning, but they damn sure were going to get cussed out if Jesus wasn't personally at their doorstep telling them it was time to go into the white light.

"Hello?" I answered.

"Miracle, it's Nikki. I need your help," she said.

It sounded as if she was whispering into the phone.

"Nikki?" I asked, sitting up. I turned to my left to see Black still asleep. He and I had gone out clubbing that night, and we decided to go back to his place. I snuck out the bed and walked into the bathroom. "What's going on?"

"Um, I know you said to call you if I need help."

"Yeah, of course. What's up? You okay?" I asked.

"No," she answered beginning to cry. "I need your help. Can you come get me please?" she pleaded.

"Okay, Nikki, what's going on?" I asked.

"He's flipping out. And I don't want him to hit me again. I can't be here, Miracle. Please come get me," she begged.

"Okay, calm down," I told her. "Where are you at?"

"Uh…I'm at the Knights Inn," she whispered. "Miracle, please hurry. He's passed out drunk, and if I try to leave I don't know what he'll do. I locked myself in the bathroom but—"

"Okay, I'll be right there, Nikki. Just hang tight. You at the one on Empire Central?"

"Yeah," she answered.

"Alright, I'll be there in a minute."

It wasn't that far away, so I knew at this time of night there wouldn't be hardly any drivers on the road so I could get there in less than ten minutes. I tiptoed back into the room to get dressed and grabbed my gun. I've been holding on to it just in case Chris came back, plus being with Black, even though he really didn't have enemies like that, you never know. So I always had it on me. But I knew I might need it tonight. I pulled it out of my bag, making sure it was still loaded and went to borrow Black's car keys since my car was still at my apartment. Black slept heavy, so I knew it would be at least a few hours before he even thought about getting up.

I drove to the hotel thinking about what would be there awaiting me. I should have woken Black up. But I knew he wouldn't want to help Nikki. Even though she was a friend of mine, he wouldn't get it. I called the only other person that I knew to call that would help me no questions asked. He answered the phone groggy.

"Hey, Goody, it's Miracle. I'm sorry to wake you up in the middle of the night. But um…I'm in a little bit of a situation. I'm on my way to the Knights Inn off of Empire to get my foster sister. It's a long story, but she's messing with some pimp now and he's got her out here hooking. She just called me about ten minutes ago crying and asking me to pick her up. I'm strapped, but I don't know what I'm walking into, so I need your help."

He agreed after fussing for a few minutes.

"Alright if you can just try to meet me there as quick as possible."

I told him where to meet me and he said he would meet me within ten minutes and I hung up satisfied. I really should have woken Black up, but he didn't understand that Nikki couldn't stay there. His thing was he didn't want to step on any toes. He wanted to stay low key and I understood that; the less attention the better. But the good thing about Goody being who he was is that everybody respected him. So if this fool didn't want to let her go, I was going to make him the only way I knew how.

I pulled up into the parking lot of the hotel and killed the lights sitting antsy waiting for Goody to show up. About five minutes later, he pulled up and got out the car.

"Why the hell are you out this late, Miracle?" he asked. "Why the hell you involved in this?"

"Goody, I promise you, it's more to it than you know. Like I said, it's a long story. But Nikki was there for me. And I need to be there for her. She was the closest thing that I had to family at that damn hell hole. And I can't let anything happen to her."

"All right," he said, scratching his head and yawning.

I got out the car and slammed the door, and he froze.

"Rule number one, if you try to sneak up on somebody, don't slam the damn door," he fussed. "And why the hell are you strapped? Where the hell you get a gun from anyway?"

I looked away seeing how upset he was.

"A friend gave it to me."

"So you taking guns from friends now?" he asked.

"Yeah but—"

"Give me the gun," he demanded. "I don't know what kind of damn friends you got that give you guns and shit."

I pulled the gun out of my bag and handed it to him.

"We gonna talk about this shit later. Come on," he said. "You know what room she's in?"

We started walking towards the doors in front of us.

“Yeah, I think she said she was in 113. She sent me a text message after I hung up with her telling me what room she was in from the bathroom. She’s scared to come out.”

We walked to the door and knocked, waiting to see if someone would answer. After a few minutes, a man answered the door who was clearly drunk. He was tall and looked to be in his late thirties with salt and pepper in his beard.

“Who the hell are you?” he asked.

“We need to talk business,” Goody stated.

“Nigga, I don't know you!” he spat. “I ain’t got to talk to you about shit.”

Goody pulled the gun and held it to his face, forcing himself inside and I followed.

“I beg to differ. Now, according to my baby girl over here you got a friend of hers here against her will, and she doesn't want to stay with you. She don't want to be up under you anymore. So, it would be in your best interest if you just let her leave without fighting me on this.”

“Nigga, fuck you! Nikki get your gawd damn ass out here right now!” he screamed. He was staring at Goody like he wanted to swing but with the gun to his head, he was playing it smart. “Your muthafuckin’ ass tryna run up in my shit like you some fuckin’ superhero. Hell nah. I ain’t with that shit.”

“Look, my nigga, all that talking don’t mean shit to me. Now I said we came to get her, and we ain’t leaving without her. So make it easy on yourself, bruh,” Goody advised.

I stood to the side watching. I was studying this man trying to figure out what the hell made him a monster. He was nothing more than a drunk to me. He must have had Nikki’s mind twisted.

“You got my sister thinking that she got to be out here fuckin’ around to take care of your ass,” I hissed.

He turned his attention to me unfazed.

"Little girl, please. I can make any bitch do with the fuck I want. Hell, if I had gotten your ass, you'd be one of my top money makers. I'll gladly take you over that bitch. You a pretty one."

He puckered his lips at me and Goody got hot. He punched him in the stomach hard, causing him to slump over.

"Watch your fucking mouth, nigga!"

He coughed and held his stomach and I smirked.

"I would never do no shit like that," I said. "Niggas like you ain't nothin' but bitches to me." I walked over to the bathroom door and knocked on it. "Nikki, it's Miracle."

"She ain't leaving," he strained. "She still got money to make."

"She's leaving. She's done with you," Goody told him.

"You wouldn't be saying that shit if you ain't had a damn gun," he responded trying to appear tough. "And you see her ass ain't came out the bathroom."

"Young blood, this gun don't make me. I run these streets, and you might want to ask about me next time you try to challenge me."

"And, nigga, who the fuck are you?"

"I suggest you ask the streets about Goody."

I saw a slight nervousness in this idiot, and I knew he had knowledge of who he was. That was the first time I had ever seen my godfather like that. Usually, when I was around him, he was nice and sweet. But this was the first time that I had seen him in this nature and it shook me to the core.

"See, what you fail to realize is, I've been in these streets for a long time now. I know all about the niggas like you. And with a snap of my finger, your ass would be dead. I murk niggas like you for fun. Now on the strength that I got my baby girl with me, I ain't gone dead your ass. Otherwise, I would have just come through that door and popped your ass. So, this is how this shit is going to go. Nikki's going to walk up out of here, and you going to leave her the fuck alone. And if I see you talking to her, or anything so much as happens to a hair on her body, then I'm coming for you. And believe me, you don't want me as an enemy."

I tapped on the door again, and Nikki opened it slowly stepping out.

"Are you okay?" I asked, looking her over.

I could tell that she had been crying, and her eyes were swollen. She had a bruise on her face that I'm assuming he gave to her. She walked past him slowly and he scowled at her. I could tell he wanted to grab her, but Goody's eyes were trained on him.

"You little bitch," he sneered. "You think you can make it without me? You think anybody's gonna want your ass? You ain't nothing but a washed-up ho. You ain't never been shit. You gone always be a two dollar hoe. You gone always be mine. You'll come crawling back in a couple of days. You calling your little friend over here to come save you ain't gon' do shit. So don't think that these muthafuckas coming up in my spot trying to get you got me shook. 'Cause you'll be back." Nikki stood eyes full of tears and moved away from me. She was believing everything that he was saying. "I should have gotten rid of your useless ass a long time ago. Hell, you ain't made me no money like that anyway. So go on. Get the fuck out. I can get another bitch just like you."

Nikki looked tearful and resistant and I snapped her towards me.

"Don't listen to shit that this asshole is saying. Because, clearly, he needs you more than you need him. Otherwise, he wouldn't have you doing half the shit he was doing. So don't trip. You good. You ain't got to worry about this nigga no more, trust me," I promised.

She looked at me her feet frozen and looked back at him.

"Y'all go get in the car," Goody told me.

I grabbed Nikki's hand and led her towards the door.

"Hold on."

She broke free from my grasp and walked over to him. She looked at him and he stared down at her. If he could, he probably would have choked her right there, but he knew that Goody wasn't going to let that happen. I could tell he was scared shitless but trying to act like he wasn't fazed. She stood for a few more seconds and then spat in his face.

"I hate you," she cried out. "I fucking hate you."

His hand went up to hit her, and Goody quickly pushed her out the way and I grabbed her hand pulling her.

"Let's go, Nikki," I said.

I dragged her out the door, closing it behind me. We got in the door, and I heard the gun pop. Both of us jumped, and my heart began to race. I prayed that Goody came out the door. A few seconds later, the door opened and Goody walked out cool, calm, and collected and walked over to my car. We both stared at him anxiously.

"Is he dead?" I asked.

"No, he ain't dead," he answered. "But trust me he got the message. Y'all need to get home now. And, Miracle, we gone talk about this shit later," he told me. "I'm going to follow you home and make sure you get in okay."

"Okay," I replied.

I didn't know what to think at that moment. I cranked my car, and drove home quietly, not sure what to say. Goody followed like he said and walked us to the apartment.

"Don't be out here trying to do no shit like that again," he warned. "You don't need to be involved in no shit like that. And you," he said, turning to Nikki. "I suggest that you get yourself together. Because niggas like that are ruthless. He could have killed you. Now that you're out, don't you ever think about going back to that shit you hear me?"

Nicki just nodded her head and let the tears fall.

"Thank you," she whispered after a few seconds.

"You straight," he assured her. "I got to go back home. I'm sure Tori's probably looking for my ass right now so let me get home before the sun comes up."

"Okay," I told him. "Thank you, Goody."

I gave him a hug.

"I always got you, baby girl," he said. "We'll talk tomorrow. Get some sleep. Oh yeah," he said. "Here." He handed me back my gun. "Put that shit up. Don't let me see it again."

I nodded and put it back in my purse. He left and I locked the doors. Nikki sat on the couch crying, and I walked over to her and held her in a hug.

"It's going to be okay," I told her. "I know this is hard to handle. And I know you been going through a lot. But I'm here to help okay?"

"I'm just tired of people hurting me. I just want things to go back to normal," she sniffed.

"I know," I told her. "Trust me I know. But we got to play the cards we're dealt. Don't worry, it can only go up from here." She sniffed and I wiped her eyes.

"Come on. I'll get you some clothes so you can take a shower and get you some sleep," I told her, walking her to the bedroom.

It just dawned on me that I had spent the night at Black's house and I had his car, so while she was in the shower, I grabbed my phone and shot him a quick text message.

Miracle: Hey, babe. Had an emergency. I had to go help Nikki. But we're good. At my apartment. Will be there in a few hours to give you back your car. Unless you can get one of your boys to bring you over here. I'll explain everything in a few. Going to try to get a couple hours of sleep. Love you. TTYL.

I waited for Nikki to get out the shower and laid in the bed. I looked over on my nightstand at the picture of my father and me and sighed.

"Shit has been really crazy, Daddy," I said. "Nothing's the same without you. But I'm trying to do right. I really wish you were here right now. I know if you were, none of this would be happening. But don't worry. I'm going to get answers. I'm going to find out who did this to you."

"Who are you talking to?"

I turned around to see Nikki standing at the bathroom door wrapped in a towel.

"Nobody," I dismissed. "I put some clothes over there on the nightstand for you," I said, motioning towards the other side of the room.

"Thanks," she mumbled.

She walked over and grabbed the clothes and put them on. I tried not to look but I noticed all of the bruises on her body.

"He did that to you?" I asked.

She looked away ashamed.

“Yeah,” she answered. “But it was my fault. It was because I didn't do what he asked.”

“Oh.” I don't want to push because I didn't want to question her too much. “Well, let's get some sleep,” I suggested.

She finished getting dressed and climbed in the bed with me.

“Tomorrow, we'll see about getting you some clothes and stuff,” I told her.

“Okay,” she agreed. “Miracle, I'm sorry that I got you in this mess.”

“Girl, don't apologize,” I told her. “When I saw you on the street that day, I was so happy because nobody knew what happened to you. You were there one day and gone the next. So I'm glad because I got my sister back. And I'm going to make sure that nothing else happens to you. I can promise you that.”

She nodded and smiled slightly.

“I really missed you, Miracle,” she said.

“Me too.” We hugged again. “Now come on let's get some sleep.”

I turned out the light and within a few minutes we were both passed out.

*****

The next couple of days Nikki barely did anything but sleep. I had to drag her out of the house just to take her to get some clothes, but it seemed like all she wanted to do was just rest. I couldn't blame her. She had it hard the last several months. Black was a little pissed at me because of the fact that

I went and didn't tell him, but it wasn't like I went by myself. I had Goody with me.

He hadn't talked to me the entire day, and he finally texted me after I had been blowing up his phone to let me know that he was going to come over. I was cleaning up the apartment and fixing something to eat when he walked in. We have keys to each other's place, but we still always let each other know when we were coming by. Even though I knew everything that he was doing, I never just wanted to pop up on him. I wasn't that type of girlfriend.

He walked in and tossed his keys on the counter and came over to where I was at the stove.

“Hey,” he greeted me.

“Hey, baby,” I responded.

I could tell he was still feeling some type of way. I put the phone down that I was stirring with and turned to him.

“Look, Black, I'm sorry, okay? I wasn't trying to put myself in a situation where I could have got hurt or anything like that. But Nikki called me and she needed my help. And it wasn't like I went by myself. I called Goody and he came through. I just didn't want to bother you with it,” I explained.

“Miracle, I'm not mad at you or nothing, but you can't keep doing dangerous shit like that. You not bout that street life. Yeah, you hustle here and there, and you help me with my weight, but you're a suburban girl. You've only been living this life for like a year. You not about getting into it with these niggas out here. And I ain’t tryna have nothing happen to you,” he said.

“And I'm not going to let nothing happen to me either,” I told him. “I'm stronger than you think, Black. I know I'm not all hood or whatever, and no I'm not from the streets but I know how to handle myself. I took my gun, I called Goody, we went over there, and it got handled.”

“Oh it got handled?” he pushed. “So the nigga getting shot and talking about how he going to run up on your godfather ain't nothing that I need to worry about?”

“What are you talking about?” I asked.

“See that’s what I’m talking about, Miracle. You ain’t in the streets like that to know that. Come on now this is Oak Cliff,” he fussed. “You ain’t think a nigga was gonna retaliate? You don't think he wasn’t gone pop off? He running around telling everybody how yo’ godfather father ran up in there and snatched one of his girls.”

“But that's not what happened,” I told him.

“It don't matter, Miracle,” he stressed. “Niggas is gonna say whatever they want to. They don't give a fuck about the truth. This fool can walk up in this muthafucka and shoot you. Then what? You got to think about that you doing. You could have handled that shit a whole other way.”

I knew he was right, but I just didn't know what to say in that moment.

“I just wanted to help her,” I whispered.

“And I know you did. And that's why I love you. You always want to take care of everybody else.” He walked over and hugged me tight and I relaxed. “You a good girl, baby. You just got to be careful. I can't let nothing happen to you.”

“Look at you,” I smiled, lightening up. “Trying to be a sensitive thug.”

We both laughed and he patted me on the ass.

“It's all ‘cause of you. I wasn't even trying to be with nobody ‘til I met your ass. One day I'm out there hustling on the corner, next thing I know I see some cute ass bougie little girl skipping school. Next thing I know I'm all sprung and shit,” he laughed.

"And you know you couldn't let this go," I joked.

"Whatever," he said. "You gave me a hard time, but I knew you were gone come around."

"Oh really?" I inquired.

"Hell yeah. Fine as I am," he smiled.

"Boy, shut up. You want something to eat?" I asked.

"Yeah, that's straight. Oh but yea, I was coming over here to tell you about something," he remembered.

"What's up, babe?"

"Aight so remember how I was telling you the other day that I may know the guy that was driving that truck?"

"Yeah," I said, turning to him and stopping what I was doing.

"Well, turns out that nigga got locked up in County. He's there waiting on his trial date or some shit like that. So, I figured the best way to find out is to go holla at him," he suggested.

"You think he'll tell us?" I asked.

"I mean I don't see why not," he said. "Worst thing he can do is say no. But it's a step towards finding out about what's going on."

"True. Alright well, when do you want to go?" I asked him.

"I'm gonna holla at my boy to see what day he can have visitation and we can go from there.

"That's fine," I agreed. "Babe, I was thinking, I was going to try to get Nikki in school or something. I mean the last couple days mostly she just slept, but eventually, she's going to have to do something."

“I feel you. Maybe she can get a job or something.”

“Yeah, but how? She doesn't turn eighteen for another couple of months. And I can't risk somebody finding out where she lives and then I catch a charge or something like that.”

“That's true,” he said. “We can figure something out. What she doing now?”

“Sleep,” I laughed.

He shook his head.

“That girl must have had it hard.”

“Yea, she did,” I agreed.

I finished fixing his plate and we sat down to eat.

“So have you talked to your godfather?” he asked, changing the subject.

“Yeah. He came over the next day after everything. I mean for the most part he was cool, but I guess he just wasn't used to me being out there like that. When I really sat down and talked to him and told him some of the things that I've dealt with, I think he got a better understanding.”

“What did you tell him?”

I could tell that his wheels were rotating.

“Relax. I didn't tell him about Ms. Patricia. I mean I don't think that he would trip off of that. Especially considering that this nigga shot somebody basically in front of me. And I mean hell, he is known for being lethal. But I didn't say anything. The less people that know the better.”

“What happened to Ms. Patricia?”

We both jumped and turned to see Nikki standing at the door.

“Hey. I thought you was sleep,” I told her.

"I was. But y'all kind of woke me up," she told me. "So what happened to Ms. Patricia?"

"Oh no, I was just telling him about the whole fire and everything and how Whitney had gotten shot."

"Oh," she said, walking over to the stove and opening the cabinet to get a plate. "Can't say that I feel sorry for them."

"Yeah me either," I told her.

"Well, at least now Kim will be in a better home."

I dropped my head and felt that lump in my throat. I thought she may have seen it on the news or something or heard it in the streets, but I guess not.

"Um... Kim died, Nikki," I told her.

She put the plate down and turned around and looked at me.

"Wh-what?" she asked slowly.

"Yeah. It all happened within like a day. A lot of stuff happened after you left. We got another girl that was living in the house; Natasha. Y'all were pretty much the same age. One day, me and Natasha were going to school and there was a shooting. We didn't know who it was at first until Ms. Patricia showed up screaming and hollering. Then we found out it was Whitney. When we got home, the case workers showed up, and they were doing one of those routine visitations or whatever. Well, Kim was upstairs coloring, and she got a hold of a gun."

"A gun?" Nikki ask. "Where the hell did she get a gun from?"

"I don't know," I lied. "But we all heard the shot, and they went running up the steps and she was lying there bleeding." My voice cracked and I cleared my throat to try to get myself together. "They took her to the hospital, but she didn't make it. So, the social worker told us that we were leaving because it was unsafe."

"Damn," she whispered taking everything in. She leaned against the counter and I could tell that she was sad. "She was so innocent. I tried to protect her as much as I could."

"I know," I told her. "We both did. But the good thing is she doesn't have to deal with any more of that trauma and abuse that that woman put us through. Now she can rest. She can be with her mama and daddy in heaven."

I felt horrible because I knew I was the reason why she was dead. I should have thought about taking that gun out that bag before I took my backpack up those stairs. But I didn't. Kim was dead because of me, and I was going to have to live with that for the rest of my life. I told myself that I was going to find out where she was buried and go visit her grave and apologize.

"So what happened to Ms. Patricia?" she asked.

"I don't know for sure," I rushed. "I saw it on the news a couple of days later that the house had caught fire. They said that they thought that she had gotten drunk and was smoking a cigarette and that's how the fire started."

"Damn, are you serious?" she asked shocked. I nodded my head. "Good riddance."

"Exactly. So I guess in a way, karma kind of worked itself out. Now they're gone, and nobody else has to deal with that."

"You're right," she said. "You think maybe we can find out where Kim is buried? I wanna go see her."

"I was thinking the same thing," I smiled. "I think that would be good. I'm sure she would like that."

"Okay cool. I'm going to leave you guys alone," she said, grabbing her plate and walking to the room.

"Oh nah you're fine," Black spoke up. "You ain't bothering me. How are you feeling anyway?"

"I'm okay I guess. I'm just really not trying to leave the house like that because I don't know who he's got out there looking for me," she said.

"Nikki, I told you that you ain't got to worry about that. We got you. He won't touch you again trust. He got the message the other night. And if he's smart, he'll listen."

"And if he doesn't?" Nikki asked.

"If he doesn't," I said, looking over to Black. "Well, if he doesn't, can't say we didn't warn him. But let's not worry about that right now," I said. "Come on, let's finish eating."

We all sat down, ate, and caught each other up on how things have been going since we had been separated. I was determined to make sure that we both came out on top.

We finished eating and Nikki went to lie down to watch TV. I heard her turning on *Real Housewives of Atlanta* on demand. She was hooked on that show. Black and I left to go meet up with his boys in Arlington and get some work done. The whole time my mind was on that meeting with that boy. I wanted to know what he knew. I wanted to know if he was a part of it. That day couldn't come quick enough.

*****

Chapter Fourteen

Going to that jail to see Lorenzo was pointless. He kept saying he didn't know anything. Either he was lying, or he really was that stupid to just give a random group of niggas carrying guns a damn ride like he was some ghetto ass Uber. All he said was that he was told to bring a group of guys with him to a delivery. Black questioned him up and down, but he just sat and moped. I was pissed off, and Black knew it because he held onto my belt loop the entire time. I swear I wanted to reach across the table and smack the fuck out of him for wasting my time. Now it seemed like I was back to where I started.

I was supposed to be meeting up with Goody in a few. I told him that I had to talk to him about some things. After that bullshit with Lorenzo or Loco or whatever the hell his name was, I had to handle things differently. I wanted to talk to him about Black working with him. I didn't understand why Black was pushing it so hard at first, but it did make sense. If he was right up under Goody, then he could find out things that I would never know. I just had to get Goody to trust him. I felt like Goody was keeping things from me to try to protect me, so if this is the only way I could get the truth, then that's what it was gonna be. The problem was going to be convincing Goody to go along with it. If he is keeping something, then I know more than likely he won't trust Black. I had my fingers crossed that he would go along with it.

I had wasted a year of not getting any answers. It's not that I could have tried anyway. But I had to find out something. I couldn't waste any more time. I was pulling up to Goody's house when my phone buzzed in the cup holder. I looked down to see that it was a text message from Chris. I hadn't heard from him in a couple of months so I prayed that he was okay. I had really missed him.

Chris: Hey, I'm in town. Hit me up when you get a chance.

I got so excited knowing he was in Dallas. I hadn't seen him in months after the shooting, so for him to be in town, I was going to take time to see him because I didn't know how long it would be before I saw him again. I figured that I would wait until after I left Goody's house before I called him, so I sent him a quick message to let him know that it would be a while before I could get free.

Miracle: Hey, I got your message. Just sit tight. I'm at my godfather's house right now, so it'll be a while before I can hit you up.

Chris: Aight cool.

I got out and knocked on the door. Tori answered smiling.

"Well, hey you," she greeted me. "Once again looking cute."

"Thanks, Aunt Tori," I said, walking in the house.

The girls ran up and hugged me.

"Hey, munchkins," I smiled.

I'm guessing that Goody must have had a conversation with his crazy ass baby mama because his daughters were back home with him. They giggled as they jumped all over me.

"Look at y'all! Y'all have gotten so big," I cooed.

Goody's girls had always been adorable. I love kids. They're so damn cute, but they are full of energy! Me and Black joked around about having babies, but that wasn't happening no time soon! I would settle for just being a babysitter. That way I can give them back to their mommies and daddies when it was time to.

"Miracle, we watching *Frozen*! Come watch with us!"

They grabbed my hand and dragged me to the living room where *Frozen* was playing on the TV. I sat on the couch and they curled up under me while Tori sat with the baby on her lap. I enjoyed having them up under me. They were so sweet. Goody came in after the movie started and gave me a quick pat on the forehead. We sang every song in the movie to the top of our lungs. This movie had them hooked because I swear when I looked down at them, I didn't see them blink not once. The TV had them in a trance.

When the movie was over, they stood up and began to sing loudly around the room.

"Okay, girls, let's calm it down a little," Goody suggested.

They kept giggling and singing, ignoring him.

"Come on, girls, let's go upstairs," Tori said.

"Baby, why don't you take the girls and y'all go get a pizza or something and bring it back to the house?" Goody asked, giving her some money. "That'll give me and Miracle some time to talk. "

"Okay, she agreed. "You good?"

"Yeah I'm straight," he told her. "I just didn't want any distractions or anything like that. Y'all go ahead. We won't be long."

"Okay. Girls, get your shoes on and everything. We're going to go get a pizza for daddy," she told them.

"Yay pizza!" they squealed.

They ran to put their shoes on and a few minutes later they were out the door.

"So what's on your mind?" he asked, cutting to the point. He sat down on the couch across from me and sighed, turning off the television the girls had left on. "What you need to talk about?"

I took a deep breath and began.

"Okay, so I'm not sure really where to begin with this," I started.

"Girl, just talk. Quit acting like you on a job interview or something," he laughed.

"Goody, I wanna know what happened that day that daddy was killed. I saw you and him arguing before that truck showed up. Before I came outside, I was in Daddy's office, and I looked out the window and I saw you two arguing. What were you arguing about?"

Goody just sat there, and I looked at him, waiting for an answer.

"Did you hear me?"

"Miracle, honestly I can't remember. That was over a year ago. I can barely remember what happened a few days ago," he explained.

I knew he was lying.

"It had to have been something because y'all never argue," I said. "So, stop trying to protect me and treating me like I'm some little girl and just tell me."

"Miracle, I honestly don't remember, okay. Why are you bringing this up now?"

He seemed like he was agitated with me, but what the hell for?

"Because somebody set my daddy up. And I want to know who," I said, raising my voice. "Somebody killed my father, YOUR best friend. Right in front of you. Don't you want to know who did it?"

"Of course I do," he answered calmly. "But what does that have to do with some random conversation that I can't even remember?"

"Because I know you're keeping something from me! I feel like that argument has something to do with why he was killed."

"Well, like I said I don't remember it," he answered nonchalantly.

I opened my mouth to speak but he cut me off.

"Look, Miracle, you can't waste your time stressing over stuff that happened a year ago."

"I'm not," I told him. "In fact, I found out who the nigga was that drove the truck."

"What?" he said, sitting up.

"Yeah. I found out that there was some dude named Lorenzo that goes by Loco or something like that that drove the truck that day. I went to see him in jail the other day. He told me he didn't know anything and that he was just told to be the driver for a group of guys that had a hit. So somebody came after my daddy. And I'm going to find out who it was. And I would think you would want to know that, too," I hissed.

"How'd you find that out?" he asked.

"I asked around," I replied. Got his name, went up there. That's it."

"Well, what exactly did you ask? And what did he say?"

"I asked him who ordered him to do it. He gave me a name after I kept pressing him, but I asked around about it and haven't heard anything. So I think the nigga was bullshittin' or whatever," I informed him.

"Who was it?" he questioned, leaning towards me.

"He said the guy's name was Marcus. But because Dallas is filled with a thousand men named Marcus, it really doesn't help me at all. I asked around but wasn't nobody talking."

He stood up and started pacing the floor, turning to me in frustration.

"Miracle, have you lost your damn mind? Don't you go do no stupid shit like that again. I honestly I don't know what's gotten into you. You popping up at hotels with a gun, now you going to jails to see some nigga that you don't even know because somebody told you that he drove a truck?" he asked.

"He did!" I yelled in defense. "He admitted to it, Goody, so what's the problem?"

"The problem is you ain't grown, little girl," he snapped. "You can't be doing shit like this. For all you know that nigga lied to you to get you off him, and now you got a target on your back. You don't know who he knows. He can make a phone call and it's over," he said.

I was getting fed up with the way he was talking to me. He wasn't my damn daddy!

"That's just a risk I gotta take," I told him. "I'm not a little girl anymore, Goody. I'm eighteen, and I'm on my own. I've dealt with a lot more than you think I could handle. So trust me, I'm not putting myself out there, and I know how to watch my back."

"Okay. Now you wanna be grown? Let me know how that turns out for you."

This shit was agitating, so I quickly switched subjects.

"So are you getting back into the game?" I asked.

"Where did that come from?" he asked.

I couldn't believe he was sitting here acting like I didn't know what's up.

"Seriously? I know that you were still hustling. Yea, y'all were businessmen and everything but you weren't a hundred percent legit. So… I was thinking maybe you could work with Black," I suggested.

"Your little boyfriend?"

"Yeah. I mean think about it. He stays low key, he's not really out there like that. He's making good money. He doesn't bring attention to himself," I added. "He's never been caught up in no shit. So that's the type of nigga you need. Somebody to get you back in and to help you stack your coins back up."

I guess I was talking a foreign language because he was looking at me like I was stupid or delusional.

"First of all, little girl, you don't know what you're talking about."

It was my turn to look at him like he was speaking a foreign language.

"I mean do you really expect me to believe that you're not still hustling? So…the money that I was getting from you while you were locked up, you keeping the bills paid here at the house, and all that, and the whole time your accounts were frozen?" I reminded him. "Tori wasn't working, so I already know the answer."

He sighed and walked over, sitting down next to me on the couch.

"Miracle, it's not as easy as it sounds. I'm not trying to live that life no more. Hell, you see how it ended for your daddy. Feds are watching my ass every damn minute. And no offense to your little wanna be thug boyfriend, but if I want to be in the streets, trust me I can do it without his help."

“Fine,” I huffed. “Then I guess I'll just have to do it myself.”

“The fuck you will,” he argued. “Listen, I don't give a damn how old you think you are or how grown you think you are, but your ass ain’t about to be out here in these streets, Miracle. It ain't going to happen. Now your father gave me the role of godfather for a reason. So that if anything happened to him, I would look after you. And I plan to do just that. And ain't no way in hell that your ass is about to be out here in these streets,” he threatened.

“I don't have to be,” I cried out, jumping up from my seat. “I've been staying up under the radar all this time and nobody has caught on. I know what I'm doing,” I said.

I was starting to believe what Black had warned me about. He was right. I grabbed my purse and headed to the door. But I had to let him know how I felt before I left.

“You know, he was your best friend. You would think you would wanna see the killer handled. But you don’t have nothing to worry about, Goody. Because, eventually, everything gone come to light. See you later, Godfather.”

I walked out the door and got in my car. All of my faith and trust in my godfather was now gone. I was going to get to the bottom of it and if I found out he had anything to do with it, I hated it for him. Somebody was going to answer; even if that somebody was family.

*****

“I can’t believe you’re back,” I said.

I smiled looking at Chris. We had met up at the food court at Valley View Mall. We had a quick conversation on the phone a few days ago after that bullshit with Goody and agreed to meet here. It was easy not to be noticed because it was damn near empty. I didn’t think anyone was looking for him anyway but he was still on edge, so he wanted to meet here which was fine with me. The mall was huge and used to be popping, but now it was slow as hell.

“Yeah, man I've been back in town for a while,” he said. “I was lying low you know.”

“Yeah,” I told him. “I'm glad you're back, though.”

He nodded his head, eating his food.

“And you straight. The cops haven’t said anything, and as far as they know, they don't have any witnesses to the shooting,” I told him.

He took another bite of his food, still looking around.

“What you running from somebody or something?” I asked.

“Nah, I'm chill. I just pretty much learned to never really relax,” he explained. “I always got to look over my shoulder and shit because you never know who's lurking.”

“Well, you good,” I told him. “So what are your plans now that you're back?”

“Well, right now, I'm crashing at this chick’s crib,” he told me.

“Word? Let me find out you got a girl,” I smiled.

“Nah, it ain't like that,” he corrected me. “She just this chick that I met through my homie that's all. She knew a nigga needed a place to stay, so she let me crash. I broke her off a few times to keep her happy. Nothing else.”

For a second, I felt a twinge of jealousy. I don't know why, but it was weird.

“So you basically fucking for a place to stay?” I asked.

“Something like that,” he admitted. “But I was wondering if maybe your boy could let me back in.”

“Who Black?” I asked.

“Yeah,” he said. “I mean since I’m not being wanted by the cops and shit, a nigga needs to get back on his paper. I tried to hustle here and there when I could, but it wasn't steady. And I got to get up out of where I am. Try to get my own,” he said.

“Okay,” I agreed. “I can talk to him. I'm sure he ain’t gonna care. I mean, hell, he was down before, so it ain't like he don't know what you can handle.”

“Aight, cool,” he grinned.

“So what else has been up with you?” I asked.

“Man, not much,” he told me. “Just hustling to survive. And what about you? I see you living good,” he observed. “And you still looking good.”

“You too,” I told him.

I wasn’t lying. I was sitting across staring at Chris. It had been eight months since I had seen him. I had to admit he was looking damn good. He put on a little weight and wasn’t as scrawny and he had these short curls in his head. I knew he probably had hoes all over him. He looked like one of those pretty boy types. Who would have thought he would have changed so much in a few months? I was trying not to stare, but I'd never really paid attention to him like that before. He was kind of fine, but I couldn't go there. Besides with what I was about to tell him, it would mess up everything.

“Look, Chris, there's something that I've been meaning to tell you,” I said.

“Aight, what’s good?” he asked in between bites of his food.

“Nikki's back,” I told him.

He dropped his food and looked at me surprised.

“For real?”

"Yeah."

"Is she okay?" he pressed. "What the hell happened to her?"

"Long story short, Patricia's boyfriend did something to her and she walked in on it. Patricia got pissed off and blamed Nikki for what her perverted boyfriend did. So, she told social services that Nikki was a danger to the house and they took her," I explained. "Wherever they took her, she ran away and met some pimp. And he basically turned her completely out and had her out in the streets. When I saw her, she was with one of her tricks," I told him. "She called me a couple weeks ago and asked me for help, so me and Goody went over there to take care of it. And well…she's been living with me ever since."

His jaw was clenched so tight I thought it would break.

"So you mean to tell me that this bitch let her boyfriend fucking rape this girl and she didn't do shit about it?" I nodded my head and watched as he balled up his fists. "Damn, man. I should fuck his ass up."

"It's handled," I promised him, knowing that Black went to pay him a little visit. Nobody knew about that except us two. "You know she can't do shit to nobody else. So let's just be happy that Nikki's okay now," I begged him.

"Man, fuck all that," he snapped. "If it wasn't for Patricia's bitch ass, none of this shit would have fucking happened in the first place."

A few stragglers walking past heard him raise his voice and looked over.

"Chris, calm down," I said. "Like I said, me and Goody went to talk to ole boy and we handled it okay? He got the message. He ain't messing with her again. And she's good. I told you, she's been staying with me, and she's getting better. She's almost eighteen, and she wants to go to school. She's studying for her GED right now. She wants to study over at El Centro, so I told her I'd help her. So, she's okay. And I'm pretty sure once she knows that you're back, she will be ecstatic."

"So y'all handle that nigga, huh," he said after few seconds.

"Yeah," I told him. It was like a light bulb went off when the idea suddenly came to me. "You know what? I think I got a way that you could make some more money."

"How?" he asked. "What? Work with Nikki?"

"No," I answered. I leaned in to make sure no one could hear. "Okay, so you know how I was talking about how me and Goody went to handle Nikki's boy right?"

"Yea, so?"

"Well, I need to get some information, but I don't think that he's gonna to give it to me. He's hiding something, but I don't know what. And I know it's got to do with killing my daddy," I told him.

"Damn," he murmured. "That's shady as hell."

"Yeah," I agreed. "So, I can put you on with Black like you asked, but if you can get close to Goody, and start working with him, then I can get the info that I need."

"He ain't tryna find out who did it?" he asked.

"Nah, man," I told him. "Not the way he's acting."

Chris shook his head.

"Damn, man, that's fucked up. If a nigga murked my best friend in front of me, I'd be hunting that nigga down and putting that lead in that ass. Something ain't right about that shit," he expressed. "If that's your nigga like that—"

"I know. Black said the same thing," I told him. "I don't know, Chris. It's just weird. Like, I just can't let it go. I mean my daddy was my everything. And now, nothing is like I thought it would be. And Goody… it's like he don't even care no more. When he was locked up and before he got locked up, all he kept saying was he was going to find out who did it. But now, he acting like he don't give a fuck. And I can't go for that."

"Better watch that nigga. The way he acting, he probably did that shit himself," Chris suggested.

"Nah. He was right there dodging bullets, too. He couldn't have pulled the trigger."

"Don't mean he still didn't do it," he argued. "You can murk a nigga without touching him yourself."

I never even thought about that. He couldn't. Could he? Why would he have my father killed?

"Nah. I don't think so. That was his boy. I mean my daddy was his partner. They did everything together. And they don't have a reason to have beef. Everything my dad had, Goody had," I defended him.

"Yeah, but you know niggas are ruthless," Chris said. "Everybody wants to be at the top and they don't care who they gotta climb over to get there. Trust me, I done seen it."

"That's true," I said. "But I don't think Goody would do that."

Could he? Could my own godfather have something to do with it and that's why he doesn't want to answer my questions? Is that why all of a sudden he just doesn't want to find my daddy's killer? Now, I got more shit to worry about.

"Well, you know I got you," he offered, interrupting my thoughts.

"Thanks," I smiled. "Now hurry up and finish your mini buffet that you got on this tray here so we can go. I know Nikki will flip when she sees you," I laughed.

"My bad," he apologized, rushing to finish eating.

"You gone give yourself a heart attack eating all that damn fast food," I told him.

"Can't help it. Got to eat."

"If you say so."

He finally finished eating, and we headed to my car. Once inside, I opened my purse.

"I think I got something that belongs to you," I told him.

I pulled the gun out and handed it to him.

He took it and tucked it in his pants.

"Man, 'preciate you holding it for me," he said.

"No problem," I told him. "Hell, it came in handy."

"You learn to shoot any better?"

"Yeah. I'm going to the gun range every now and then. And of course you know Black is showing me," I said.

"That's what's up," he said. He looked out the window as I drove to the apartment. "Look, Miracle, about that night before I left…"

"What about it?" I asked.

"I just…I wanted to apologize for the shit that I did that night. I know you rolling with your boy and everything and I guess a nigga just let my personal feelings get in the way. I mean, we not blood or nothing but I ain't tryna put you in no weird shit or whatever," he said.

"It's cool," I told him as I drove. "I'm not trippin'. As long as you good, we straight."

Hearing him apologize did make me feel better, but then it did make me think about that kiss. I quickly dismissed it ‘cause I shouldn’t be thinking about anybody other than Black anyway. He was more than enough for me.

“Black seems like he a cool nigga anyway,” he admitted. “But as long as a nigga treating you straight then I'm cool.”

“Oh, now you want to be the protective big brother?” I laughed at him. “Aww that’s so sweet.”

“Man, whatever,” he groaned. “Go on ‘head with all that. I’m just saying. I got you, and I’m glad you got a nigga that’s taking care of you and shit.”

We pulled up to the apartment complex and he followed me up the stairs. I opened the door and Nikki was lying on the couch, watching TV.

“Hey, girl,” I said, walking in. “I got a surprise for you.”

I moved away from the door and Chris walked in. She turned, looked, and her eyes large.

“Oh my God!” she screamed “Chris!”

She jumped into his arms and he hugged her tight. I couldn't help but to let the tears that were forming fall on my face. Nikki was crying, and Chris was trying to hold it together.

“I thought you were gone forever,” she wept.

“I'm okay,” he said. “I’m here.”

“Why did you leave me?” she asked.

“I’m sorry, Nikki,” he apologized. “I just…I couldn't take it anymore. And I didn't want to tell you ‘cause I didn't want you to worry.”

“You just left me, Chris! You left me in that house,” she cried.

“I know,” he acknowledged. “And I’m sorry. I know it was real fucked up. I ain’t really think about it when I did it. I was just trying to get away. If I'd stayed, that shit that popped off with you wouldn't have happened.”

She stood there and cried as Chris grabbed her in another hug.

“I promise you I won’t let nothing else happen to you. And I'm not leaving again, you hear me?”

“Okay,” she sniffed.

Eventually, she stopped crying and dried her eyes.

“See all this crying and shit, y’all got me over here messing up my makeup,” I joked, trying to lighten the mood. We all laughed and hugged each other. “You know I never really had anybody that I was close to besides my best friend,” I told them. “And I know we met through some crazy mess, but y’all are really like family to me. Y’all are like my sister and brother. And now that all of that drama is behind us, we can move on.”

They both lowered their heads and agreed.

“In a way, I guess we got that crazy ass woman to thank, huh?” Chris said.

“Yeah,” I shrugged. “But that's as far as it's going to get for me.”

“You right.”

We promised each other that we would have each other's backs no matter what and spent the rest of the night talking and catching up. It felt good to have a family. No matter how messed up our lives may have been.

*****

Chapter Fifteen

Myesha had talked me into going to Lancaster with her to go to the club. We hadn't hung out in a while, so I didn't mind it. I needed to catch up with her. Ever since me and Black got together, it seemed like our friendship was drifting apart a little. Myesha had been my girl since day one, so I never wanted to make it seem like I was neglecting her. Hell, she held me down when I was caught up in all that bullshit. I wasn't about to leave my girl behind now that I was doing good.

"Girl, it's about time you brought your ass out the damn house!" she said over the music.

We were dancing in the middle of the floor, and of course, she had every nigga in the club watching her ass. I guess she was always going to be a party girl. When she graduated, she went to school for two weeks before she got into a fight at a house party and was expelled. Her mom was pissed, but all Myesha did was call her daddy to save the day as usual. She moved into one of his apartments and spent all his money. She was spoiled rotten. I don't think the girl ever heard the word no. She got what she wanted, when she wanted to. And it looked like tonight she was going to get every nigga in the club. Every time I turned around, a dude was in her face trying to get her a drink. Of course, I had a few people in my face, but I wasn't impressed. Hell, I could buy my own damn drink. Plus, Black had been texting me and I was ready to get back home to my man to get some good dick. I think he got a kick out of messing with me when I was out. If he could keep me all to himself, he would. I didn't mind it either.

"Girl, you better let one of these niggas get you a drink!" she said.

I laughed at my drunk friend.

"I'm good," I told her. "Besides, one of us has to drive home. And it's going to be real bad if both of our asses are underage and drunk driving."

"Whatever!" she said, taking back another shot of Patron. "I'm just glad your ass is out the damn house."

"I know. I know. Girl, I been so busy," I admitted.

"You ain't been busy. Your ass getting that dick, hell. Then you over there playing Mama to that crazy ass prostitute foster sister of yours," she laughed.

"Don't do that," I said. "I know you don't like the girl, but damn."

"What?" she asked. "You got cray at your house."

I was trying to stay cool, but she was starting to piss me off. She didn't know what it was like in that damn foster house, so for her to be making light of it was pissing me off.

"Anyway," I said, changing the subject. "How's it going with you and Wood? I heard you were getting back with him."

"Girl, bye! Ain't nobody worried about that nigga," she huffed. "I ain't talked to him in weeks."

"Oh okay."

I thought about that text message that she sent to Black.

"Come with me to the bathroom real quick I gotta pee," she said.

I laughed. She had no type of modesty whatsoever.

"All that damn liquor you been drinking of course you do!"

She started to the bathroom and I followed behind her.

"Girl, that Henny got me feeling right!" she said, walking into the bathroom stall.

"I bet," I said, looking at myself in the mirror making sure I was still straight.

"Girl, you see how many niggas is up in here?" she asked, walking out of the stall. She washed her hands and fixed her hair and makeup.

"Yea, it's a couple of fine one's up in here," I admitted.

"Yes, girl. I met this dude named Rizz. He's fine as hell! I was dancing up on him, and all I could feel was dick. It's taking everything in me not to fuck him like right now," she moaned. "But I gotta make him wait for it just a little bit."

I fluffed my hair. I had just gotten some new bundles installed and it was laid!

"You are such a hoe," I laughed.

"Whatever," she sucked her teeth. "Shit, how long it take you to lose your fucking virginity? And you only been fuckin' one nigga. Man, you have no idea how good new dick can be!"

"Trust me I'm good. Black handles this very well," I told her.

"Yea okay. You just saying that she 'cause you ain't had another nigga yet. But trust when I get Rizz, that nigga gone be bae," she promised.

"I believe you. So you gave him your number?"

"Hell yeah!" she said. "He had to leave but he said he would give me a holler tomorrow. In the meantime, I'mma get my ass back out on that dance floor and let these niggas get me wasted! So come on, girl!"

I shook my head and followed her back out to the dance floor and we partied like we used to. We tore up the dance floor and had all eyes on us. I danced 'til my feet hurt. I missed hanging out with my girl. We stayed 'til the club closed and then headed to get something to eat. I texted Black to let him know that I would be back in a couple of hours and that he needed to be ready for me. All this dancing and grinding and shit in the club had me ready to ride his ass.

When we got to the restaurant, of course, Myesha couldn't just let us eat in peace. She had some random ass nigga sitting with us at the booth trying to spit game, and I was ready to go. It was damn near three o'clock in the morning.

"I'll be right back," she said, getting up. "I got to go to the bathroom."

, She got up and walked away, leaving this idiot sitting at the table with me.

"So what's your name?" he asked.

"Taken," I snapped.

"Damn, my bad," he snorted. "I'm just tryna get to know you is all."

"Well, a minute ago you was tryna get to know my friend so I'm straight," I told him. "Matter fact, why don't you just go ahead and like leave your number or something, and then when she comes back I'll give it to her 'cause we got to go," I told him. I was getting tired of looking at this thirsty ass nigga.

This fool actually wrote his number down on a napkin. I can just see Myesha's face laughing when she saw that. He handed it to me and got up and walked off like he had just won the lottery. I rolled my eyes and tossed it inside of my glass and got up, heading to the bathroom to get her.

"Girl, you won't believe this shit."

Myesha jumped and I almost lost my damn mind.

"What the fuck are you doing?" I yelled.

She tried to hurry to wipe powder away from her nose. There were two white lines of powder on the counter though that she couldn't hide.

"Myesha, what the hell?" I said.

"Girl, will you relax," she said with her eyes half closed.

"You in here sniffing shit up your nose and talking about relax? Bitch, are you insane?"

"Damn, this ain't no after school special commercial, Miracle, shit," she dragged. "You buggin' the fuck out and it ain't even necessary."

"I walk in and see you in here sniffing cocaine! How the fuck am I supposed to act right now?"

"It's not that serious," she tried to reason. "I don't even do it like that. Just like every now and then."

"I knew something was up with your ass," I said.

"Here we go," she complained.

"Yeah, here we go. I'm supposed to be cool when I come in the bathroom and see my best friend snorting powder?"

"Miracle, I've only done it twice, this being the second time," she explained. "I told you I don't do it like that. I get blazed."

"I don't give a fuck, Myesha! Like, come on now, that's some shit you don't need to be doing."

"Oh, so now you give a fuck?" she said, fixing her face.

"What the hell you mean?" I asked caught off guard.

"Seriously, Miracle? I have barely talked to you on the phone in weeks. This is the first time I've seen you in what, two months? And you want to act like you're so perfect? You kick it with them rejects more than you kick it with your best friend. I was the one that was holding you down and helping you when you were going through your shit. But the minute that you got Black, you act like you didn't know nobody no more," she exploded.

I was surprised at how she flipped out. She was right though. But it wasn't like I did it on purpose.

"Myesha, come on now," I told her. "You know it's not like that. You my bestie all day, every day. I'm sorry, okay?" I said.

"Yea, okay," she mumbled, rolling her eyes.

"No for real, Myesha," I urged. "You been my girl since day one. Hell, we've been best friends since forever and ain't nothing gonna change that. But this?" I said pointing to the remnants on the counter. "You can't be doing this. I lost enough people. My father, and then that bullshit with the foster home. The last thing I want is for you to get strung out on drugs and be one of the people that we see on the corner. One of them damn dope heads that can't go a day without a fix," I told her.

She got tearful and sniffed.

"I wasn't trying to do that," she said. "I tried it one time with Wood, and I still had some extra, so I figured why not. It was something that made shit seem fun."

"Girl, you don't need that shit to have fun. You are always the life of some damn party, so don't ever let me hear you say no dumb shit like that," I fussed. "So, if I got to come over to your house every day and annoy the hell out of you, then that's just what the fuck I'm going to do. And besides, you can't be getting skinny doing no drugs. You know these niggas like them thick girls," I laughed, trying not to cry.

I couldn't believe that she was doing this shit all because she felt alone. Myesha was always the center of attention. I never thought that she would be feeling like she didn't have anybody cause she always had somebody in her face. That's just how she was. I felt like shit knowing that I had been neglecting my friend. I had to do better. Because if I lost anybody else, I couldn't deal. Chris and Nikki may have been like family, and that will never change, but Myesha truly is family, and family looks out for each other.

*****

What the hell was going on? Why am I standing in the yard? Lorenzo was getting out of the truck with the flowers in his hand. What the hell am I not seeing? Why do I keep having this nightmare? What does all of this mean?

"I didn't order no damn flowers." I heard my daddy say.

I looked over at him, but he couldn't see me.

"Goody, what's going on?" I asked. But he didn't answer me either.

"Did you order flowers?" I heard my father ask my godfather.

"Nope. Didn't order any," he answered.

The door to the truck opened and the bullets started to fly. I looked at Goody and my dad and I watched as he turned to run to cover me, but I wasn't standing there. Goody pulled his gun out and started to fire, but he shot away from everybody.

"Miracle! Get down!" Daddy yelled.

But I wasn't there. Why couldn't he see me?

"Daddy!" I screamed.

Why couldn't he see me standing there? What was Goody doing shooting at nothing? What was going on? I stood and watched as my daddy bled out in front of me. I kept crying, but neither one of them would respond. And just that quickly, everything faded.

*****

I woke up screaming and Black was shaking me.

“Miracle, baby, wake up!” he said.

I could feel the tears on my face as I looked around the room and realized that I wasn't at my father’s house anymore. I was in bed, in Black's apartment, and he was looking at me like I was crazy.

“You okay?” he asked.

“I'm sorry,” I apologized. “It was just…I had that damn dream again.”

He sighed and yawned.

“It’s aight. You couldn't help it.”

“No, Black, it was…something was different about this. I kept trying to figure out what the hell was wrong that day and what was off about it and I think I know,” I told him, recollecting on the dream.

I thought about how Goody stood there shooting at nothing.

“Okay, what's good?” he asked.

“Well, in the dream I was standing there like I was before but Goody and Daddy couldn't see me. It was like they were looking right through me. It was weird. Like…I watched the bullets tear through Daddy, and I watched Goody shooting,” I explained.

"Okay," he said confused. "I mean it sounds like what you told me what happened."

"But that's just it," I continued. "He wasn't shooting at anybody. He was shooting away from everything."

"What you mean?" he asked.

I looked at him and knew that my baby was right about that gut feeling that he had. So was Chris.

"I think it has something to do with my dad being killed."

"Why because he was shooting and didn't hit anybody?"

"Exactly, Black. Think about it. This is Goody. And I mean he's meticulous. He's detailed. If he was going to shoot you, he would have killed you with one hit. So for him to just be shooting at nothing? Think about it. Bullets are flying, people are running and ducking. He pulled out his gun and start shooting to make it look like…like…like he was defending Daddy. But I remember. I remember looking at him and he was shooting away," I recalled. "Goody had my father killed."

Saying it out loud was still hard to believe.

"Yeah, but you don't know that for sure right now," he said.

"You right," I told him. "But I will soon. But I know I'm not crazy, Black. The fact that I remember that means something. And it means Goody had something to do with it. Goody had my father killed."

*****

Some Time Later… (I Told Y'all Stuff Don't Just Happen In a Week! Lol)

Chapter Sixteen

I was meeting Chris at our usual spot at Valley View Mall since he had some information for me. It had been six months since all of this shit had happened. A lot of stuff had changed. For one, me and Black were still together, but I never saw his ass. Every time I turned around, his ass was out late, and when he was home or I was with him, he was always on his damn phone. He would say that it was work, but I just wasn't sure. I didn't want to think that he was out there cheating on me because he'd been the only man I've been with, and I loved him but he was starting to work my damn nerves.

I was still hustling, but it seemed like I was doing my thing without Black. His operation was getting a little bit bigger, which was good, but because of it, he was gone more. I know a man got to get his money and got to get on his grind but damn even Nino Brown had Selina by his side. We were supposed to go out later on and spend some time together but I doubted it would happen. He had broken his last three dates with me in the last month. So if we actually went out, I'd be surprised. I wasn't asking him to take me around the world, but damn, spend some time.

Then, I had to deal with Nikki. She finally turned eighteen of course, but then her ass turned around and got pregnant. She was kind of tight-lipped about it, so I just let it be, but I damn sure let her know I ain't taking care of no babies. She was family and everything, but my apartment wasn't big enough for me, her, and her baby. She said that the baby's daddy was going to move her out and help her get her own spot, but what nigga ain't tell a bitch anything she wants to hear when he trying to get some pussy, and she fell for it hook, line, and sinker. Now her ass was three months pregnant and only working a part-time job at Burger King. She promised me that her baby daddy was going to be involved, and he told her he would be there every step of the way, but I never saw his ass at the doctor's appointment.

Even though she wasn't out hooking anymore, she was still wild. She went from staying in the house and doing nothing but watching TV to partying and clubbing damn near every night. She had started hanging out with her coworkers and just took off from there. I wasn't hating 'cause I wanted her to have her own life, but I really thought she would do something different. She got her GED, but working at Burger King was not my idea of stacking paper. I told her ass to go and apply for food stamps, Medicaid, WIC, and everything else, but she swears up and down that this baby daddy is going to be there to support her. I can only do but so much, so I said fuck it.

Me and Myesha were still tight of course. We don't really see each other as much anymore because her father finally got into her ass and made her get her shit together. He came home to find some random nigga in the crib, so he told her either get a job or go to school. She goes to Texas A&M now and is majoring in Mass Communications. I'm happy for her. Sometimes I'll ride down there and go kick it with her when Black is working, and when she comes home, we still hang out like we used to. She ended up hooking up with this Rizz nigga that she met back when we were at the club, but I hadn't met him yet. Everybody had all these secrets. I'm sure whoever it is she probably walks all over them and they worship the ground she walks on. But as long as he's not putting his hands on her or hurting her in any way, I'm cool.

And then, of course, there was Goody's lying ass. I still had to keep up appearances with him. Far as he knew, I had dropped the whole idea of daddy being set up. But I wasn't. And I hadn't. That's why I was meeting Chris today. Goody was so worried about keeping me off his tracks, that he didn't think I would have somebody else do it. For him to be such a legend, he damn sure didn't think about that possibility.

Chris did everything I knew he could. Just as I thought, Goody's ass was still hustling. Why he chose to lie about that shit I will never know. It took him a few months before Chris even met him, but Chris was out there hustling hard trying to get close and it worked. Within a couple of months, he had met with him and Goody offered him a job. After a month, he was doing runs for Goody personally. And all the while he had no clue that I was behind any of it.

Chris and I had become close of course. We would hang out whenever Black would blow me off or when he wasn't out hustling and handling business for Goody. He was a completely different person now that he wasn't under the spell of Patricia and that bitch, Whitney. He always had me laughing over some dumb shit. And he kept me from killing Nikki a couple of times. I like the fact that he was so protective over her. When he found out she was pregnant, he was pissed off just as much as I was, but he came around eventually, and just like I had, he told her he would be there.

I don't really think Black likes the fact that we were tight, but I don't think it had to do with him feeling threatened. I think it had to do with the fact that Chris wasn't working for Black and was working for Goody. I told Black the reason why I was doing what I was doing, and all he did was make it seem like I was trying to draw attention to him. He had been hustling since I've known him and had never gotten caught, so the fact that he would even think that I would be reckless like that was ridiculous.

I parked my car and rushed inside. It was fifty degrees outside which was rare in Dallas, and I didn't bring my coat. I hurried to the food court and Chris was sitting at the back, waiting on me.

"Hey, what's good?"

"Hey," I greeted him. "So what's up?"

I sat down and rubbed my arms trying to get warm.

"All right so," he started. "I'm not sure exactly what it means yet, but I overheard him talking to a few niggas that were hanging around about a job that he had them do. Remember that nigga, Lorenzo, the one that was driving the truck with the flowers and shit?" he asked.

"Yeah," I remembered. "I thought he got sent up to Huntsville?"

"Yea he did. He said a couple of months ago. Same place where your boy was locked up," he pointed out.

"Aw shit," I said, realizing what he meant. Lorenzo was sent to the same prison that my godfather was in. "So what happened?"

"Well, apparently that nigga, Loco, was stabbed like over fifty damn times in the joint," he said.

"Damn! Goody had that nigga murked?"

"Sounds like it," he answered. "And I'm assuming the niggas that he was talking to planned the shit. But he made a call and he told them they had ten grand a piece waiting on them."

"Fuck," I whispered. I remembered the conversation I had with Goody that day at his house and how he said anything could happen to him and I shuddered. I guess he meant what he said. "So what else has been going on?" I asked him.

"Not shit really," he answered. "Right now, he's still got me doing all these crazy ass runs and shit. But I do hear him talking about this nigga named Devon a lot."

"Okay," I responded. "Who is that?"

"I ain't never seen the nigga, but I hear him talking on the phone with him telling him that he got to lay low and shit. Something about some money that he was supposed to pay him that ain't came through it yet. So you may wanna have your boy look into that," he suggested.

“Okay,” I said, making a mental note. “Find out what you can on your end though for me.”

“I got you,” he shrugged.

“I appreciate it, man,” I told him. “You okay, though?”

“Hell yeah,” he smiled. “Hell, it may be for some low key grimy shit but a nigga making his money. I ain’t gone lie, he keeps my pockets lined up,” he bragged.

“I noticed,” I said. observing him in all his new bling. “I see you looking like 2 Chainz Jr. All blinged out looking like you ‘bout to go to the BET hip-hop Awards or some shit,” I joked.

He burst out laughing.

“But that nigga still paying well.”

“Well, just don't forget what the end game is,” I reminded him.

“I ain’t, Miracle. I got you,” he promised. “Shoot I can do both at the same time. I mean…once he goes down, I might take over,” he said with a serious expression on his face.

My eyebrows shot up in surprise.

“What you mean?” I asked.

“I mean I'm saying. I'm a natural born hustler. And once I learn all his ins and outs and his connects, it's only a matter of time before I can use them against him,” he expressed.

“Okay, now,” I said, stopping him. “Don't go do nothing stupid. Just play it safe right now.”

“Yea,” he answered, mumbling.

I could tell he just said that to placate me ‘cause his mind was somewhere else already.

“Anyway,” I said, changing the subject. “So what you getting into for the rest of the night?”

“Not much,” he told me. “Probably go hang out at the crib for a little bit. Me and some of my niggas were talking about going out to some new club, but other than that, nothing. What about you?”

“I’m supposed to be going out with Black tonight,” I said, rolling my eyes. “We'll see about that.”

“What y’all beefing or something?” he asked.

“Something like that,” I told him. “Just seems like lately we not really seeing each other like that; he always gone. And when we are together, he all quiet and shit. Like, used to be he didn’t want me to leave his sight. Now he doing them jobs without me, I mean he still giving me money, but it's like he don't want me to be included in shit no more.”

“Or maybe he wants you to focus on school,” he suggested. “I mean, after all, ain’t that what your daddy wanted you to do anyway?”

Thinking about it, I felt a twinge of guilt. I had never looked at it like that. Black was always on me about staying on track with my school work. I was maintaining a 3.4 GPA, but I got a C on one of my last exams that I knew I could have done better on.

“Yeah,” I admitted. “And Black has always been supportive of me getting my education. Maybe you're right.”

I had been hustling a lot more and not focused on school enough. Maybe that was why Black was so distant with me. I would talk to him about it later on.

“There you go,” he pointed out. “Instead of overthinking it, just holla at the nigga. You know he handling a whole lot more right now with him tryna expand and shit, and with Goody ass out there basically taking over, I know that shit stressful for any other nigga out there on the block. I'm sure he'll keep it one hundred with you."

I nodded my head in agreement. When he was right, he was right.

"Yeah," I agreed. "All right, let me get ready to head up out of here. Just holler at me later. I was thinking about going to Kim's grave and I figured you'd wanna roll."

I had been going to Kim's grave and putting flowers down for the last few months. It gave me a sense of peace doing that. Just being there and talking to her, I was able to get out a lot that I had built up.

"Oh yea, no doubt. Let me know about that. I'll roll with you," he promised.

"Okay, cool. Aight, I'll talk to you later," I said, gathering my things to leave.

I walked to my car, remembering him mentioning Devon. I was already trying to figure out how I was going to find out who he was. I had to find a way to get to him without getting caught and without it getting back to Goody. I had an idea, but it would require some serious acting on my part.

Driving home, I thought about the conversation that I had with Chris about Black. Chris always gave good advice. Whoever he ended up with was going to be lucky. He was a good dude with a good heart. If only Black could be like that all of the time. I missed the days that he and I would be lying up in the bed all day, fucking the hell out of each other, and afterwards, we would get blazed and talk about our plans for the future. Then we would end up going at it again. Now, I could barely get two words out of the nigga. I know he loved me, and Lord knows I love him. But he had to get it together.

I finally got home and began to get ready for my date. I turned on the shower, put my hair up, and turned my phone on to find some music to play. Beyonce's "Kitty Kat" came on, and of course, in my mind, I thought I was Beyonce, so I began to dance around the room getting an outfit together.

I was about to walk into the bathroom when I heard the song stop for a few seconds before turning back on which let me know I had a text message. I picked up the phone to see who was texting me and saw it was a message from Black.

Black: Hey, babe. I'ma have to get at you a little bit later. Something came up and I gotta go handle some business real quick. But as soon as I get back I'll come over and we can catch a movie or something. LY.

I sighed and threw the phone back on the bed.

See this is the bullshit that I'm talking about. Every time I turned around he would get my hopes up and then disappoint me. I slammed my closet door and went ahead and took my shower. I decided that I wasn't going to be around when he decided to come home. It was Friday, so I figured I'd drive down to go see Myesha and hang out with her. Yeah, it seems kind of messed up that she was a consolation kind of thing, but I just didn't want to be in the house. And I knew that if I stayed, I would have to deal with Nikki and her hormones whenever the hell she came home.

I hurried up to finish my shower and dressed to head to her campus. I packed an overnight back and tossed it over my shoulder. Let Black's ass do him. It was obvious he wasn't thinking about my ass anyway.

I was looking around for my car charger when I realized that I had left it at Black's house. I had a tendency to keep my phone off the charger all day and it was already on twenty percent, so I hurried out the door and flew to his house to grab it before getting on the highway to head to my bestie. The last thing I needed to do was have a dead cell phone and end up having some type of car trouble or something like that and be stuck.

I drove the ten minutes to get to his house and pulled up leaving the car running so that way I wouldn't have to start the car again. Plus, it would give it time to warm up. My car had a keyless entry and a push start ignition, so I could take the keys with me and not worry.

I unlocked the door and ran into the house to grab my charger. I couldn't remember if I had it in the living room or if I put it in his room, so I stopped to think about the last place I saw it. It was then that I heard the moans coming from the bedroom.

"What the hell?" I mumbled.

I didn't want to just go back there because I knew he had a few of his homeboys that he trusted in and out the apartment when we weren't there, and they would be playing video games and smoking. I didn't think any of them would be stupid enough to use his bedroom to fuck some random THOT 'cause none of them had any serious girlfriends, but clearly one of them was.

I contemplated busting in on them because nobody would be disrespecting my nigga's house like that when I heard a familiar voice.

"Oh shit! Yes, daddy, that feels good. Fuck! Black! Don't stop!"

"Shit!" I heard him moan. "Damn, this pussy is so fucking good."

I heard a smack which I assumed that he popped her on her ass. I don't even remember running towards that room, but the shit that I saw in front of me made me wish to God I had my gun. I opened the door to see my man fucking Nikki!

"Are you fucking serious right now?!" I screamed.

They both jumped, and Nikki tried to cover herself as Black pulled out of her.

“Really, Black?” I screamed. “You fucking her, really?”

“Miracle!” he yelled. “What are you doing here?”

“What am I doing here?” I snapped. That's all you can muthafuckin’ say? I'll kill your muthafuckin’ ass!”

I charged towards Nikki trying to snatch her as fast as I could, but Black grabbed me holding me back. Nikki jumped over the bed and ran into the bathroom, slamming the door.

“I'm so sorry!” she cried.

“Bitch, this ain’t no muthafuckin’ *Players Club* hoe! Bring your muthafuckin’ ass outside you thirsty bitch!” I screamed. “And you let go of me trifling ass nigga!” I said shoving, Black off of me.

“Baby, listen! I'm sorry. She came over here and was crying and shit, and I…I was fucked up. I swear to God I didn't mean for it to happen,” he pleaded.

“You didn't mean to slip your dick into her? Right. You didn't mean to fuck somebody that's pretty much my sister? My muthafuckin’ family? Get the fuck out my face,” I said.

I turned back to the bathroom door and banged on it. I could hear her from the other side, crying and apologizing over and over.

“Shut the fuck up, hoe! You wasn’t crying when you was fucking my nigga! You better be glad that I can't get to your muthafuckin’ ass! If you wasn't pregnant, I swear to God I would beat your ass. Don't come back to my muthafuckin’ house. As far as I'm concerned you two hoes can stay here together. I can't believe your trifling ass!” I said turning to Black. “You fucked her really? You done had me questioning myself and tripping and thinking that I'm wrong and that you actually out here grinding like you say, and you are here fucking some Burger King hoe? I guess you really can have it your way then, huh?" I spat.

I was pissed the hell off and was liable to say and do anything.

"Miracle, come on man. Don't do this," he begged.

"Don't do what? Clearly, you've done IT already. And obviously, you enjoyed it 'cause your dick is still hard, nigga!" I pointed out.

He looked down and tried to grab his clothes.

"No worries. You ain't got to get dressed. I'm out. Fuck you, Black. You fucked around on me for some strung out, prostitute ass BITCH!" I yelled, making sure she could hear me. "I may not have been one of these little birds that you used to fuck with, but you meant something to me," I huffed. "Clearly, I don't mean nothing to you." He tried to reach for me, but I snatched away.

"I'm done."

I ran out of that apartment so fast and to my car and sped off. I cried as I drove down the highway back to my house. I couldn't believe that he had done that. My eyes kept replaying the scene of my boyfriend, the man I loved and had given myself to, sleeping with my sister. Foster sister or not, I considered that bitch my family. How could he hurt me like that? How could she hurt me like that? Why was this happening to me? The tears were flowing so hard I could barely see. I needed to pull over and get myself together. I swerved my car into the next lane not seeing or paying any attention to the pickup truck that was there. I'm sure if I was in my right mind, I wouldn't have been speeding or driving reckless like that, but I wasn't.

I hit it so hard that I ended up flipping my car altogether. I saw the truck slam into a pole while my car flipped in the opposite direction. I flipped three more times and the last thing I saw was Black's name on my caller ID before I succumbed to consciousness.

*****

“I think she's waking up.” I heard Black’s voice.

I knew immediately I had to have my ass in the hospital. The last thing I remember was hitting that damn pickup truck and flipping down the street. But I damn sure didn't expect his ass to be there. I remember he called me during the accident, but I didn't think he'd have the balls to be here.

“Yo, sis, you good? Can you hear me?” I heard.

I opened my eyes and looked to see Chris standing over me.

“Yeah, I think she's good,” Black answered. “The doctor said she just had a couple of bumps and bruises, but he was going to keep her overnight. I think they gave her a sedative to help her sleep for a while.”

I sat up and saw that my left arm was bandaged in a sling. I was checking over my body, and everything seemed to be okay.

“The doctor said you just had a broken arm and a few bumps and bruises,” Black told me. “He said you're lucky to be alive.”

He reached out for my hand and I snatched away quickly, remembering the reason why I had the car accident in the first place.

“What the fuck are you doing here?” I hissed. “If my memory serves me correctly, I said I didn't want to see you, and I didn’t want to talk to you. So why the fuck are you here? You can leave. Go be with your bitch,” I snapped.

“That's not my girl,” he growled. “You are.”

“The fuck I am! You really think I'm going to be with you after I come in and catch you with my sister, nigga?”

Chris, who was watching from the side, turned his attention to Black after hearing that.

“What the fuck you just say?” he asked.

“Yeah,” I said. “He didn't tell you? He didn’t let you know the reason why I got into the car accident?” I asked, looking to him.

“Yo…” Black tried to explain.

“Save it,” I said. “Right now if I was you, I would get the fuck out and quick. Unless you want me to get security up here. I'm pretty sure that they would love to escort your ass up out of here,” I threatened.

I wanted to jump up and strangle him, but my head was hurting so bad and I didn't want to give him the satisfaction of seeing me in pain. Black opened his mouth to say something, but Chris walked around from the other side of the bed.

“Look, my nigga, she don't want you in here so you can hit it,” he said.

“I'm not leaving,” Black said, stepping to Chris.

I saw a look in Chris’s eyes that I hadn't seen since the day he shot Whitney. It was like he didn’t have any remorse.

“I promise you, dawg, if it wasn't for my sister sitting right here in this damn hospital bed, after what she just told me, I would have fucked you up a couple of seconds ago,” he gritted.

“And on the strength that she your sister, I ain’t rocked your shit yet. But be clear, I don't take no muthafuckin’ orders from no nigga,” Black barked.

“Well, you gone take them from my ass because I don't want you in here. So you can leave now, or like I said, I can call security," I said, picking up the remote that was attached to the bed.

Black looked at me and tried to give me this sad ass "I'm sorry" face, but I wasn't feeling it.

"Alright, cool," he conceded. "But I'll be back."

He walked out and closed the door and Chris watched him the whole time.

"Yo, what the fuck happened?" he asked the minute that Black was out of his sight.

"How'd you know I was here?" I asked him.

"I didn't know 'bout the other shit," he explained. "He called me and told me that the EMTs had answered your phone while they were getting you in the ambulance. You had him listed as your emergency contact."

"Okay. Definitely gotta change that," I said.

"Will you to tell me some of what the fuck just happened?" he asked.

I sighed and laid back so that I could explain this fuckery.

"Well, basically, all of this time that I've been thinking that he's been out working and grinding and all of this, apparently he hasn't. I was going to go see my best friend down at A&M and I needed my car charger. I remembered I left it at his house, so I went over there to get it, and then all of a sudden I hear all this moaning and groaning and ass smacking, and all this time I'm thinking it's his boy or something. But when I walk back there, I see him and Nikki fucking." Chris's mouth dropped open. "Yeah. And then Nikki's punk ass gonna go running into the fucking bathroom and shit like she trying to hide. This nigga tryna tell me that he was fucked up and that she came over there crying and it just happened. But I don't believe that shit," I said.

I was so angry that I didn't even realize I was crying again.

“Come on now; calm that down,” he fussed. “You found out what that nigga really is, and you did what you had to do. The shit’s fucked up ‘cause you got hurt ‘cause of it. Like real talk, if something else had happened worse than this I would have fucked that nigga up for real,” he said.

The way he was looking, I believed him.

“I'm just blown right now,” I sniffed. “Like Black knew how I felt about him. He knows I loved the hell out of him. So why would he go do some shit like that?” I stopped to wipe my eyes. “And then for Nikki to turn around betray me like that? Like that's some shady ass shit. You don't do shit like that! If she wants to fuck up her life, that's fine, but why fuck up mine? Like I was there for her! I helped her through all of this bullshit she was in. I saved her from that fuckin’ pimp and this is what she do? This is how she repays me?”

“I feel you,” Chris said. “I'ma holla at her.”

“Yeah well, while you hollering at her, tell her that she needs to get her shit the fuck out my house,” I told him.

He nodded his head but didn't say anything.

“Hey, where's my cell phone?” I asked.

“I think it's in the bag with your stuff,” he said, walking over to look.

I didn't even realize I wasn't in my clothes until he said that. They had me in that ugly ass hospital gown. He opened the bag and pulled my cell phone out and handed it to me. I looked to see that I had fifteen text messages. I already knew that most of them were probably from Black’s ass. I remembered my phone lighting up while I was speeding away. Opening my text messages I was right. Him and Nikki both had been blowing my phone up. I opened them to see her begging.

Nikki (Sis): Miracle, I'm so sorry. I didn't mean to do it. I just got caught up. Please don't ignore me. Please just call me so we can talk. I messed up. I made a mistake. I'm sorry.

Nikki (Sis): please answer me. I know u probably mad right now but I wasn't thinking. I was just jealous of what u had & I did somethin' stupid. I know I was dead wrong.

Nikki (Sis): I guess I'll just get my stuff n go. I don't know where I'm going to go because I don't really have any money saved up, & everybody that I hit up don't have room for me. I'm sorry.

I smirked. I know this bitch was not trying to make me feel sorry for her. Clearly, those pregnancy hormones had gotten to her brain because there was no way in hell she could actually think that I was going to feel sorry for her enough to let her stay in my house after what she did. She was trying, and she better be glad I couldn't get to her. I sent her a text message back to let her know exactly what the fuck she could do.

Miracle: U should have thought about that before u decided to fuck my man. I ain't got no sympathy for u or ur bastard ass baby. So get your shit and get the hell out. & I'm not playing. Must have been crazy to let a cracked out hoe in my house. As far as I'm concerned, u can go back to that whack-ass pimp that I saved ur ass from BITCH!

I tossed my phone and laid-back.

"Yo, you good?" Chris asked.

"No," I said, feeling myself about to cry again.

Chris looked completely uncomfortable but he held my hand and tried to comfort me the best he could. I let the tears fall. Me and Black had been together over a year, and for him to do something like this was just unimaginable. I could never hurt him on that level but I guess my feelings didn't mean anything to him.

I just wanted to wake up from this nightmare. Two of the people that I trusted the most, two of the people that I loved the most hurt me to my soul. At what point would things get better? At what point would people stop hurting me? Chris's phone buzzed in his pocket and he pulled it out and gave a frown.

"My bad," I apologized. "I'm pretty sure I'm keeping you from whatever you were doing."

He gave me a little smile still looking down at his phone.

"Nah, you straight," he said his fingers busy typing away on the keyboard. "That's Goody. He needs me to meet him somewhere." He put his phone in his pocket and straightened up. "I'ma go handle this real quick, and then I'll be right back."

"Where am I going to go?" I said sarcastically.

He gave a half smile and kissed my forehead.

"Just try to get some sleep or something. And stay off your phone. Matter fact…" He picked my phone up off the bed and put it in his pocket.

"Um excuse me?" I asked. "What the hell you think you doing?"

"Keeping you from losing your damn mind," he said. "Look, I ain't into all of that girly shit, but I know you talking to either one of them right now ain't going to do nothing but make the situation worse. So, I will take your phone, and I'll bring it with me when I come back. That way, if they hit you up, you ain't got to see it, and you ain't gone be damn near breaking your fingers to be having some text message war," he laughed. “But, don't worry, I won’t be gone long. You need anything? You hungry or something?”

Now that I thought about it, I was a little hungry. Me and that bitch ass nigga was supposed to go get something to eat, but he canceled the date so that he could fuck my sister.

“Actually yea. Can you bring me something light?” I asked. “Ooo better yet, you know what, I would love some Taco Cabana,” I smiled.

“You're trying to blow the damn hospital room up,” he joked.

I laughed a little. Taco Cabana was bomb.com, but thirty minutes later you in the bathroom on the toilet.

“Okay, then just bring me some Jack in the Box,” I said.

“Aight, cool,” he said. “I'll be back in a little bit. Try to get you some sleep.”

He walked out closing the door behind him and I laid back against the flat pillow on the bed. I sighed and replayed everything. It seemed like everybody that I trusted and loved did nothing but break my heart or lie. I can't trust anybody. At this point, if I ever saw Black or Nikki again it would be too soon.

I turned the TV on just to see what was on and one of the nurses came in.

“Well, look who's awake,” she said.

“Hi,” I said not looking at her and keeping my focus on the screen.

“So how you feeling?” she asked.

“I'm okay,” I told her.

"Well, that's good. You know you're lucky. Your car was pretty much totaled. And for you to only have a broken arm and a bump on your head, you got extremely lucky."

"So I keep hearing," I mumbled, thinking about Black saying it earlier.

"Yea, you were. Unfortunately, the other driver didn't make it."

I turned my head to her once I heard that.

"What?"

She nodded her head slowly.

"Yea. Unfortunately, when the ambulance brought them in, the internal injuries were too bad. They died on the operating table. Yours was just as bad. They had to cut you out with the jaws of life," she informed me.

Hearing that the other driver died because of my carelessness immediately fucked me up. I really didn't mean to hurt anyone. I was just so upset from everything that had happened. I didn't think about anything that I was doing at the time. I felt like I was a curse. Someone was dead because of me. I hated Black and Nikki even more because this was all their fault. I guess the nurse realized that I was upset because she tried to comfort me.

"It's okay, sweetie," she soothed. "It was an accident. You didn't intentionally hurt him. You just relax okay?"

I sat there numb once again not knowing how to feel. I'm surprised I still had a heart as much pain as I endured.

"Well, we gave you some morphine for the pain, so you may still be a little drowsy. It'll probably wear off in a few hours. We'll bring you another dosage in about six hours if the doctor thinks it's okay," she advised. "If the pain gets unbearable before then, though, just let me know, and we'll see what we can do okay?" she said.

“Okay, thanks,” I mumbled.

“Do you need anything? Can I get you some water or something?” she asked.

“No,” I told her. “I’m fine.”

I just wanted to cry and kick and scream, but I couldn’t move.

“Okay,” she agreed. “Well, I'll let you get your rest. You want your light off?” She asked as she headed to the door.

“Yes, please,” I sniffed.

She hit the switch, and I closed my eyes to think. She was dead on about the morphine because within a few minutes I was out. I woke up several hours later to a dark room. I looked over to see if Chris had returned. He must have because there was a Jack in the Box bag sitting on the tray next to the bed. I sat up and rolled it towards me and saw the note underneath.

Hey, Big Head,

You were knocked out when I came back.

I had to go run out and take care of some things, but I'll be back in the morning. Make sure that you go your ass to sleep. I kept your phone because you really don't need it right now. Don't worry. I'll make sure I'm here before you wake up in the morning. Now eat the damn food and go to sleep!

Chris

I shook my head. At least I still had somebody in my corner. The smell of the food was taunting my stomach. I knew it was cold, but I didn't care. I pulled it out the bag and begin to eat devouring every bite. I was so into the food that I didn’t notice the woman standing at the door watching me.

“Can I help you?” I asked her.

She didn't say anything and just stood there.

"What? You don't speak English?" I knew she understood me because she frowned at me like I said something wrong. She was black and looked to be in her late thirties. She was pretty but the way she was just staring at me was creeping me the hell out. "Look, if you not saying nothing, can you please leave me the hell alone and go stare at someone else?"

She stood for a few more seconds and finally spoke.

"Watch yourself."

And just that fast she walked off.

What the fuck was that about? I hope the hospital didn't tell the family of the guy that died what room I was in. That shit is just not cool.

The nurse came back in and gave me hydrocodone.

"Well, I'm glad that you're eating," she observed. "That's good. Here take this. It's not as strong as the morphine, but it'll help with the pain and help you sleep," she warned.

"Thank you," I said, popping the pills in my mouth and downing it with the soda from my meal. "So, I'll be able to go home tomorrow 'cause some lady just came to the door just now, and I don't know if y'all make it a practice to just give my information out, but I don't like that kind of shit."

The nurse looked confused.

"Um, I'm not sure what you're referring to, but I can assure you that hospital staff does not give out information on patients. It's against policy."

"But you gave me information on the other driver and I didn't even ask so…" I said, calling her on her bullshit.

"Yes, ma'am, I did," she acknowledged. "And I apologize about that. It was in error. But I promise you that we did not give out your information to anyone. I can have security make sure no one is allowed in here unless it's staff or family."

"Well, I'm going home tomorrow, though, right?" I pushed.

"More than likely, yes," she answered. "The doctor said he's going to come in and do a final examination and if everything checks out, you'll be able to leave in the morning."

"Good," I said.

This day had been so messed up. All I wanted to do was go home, climb in my bed, and cry my eyes out.

*****

Chapter Seventeen

I was so glad to be out of that damn hospital. They ended up keeping me an extra day just to be on the safe side, and I was bored out of my mind in there. Chris had picked me up to take me home since my car was totaled. I had a million thoughts running through my head, but the main one was that if Nikki was at the house, I was going to go to jail. Chris said that he had talked to her, but I just hope she wasn't that stupid.

I walked in the house, and it looked like she took his advice and got the hell out. Fine by me; I had been footing the bill for her ass long enough for her to betray the hell out of me.

“You straight?”

“Yea. I’m straight,” I assured him. “Right now I just want to lay down. These last few days have been crazy as hell.”

“I feel you,” he said, looking around. “But at least you aight.”

“Yeah,” I agreed. ‘Now, I ain't worried about nobody else but me. I've been sitting up here worrying about Nikki ass all of this time when I should have been worried about my damn self. And I ain't got time for that no more. So, I'm just gone do what I got to do.”

“Without Black?” he asked. “What about him?”

“I ain’t got shit to say to him. And as far as I'm concerned, we're done. Like for real, they can have each other. I don't care.”

“Yea,” he said, looking as if he didn’t believe me.

I know he had probably heard that before with other females, but I couldn’t be with somebody that would outright disrespect me like that.

"Well, anyway, you know I got you if you need anything."

"I mean I'm good. I got money stashed in the bank. I mean, granted, I don't have a regular job or anything, but I got enough to last me a while. Plus, I got a little bit stashed here in the house," I told him. "I keep a little bit stashed in cash just in case something ever happened and I couldn't get to my account."

"That's smart."

"As far as Black, I really don't need him. I'm sure he probably still thinks that I'm going to be hustling with him, but I do not want to see this nigga."

"Well if it gets too rough you know you can hustle with me," he offered. "I'll work it out. Goody ain't gotta know nothing."

"No," I refused. "That's too much of a risk. Besides, eventually he will find out and it would be some more mess. Right now, it's better that you just keep doing what you been doing and staying on his good side. The less he knows, the better it'll be."

"Speaking of Goody, I needed to holler at you about that, too," he said. "Remember what I was telling you about before you went into the hospital and shit? About that nigga that's been laying low? Devon?"

"Yeah, I remember. What's good?"

"Well, I asked around, and Devon was in the truck that day with that nigga, Lorenzo, and Goody's two niggas, Cisco and J.D., and some other nigga."

"You sure?" I asked.

"Yep. And on top of that, he was the one that pulled the trigger. But this nigga is like on some runaway slave type shit. Like nobody can find this nigga. But Goody was talking about how this nigga wasn't getting nothing from him. Then J.D. was talking 'bout how this nigga, Devon, talking reckless and that's why Goody got them two going to holla at him," he informed me.

"So, in other words, we need to get to him before they do," I said.

"But is that what you really want to do, though? I mean if he pulled the trigger, what's your game plan?" Chris questioned. "Because, if this nigga really is behind this, and he ain't getting paid, it could work in our favor." I wasn't following so he continued. "Think about it. If I paid you to go and kill somebody, and you go and do it, and then I don't give you your money and I try to kill you. If somebody else comes along to kill your ass, you going to be more than willing to help them."

"True," I agreed. "Alright so, we gotta find him quick."

"Aight, I mean I can see what I can do," he said. "It's going to be a little hard, though. Cause if he already got them fools on him, ain't gonna be a lot of time to find him."

"Alright, so how 'bout we follow them?" I suggested.

"What you mean we?"

"Did I stutter? Just what I said, we."

"Miracle, you can't hang with these type of niggas," he warned.

I was so tired of people underestimating me.

"Look, I know you don't think I can handle this but I can. And on the real, this ain't something that's really up for debate," I said.

"Man, calm down, sistah soldier," he said. "I didn't say that you couldn't handle it. I'm just saying that it's going to take more than just me and you. These niggas are pretty much professional hood hitmen. So I know we ain't gonna be able to stop them by ourselves."

"Okay, I get you." I understood. "But I got people."

"People like who? Black?"

"Don't worry about all that," I said. "Look, I'm not saying that we going to follow them and then go to confront them and nothing like that. I just said we follow them and find out where he is. That's the first thing we need to do. I mean, I don't know about you, but I'm trying to dead this shit."

"All right," he agreed. "But I'm just saying we got to be real careful with this. I done seen first-hand what type shit this nigga is capable of. One wrong move and it's over."

"I know that, Chris," I sighed. "I'm not stupid. I grew up with this man. I know what he's capable of okay? But I also know what I'm doing. So you either with me or you're not. Right now I don't need any uncertainties."

"Yo, if I wasn't with it I wouldn't be doing what I'm doing now. So don't ever question me on that again," he snapped.

I hadn't seen Chris like that since we were living with Patricia. I knew I was wrong for it 'cause he really was going to bat for me when he didn't have to.

"Alright cool," I said. "My bad."

For some reason, the woman in the hospital popped into my head.

"Oh, I forgot to tell you about some crazy shit that happened the other night," I said, changing the subject.

"What's up?" he asked.

"Aight so, after you brought me something to eat, I woke up or whatever and I was eating my food, and it was just this chick, standing at the door."

"What you mean?" he asked.

"That's what I said," I told him. "I mean the shit was weird. Like…it was just like she was standing at the door watching me. And then the next thing I know she's telling me that I need to be careful and then she just walked the hell off."

"Damn. And you sure you ain't know her at all?"

"No!" I told him. "You know I don't mess with a bunch of females like that. Besides, this looked like some grown ass woman. So I definitely don't know her. At first, I thought she was from Social Services or something, and for like a second, I thought maybe she found out what I did, but that wasn't it. Like I don't know this chick," I reiterated. "I told the nurse about it, but she was just like she could get security or whatever."

"Damn, that's kinda crazy."

"No shit." I got quiet for a second remembering something else from the hospital. "They told me that the guy I hit didn't make it."

"Oh damn," he whispered. "Sorry to hear that."

"Yeah, I know right?"

"You think the chick that you talking about, maybe it was his wife or something?" he asked.

"Honestly, I don't know."

"Well, just don't go blaming yourself," he added.

"I mean I'm trying not to think about it," I told him. "But I wasn't thinking when I was driving and... I mean, if I was in my right mind I know I wouldn't have done that. And now." I felt myself getting choked up and tried not to cry. "Now this man is dead because of me."

Chris rubbed my back trying to comfort me.

"It's okay, Miracle. Maybe it was quick."

“Something about internal bleeding or something,” I sniffed. “The nurse wasn't supposed to tell me, so I don't know what to think. But I know the minute that I told her that the chick was at my door, I asked her had she given her my information, and she said swore up and down that the hospital didn’t release any information.”

“So how’d you find out about the guy? I didn’t see any cops or anything,” he pointed out.

“She told me.”

“But I thought you said—”

“Exactly,” I finished. “So, now you see what I'm saying.”

“Well, I don't think she’d be stupid enough to give his family your room number,” he reasoned. “Besides, if that was the case, she would have said more to you than just be careful.”

“You right,” I said.

I hadn't really had a chance to think about it because I was so wrapped up in everything else. My phone was buzzing and I already knew who it was.

“Remind me to change my damn phone number,” I said.

“You should have done that already,” he laughed.

“Whatever.” I rolled my eyes. “I'm glad you think it's funny.”

I looked to see Myesha had sent me a message asking me what happened to me the other night. I needed to call her, so she wouldn’t be worried. But knowing her she wasn’t too fazed because she was just now sending me a message, so I would skip the details of what happened and just let her know I would come down later.

“So what you going to do?” he asked.

“Well, first thing I’m gonna do is take a nap,” I laughed. “Then, I’m gonna try to see about going to get a rental car for a while so I can get around.”

“I mean you can borrow my whip if you need to,” he offered.

I laughed again.

“Nah, I'm good,” I told him. “Besides, I'm not trying to be driving that big ass gas guzzler that you call a car.”

“Aye, man, don't sleep on the Eldorado.”

“Whatever. But other than that I'm probably just going to chill out for the day,” I told him.

“All right. Well, you need me to get you anything?” he asked.

“No,” I told him, shaking my head. “I should be straight. Go ahead and handle your business. I'm pretty sure that you got a lot of work to do. And I ain’t tryna hold you up.”

“You right,” he grunted, getting up off the couch and walking into the kitchen. “Yea I got a couple of moves I do need to make. You got anything to drink?”

“Negro, you already in my kitchen go look in the fridge,” I joked, walking in behind him. “And while you at it get me something, too.”

I needed to get something to drink, too, so I could take some of these pain pills. He opened the fridge and grabbed a Pepsi, and gave me a bottle of water. I leaned against the counter and took a long swallow so that I could get the pills down. I barely noticed that one of my cabinets was still open. But when I did, I got this strange feeling and something told me to check. I stashed some of my cash in an empty box at the back of the cabinet. I had always seen it done in the movies, so I thought it would be cool when I started doing it but then it became convenient, especially as much hustling I was doing with Black. So I put it in an empty box of sugar hidden at the very back of the cabinet. That feeling in my gut was telling me Nikki did some dumb shit. Of course, when she was here, I never hid my money in there because I never thought I it would be a problem. I prayed to God that she hadn't stooped that low.

"What's wrong?" Chris asked, noticing my face change.

"Hold up," I said. I walked over to it and pushed all of the other boxes out of the way to grab it. "Please tell me she didn't." I prayed silently. I opened the box and sure enough, the $5,000 that I had stashed was gone. "This bitch!" I screamed.

"What?" Chris asked still drinking his soda.

"This bitch stole my money!"

"You sure? I mean, did you put it somewhere else?" he asked, walking over to the counter where I sat the box.

"What the fuck you mean am I sure?" I yelled. "Chris, I know where the hell I put my shit. This money been sitting here since I moved in. I didn't even think she knew where the hell it was, but clearly, she was paying attention. Nobody else could have taken it but her," I said.

"I'm just saying you ain't got no proof. And y'all shit already fucked up, so you don't wanna go running off at the mouth."

"Nigga, please! I KNOW her ass did it. Especially when she sends me a text message talking about she ain't got no place to go, and how she ain't got no money. Hell yeah, I would think that she would do some shit like that. Yes, she took it!" I screamed. I was so fucking mad I was pacing back and forth. "I know this much, she better run me my shit!"

"You got an idea where she went?" he asked.

"Hell no! For all I know she probably staying with one of those crackhead friends of hers. Or this mysterious baby daddy that she got." Chris gave me a look that caught me completely off guard in the middle of my rant. "What?"

"You sure this nigga and Nikki only fucked around one time?" he questioned.

"Huh?"

"You said she ain't never brought this baby daddy around, and he got all this money and shit, right?"

I hadn't even thought about that shit. The thought of it just made me sick to my damn stomach. I picked up my phone and I called him.

"What you doing? That nigga ain't bout to tell your ass the truth, yo," Chris fussed.

"Oh I'm gonna find the shit out," I said. Of course, Black answered sounding all desperate and eager. "I need you to come to the house like ASAP. It's urgent," I rushed.

"What's wrong?"

"Just get to the house please," I said.

"Alright," he agreed. "I'm on the way."

I hung up and Chris looked at me puzzled.

"What's good?"

"Oh, he on the way," I confirmed.

"Why you even trying to see the nigga?"

"Because I want him to look me in the face and tell me that he ain't get this hoe pregnant," I explained. "'Cause if he's her baby daddy, that means they been fuckin' for a while, considering that she's what four months pregnant now? So that means they were fuckin around on the low for a good minute, and if they have, then I hate it for his ass. Because he didn't give a fuck about fuckin' this hoe raw and could've brought me back some shit. You know how Nikki got down. How the fuck I know she ain't have shit?"

"Alright, come on now you gotta calm it down a little bit. I know you mad, I know you ready to pop off, shit I would be, too, but tryna come at her right now really ain't going to do nothing," he tried to reason.

"Oh, it's going to do plenty," I said. "Because this nigga claimed that it only happened one time because he was drunk. So if he lying, trust me I'ma know it."

"Aight, whateva. I don't even know why I'm telling you. You ain't gone listen no way," Chris said, sitting back down at the table.

"Nope. Not on this."

"Alright, well I'ma stick around just in case ole boy get reckless," he said.

"Please, he ain't stupid," I scoffed. "I'm good. Go handle your business. Trust me. I'll call you if I need you," I told him.

"You sure? Cause I ain't tryna body no nigga for acting stupid."

"Nah. I'm straight," I assured him. I had gotten another gun when I gave him his back. So if Black even thought about going left, that ass would be done.

"Alright," he gave up. "I'm gone. Holla at me if you need me."

"I got you," I said.

He walked out the door, and I locked it behind him. That only reminded me that there was something else that I needed to do; get my damn locks changed. 'Cause ain't no way in hell I'm about to have Black just walking the fuck up in here when he felt like it; especially if he tells me an answer that I don't want to hear. No sooner had Chris left, then Black showed up, opening the door. He must have sped his ass over here.

"Hey. You okay? How you feeling?" he asked, walking in.

"First of all, I need you to give me my key," I said. "And I'ma give you yours don't worry."

I reached for my keys, so I could make sure he got his, too.

"That's what you called me over here for? Come on, man, can we talk about this shit, please?" he begged.

"Yea, we gone talk," I agreed. "Cause I got a whole lot of questions."

"Miracle, what are you talking about?" he asked.

I had to get his phone to confirm my gut instinct, and I had an idea.

"Hold on a sec." I picked up my phone and pretended that it was dead. "Let me see your phone real quick. My phone died and I don't have my charger. That was why I came back to your house that night."

My phone was just fine. But I knew that there was a possibility Black's ass was going to lie to me so, I figured I'd go to his phone. And I knew his ass wasn't smart enough to think about that. Sure enough, he handed me the phone.

I pretended to be typing a number, but instead, I opened up the text messages and went through his messages. My heart dropped to my chest when I saw that he had been messaging Nikki for days. Their messages were very much more than friendly.

"You trifling mutherfucka!" I whispered.

"Say what?" he asked.

I threw the phone at him hard.

"Miracle, what the hell is wrong with you!"

"So you been fucking her more than one time OBVIOUSLY," I accused. "So that baby is yours?! That's your baby."

I tried to take a swing at him.

"Miracle, calm down! What are you talking about?!"

"The fuck you mean?" I yelled, picking up my remote and throwing it at him. I wasn't gonna stop 'til I knocked his ass out. "I'm talking about the messages in your phone from that bitch, Nikki! I'm talking about how y'all been smashing obviously longer than you said. You lied to me! You told me you only smashed this bitch once! But I'm looking at your phone and I see you been hitting her for quite a while! And you got this chick pregnant? A bitch that used to be a fucking prostitute? But you want to say that you love me? She's having your baby! How long you been smashing her, huh? What? Since the first day you met her?"

"No!" he yelled, trying to grab me to calm my ass down. "Come on, man, it's not like that!"

"It's not like what? Nigga, what the fuck is it not like?" I couldn't believe this fool was still trying to debate me on this. "I saw the messages in your phone. I saw where you told her that you wasn't trying to be no daddy. I saw where you told her that you was going to give her money to get rid of it. Well, guess what? She didn't get rid of it! So what? You trying to pay her money to get rid of the evidence of the dirt that you did? Too late! I can't believe your trifling ass! I can't believe I trusted you and that hoe!"

"Baby, I'm sorry," he pleaded.

"Yeah, you sorry alright! You sorry you got caught! I NEVER thought you would do no shit like that. Here I am being loyal to your ass, but you out here fuckin' my sister? My family? And you made a baby with this bitch?" I sobbed.

At this point, I was so mad I was crying uncontrollably.

"I promise you, it wasn't supposed to go there like that. I wasn't really messing with her like that. It was just a couple of times," he tried to explain.

"A couple was more than it should have been, Black! It shouldn't have been any times! I shouldn't have had to worry about my man sleeping with my sister. But you know what? I'm good," I sniffed.

"Miracle, come on, baby. I love you."

"And I loved you. But I don't know more. So you can bounce," I told him. "I know what I need to know. I'll bring you all your shit. Just give me my key, and as far as I'm concerned, we got nothing else to say to each other." He looked at me all sorry and pathetic like he thought I would take pity on him. "What you got a hearing problem?" I snapped. "I told you, I'm done. Run me my key," I said, holding my hand out.

He continued looking at me as if he wanted to say something but opted not to. He placed the key in my hand and I snatched away.

"Miracle, please, just please give me a chance to explain," he sighed. "You know how much I love you. You know I would never try to hurt you."

"I don't know that," I said, shaking my head. "I don't know what you would do anymore. I thought I did. I thought that you would be faithful. I thought that you would never hurt me considering everything that you knew I had been through. I thought that you would be considerate of my feelings, knowing that I gave myself to you. I lost my virginity to you. I thought that meant something. I thought that me being down for you since day one meant something, but apparently, pussy means more to you. So no, Black, I don't know you."

He got so close to me, and I was a ball of emotions. A part of me wanted to believe him but the level that he took it to was so hard.

"Come on, baby," he whispered. "I promise you I will never do anything like that again."

I looked in his eyes and I just didn't know anymore.

"You know my daddy used to say that if they mess around on you once, then they will do it again. And I'm not about to be somebody's damn doormat. So I hope you and Nikki are happy together. Oh and by the way, you need to tell that hoe that I know she stole my shit."

"Huh?" he asked caught off guard.

"The bitch stole my stash."

"What stash?"

"You heard me. $5,000 is gone. So you better tell that chick that if she don't run me my shit, I will find her, and I will get in that ass, pregnant or not. I'm pretty much going to do that anyway."

This bitch thinks she's invincible apparently. Fucks my nigga, living in my crib, and now she done stole my shit? Clearly, she don't give a fuck about her life.

"Miracle, I swear to God I'm sorry. I never meant for any of this to happen," he tried to reason. "You're my girl. I love you. I don't care what I got to do. I'll do whatever it takes to get you back."

Sad thing is, I really felt in my heart that he would, but too much damage had been done.

"Just leave me alone, Trevon," I said.

He dropped his head. He knew the only time I called him Trevon was when I was mad at him, which had only happened a few times.

“Miracle,” he begged. “Don't do this.”

“You made the choice for me,” I said, closing the door on him.

I locked it and broke down. Over a year into this relationship and he threw it all away. How could he do that? Wasn't I enough for him? The fucked up thing was, I don't think it would have hurt as bad had he just messed with some random chick on the street. Yeah, I would have been upset, but to know that he didn't even care that it was my sister, tore me to the core. And now they're having a baby together? This can't be life right now. I wanted to break everything in my sight. But I couldn't. I had to hold it together. I picked up my phone and sent a message to both of them. I meant to say it to him when he was in the apartment, but I was so emotional over the pain I didn’t think about the anger as much.

Miracle: Triflin ass bitch! You stole $5,000 from me, Nik. On top of being a hoe, and on top of being ungrateful, you stole from me. Really bitch? You aint done enough shit? Either you get it to me, or I take it. And if I take it, game over. You dead bitch.

I knew her ass wouldn't respond. But that bitch got my message. I know she did.

I cut my phone off, laid down on the couch, curled up into a ball, and cried my eyes out. I had nothing anymore. The only person that I had that I could trust was Chris. And there was no telling how long it would be before he betrayed me.

Maybe it was just meant for me to go through life miserable. I've always been told that you're as strong as what you can handle. But clearly, I wasn't as strong as I thought I was. This heartbreak thing sucks.

*****

Chapter Eighteen

I was sitting in this hot ass car with Chris across the street from some restaurant that Goody's so-called goons were eating at. Chris had been tailing them for the last couple of days, so I came along 'cause I had to get out the house. From what I can see so far, there was no type of indication that they even planned on getting this Devon guy. What few connects that I did have, I had them keeping their ears to the streets, but it was like this guy was non-existent.

I was starting to wonder if Goody had set Chris up because one minute, this mysterious dude's name is on everybody's lips, and then the next he's not. Now here we are sitting across the street for damn near two hours. I was bored out of my mind. I was passing time playing Candy Crush on my phone while Chris kept watch.

"Yo, you are addicted to that damn thing," he observed.

"I know," I laughed. "But it keeps me occupied."

It had been a week since me and Black had broken up, and I kept my word. I took all of his stuff to his apartment and left it on the front door. I changed my locks, and changed my phone number. I thought Goody would have had something to say, but he didn't really pay it any mind. He and I hadn't talked as much lately, and majority of the time if I went to see Tori and the kids, I would wait until I knew he was gone. He questioned me on it, but I just told him that it was because I was dealing with me and Black breaking up. As far as he knew, me and Black had been apart for a while. But I'm pretty sure that he knew why I was avoiding him since our last conversation.

I was careful with everything that I said around him. Because the more that I looked at him, the less trustworthy he seemed. He wasn't nothing more than a snake to me at that point. Every time I saw him or talked to him I got happy because I knew I had a secret weapon right under his nose, and he was none the wiser. I couldn't wait to catch him in the middle of his shit. The minute that these idiots led us to Devon, I was going to know all I needed to know, and if Goody was behind it like I knew he was, he was dead.

I constantly questioned myself as to if I would have the guts to pull the trigger. After all, he was my godfather, but why murder? I thought of a thousand different ways of handling it. Either way, I knew I was so close to finding out the truth. But what I was going to do with it once I found out was what was troubling me. Could I really kill my own godfather? Even though this man had a large help in raising me, in a sense, it was like I didn't know him; especially keeping this big of a secret. Why say he loved me like I was one of his own and kill my daddy? That question haunted me every day.

"Something's going on," Chris said, interrupting my thoughts.

I looked over to see the one Chris said was called Cisco on his phone and rushing to throw stuff in the trash.

"Looks like they're on the move."

"Cool," I said. "'Cause I'm getting bored sitting here."

"You talk to your boy?" he asked.

"Nope and don't want to," I sneered. "You found Nikki?"

"Nah," he answered.

"Seems like this hoe just up and disappeared," I said.

I was still furious that she had taken my money from me. To me, that was the lowest shit she could have ever done. It means that she didn't give a fuck about me at all, especially after everything that I've done for her. I had gone to the bank a few days ago and saw that there was $10,000 more in my account, and I knew Black's ass had something to do with it.

Nikki's ass didn't have that kind of paper, otherwise, she wouldn't have taken my shit, but he saving her ass. But she was Black's problem now.

I wasn't going to get Black his money back either. I'm sure he did it to try to get me back but that damn sure wasn't happening. Shit, it's the least that he could do after all the pain he's caused. He owes me that much. He may not realize it now, but his money wasn't going to be the same without me. I helped his hustle grow and was having his money doubled. Couldn't nobody handle half the stuff I could and stay under the radar. Don't get me wrong, his boys worked for their money and everything, but their mindset was on the then and now. They were doing all the street hustling. I always thought about the future and was behind the scenes. I always made sure to set his money up to make more money. That's what my father did. And I am my daddy's girl. But I damn sure wouldn't be doing that shit no more for him.

The downside was with me not working with Black, I wasn't going to be able to just relax anymore. My ass was going to have to get a job or something. Black had paid for my tuition for school so that I wouldn't have to worry about taking out student loans and everything, but I was going to have to figure out what to do at that point because, once the semester was over, I was on my own. I didn't want to drop out because I know how important it was for my father for me to get my education, plus I was doing really good in school. Even despite all of this with Black, I was still making A's and B's. But now I have to make sure that I could provide for myself.

For the first time, I was really on my own. Going straight from the foster home to Black taking care of everything, I never really took care of things myself. I always tried to, and with Black, I would tell him that I could do it, but he always did everything because he said he didn't want me to have to worry. I had money saved up, a little over fifty thousand, but considering that my rent was damn near $800 a month, and I had to get a new car now because my car was totaled, and I know had school to add to the list of worries. Not to mention that the guy that I killed in the car accident family was suing me.

Officers had come to question me a few days after I'd gotten home, and I told them that I didn't see the truck, which I technically didn't. But the police didn't have enough to charge me with anything, so naturally, the family was upset. No sooner had he been buried then I was served with papers saying that I was being sued for wrongful death. I had hired an attorney because I knew that a situation like this could get very bad and quick. I just prayed that my name would stay out of the papers. I was always a bit jittery and nervous about social services seeing my name in the papers and connecting me to Patricia, but it's been over a year and so far nothing. My attorney had told me to prepare for the worst because I was lucky enough to not be charged. But there was no way I was going to walk away from this without paying some type of restitution. So I had to get money and fast. Otherwise, my entire savings could be wiped out.

After I was served, I remember wanting to kill Black. I blamed him for everything. If he had never fucked Nikki, none of this would be happening.

I snapped out of my thoughts to notice that we were going through a very familiar neighborhood.

"I know where we are," I said, looking around at the familiar surroundings.

"Okay?" Chris said.

"My dad and Goody used to own a restaurant and nightclub out here a few years back," I told him. "We used to come to this neighborhood all the time. I would hang out and go shopping while they handled business."

"Oh okay," he listened.

"You know what? I got a feeling that I know where they're going," I told him remembering where the restaurant was. "Turn right down this next street." I watched as their car kept straight and Chris followed my instructions. "Park over here," I said, instructing him to park in the alley a few blocks down.

I had him take the shortcut and park away from the restaurant. Something told me that's where they were going. I got out the car, and of course, Chris followed. I ran to the building across the street from the old restaurant. I looked to see if there was a way to get in and found an old ladder which was even better. We climbed the ladder and crawled on the roof lying flat so that we could watch what was going on across the street without being seen.

"Let me find out you like a low-key Navy SEAL or some shit like that," he teased.

I looked at him with a smirk.

"I told you, I know this place. My dad used to bring me here all the time when him and Goody would be handling business. But what I'm wondering is why they're here. The only way they could have known about this place is Goody," I told him.

We weren't there for too long before we saw the car pull up and Cisco and J.D. got out. They stood outside for several minutes smoking a blunt, and I wondered what I was missing.

"Okay, so what the hell are they stopping here for?" I asked.

"I don't know," he shrugged watching intently.

But my question was soon answered. A few seconds later this black Honda Accord pulled up, and some heavyset, light-skinned nigga got out. He looked around to see if anybody was watching and approached the other two.

"Damn, I wish I could hear what they were saying," I whispered.

They were carrying on a conversation and I saw one of them return to his pockets to hand him an envelope. If this was Devon, he was not what I expected. He looked completely shook. I could practically see him shaking like a bitch from up here. I know they saw it. One of them touched him, and he jumped. What the hell had him so nervous? This couldn't have been the man that shot and killed my father. How?

I scooted more towards the edge so that I could try to hear.

"Look, man, I got to do it." I heard him saying. "Shit is getting too heavy, man. Everybody asking questions and shit."

"What you mean questions?" J.D. asked.

"Nigga, did I stutter? People asking about me!" he said. "So your boy's squad ain't as tight as he thinks it is."

Chris and I looked at each other and I felt a little nervous.

"Is that him?" I asked in a whisper.

He nodded his head.

"That's Devon? For sure?" I pressed.

He rolled his eyes and gave me a look as if to say "bitch shut the fuck up".

"Just listen, hell."

Something wasn't adding up to me about this Devon nigga. If he knew people were asking questions about him, then that means somebody was running their mouth. I just hoped that it didn't get back to Goody before we could get the answers that we needed.

“Look, D man, you wrapped too tight right now. Just chill the hell out,” Cisco snapped.

I noticed that Cisco was the more vocal one and seemed to be the one in charge. Devon kept backing away from him, but Cisco was staying on him.

“You just being fucking paranoid. You need to go home, you need to chill out, and you just need to relax. I’m tryna tell you,” Cisco warned.

“I know what the hell I need to do, and that is to get the hell out of here before the questions turn into something else. Dawg, I don’t need this kind of shit,” he ranted. “Goody said this shit would go off without a hitch. I didn't even want to fucking kill him. Your boy is the one that said that we were all going to come out paid. I sat there and waited on his ass for damn near a year while he was in jail.”

“The nigga had to get locked up. Otherwise, it was going to make it look like it was a setup,” Cisco said, lighting another blunt and taking a long drag of it. “But you run around here, shaking like a bitch ain't gone change shit either. You just drawing attention to yourself and us muthafucka!”

“Who you callin’ a bitch?” Devon asked, getting mad.

“Aye, partna, you squaring up at the wrong one. I'm just trying to tell you what it is,” Cisco said. “Now, boss, said we had to wait for shit to die down. What would it look like that this nigga dead, then all of a sudden everybody ballin’? You wasn’t complaining when you got your half up front after the damn job was done. Now that’s how shit gotta be done.”

“I don't give a fuck about all of that!” Devon snapped. “Bruh, you not the one fuckin ducking and dodging and living in hiding and shit. I fucking did that shit over a year ago, and I’m just supposed to twiddle my thumbs waiting on this nigga?” That was what I needed to hear. He really did kill my daddy. “Fuck that shit, man. Y’all act like this nigga is God or something! I coulda taken my ass to the cops a long time ago, but he stalling me out? Man, fuck Goody!"

Devon pulled his gun, but Cisco was quicker. Two shots rang out and blood poured from Devon's chest. I screamed before I realized they didn't know that we were up there, but it was too late. Both Cisco and J.D. looked up to see us on the roof.

"Shit!" Chris said, knowing what was about to happen. "Come on we got to get out of here!"

He grabbed me and we ran and I prayed to God the entire time that we didn't get shot. J.D. and Cisco started shooting up at us and we were running hard as hell. We hurried down the ladder and ran towards the alley where the car was parked. I knew they probably ran towards the door of the building and didn't think to go around back so that bought us a little bit of time, but not much.

We jumped in the car, and peeled out of there so fast! But not fast enough because a bullet shattered the back of the windshield. Chris drove faster, but I already knew it didn't matter. They knew who we were.

"Damn it!" I screamed. "What are we going to do?"

"Be quiet. Just… just let me think for a second," he rushed.

"These niggas know who we are! They saw us!" I told him.

"I know!" he yelled, driving and trying to shake the two. "Shit! And by now Goody knows. Which means ain't no point in going back to the crib 'cause he gonna have niggas waiting by the time we get there."

He was right. And I knew my spot would have niggas lurking, too.

"Alright, we gone have to ditch this car or something," I told him. "Because riding in this thing, we are a damn moving target."

"And go where? That nigga gonna have everybody in the hood watching for our asses!"

My mind was racing trying to think of a plan.

"Alright so, we ditch the car somewhere far, and take the train, hideout for a bit. Then go get a rental car or something. But we need to get the fuck away from this car now. We gotta hideout somewhere where he can't find us," I rattled off.

"Alright cool," he agreed. We drove in silence for a few minutes as he sped on 635. "I think we lost them," he said, looking in the rearview mirror. "Maybe they didn't see our faces."

"Chris, it don't matter! Your car is not some fucking average ass car. You the one that decided to get this damn El Dorado!"

Chris' car was a damn black and red '89 El Dorado with unbelievably big ass rims. I should have thought about that shit when we left, considering the car was an attention getter, but I didn't. Hell, I don't even know how the hell we went undetected all of this time. They probably spotted our asses a long time ago.

"Alright, so this is what we going to do," he spoke. "We take the car out to Plano, get rid of it, and catch the red line. Arlington is probably gonna be our safest bet right now for a place to chill for a bit."

"I guess," I said. "I can't believe this shit is happening," I sniffed not even realizing that I was crying. "Chris, it wasn't supposed to go down like this, man."

“Just try to calm down. Once we get to a spot, we can sit down and think of the best plan,” he suggested.

“We don't have much time!” I stressed. “By now, they're probably going to tell Goody, if they haven’t told him already, which means that he knows that you and me know each other and that you ain’t really got his back. Even if they didn't see us, they saw your car. And I’m sorry but ain't that many niggas that drive a fuckin’ ‘89 El Dorados with big ass rims!”

“I know,” he nodded. “But look, yelling at me ain’t gonna change shit or make shit happen. We got to think smart.”

“No, right now, we got to stay alive!” I said.

My heart was racing and beating so fast I thought it was going burst out of my chest. What the hell was I going to do? I couldn't just go home. Goody would damn sure have people at my apartment. And we damn sure couldn't go to Chris' spot, because since they saw his car that would have been one of the first places that they went.

I was shaking I was so scared. We hurried to Plano and ditched the car like he said. It took us almost three hours, but we finally got to Arlington and checked into a hotel. Of course, we made sure that no one was able to get access to the room and made sure no one could disturb us.

Once we got settled, I sat down on the bed and tried to calm my nerves. But I couldn't. Everything had fallen apart in a matter of minutes. I actually got shot at. Chris tried to call me down, but I couldn't stop shaking. I was losing it.

“Chris, what are we going to do?” I sniffed.

“I don't know,” he admitted. “But I need you to relax for me for a minute, okay? You shaking real bad, and you making a nigga nervous.”

“I'm sorry,” I apologized. “I'm just kind of blown right now. Like we are fucked.”

Chris grabbed me tight and held me while I cried. And I mean I balled hard. Like a baby getting his bottle taken away hard. But he wouldn’t let me go.

“No, we are not,” he soothed. “Just breathe and try to calm down.”

“Calm down?” I sniffed. “We're in a fuckin’ hotel, you had to ditch your car, we were shot at, neither one of us has any clothes, we don’t know how much longer we got before they find us, we can’t go home. This is just all messed up.”

“Miracle, I was right there with you,” he reminded me. “Don't you think I know that? But you freaking out right now and this is when I need you to be on your game. Right now we gotta be on point.”

“We have to go to the cops,” I blurted out.

“And tell them what?” he asked, letting go of my hand and looking at me as if I was deranged. “What that we saw two random ass niggas shoot and kill somebody? Two niggas who, if they get caught, will either take me down with them or have every fuckin’ savage nigga in Dallas tryna kill me. And you! Besides, Goody wasn’t even there. So we can’t place him to anything. And Cisco ass ain’t gone roll on Goody.” He stopped talking and grabbed my hand again and looked me in my eyes. “If you call the cops, you might as well kill your damn self. And you know I'm right.”

“I know,” I sighed. “But, Chris, I'm scared as hell. He's gonna find us eventually. Then what? What are we going to do? What are we going to say to him? What excuse could we possibly have as to why the hell we were on the roof of a building watching Cisco and J.D. kill the man that pulled the trigger on my father? Huh?”

“Miracle, I’m just saying that we can’t go to no cops and not be able to explain the shit. If we say we saw that shit go down, we are dead,” Chris pressed.

“Okay, so we get some evidence or something,” I suggested.

“I don't think that's going to work,” he said. “Think about it. You get cops involved and then you got them looking at all of us. I've been doing dirt with this nigga. If we get the cops involved, then I'm going down, too.”

He was right. There was no way that we could go to the cops. If we did, Chris, Black, and everybody would be locked up. Although Black’s ass being in prison was something that I wasn't mad at. But I had bigger fish to fry.

“So then what can we do?” I pushed. “Because we gotta do something.”

“That, right now, I don't know,” he admitted. “We just need to chill and lay low for a couple days and see what happens.”

“Okay,” I caved.

I damn sure wasn't liking the idea of just sitting tight. It was too much.

“I need to get some clothes,” I said. I looked down and saw that I was bleeding from when I fell.

“Well, I saw a Walmart a couple of blocks down. I can walk over there and get us some stuff.”

I guess he saw the worry on my face because he rubbed my back and patted my leg.

“Don’t worry, I will be straight.”

“Okay,” I said.

"Don't worry, I will be back before you know it. It ain't like they followed us all the way here. If they did trust me we'd be dead by now. So I'm gonna run over there get some stuff, and we'll be good," he promised.

"Okay," I nodded. "You got cash on you?" I asked him.

"Yeah. I got a couple bands on me," he told me. "But eventually I'ma have to get to my stash and my key, if they ain't got it already,"

I had a feeling that I'd be using my savings to get us up out of here 'cause I know there ain't no way in hell my black ass was going back to his house.

"Okay. Just please be careful," I said.

"I got you," he promised. "Lock the door. Put the chain on. I'll knock twice when I get back, so you'll know it's me."

"Okay."

I watched him walk out the door and locked it behind him like he said. I sat down on the bed and dropped my head into my hands. We had gotten our asses into a big ass mess. I just didn't understand how it went bad so fast. I didn't know he was going to pull a gun. And now, I would never know why the hell Goody wanted my father dead because the man that killed my dad was now dead.

I had been sitting and thinking about everything for damn near an hour when my phone started beeping with notifications taking me out of my thoughts, and I damn near jumped off the bed. I had forgotten that I had it in my back pocket. I looked at the home screen and saw it was my Facebook messenger. I saw Black messaged and opted to ignore him, but they kept coming. My curiosity getting the better of me, I picked it up.

***Trevon:* Yo, you need to hit me now! Are you okay? Why the hell is your apartment trashed? Where you at? Call me now!**

Shit! Goody had already gotten to my fuckin' apartment. Why the hell did they trash my shit? That means if I even thought about going back to my apartment, it was a wrap. Even though I changed my phone number, and deleted his phone number from my phone, I still knew his number by heart. I called him to see what he knew. The minute that the phone rang he answered.

"Where you at? Are you okay?" he rattled off.

"I'm good," I answered not really pleased to be talking to him. "What's going on? What are you talking about my apartment was trashed?"

"I rode by your spot to come and talk to you and the door was wide open. I walked in the joint, and it was shit everywhere. What the fuck is going on?" he said.

"It's a whole lot of shit that's done popped off," I told him. "I can't really get into everything right now."

"What the hell does that mean? Miracle, where are you? Your neighbors talking about some niggas broke in your shit. What the hell did you do? Was it a deal that went bad or something? I mean what you get caught up what? Just let me know," he rambled.

"Look can you please stop yelling?" I sighed. "I done had enough shit happen tonight. I don't really need the attitude right now."

"I ain't got no attitude, babe," he quickly tried to correct. "I'm just trying to make sure you okay."

"Well, physically I'm fine," I told him. "It's just really been a fucked up day."

"Okay, what's going on? Tell me."

"I can't do it over the phone," I said.

"Okay, well where are you at?" he prodded.

I heard a quick two knocks at the door and knew that it was Chris.

"I'll call you back," I said, hanging up.

I tossed the phone down on the bed and rushed to the door to open it. Chris came in carrying several bags, containing clothes and food.

"I figured we'd be here a couple of days, so we might need other stuff," he told me.

I helped him bring everything in, and went through the bags.

"You brought me hair dye?" I asked confused.

"I mean I figured you might want to go rogue or something like they do in the movies," he joked.

"Not the right time," I said. "Did you see anybody watching you or following you or anything?" I questioned. "You were gone for a while."

"Nah. I was in and out. It just took awhile 'cause I had to walk with all these bags after waiting in line for like thirty minutes," he huffed. "Besides, you know them damn Walmarts only have like three lanes open and the stores be packed. Plus, ain't no niggas out here like that and the only folks watching, was watching me."

It was true. We were in a predominantly white neighborhood so if any hood niggas rolled through here, it would be very easy to spot. That put my mind at ease a little. Maybe I was overreacting.

"But we got a problem," I said.

"What?" he inquired.

"I just talked to Black. He said that my apartment was trashed. And apparently, the neighbors said that two niggas ran up in there and trashed the place." I updated him. "I'm pretty sure it's probably crawling with cops."

"Yeah," he nodded. "More than likely. Wait, how did that nigga know?" he asked.

"He said he came by to talk to me, and when he got there, the door was wide open or some mess. He couldn't call me 'cause I changed my number so he messaged me on Facebook and I called him," I told him.

"Oh," he said.

It was a strange look on his face, and I couldn't help but push it.

"What's the matter?" I asked.

"Just don't understand why you still dealing with this fuck nigga," he spat.

"Well, damn, tell me how you really feel," I mumbled.

"Man, look, you gone do what you wanna do at the end of the day, but shit, I wouldn't never do no shit like that to somebody I love and that's held me down."

I didn't know where this was coming from. I knew Chris had some type of feelings there, but the way he was acting, it almost seemed like he was jealous.

"Chris, why are you acting like this?" I asked.

"Just forget it," he answered. "Never mind."

"No," I disagreed. "Obviously, you got something that you wanna say so, out with it."

I wanted to know what the hell was wrong with him.

"I'm just saying. I don't know any nigga that's gonna fuck around on they girl and do some foul shit like that. And you still talking to this nigga calling him and shit," he explained.

"Yes because he saw what happened!" I stressed. "But it's not like I'm tryna fuck with this nigga."

"Yea okay," he mumbled.

"Seriously, Chris, what the hell is eating at you? You really trippin' right now."

"Because you wasting your time worrying about some nigga that ain't shit. Like what the fuck you call him for? Real talk I'm here with you now. Not that nigga."

I didn't know what to think. He was so amped, and I was in utter shock. I knew he had feelings, but I thought we had squashed that when we talked. I mean hell it had been over a year since we had kissed. I wanted to say something, but I wasn't even sure where to start. Now, this was something else that was gonna be on my brain.

"Look, I'm about to hit the shower. I saw your leg was bleeding, so I bought some peroxide and some Band-Aids. They in the bag," he added.

"Thanks," I said blankly.

"No problem."

He took off his hoodie and pulled his shirt off. Damn! This nigga's body was perfection. How the hell did his body get like that in a fuckin' year? My ass wasn't gonna be able to focus on tryna get out of this mess, looking at him like that for the next couple of days. But shit, I couldn't help but to stare. My body woke the hell up and quick. My pussy was practically screaming and I was trying my damn best to calm her down.

"Will you hurry up and get your ass in the bathroom?" I rushed him.

He turned around and smirked.

"It's cool. I know you like what you see," he teased.

"Man, whatever. I'm just trying to take a shower and you stink," I mumbled.

"Yea okay."

He walked into the bathroom and closed the door, and I sighed a sigh of relief. Thank God we had separate beds. I went rummaging through the bags to occupy my time. With everything he bought, it looked like we weren't going to be leaving the room for a couple of days at least. I just needed to focus, but my mind kept wandering back to that conversation and his fuckin' body. He better keep his ass dressed 'cause otherwise I was in trouble.

The shower turned on and I picked up my phone to call Myesha. I doubt that Goody would go after her, especially since she was at school, and he never really had much to say about her, but I had to be on the safe side and just warn her to be safe. Her phone went straight to voicemail, and I left her a message.

"Hey, I need you to call me back when you get this. It's important."

I hung up and contemplated calling Black back. I decided against it because of how Chris reacted. To him, I guess I was leaning on Black to fix everything, and that's not what I was trying to do. I didn't want him to feel like I wasn't appreciative of everything that he had done for me because Chris really had my back these last few weeks with everything. But now I'm wondering, was he doing everything to get closer to me or because of his feelings for me?

I had never even thought about him in that way other than that one situation, but I shut it down because my heart belonged to Black. Maybe that's why he hated Black so much because of the fact that I wasn't looking at him like I did Black.

But I never thought about it because, hell, he was my foster brother at one point, and I just always looked at him in that way. But did he?

The more I thought about it, Chris was really there for me. He was putting his ass on the line to help me when he didn't have to. I had to let him know that I appreciated that and that I had his back too. I just didn't know if I could cross that line with him.

"This shit is just too much for one day," I said to myself.

As much as I knew he would be there for me, I knew we had to get help from someone. It wasn't like we could hide in here forever. And now that Black knew what was going on somewhat, as much as I hated him, we were going to need his help. I felt like I was asking Satan for his help by going to Black, but we were in a corner and it wasn't much we could do.

I went through the bags and found a pair of pajamas that I was assuming were but for me. It was basically an oversized Minnie Mouse shirt, but I was grateful. I waited for Chris to hurry up so I could wash my own ass. I was tired, hungry, and I felt like I had walked all over Dallas.

Chris walked out of the bathroom with his towel wrapped around his waist, and I knew he was starting to do that shit on purpose. Why the hell was my body reacting like this? All the time that I had been around him before and I never even thought about like this.

"Nigga, you ain't slick," I smirked.

"What?" he asked, grabbing some lotion. "I left my shit out here."

"Whatever," I grunted, brushing past him in a hurry before he could notice my flushed face.

I got in the shower and let the hot water hit my body. It was so relaxing and well needed. I swear I'd had the most stressful life any eighteen-year-old has ever known. I had two months before my nineteenth birthday, and I had experienced damn near everything and then some. I thought about how simple life was when my father was alive. I missed that. I didn't have a care in the world.

I wanted to wake up from this never-ending nightmare. I wish I had never started asking questions. They say curiosity killed the cat, well my black ass damn sure almost got killed tonight.

The door opened and I jumped.

“Calm down, it's just me,” he said.

I glared at him from behind the shower curtain.

“Nigga, you know my nerves is shot! What?” I snapped.

“My bad. I didn’t even think about that,” he apologized. “I was just trying to see if you wanted me to heat up one of the little microwave pizza things.”

“Oh,” I said “Yeah that's fine. ‘Preciate it.”

He closed the door, and I hurried up to finish my shower. What if he had opened that door when my ass was getting out? Awkward…

I grabbed my towel and dried off, and threw on my oversized shirt. I smirked at the big as granny draws that he got me. But I had to be grateful. I tied my hair up and walked out to find him sitting on my bed.

“Excuse you, your bed is over there thanks,” I said, pointing towards it.

“Damn, my bad.”

He got up and walked to his bed. I was trying not to stare, but he was making it really difficult walking around in a wife beater and some basketball shorts. His calves were amazing and his muscles literally came from nowhere. I'm wondering if this nigga did nothing but lift when he wasn't grinding. And you could see his abs through the shirt.

See this is how white folks get killed in the fucking movies. They running for their life and end up fuckin' at some random ass spot at the wrong time and get killed. I had to keep my mind focused on any and everything but him.

I climbed into bed and started eating my pizza, and we both sat in silence.

"So, what do you think about leaving Texas?" he asked after several minutes of us munching and looking at some random television show.

"I hadn't really thought about it honestly," I admitted. "At this point, it's either leave or stick around and wait to see what happens," I said. "And I mean, honestly, leaving might not be a bad idea. It's not like we really got much here anyways."

"That's facts," he agreed. "Only thing really, keeping me here is you and Nikki…"

He paused, seeing the frown on my face.

"Yeah I know," I said.

"You think maybe we should call her?" he questioned.

"And by we, you mean you?" I corrected. "I don't know. I mean don't get me wrong, I can't stand her ass right now, but I mean I don't want nothing to happen to her either; especially now that she's pregnant with his baby."

Shows how much of a caring person I was. Despite all the shit that both of them had done to me, I actually gave a damn about her still.

“Chris, do you think I’m a bad person? I mean like…really?”

He came over and flopped down next to me.

“No,” he answered. “That just means that you not like these other broads out here. You actually give a damn about people. It's not a bad thing, Miracle. It just means that you human. It means that you have a kind heart. It means you're a good person.”

I was trying not to look him in his eyes because I knew my ass was having them crazy thoughts about him.

“I have never heard you talk like that,” I said.

“I never had the opportunity to until today,” he said.

Before I knew it, he grabbed me up and placed his lips on mine and I swear it was like one of those kissing scenes out of those romance movies. That nigga was tonguing me down so good I forgot where I was. It took me a few minutes before I could get myself together and I pulled away.

“Chris, wait,” I murmured.

“Come on, Miracle,” he said. “You know I been feeling you for a minute. I know it sounds fucked up, but being alone with you like this got me seeing what I been missing all this time.”

I was so flustered. Was this really happening?

“I mean…I don’t know, Chris. I didn’t know it was this deep. I thought…I thought when you kissed me before it was just that moment. I didn’t know. Like, where did this come from?” I asked, sliding away from him

I needed to be able to think clearly, and I wasn’t going to be able to do that with him right there under me.

“Miracle, I’ve been feeling you since you came to Ms. P’s,” he confessed. “I didn’t wanna let it be known like that because I knew Whitney would torment you more than she already did, and so I kept it chill. But, yo, you was bad as hell then and now."

Hearing that, I couldn't help but to smile a little. I never thought he paid me any attention like that.

"I never thought you felt that way."

"I couldn't let her hurt you, so I had to be cool," he told me. "But you deserve somebody that's gonna really be there for you. Now I ain't throwing salt in that nigga, Black's, game but he don't know you like I do. And I ain't saying you gotta just jump into it or no shit like that, but I ain't gonna just keep ignoring this either. You the type of chick that holds her man down and you showed me that from day one when you covered for me when I left."

I was shocked. There was so much and I didn't know what to say.

"Chris…"

I looked at him and it was over. He scooped me up completely off the bed, placed me in his lap, and kissed me hard. I moaned and relaxed and felt the bulge in between his legs growing as his hands ran over my ass and up my sleep shirt.

And I got these big ass draws on.

But I guess that didn't matter because he slid his hand inside of my panties and I felt him massaging my pussy with his fingers.

"Sssss…" I hissed as he continued to cover my lips with his.

I finally broke free and tilted my head back feeling the pleasure.

"Look at me," he whispered.

I held my head back down as his fingers worked their magic and looked at him as he instructed. He dug deeper and I felt the familiar sensation. I got ready to close my eyes, but he tugged at my hair catching me completely off guard and stared intently at me.

"Uh uh. Keep them open. Look at me," he ordered.

The shit was feeling so good, that I was whimpering.

"Chris, please," I whispered.

He continued to tease my clit with his fingers and began to speed up making my body get hot all over. I knew I was about to cum and so did he.

"You better keep them eyes open," he warned. "Let it out."

"I'm cummin," I moaned.

He kept going and I began to move in a circular motion until I felt the cum seeping my panties and a large grin formed on his face. He grabbed me again and we tongue wrestled until we both had to come up for air. He stood up with me gripping him and laid me down on the bed. I tried to snatch his clothes off, but he stopped me.

"Uh uh," he said, stepping back. "Not yet. I want to take my time. I want to really please that pussy when you ready."

What the fuck? Who the fuck he just gonna finger fuck me like that and then stop? What the hell?

"I am ready!" I damn near screamed.

He smiled and leaned to kiss me again.

"Not yet. I want to take you when you know you are ready to be mine."

He sat back down on his bed, and I tried to collect myself because my nut was all in my panties and my face was on the floor.

This was a bizarre fucking day. All of this going on and now, Chris confesses how he feels for me, makes me nut, and then decides he doesn't want to fuck. I got up and went to the bathroom and cleaned myself up. I took a few minutes to get my thoughts together. I was going to go out there and just act like nothing happened.

I walked out of the bathroom and got back in the bed and grabbed my now cold pizza.

"So where would we go?" I asked, smacking.

"I don't know," he answered. "But the further we get out of Texas, the better. Maybe we can go to Atlanta, you know it's easy to blend there. It's so many black folks there, hell he wouldn't know where to look."

"True," I considered. "Maybe Louisiana?"

"Nah too close," he disagreed. "Like we need to get the hell out of this area altogether."

"Okay, so what about Florida?" I asked.

I could see him contemplating it.

"That could work," he said. "Miami is lit."

"I probably wouldn't suggest Miami if we doing Florida. Definitely don't want to go to the city that's known for drug lords and we tryna get away from one," I explained. "If we go to Florida, it needs to be in a town where there ain't nothing but snowbirds."

"What the hell is a snowbird?" he asked, looking confused.

"You know where the old people go to retire. Towns where it's mostly elderly?" I told him. "The less attention we draw to ourselves the better. I mean I'm not saying we got to live in a retirement village and nothing, but that might make stuff easier. We can go legit, get regular jobs. I could keep going to school. I mean, I got enough stashed away. And, worst case scenario, I'll just take out student loans or something."

He nodded his head. I could tell he was getting with the program.

"If I can get to the stash at my crib, we'd be set," he said to me.

"Chris, no!" I argued. "That is gonna be entirely too risky. You see these niggas fuckin' tore my shit up within an hour of us leaving. So I know they got people watching yours if they ain't trashed it, too," I said. "Hell, they could've found the stash."

"Doubtful," he said. "I hid that shit well. Plus, there's a key to my deposit box that's got most of my paper in it."

"You got a safety deposit box?" I asked surprised.

He laughed when he saw how shocked I was.

"Thugs can have bank accounts, too."

I laughed at his joke.

"My bad."

"You good," he assured me. "But we gonna have to figure out something. I mean it seems like a lot, but you think about all the stuff we gone have to do."

"Yeah," I said. "But I'd much rather we tough it out then you try to go get your shit and something happens."

"I got you, but we gonna need it if we gonna get away," he told me. "I'll hold off for now, but I ain't leaving without it. But as far as everything else, let's start making plans. Tomorrow, we'll start looking for apartments online or whatever. And I can find a cheap car real quick."

“Okay.” I agreed happy that he wasn’t going to do anything stupid. “Most of it I can do from my phone. I’ll get up first thing and start looking,” I said. “Oh shit. I don't even got a charger.”

“It's one in the bag,” he said.

“Look at you,” I said in awe jumping up out the bed to retrieve it. “Thank you.”

“Yeah, I figured you’d need it. It's not like we both had a chance to really grab anything.”

I grabbed the charger out of the bag so that I could charge my phone.

“Tomorrow I'll start looking online for some cheap spots,” I informed him.

“Aight, cool.”

“Alright I'ma try to get some sleep,” I yawned as I climbed back in the bed.

I was more tired than I thought because the minute I laid down my body went into shut down mode and I fell asleep with thoughts of wanting to feel Chris’ body pressed against mine.

*****

Chapter Nineteen

I jumped out of my sleep, trying to catch my breath. I had been having the worst nightmare. Chris and I were back on the roof across from the restaurant and Cisco and J.D. were shooting at us. We were running just like we had that night only we ran to the car and my father was seating in the passenger seat and Goody was sitting in the driver's seat. When we ran up, Goody pulled the trigger and my father began to spew blood. We tried to turn to run, but at that point, Cisco and J.D. were behind us and started shooting. Chris jumped in front of me and his body was riddled with bullets. I tried to save him, but he was slipping from me. The next thing I know I woke up with my trying to breathe. I started crying because it just seemed so real and so scary. Was this a premonition of what was to come? I had to make sure nothing happened to Chris. He may not like me calling on Black for help, but if it meant keeping him alive, he would have to just deal with it.

I looked at the clock to see that it was four o'clock in the morning, and I looked over to hear Chris snoring. This nigga sounded like he was sucking down the ceiling. There was no way in hell I was going to be able to go back to sleep.

I got up and went into the bathroom not wanting to wake Chris up with my sobs. I wished I could just lay down, go to sleep, and start this day over. I would do things so differently. I was petrified. I cried and prayed, wondering if God still heard me. There was a light tap at the door and Chris opened it, rubbing his eyes.

"What's the matter? Why you crying?" he asked.

I tried to hold it together but once again my emotional ass broke.

"I had this bad dream, Chris. Goody shot daddy in your car…and….we were running from them two fools and then…"

He pulled me up and hugged me tightly.

"I'm good. I'm here, aight?" he said, trying to comfort me.

"They shot you, Chris!" I cried into his chest. "They shot you in front of me and you died. And I don't want nothing to happen to you."

He let me cry and walked me to the sink to put cold water on my face.

"Chill with the tears," he said. "Ain't nothing gonna happen to me. It was just some crazy ass dream. It was probably cause of that pizza you ate," he joked, trying to make me laugh.

I gave him a half smile as he wiped my tears.

"Come on, let's get you back in the bed."

I walked back over to my bed and climbed in and Chris lay next to me on top of the covers. He picked up the remote, turned on the TV, and started flipping through the channels trying to find something to watch. It wasn't anything to watch on the few channels that the hotel did provide, so I just grabbed my phone to play Candy Crush while he stared at the screen. I was so busy playing that I didn't even notice the notifications on my phone.

I stopped playing and looked through my text messages. Black had messaged me a few times, but so far nothing from Goody. A message from a five digit number was also there, and when I opened it, it was a picture of Nikki sitting at a Checkers eating with some of her little friends. Whoever took the photo, must have been far away enough that she didn't see them. I knew that was Goody sending me a message.

"Shit! Chris, look."

He turned his attention from the TV to me, and I showed him my screen.

"Goody sent me a picture of Nikki."

I watched as he stared at it.

"She looks okay," he mumbled.

"Yeah, but what if they got her by now? What if she's hurt or something? I mean I know I was mad at everything, but I ain't trying to have her getting caught up in this," I nagged.

He yawned and put his arm around my waist.

"Relax, girl," he said. "Look, I don't think that he's going to hurt her. I think he just did that to scare you. And right now it's working. But we got think smart. Okay? If we go to him right now, we're doing exactly what he wants us to do and we're both dead. Nikki's going to be okay. I'll hit up a couple of my boys and make sure that they keep her eye on her."

"But what if it's too late?" I pushed.

"It's not. She'll be fine," I huffed and he pulled me closer to him. "It's going to be straight. Just try to get you some sleep. I know it's hard, and I know you got all that shit running through your head even though I told you it was gonna be okay, but yo, I got you. Okay?"

"Okay." I gave in lying back and pulling the covers over me.

I thought he would have got up and gone back to his bed, but he stayed right where he was with his arm around me. I missed having someone holding me like that. I just didn't expect it to be Chris. But I felt safe for the first time since all this crazy shit started. I drifted off to sleep knowing that I had at least one person that had my back.

*

I slept some but woke up a few hours later. Chris was still lying next to me, holding me. I'm surprised he wasn't snoring. I closed my eyes to see if I could get a few more minutes to sleep, but my mind had already started racing. I tried to move, but Chris was holding me so tight I could barely move. I had to admit, it did feel good, though. Of course, I was trying to ignore the fact that his dick was basically in my ass. I tried to move a little and ended up grinding against him. He groaned and moved in his sleep, waking up.

"Sorry," I whisper. "I wasn't trying to wake you up."

"Nah, you good," he grunted. "I wasn't really sleep like that anyway."

He moved and I felt him getting hard. He could tell me all day long that he wanted to wait until I could be his only, but his dick was saying otherwise right about now. I knew that this was bad timing, but my curiosity was just getting the better of me. So I said fuck it. I started to wiggle a little bit more, giving him the hint that I wanted him to take it further. Any man that is lying next to a woman knows then when she starts wiggling and grinding on him she's trying to fuck. And it definitely didn't take him long to pick up on the hint. He continued to grind me and soon I felt his lips on the back of my neck.

"I told yo' ass that I wanted to take that pussy when you were ready to be mine," he whispered in my ear.

That shit turned me all the way on. I turned over and pulled the covers off me exposing my legs. We began kissing while he squeezed me ass. He began to massage my thighs and my pussy went from zero to one hundred! I reached my hand down to pull at the string of his shorts and he stopped me.

"Are you mine?" he asked.

"Huh?" I asked, trying to snap out of the pleasure zone he had me in.

"Are you mine?" he asked more seriously.

"I...uh…I don't know, Chris," I whispered.

I just wanted him to take me. I don't know if I could be with another savage nigga like that. Why in the hell did he have to ask me that? Why couldn't he be like most niggas and just get pussy and be good?

I leaned in to kiss him, and for a few seconds, we tongue wrestled before I tried again to pull at his shorts. He pulled my hand away and flipped me on my back, pulling my hands over my head and holding them down. He kissed me hard and began to bite at my neck. He moved his hands from holding mine and began to pull at my panties. I reached down in eagerness to help him and he slapped my hand away.

"Put your damn hands where I had them."

I did what he said and lied back as he took my panties off. He threw them to the side of the bed and began to kiss my panty line. He sat up and looked at my pussy and smiled.

"Is it mine?" he asked me.

I had no words I was so damn zoned out.

When he saw I didn't answer, he took his fingers and slowly inserted his pointer and middle finger inside of me, moving them in and out, instantly getting me wet. He laid on his stomach and took his tongue and began to trace it from the top of my lips making me shudder.

"Oh shit," I moaned. "Chris!"

He continued the motion of fingering me and flicked his tongue vigorously across my clit. This nigga was driving me crazy! I couldn't take it. He rose up and demanded me to open my eyes as I now had them shut and was grasping the sheets in my fingers. I opened my eyes and he stared at me, making me weak.

"Are you mine?" he asked again.

I opened my mouth to answer but nothing came out. Seeing that I did not respond he stopped his rhythmic massage and quickly grabbed my legs pushing them up in the air and spreading them wide while diving his tongue into my pool of wetness.

"Oh gawd!" I cried out.

He explored my entire pussy with his tongue and I felt all the heat rush through my body. He dug deeper with his tongue as he took his hands and ran them up my sleep shirt to massage my swollen titties.

"Oh!" I screamed.

I looked down to see him grinning as he continued to feast on me. He tortured my clit as he sucked on it. I arched my back feeling like my body was going to collapse. I was moaning so loud and it felt so good. If this was one of those romance novels or movies, this would be the time that the girl would let out the single tear from passion. But my ass was in here about to go into a seizure the way he was eating my pussy.

"Yes, Chris! Yes, I'm yours!" I screamed.

I don't know where my voice came from 'cause I was damn sure in shock, but he had me hollering.

"Say it again," he demanded, holding my legs back and licking me all over.

"It's....it's..."

I was trying to speak, but it was feeling so good that I couldn't. He plunged his tongue into me once more and I came so hard that I was seeing double.

"I'm yours!" I cried.

He lapped up my juices and kissed my clit as I whimpered and came down from my high.

"Good," he whispered finally coming up from my extra wet opening. "I've wanted you for so long, baby. And now that you're mine, I wanna please you like this all night and every day after."

I locked eyes with his, and it was just something there that clicked. I knew that he was sincere. Fear rose in me because I didn't want to hurt him. I didn't want to fall for another savage ass type nigga. I didn't know what I had just agreed to, but I knew that in that moment I wanted him to make me feel the pleasure I had been deprived of because of Black's cheating.

He climbed up on top of me and we continued to stare at each other and he removed his wife beater, showing me his chest.

"Are we really about to do this?" I asked.

He nodded his head and placed his lips on mine. That fast I was reminded of how good it felt kissing him.

"Sit up," he ordered.

I did as he instructed, and he raised the shirt above my head, exposing my body that was now completely naked. He smiled, and I looked at him nervously.

"You know you have the perfect body right?" he asked.

I let out a small smile and looked away. I was a little nervous considering that the only other nigga that had ever seen my body was Black and I didn't know if Chris would like it. But the way he was staring at me had me blushing.

"I would hope so seeing as how I'm laying here naked," I giggled nervously.

"I just want to look at you," he murmured, staring at my body up and down. "Miracle, ever since that day that we kissed, I know I've wanted you. I know it sounds real trife 'cause that's some shit any old nigga would say, but you are special. You not like these other broads. You…" he stopped and looked at me and sighed. “You somebody I gotta have for me.”

“Are you sure?” I asked.

“I’ve never been more sure of anything,” he said, looking at me. “I tried not to look at you as more than just family, but I can't. Chilling and everything with you since I been back had me thinking. And when your boy fucked up I ain’t gone front, a nigga got excited. I figured I had a shot. And I tried to be respectful and everything and give you space, but yo, when I get around you all that shit goes flying out my mind.”

I don’t know if I was just emotional or what but everything that he was saying had me feeling some type of way. I grabbed him and pulled him to me and kissed him giving him all of me. He placed his lips on every possible inch of me that he could get and I became weak. He was making me feel so good.

It had been a while since my body felt any type of pleasure because, even though Black and I were together, we weren’t fucking like we used to. I didn’t want him to stop. He cupped my breasts and began to massage them placing each nipple in his mouth, flicking his tongue against it.

I moaned at his touch and he kept sucking them like he was a breastfed baby.

“So beautiful,” he murmured.

He stood up and pulled off his shorts.

Damn! I don’t even know why I expected anything less from him. The dick that I was looking at was amazing. It put Black’s to shame. I know I wasn’t a dick expert or nothing like that, but Chris DEFINITELY was working with a monster. As weird as it sounds, I can see why Whitney was acting the way she was.

He climbed back on top of me and I spread my legs around him, bringing him closer to me. I traced my fingers down his chest. I tried to sit up so that I could kiss it, but he pushed me back down.

"Uh uh," he teased. "I want to enjoy every minute of this. I've been waiting forever."

"Okay," I agreed. And then I remembered. "Wait a minute." I managed to get out. "What about your girlfriend?"

"The only girlfriend that I want is you," he said.

I gave him a 'nigga I ain't stupid' look and he sat up.

"Miracle, I'm for real. I ain't that type of nigga to be out here playin' females. Me and her ain't really work like that 'cause she was mad I was always in the streets. She knew what it was when we kicked it. Besides, I was always thinking of you," he added, stroking my face.

"Chris, don't lie to me," I warned. "I done been through enough bullshit with Black's ass."

"And that's exactly why I'm being truthful to show you that not every nigga is like that dumb ass fuck nigga that lost you," he said with sincerity.

Damn. He knew how to say all the right things. How could I not believe him? He hadn't really given me any reason not to. But then again, Black had never given me a reason not to trust him either, so I was going to take that shit with a grain of salt.

He watched me with those dark eyes of his, and I nodded my head letting him know that I was okay. I wrapped my arms around him and allowed him to devour me.

His mouth found its way back to my pussy and he started to explore me like he was searching for the Black Pearl. Damn, it feels so good!

"Chris!" I moaned. "Please don't stop."

And he didn't either. He worked every inch of my pussy: clit, lips, and everything. I couldn't stop cummin' even if I wanted to. He was doing things to me that Black never had. I damn near jumped off the bed when I felt his tongue going further past my clit and into my ass. I gasped so loud that he stopped and looked at me worried.

"You okay?" he asked.

"Ye-yea," I stuttered. "I just didn't know..."

He gave me a wicked grin and spread my legs going right back to his feast going faster and faster slurping me up.

"Oh God! Chris, I think I'm about to lose it!"

"Go ahead baby," he whispered coming up for air. "Let it out. Give me every drop."

I did as he said, and my body convulsed so hard that it felt like my chest had caved in. I was panting and gasping for air. He got up and walked over to his wallet and grabbed a condom. He quickly put it on standing over me.

"Damn, Chris, I don't even know if I have the strength." I huffed, still trying to get myself together.

"Don't worry," he assured me. "I'm going to take my time. You don't have to worry about anything."

The fuck I didn't. I looked at that dick as he positioned me, and I knew I had to worry. He eased in between my legs, and my girl had to seriously adjust to the size of his girth.

"Oh shit," I groaned, wiggling underneath his body.

"Don't worry, baby, I'm going to go slow, okay?" he promised.

"Okay," I whimpered, trying to adjust as he continued to push his way in.

“Just let me know if I'm hurting you,” he requested.

“I'm fine,” I assured him.

He began to stroke and move slow and easy. My pussy was grasping him so tight.

“Damn you feel so good,” he whispered in my ear and kissed me on my neck. “You are so perfect.” He kept going slowly, quickening his pace. “Miracle,” he whispered.

Hearing him moan like that only made me want it more. Matching my rhythm to his, and squeezing my lips around his massive dick I was torturing him to cum.

“I know what you're trying to do,” he said, smiling looking down at me. “But you can't beat me.”

I took that as a personal challenge and begin to grind harder. I may be new to the sex game, but my pussy was tight and right and would have him in shut down mode. Before we both knew it, we were going heavy, and I was screaming from pleasure. At that moment, I felt like my soul had left my body and was floating around the room watching us. That's how good the shit was.

“Shit, I'm about to cum,” he growled.

“Me too, baby,” I said. “I’m cummin’ again.”

Hell, that had to be like the tenth time that I came. Chris's dick game made Black look like an amateur. I felt that tingling feeling again, and dug my nails into his back.

“Nah, I ain't cummin yet,” he laughed. “I lied. I gotta make that pussy come one more time,” he smiled as he pounded me harder.

This nigga was fucking me like he was the Bionic Man or something. I don’t know if he had a Red Bull or what, but damn! The sounds of his balls slapping against my ass and his dick going in and out of me made me go crazy. Within seconds, I exploded and squirted all over him and the sheets. He growled and gripped my shoulders and I knew he was cummin' too.

"Fuck!" he moaned out loud. His body tensed up, and I smiled, feeling his body shake. "Damn," he whispered.

He got up from on top of me and stood up to go to the bathroom. I heard the faucet turn on and he grabbed a towel, wetting it with warm water and walked back to me.

"Open your legs," he instructed and I obliged.

He wiped in between my legs, paying special attention to my lips and wiping them slowly, sending me into aftershock and of course I shuddered.

"Thank you," I said.

"You good," he nodded. "I figured I'd do it since you'd probably be numb anyway," he joked. "You looking a little tired."

"Whatever," I said, rolling my eyes.

He walked back over to the sink and cleaned himself up.

"We might as well just stay awake now," I laughed looking at the clock and seeing that it was close to eight in the morning.

"Yea," he answered with a wicked grin, climbing back in the bed and pulling me to him.

Clearly, sleep was the furthest thing from his mind. My ass was drained and felt like I had ran a marathon, but this nigga was just getting started. His dick game was unbelievable! But I wasn't complaining. I had fallen for another savage. Damn.

*****

Chapter Twenty

I woke up and the room was empty. I was lying in the middle of the bed, trying to remember the events that had taken place. Looking around the room, everything came flooding back that Chris and I had run for our lives the night before. I also remembered that Chris had worn my pussy out and caused me to sleep until almost three o'clock in the afternoon. But considering that we didn't go to sleep until almost eleven, I was fine. That just means he got some good dick to put me in a coma.

I sat up and pushed my hair out my face. I felt hungover and knew I hadn't drunk anything. I thought about everything that happened and started questioning myself. Did I just sleep with him just 'cause I was lonely? Did I really agree to be his girl? How could I be with another savage ass nigga? Black was savage as hell, and it didn't turn out good. But then again, Chris was different than Black. I could always be chill with him. He looked out, and let's be honest, the dick game? Damn. But I didn't wanna be caught up in another relationship like the one with Black.

I got up and headed to the bathroom so I could take a shower. I was supposed to get up early that morning to look for apartments so we could get the hell out of here, but clearly, I slept through half the day and would only have a few hours to call around to some places. I hurried to shower and threw some of the sweats on that Chris had picked up and threw a hot pocket in the microwave to put something on my stomach. My mind went to the night before, or morning rather and I couldn't help but to smile. He definitely surprised me. I went to pick up my phone to call him to see where he went.

After a few rings, he picked up and I smiled again.

"Hey, where'd you go?" I asked.

"I had to go to the crib to try to get the stash and my key," he answered.

"What? Chris! I told you don't do that. Are you tryna get yourself killed?" I shrieked.

"Relax, babe. It's cool. I hit up some of my boys and had them meet me down the block from the crib. I told them what to look for, so I wouldn't have to go in there," he explained. "I'm good."

I sighed slightly.

"Don't scare me like that. Damn, man, why didn't you wake me up? I would've gone with you!"

"Nah. It was better that I went by myself instead of you tryna roll. We would've been spotted a lot faster if we were together," he said.

"Well, did they get your stuff?" I asked. My stomach was in knots, hoping he made it back okay.

"Yea I got it," he answered. "I had about ten thousand in cash, but most of my shit is in that box."

"Okay," I said. "Well, where are you now?"

"I'm at the station waiting on the train," he told me. "I think it's running late. But I should be there in like maybe an hour."

"Okay well just be—"

"Ah shit!" I heard.

"Chris? What's going on? What's happening? Chris?"

I could hear a lot of noise that sounded like wind. Was he running? What the hell was going on?

"Aye, man, hold up," he screamed.

BANG!"

"Ah!"

Chris was screaming loud, and I started to lose my breath. He had been shot. I know he had. I couldn't hear him anymore, but I heard Cisco. I couldn't deal. This shit could not be happening again.

"Chris, please answer me!" I cried.

I knew that he wouldn't. Even though the words came out my mouth, I knew that he wasn't going to answer. He was gone.

I knew I needed to call someone, but who? If I called the cops, I had no idea of what I was going to tell them. All I knew is that he was at a damn train station and I don't even know which one. Hell, I couldn't even give them a description of what he was wearing because he left while my ass was asleep.

I called Nikki to see if she had heard anything from him.

"Hello?" Nikki answered.

"Nikki, it's Miracle," I announced. "Listen, it's really important. Have you talked to Chris at all? Has he called you?"

"Nah," she answered, smacking on something loud in my ear.

"Damn it!"

"What's the matter?"

I was trying to choke back the tears and toughen up because now was not the time for emotions.

"Um I'm not sure. I'll call you back when I find out," I said.

"Wait uh…Miracle. I just, I wanted to say I'm sorry. I'm gonna get an abortion," she rushed.

I didn't even have time for her bullshit.

"Don't kill y'all's love child on my account," I snapped, hanging up on her before she could respond.

Why she thought now was the time to talk to me about that I don't know, but I wasn't even trying to deal. I had to figure out something. I had to get out. They got Chris, which means they could easily get to me. I knew I didn't want to, but I called the only person that I knew would help.

"Black, hey. It's me. Listen I really need your help. Like life and death," I told him.

"Where you at?" he asked.

"I'm at the Sheraton out here by the AT&T stadium. Like I need you to get here fast," I pleaded.

"Okay, don't worry. I'll be there soon. I'm finishing up with something here real quick, but I got you," he told me.

"Okay, just please try to get here as soon as you can."

"Aight."

I hung up the phone and flopped down on the bed in frustration and fear.

"Really, God? Are you really just trying to take away everyone from me?" I said out loud. "Everybody that gives a damn about me is taken. My daddy, Kim, and now Chris. Haven't I dealt with enough? Huh? Did I do something that is so harsh that everybody I love is snatched from me? Am I supposed to be just miserable for the rest of my life? Chris was all I had. He looked out for me. He loved me. He can't be gone. He just can't be."

I broke down and I just cried. I mean really cried so hard that I could barely see there were so many tears. I never thought I would be one of those people that spend their entire lives fighting, but since I lost my father, that's all it had been. I had enough. I couldn't take it anymore. If this is how it was going to be, then I wasn't hiding anymore.

I was done living in fear. I was done guessing. I was giving him everything that he wanted by hiding. But I wasn't about to give him the satisfaction of me being afraid anymore. I was going to Goody, one way or the other.

"Enough of this shit," I promised myself. "You took my life, now it's time to take yours."

*

I had all my stuff packed up and Chris things, too, as I sat waiting for Black. He had texted me telling me he was less than five minutes away and I gave him my room number. I pulled the .320 out my bag and checked the clip to make sure it was loaded. I was going to use every bullet that I could to watch Goody's ass drop. I had it in my purse the night we ran and didn't even think to use it. But I was now. I put it behind my back, so I wouldn't have to fumble to go through my purse for it.

Black knocked at the door, and I let him in.

"Hey, thanks for coming," I greeted him as he walked past me.

"Well, it sounded important. What's good?" he asked.

"I think Goody's boys shot Chris," I told him.

His face changed to concern.

"Damn. When this happen?"

"A few minutes before I called you," I told him. "I woke up and he was gone and…I called him and he said he had gone to get his safety deposit box from his crib even though I told him not to and the next thing I know, I hear him screaming, and I hear Cisco's voice and then a shot."

"You sure it was a gunshot you heard?" he asked.

"Trust me. I've heard enough of them in the last year," I said. "I think he's dead." I dropped my head and felt the tears stinging my eyes. "I gotta find him, Black. I gotta. He's all I got."

I saw a pang of jealousy cross his face, but I dismissed it.

"And you don't know where he was?"

"No!" I huffed. "When I woke up he was gone. We were up all night, and I don't think I went to sleep til' like nine o'clock this morning."

He looked around the room and noticed the messy bed and condom wrapper on the floor. Shit. I didn't even realize what I said until it was too late. But it wasn't like I cheated. He was the one that pushed me away into another man's arms. Why was I even thinking about this anyway?

"Well, I guess you moved on," he mumbled.

I rubbed the temples of my forehead.

"Look, Black, I know you're probably pissed right now, but I'm so not even in that mindset right now. I just need to get to him," I explained.

He looked as if it was something that he wanted to say, but he didn't.

"Black, please," I stressed. "I need your help."

He hesitated and eventually agreed.

"Thank you," I said.

I knew he was upset about me and Chris, but the only way to save my baby was with his help.

"Aight, well let's get your stuff and roll out," he spoke up. "One of my boys hit me and told me the other day where his boys might be at."

"Yea, and I bet one of them is the restaurant," I told him.

We grabbed the bags and walked out the door to his car. I was nervous looking around the entire time, hoping that no one would just pull up and start shooting. My nerves were completely shot and all I wanted to do was kill this muthafucka. I thought about how much hatred I had for Goody the entire time Black drove. He was the reason for all of the fucked up shit that I went through. And if Chris was dead, he was going to go slow. He was going to feel the pain like I felt.

We drove to Black's house and went inside. As soon as we walked in, all of his boys left.

"What's going on?" I asked, noticing.

"They know I got business to handle so they out looking. They all got different folks they can hit up and look, so I told them the minute they find out something to hit me up," he informed me.

"Oh," I answered.

He walked to the other side of the living room and sat down on the couch.

"So how did this thing happen with you and your boy?" he asked.

I sighed. I really wasn't trying to get into all of this with him.

"Not that I owe you any explanation, but I mean it just did," I admitted. "No, it wasn't on no revenge shit or nothing like that. Honestly, I wasn't expecting it, but it just kind of happened."

He nodded.

"You know I never meant to hurt you, right?" he asked.

“No. I don’t,” I whispered. “Everything that I thought I knew about you and who you were, turned out to be a lie, Black. And I can’t be with nobody like that.”

“But you can be with this nigga that’s supposed to be your brother?”

“Don’t do it,” I warned. “Like I said, I’m not with him for no revenge type shit over you. I ain’t one of these chicks that’s gone pine away over someone that did me wrong. I’m with Chris because he’s been down for me since day one. He’s always there for me, and even though I really didn’t understand it, he cares about me as more than just a ‘foster sister’.” He sat looking at me like he was upset. “This was a bad idea. Look, I’m gonna go. I’ll just have to handle this myself.”

I stood up to leave and he stopped me.

“No. My bad,” he apologized. “Look I just thought that maybe we could’ve started over. I don’t love Nikki. I don’t want that broad. I don’t even know if I’m the damn daddy. She wasn’t nothing but a moment of weakness.”

“Yea well, it looks like you’ve had a few moments of weakness based off the messages between y’all. But, look, I really don’t wanna keep talking about this,” I said. “I just really need to focus on finding Chris and this nigga, Goody.”

“Aight,” he answered, sounding defeated. “Well, for what it’s worth, I’m sorry.”

“I know.”

He looked at me like he expected me to say something different.

“I’m gonna uh…go get something to drink real quick.”

He got up and went into the kitchen and I sat in that chair trying to understand everything. My mind was on Chris, but now my ass was starting to wonder if maybe Black deserved another chance. He seemed genuine in his apology, but I didn't want to just run back to him. Maybe after all of this shit is over I would think differently, but for now, all my energy and thoughts needed to be in saving Chris.

I heard vibrating in the room and looked at my phone. Mine was still locked, so I was trying to figure out where it was coming from. I got up and walked to where the noise was coming from on the couch and found a phone wedged in the cracks of the couch.

"What the hell?"

I picked it up and opened it. This didn't look like Black's phone. This shit was a burner phone.

"You want something to drink?" Black called out.

"Nah I'm good," I answered, stuffing the phone in my pocket. "I just need to pee."

"You know where it is."

I walked past him to go to the bathroom. My curiosity had gotten the better of me, and I wanted to see who he was talking to. Was it more females? Maybe it was one of his homeboy's phones or something.

I never thought I would be one of those snooping females, but here I was. I looked through the call history and saw a few numbers. This shit was a burner phone. It's not surprising that he would have one, but I didn't even know about it. I opened the text messages and only one number was popping up; one very familiar number. I pulled my cell phone out of my back pocket to check to make sure I was right and I was. It was Goody's number.

What the hell? Why the hell was Goody messaging Black? The better question was, why was Black messaging Goody? He claimed he didn't like Goody's vibes so I was trying to figure out why they were even talking. I started looking through the messages and my heart sank. They had been talking to each other all this time! Goody had called him. That was why I heard the vibration in the couch. The last message shook me to the core.

Black: She called. On the way to go get her.

This shit couldn't be happening. He's in on it. He's helping Goody. Fuck!

An incoming message came in from him and I froze.

281-943-7500: Why u not answering the phone? U got her?

I had to answer. I had to find out what Black was up to.

Black: Yea. That's why I didn't answer. My bad.

I waited to see if he would respond, but I didn't have to wait long before the phone vibrated again.

281-943-7500: Good job, son. Bring her to the spot. Don't let her out of ur sight.

Son? Like his for real son? Black was Goody's son. I had known Goody my whole life and never knew that he had a son. I knew about his daughters, but he never mentioned having a son. So was Wood his brother? So Black knew who I was from jump. Shit. This nigga set me up! They were going to kill me.

I had to get out of there and fast. But how? I had his phone and I knew he would be looking for it. I turned the power off and dropped it in the dirty clothes hamper that Black had in the bathroom stuffing it under a bunch of dirty clothes. I was shaking I was so scared.

"Yo, you aight in there?" I heard.

I damn near jumped out my skin when he knocked on the door.

"Y-yea!" I called out. "I think I ate something bad last night and my stomach is a little upset is all."

"Aight, well make sure you use some air freshener," he joked.

I sat down on the toilet rocking. What the hell was I going to do? I had to get out of here. How the hell did I not see this? How did I miss all of this? I was sleeping with the enemy; literally. I trusted Black and thought he loved me. But he was Goody's son! He had been bullshitting me all this time.

I wanted to cry. I wanted to run. But right now, I wanted to live. I pulled my phone back out and texted Nikki.

Miracle: If u get this, I need u to call the cops! It's an emergency. Call the cops & tell them to track my phone. I'm gonna turn the locator on. But make sure to give them the info to track me. Please just do it! Please.

I prayed to God she wasn't in on this, too. She had been fucking Black, so I didn't know who to trust. I didn't mention Black or Goody just in case. Every move I made at this point I had to be careful.

I sat a few more minutes trying to figure out how I would get away from Black without him getting suspicious. I couldn't let on that I knew that he was in with Goody. I was going to have to come up with something.

I opened the door and walked into the living room, but he wasn't there. He must have been in the bedroom or something, so I took my chance and grabbed my purse off the chair and headed to the door.

"Where you going?"

I turned to see Black standing at the entrance of the kitchen drinking a soda. He was standing in his wife beater now showing off his muscles.

"Oh…I uh, I just needed to get out and get some air. I'm just feeling a little upset right now," I lied.

He walked over to me and pulled me away from the door. Shit.

"I don't think it's a good idea for you to go outside by yourself," he said. "My boys said Goody and his folks are out looking and they could be heading here. That's why I was about to come get you to tell you we need to be out. They out looking so you know they gonna come here."

"Where we gonna go?" I asked, trying to find out a clue.

"We gonna go hide out in Richardson. I got a spot out there," he said.

"Black, maybe I should just get out of town," I rushed trying to back towards the door. "If I leave now, I can get a head start."

His cell phone rang and he pulled it out and frowned. My heart sank to my stomach when I saw his expression.

"Hold on," he said, answering the phone in front of me. "Yo?"

He stood listening for a second, staring at me the entire time. If I made a run for it, I could get away fast.

"I'm on the way now," he said.

He hung up the phone and looked at me.

"We need to go," he said. "Now."

"Black, I don't know…"

He smirked and walked up to me and snatched me.

"You texted him, pretending to be me," he smirked. "You almost got away with it."

"Black, what are you talking about?" I feigned ignorance.

He pulled the gun from his waist and put it to my side.

"Shut up," he demanded. "No need to deny it."

My heart was beating so fast I thought it was going to explode.

"Now we got somewhere to go," he continued. "So I'm gonna open this door and we gonna walk up out of here. I don't think I need to warn you about tryna draw attention to yourself."

I shook my head.

"Good." He started, patting me and felt the gun that I had in the back of my pants. "Don't worry. You ain't gonna need this."

He took the gun and tossed it on the couch then reached in my back pocket to take my phone and placed it in his pocket. At least he didn't throw it so that way if Nikki did what I asked, the police could track me.

"Black, please," I whimpered. "Just let me go. Like I said, I will leave town and y'all don't have to worry about nothing," I promised.

He shook his head and grabbed his keys.

"Nah. It don't work like that. Let's go."

He opened the door and walked me down the stairs to his car.

"Get in," he ordered.

I followed his instructions and climbed in and he closed the door. He walked to the other side and got in, cranking the ignition and heading to this secret location where I was sure I was going to die.

"So you're his son?" I asked after a few minutes of driving in silence. He didn't answer and kept driving. "How come he's never claimed you?" I pressed. "Did you have something to do with my father being killed? Did this Devon dude really do it or was it you?"

"Shut up," he finally said.

He drove and I wondered where we were going. Please dear God let Nikki have called the cops.

"So did you ever love me?" I asked, trying to get some answers. "Or was this all a lie?"

He looked at me with what I thought was some remorse, but as much as he had been acting for the past year, I wasn't sure.

"So it was all a lie," I whispered.

He used me. He lied to me. He only got close to me because he was trying to steer me from Goody. And now that I knew everything, there wasn't anything stopping him from killing me.

"I do love you," he spoke up.

I looked at him, but he kept his attention on the road.

"Then let me go," I begged.

He gripped the steering wheel and kept driving.

"You should have listened," he said. "I told you to fall back from that nigga, but you didn't. You kept coming at him. He tried to tell you to let it go. I told you to stay away. But you didn't listen."

"Would you?" I asked. He didn't respond and instead hopped off an exit. "You know he's never said anything about you, right? I've known Goody since as long as I was alive, and he never said anything about you. What kind of father doesn't claim his own son?"

His jaw clenched, but he remained quiet. I was hoping to push him to the point that he would feel sorry for me and let me go.

We drove for a few more minutes until he pulled up to this large house. He pulled the car into one of the open garages and waited.

"Black, I'm begging you. Let me go. Please!" I pleaded.

I wasn't trying to die.

"Get out," he said.

"Black, please—"

"Get out now!"

I jumped and opened the door doing as I was told. He came around and grabbed me and walked me inside the house. I looked around and saw the house was mostly empty with a few pieces of furniture scattered here and there. It looked as if no one was living there with the exception of the small things. He led me down the hall and I could hear someone talking.

We walked around the corner and Goody stood in the middle of the room, looking like Lucifer himself.

"Well, well, well. Welcome to the party."

*****

Chapter Twenty-One

"I knew it was you." I looked at this man that I once thought the world of and now I loathed. "I knew that you had something to do with it. All of this time, I kept trying to convince myself that you was his boy. I kept telling myself that my father wouldn't have a fucking snake ass shady ass best friend. I told myself that my godfather, my father's partner, couldn't be that way. But clearly my gut was right," I said.

"Are you done?" he asked unfazed.

Cisco and J.D. came from around the corner, and I knew it was over. But I needed to know why. I was going to die anyway.

"Why?" I asked. "Why did you kill my daddy? Why would you take him from me? Why did you make me think all this time that you cared about him? You were his best friend."

He sucked his teeth and walked up to me, laughing. His face was so close to mine, I could smell the nicotine on his breath.

"You see that's your problem, Miracle, you just like him," he started. "You ask too many fucking questions. That's what got your daddy caught up. He always questioning me on shit that I was doing. My nigga gone sit there and question me on what the fuck I'm doing." He started pacing the room laughing while Black kept his gun on my back and Cisco and J.D. watched. "I was the one that handled all the business, but your daddy, that nigga wanted to play it safe all the fucking time. Everybody swore he was a fucking legend, but truthfully…the nigga was a coward. I did all of the fucking work, but your daddy wanted to spread the love around. He wanted everybody to get paid. But everybody wasn't out there doing the work, Miracle."

"So you killed him because he wanted to make sure everybody was living good? Really?" I screeched.

"No!" he shouted. "I killed your fucking daddy because he was stupid. He didn't know good business moves when he saw it. We could have been paid, but he wasn't trying to go to the next level. He was happy where he was at and keeping the rest of us down. But that didn't matter to him no matter how many times I tried to convince him otherwise. I'm about making money. And, unfortunately, your daddy didn't see it that way. He had a perfect opportunity to walk away with millions and he didn't. And when I offered to let him out, he laughed at me. So, he had to go."

"So you just pulled all the strings, huh?" I said, letting the tears fall. I had heard an answer, but it damn sure wasn't one I wanted. "You set him up and made it look like someone else was trying to kill him and all along it was you. You even went as far as killing somebody else to make it look like you had his back! And you just did this shit in front of me?"

"You wasn't supposed to see it," he shrugged. "But like father, like daughter I guess. You were somewhere you shouldn't have been. Always sticking your nose where it don't belong. That's why your daddy got killed. Because if he would have just let me do my thing, then he would have never got caught up in it." He paused and smiled. "Just because he wasn't trying to get paid doesn't mean the rest of us weren't. But your daddy being the nosey ass muthafucka that he was, he threatened to get rid of me. Me? He really thought I was just gonna walk away."

He started laughing like a damn maniac and I didn't know what to think. I didn't understand how all of this shit was happening and I didn't see any of it. Whenever I saw Goody and my father, they were like they always were. They always seemed like everything was good. But then again, my dad kept me from a lot of stuff, so I was probably completely oblivious to it.

"So now what?" I asked. "You kill me, too?"

"Once again," he pointed out. "Being nosy. Haven't you learned yet? You sticking your head where it don't belong is the reason why you're here."

"No," I corrected him, trying to move away from Black. "Your son is the reason I'm here."

"Ah yea, well that's true. You almost had me thinking it was Black I was texting. Until he called me and told me he had you," he mentioned.

Well, that explains how he found out. I turned to Black.

"You knew all of this time, and all of his time I'm thinking that you loved me and cared about me," I said.

He just looked at me with this blank expression and Goody started clapping.

"Well. if you're done with this week's episode of 'The Young & the Stupid', Trevon take her downstairs. Let her sit down there with that other muthafucka," he told him.

Black nodded and grabbed me by the arm.

"Let's go," he mumbled.

"Don't touch me!" I snapped, snatching away as he pushed me down the stairs.

"Tie her up, and make sure you gag that big ass mouth of hers. When you finished, come back up here. I got something for you to do," Goody ordered.

Black didn't even say anything. He just pushed me down the stairs and did as he was told. It was like he was a completely different person. He did whatever Goody said as if he was under some kind of spell or something. I knew he was his son, but damn.

"So that's what you do?" I said, walking. You do whatever the hell he tells you to like some little bitch?" I pushed.

He shoved me harder almost making me fall. I looked to see Chris lying in the corner blood all over the floor.

"Oh my God!" I cried out. "Chris!" Running to his side. His face was all bruised, and he had blood stains everywhere. "Chris, it's me, baby. It's Miracle. Please answer me. Please."

I touched his face, and he was still warm. He groaned and lifted his head.

"I fucked up, baby," he moaned.

"Thank you, God," I whispered, grabbing him. "I told you not to go, Chris."

"I know," he grunted. "I was just trying to get us up out of here..."

Black, agitated, walked over, and he tried to push me back but wasn't successful.

"Sit down," Black ordered.

"No!" I said. "Black, this ain't you." I stared at him, trying to read him and see where his head was at. "Look, I…I know you love me. You couldn't have said it and not meant it. I know that he put you up to this. But I know that you wouldn't hurt me. Because if you didn't really love me, you would have killed me a long time ago," I reminded him. "And you tried to warn me that night when I first started talking about me thinking it was Goody...I mean, your dad." That just seemed weird saying it. "And the fact that he's never said anything about you? Come on now. You know I'm telling you the truth," I stressed.

"Shut up," he growled. "I don't care what the hell you got to say. Just do what the fuck I say. Now sit down!" he yelled, grabbing the rope and knocking me to the ground.

"You're just what I thought you were," Chris spoke up. "Just another one of his little bitches."

“What you say, nigga?” Black said, turning to Chris.

“You heard me, muthafucka,” he said. “I said that you a bitch, just like your daddy. You do whatever the fuck he tells you to. No wonder Miracle didn’t wanna fuck with your ass no more. She wanted a real nigga.”

I looked at Chris like he was crazy. Had he lost his damn mind? Was he trying to get killed? Something was telling me that he was doing it to get Black to leave me alone, which was really stupid but it worked. Black turned his attention away from me and punched Chris so hard that I thought it knocked him unconscious.

“Fuck you, bitch muthafucka!” he yelled.

Chris mustered up every bit of strength and grabbed Black. All I could see was fists swinging, and Black tried to pull his gun. I tried to pull him off, but I ended up getting thrown across the room.

I jumped up to try to help Chris again and the loud pop halted my feet. I stood frozen waiting to see what would happen. The next few seconds seemed to drag by. Neither Chris nor Black were moving. I could hear the footsteps above my head and they were coming quick. I looked over at Chris and Black who both were lying still. Fuck! I was scared shitless.

“Miracle, grab the gun.” I heard Chris whisper.

My eyes got big and I rushed over to his side. I pulled Black off of him and saw that he was bleeding from his stomach.

“Oh my God,” I whispered.

Chris shoved the gun in my hand, and I turned and aimed it at the feet coming down the steps. J.D. and Cisco both had guns pointed at me. I aimed right at Cisco.

“Shit!” J.D. said when he saw Black. “She shot him.”

“No,” I said “I didn't. Because if I did, I would have shot him in the fucking head. And I swear to God if you don't put that fucking gun down I won’t have a problem shooting you in yours,” I warned.

Cisco looked at me as if he wasn't fazed.

“Look, girl,” he sneered. “I ain’t got time for these games.
He took a step towards me and I shot him in his foot.

“Shit!” he screamed out in pain.

“Well, I guess that let me know that I didn't miss,” I said. “And if you try to come near me again I WILL blow your head off.”

He opened his mouth, but another shot rang out and blood came spewing out as he hit the floor. Goody came down the stairs, an evil grin on his face. Black was lying on the ground behind me groaning in pain, and Chris was slipping in and out of consciousness. I tried to keep my focus on J.D. who at this point was looking petrified. He had his gun aimed at me, but I could see him shaking from where I stood. Now that his boy was dead, he knew he was next.

“So what you going to do?” Goody asked. “The minute that you pull the trigger, one of us is going to shoot you. There's no way that you can kill us both at the same time,” he said. “And I don’t think you got it in you. If you did, you would have killed my ass a long time ago, and you didn’t, so it proves my point.”

“Pops, I need an ambulance,” Black moaned, interrupting him.

Goody darted his eyes to him and shook his head.

“See because of my dumbass son over here, I had to lose one of my men. Hell, he was more like a son to me than this one,” he said, pointing to Black.

Damn. He made it clear that he didn't give a damn about his son. I actually felt sorry for Black. I could tell that he didn't want to hurt me, but he was trying to make sure he stayed on his good side so my thoughts of putting a gun to Black to try to get out of the house were going to be pointless. Goody was so relentless, he would kill his own son.

"Black, give me your phone," I said.

"What?" he grunted.

"Give me your phone!" I said, yelling at him but keeping my eye on Goody.

He struggled to reach in his pocket, and I bent down, gun still trained on Goody to snatch it from him. I should have known better because as soon as I reached my hand out Black pulled me down and I felt the gun falling out of my hands and he snatched it. Fuck! How the hell could he still want to help his trifling ass daddy after what he just said? Goody smiled, watching, and I knew I was dealing with the devil.

Black held the gun to my head, and I knew it was over. Goody was going to have pleasure in his son killing me, and Chris was already halfway dead.

"I hope you burn in hell." I struggled through Black's arm around my neck, tears rolling down my face.

"I'm sure I will," he smiled, walking closer. "But not before you. Go ahead, son."

Black cocked the gun, and I shut my eyes tight, praying to God that I would go quickly.

"I'm sorry, Daddy," I whispered.

A loud boom shook the room and everyone including Goody was startled. But there was no time to react as you could hear footsteps everywhere.

"Freeze! Hands up! Put the gun down!" was all I heard.

There were cops everywhere as well as what I think were agents. I had never been so happy to see cops before in my life. There was no way Goody was getting out of this alive with all of the guns pointed at him.

"Marques Goodwin, FBI. Put the gun down and step away from it slowly."

He kept his gun raised and stared them down.

"Get the hell back!" he yelled, turning the gun on me and Black.

"Put the gun down," the agent repeated. "Step away and you can walk out of this alive."

"What do I do?" J.D. asked nervously. "I can't go to jail."

"Put it down now!" they shouted, seeing his weakness.

J.D. looked back and forth between me and Goody not knowing what to do. He was shaking like a leaf. Suddenly he made a move and turned his gun aiming it at the police. Before he could fire, I saw an agent put a bullet in the middle of his head. Goody ducked, and I screamed and the agents took the opportunity to move in. They shot Goody in the shoulder, and he fell to the ground.

"Ahh!" he cried out in pain.

Black had dropped the gun, letting me go, and threw his hands up in surrender.

"Please!" I cried. "Help him. He didn't hurt me." I showed them.

He looked at me and I saw his eyes filled with tears.

"I wasn't ever going to hurt you," he said as the cops put handcuffs on them.

"We need a bus!" One of them yelled out. "Get those medics in here quick."

Goody was now standing, cuffed and being read his rights, but he was staring at Black with malice.

"Weak. That's why I never claimed you," he growled. "You never pick pussy over family. But that's all you are," he taunted. "You ain't nothing but fucking weak ass pussy. You not my son!" he said as they dragged him up the stairs. "Her fucking father ruined everything and you side with that fuckin' bitch! You'll be dead without me!"

They rushed with the medics to get Black and Chris to the hospital.

Ma'am," one of the officers asked. "Are you Miracle Davis?"

"Yes," I answered still watching the medics with Chris. "Yes. Please, can they get them to the hospital?" I begged. "Chris isn't doing too good and Black's been shot in the stomach. Please get them to the hospital. I… I can't lose either one of them," I begged.

The medics were putting them on the stretcher, rushing them out.

"It's okay, they're being transported now," he advised. "Don't worry, your sister called us and told us that you were in trouble."

Thank God. Nikki actually helped. I don't care how mad I was at that girl, she had come through.

"Okay, we need to get you to the hospital to get looked at as well," one of them spoke.

"I'm not hurt," I assured him. "I'm fine. Just a couple of bumps and bruises."

I was more so concerned about Chris and Black. Chris wasn't even responding, and Black had bled out so much. I didn't want to lose them. I wish to God that I had just put a bullet in Goody's brains. I walked up the steps with the officers walking past both a dead J.D. and Cisco. I had seen enough dead bodies to last a lifetime and then some. And finally, it was about to be over.

*****

I've been in the hospital for damn near twenty-four hours answering questions and talking to police and agents. Apparently, even though Goody had been released from prison, the FBI was still watching him. They had actually been watching him for a while since before he got locked up. They were watching my father, too, but had more evidence on Goody.

Nikki had in fact called the police to let them know that I was in trouble, and they tracked my phone to his house, but from what I found out, they already had agents close by in surveillance. They had to wait for him to mess up before they could come in. Hell, I'm glad they came in when they did because one second later and I would have been dead.

I guess there was a reason why my father chose not to get into business with certain people. Goody just didn't know that. He was thinking greed instead of smart and that's how he ended up on the FBI's watch list. But everything was finally winding down after all this time and I was able to rest. I needed to get to Chris, though.

I had been asking the doctors and nurses so much to make sure that he was okay. He had a broken leg, four broken ribs, a few fractured fingers, and his face had been hit so many times, it would take several days for the swelling to go down. JD and Cisco did a number on him, but he would survive.

I was lying in my bed which I really didn't want to be in, thanking God that I was here. I was ready to go home, but I guess it was standard procedure to keep me overnight. I was lucky. I had to thank Nikki because had she not called the cops, I don't know what could have happened. As bad as I treated her, and as mad as I was, I owed her my life. She didn't have to call the cops, but she did. I had saved her life and now she had saved mine. I couldn't keep being hateful towards her. Besides, I loved Chris. In my heart of hearts, I had let Black go, especially after finding out that he was Goody's and him lying for over a year really put stuff into perspective.

I was appreciative of him not killing me and saving my life and everything, but facts were still facts. And the main fact was that he was not who he said he was. In essence, I was with a stranger. But I wished him well.

I couldn't help but be afraid that we would all go to jail though. I'm pretty sure the cops were at my house and Chris's and Black's. Black had a stash, but it would be very difficult for them to find. I didn't know about Chris, but I knew that Goody wasn't going to go down and not take everybody with him.

A knock at the door interrupted my thoughts, and another agent walked in.

"Miss Davis?" he asked.

"Hi," I said, yawning and sitting up.

"Sorry to have to bother you so late," he apologized. "I know it's been a hectic day for you, and I know you've had a lot of people asking you questions. I won't take up too much of your time, but I was just wanted to let you know that everything is going to be fine now. Mr. Goodwin is going to be going away for a very long time."

"Good," I said. Something was telling me that there was more.

"But in order for us to make that happen, we need for you to testify."

And there it is.

“So you need for me to snitch?” I asked.

“Yes,” he nodded his head. “I know it doesn't sound all too appealing, but Mr. Goodwin has been under FBI watch for a very long time, and with your help, we can keep him locked away for a very long time. In fact, we can keep him away permanently.”

“Well…what about Chris and his son Bl- uh...I mean Trevon?” I asked.

“Mr. Warner will be testifying as well in exchange for immunity. He informed us that he was working for him trying to gain information on him killing your father, in which you two were going to present to the police,” he told me.

He flat out lied, but clearly, it worked.

“So like you're not going to try to charge Chris with any of this?” I asked, trying to make sure I was hearing him correct.

“No,” he confirmed. “As far as we know, he wasn't connected to anything aside from what we were told. In this case, he was working as an informant.”

Thank God. Hopefully, they wouldn't try to charge him with something later.

“What about Trevon?”

“Unfortunately, Trevon succumbed to his injuries,” the agent said.

“Wh- what?” I asked not believing what I was hearing.

The agent nodded his head.

“I apologize I have to be the one to tell you,” he said. “That was another reason why I came in here. He passed away about an hour ago. The doctors tried to do everything that they could. They had been operating on him most of the day, but there was too much internal bleeding."

"Oh my God," I whispered. I felt the room beginning to spin, and I had to take a minute. "He's really dead?" I asked.

"Yes," the agent confirmed. "But we still have a case against Mr. Goodwin without him. We plan on making sure Goodwin never sees the light of day again, and that's why we need your help."

"I can believe it," I mumbled. Now they were in my face asking me to testify. "I don't know," I responded. "I mean I done been through enough with all this. And Goody got people everywhere. I mean LITERALLY everywhere. I was with his son for an entire year and didn't know it," I admitted.

The detective nodded in understanding.

"And I understand Ms. Davis," he empathized. "Believe me I do. But you will be protected. We won't let anything happen to you. We can put you in protective custody if need be," he offered. "But if you don't testify, there's a strong chance that he could be serving the minimum sentence meaning he could be out on the streets in matter of a few years. Even though we have enough evidence on him the more that we get and your testimony will seal the deal."

I knew that he was right, but still. With Goody, you could be looking over your shoulder for the rest of your life, and I wasn't trying to do that. I thought about how resourceful he was behind bars when he was sending me money and everything. And he kept up the façade for over a year with Black and I was around both of them on so many occasions and they never let on. But I had already come face to face with him, so it wasn't like he wouldn't see this coming. He had to know that the cops were going to come to me. I couldn't live my life in fear. What the hell was I going to do? This is why I needed to talk to Chris.

"This is just, a lot to deal with. I got to think about this," I told him.

"Absolutely," he agreed. He handed me his card out of his wallet and headed towards the door. "Think about it and give me a call," he said. "Agent Bolts." He paused for a second. "It's good to see that you're okay."

He gave me a small smile and left the room. I looked at the card and huffed. I really didn't want to testify. I just wanted it to be over and done with. I'm pretty sure that they could put him in prison without me, but I knew that me testifying would make things a whole lot easier. But if he knew where I was, it would make things a whole lot harder too. Maybe if I didn't testify me and Chris could just get our stuff and go, and with Goody in the feds custody, that would give us enough time to relocate. But if we ran, then we would have to run far and never look back.

I got up and put on my shoes and walked towards the nurses' station to find out which room he was in. They encouraged me to go lay back down, but I told them how important it was and stressed that he was all I had and they gave me his room number. There was an agent outside of his door like mine who let me in. I opened the door to find him lying in the bed with his leg in a sling.

"Hey," I whispered, trying to hold it together at the sight of him. "I'm glad you're okay."

He tried to smile.

"It's a lot worse than it looks," he said his face completely swollen looking as if it was full of gauze.

"Yea right," I argued. "If that was the case, you know you would've snuck out a while ago."

He tried to laugh and winced in pain as he grabbed his ribs.

“See?” I pointed out. “This is why I was gonna come visit you. How are you feeling?” I asked.

“I'm good, babe,” he slurred. “Just ready to get up out of here but they said I got a couple of weeks before I can be out. But I'll be cool.”

“Well, I'm not leaving you,” I said. “I’m gonna be right here.”

“Miracle, please. You know you're going to get tired of my ass complaining,” he joked.

“No I won’t,” I said. “Just like you made me tell you that that ass was yours, well, that ass is mine, and I don't plan on giving it up.”

He laughed and groaned in pain at the same time. I had to remember that I couldn't joke with him the way I wanted to.

“They asked me to testify,” I told him.

“Word?”

“Yea,” I whispered.

“Are you?”

“I don't know,” I told him. “If I do, then that means I'm a walking target. You know that nigga can make one phone call and shit will be over. He’s got so many people I don’t know who I can trust.”

“Yeah, but if you don't, then you'll be running forever,” he reminded me.

“That's true, too,” I agreed. “I don't know what I’ma do.”

“Well, whatever it is, you not gonna worry about it right now,” he said.

“You right.” I walked over and sat down in the chair next to the bed. “I got to make sure that you're good. Everything else will fall into place.”

“Speaking of fall, why don't you come fall on this dick?” he joked.

I slapped him on the arm.

“If you don't shut your horny ass up,” I fussed. “Always thinking about some damn sex.”

I can't believe he was joking at a time like this. But it definitely put a smile on my face.

“I love you, girl,” he soothed.

“I love you, too,” I smiled. I leaned in and kissed him as gently as I could without hurting him.

“Soon, this shit will be over and we can live a normal life,” he said.

Yep. My baby was right. Everything was finally over. I found out who Goody really was, and that he was the one who betrayed and killed my father. And as dumb as the reason was behind it, I had done right.

I knew my father was proud of me. He's probably pissed at the dangerous situation I put myself in, but I knew he was proud. And for me, that was enough. I looked at Chris who had dozed off and smiled. I know my daddy wasn't too keen on me dating a savage type nigga like him, but if it wasn't for this savage, I never would have found out the truth. I would have still been that scared little girl. Chris had been there from jump and loved me unconditionally. And I had to admit, I loved him too. That savage love was something else!

*****

Chapter Twenty-Two

"Okay, Miracle, you're up," Mr. Garner spoke. Two agents were standing on both sides of me and Chris. Mr. Garner, the prosecutor, had come out of the courtroom to come and get me. They had been on lunch, and it was finally, after months of filings, extensions, continuances, and other stall tactics, the day for me to testify.

"Now remember what I said. The defense is going to try everything that they can to make it look like you were in collusion with him. They're going to make it seem like you had a personal vendetta against him since your father was killed, and he lived. They're going to throw everything that they can at you, but you just remember to remain calm, and answer the questions."

"Okay," I said, nodding my head.

What a perfect way to spend my damn twentieth birthday. It had been a year and two months since Goody was arrested. At first, I was hesitant on testifying, but ultimately, I knew if I didn't, things would only get worse. Plus, once I found out that they had Goody in jail in isolation with no form of communication, it made things a lot easier for me to decide to do it.

Chris and I had been in protective custody for months while the trial was going on, and it was driving us both crazy. We couldn't go anywhere or do anything without an agent with us. It wasn't that we really went anywhere anyway because of the fact that we had to testify. We mostly stayed in hotel rooms. I didn't mind though. Every chance we got, we were going at it like we were newlyweds or something.

Chris was perfect for me. It took him awhile to heal from his broken leg and all, but that didn't stop other parts of him from working. I hated it for the agents outside of our door. They were probably thinking we were fucking like jackrabbits.

I didn’t care though. Chris satisfied me in every way, and it wasn’t just about the sex. We would stay up all night talking. He would hold me when I cried, missing my daddy, and he helped me with school. We even made plans for our life together.

He was still able to get access to his bank account before we went into custody and placed everything in a new account. I did the same. Even though I told him I didn't want him to, he paid my tuition for the next year. I had to argue him down on that, because he wanted to pay it for the full degree program. I compromised and told him that he could pay for a year, and then after that, we would see what happened. I'd learned from being with Black that I needed to learn to take care of myself. I refused to be put in another situation where I had somebody taking care of me and then something went wrong.

Nikki had her baby. She had a baby boy, and of course, she named him after Black. He was almost eight months old now and gorgeous too. He looked just like Black. Although she saved my life and I forgave her, our relationship wasn't a hundred percent. We talked about a lot of things, and of course, she apologized so many times, but we just weren't as close as we used to be. I knew over time that things would get back to what they once were. I didn't have any hatred in my heart anymore for her.

It hurt me to know that her son would not know his father though, so we helped her as much as we could. We'd only seen her and the baby a couple of times because of the fact that we were in protective custody, but I promised her that once everything was over, we would be there for her a lot more.

She got herself together, and was living on Section 8. It was better than nothing, and she seemed happy, so I was good. Even though she was working part time, we sent her money every now and then to help out with the baby, but we had to have it done through the agents so as not to risk our location. The few times we did see each other, it was in places that were nowhere near our spot.

Chris and I had been talking and decided that after the trial was over, we were going to move to Georgia. Although it wasn't as far as Florida, I knew that he was going to hate living in a town for the old folks, so I figured being in Atlanta would be a good move.

I was so ready for this trial to be over. His attorneys were doing everything that they could to hold it up since it started six months ago. He had more subpoenas and requests to postpone trials thrown. You would have thought this nigga was OJ Simpson. He even had the original judge recuse himself from the case as he had been found to have an extramarital affair with Goody's baby mama, Lisa, years ago.

Of course, when they brought in the new judge, they threw another motion for dismissal, but the judge had enough and said the trial was going to happen.

“You ready to do this?” Mr. Garner asked.

“Yep,” I said.

“Alright… let's go.”

We all walked to the door, and the agents opened it, allowing me to walk in. I walked down the small walkway and sat where I was instructed, looking back to make sure that Chris was there. He winked, and I felt better. Damn, I loved him.

I looked over to see Goody watching me. The familiar fear immediately overcame me, but I shook it off. I wasn't going to be afraid of him anymore. As far as I was concerned, he was done. Mr. Garner had told me on more than one occasion that the evidence on Goody was piling up so fast that they could barely keep track of it all. When he got arrested, the feds raided every last spot of his, thanks to the many informants, and so many of his boys flipped on him in exchange for lesser sentences. If he had any allies left, I hated it for them, because those that didn't turn on him were in the same boat that he was.

“All rise!” the bailiff called. We all stood as the bailiff announced the judge. This older white man that looked like he was in his late sixties approached the bench and looked out into the courtroom.

“You may be seated,” he said. Just looking at him, I knew it was over for Goody. This dude looked like he did not play.

“Court is now in session. Reconvening the case of the State of Texas vs Marques Goodwin.”

The judge looked at his paperwork before directing his attention to us.

“Before we begin, let me make myself perfectly clear,” he started.

“This will not be some major television spectacle. If there are any media or other communication outlets here, please remember that this is a courtroom, and it will be treated as such. With the defendant's background and knowledge of crimes, I am reminding you all that there are to be no outbursts or anything else that will be considered disruptive to the courtroom. Is this understood?”

Everyone nodded their heads or gave a quick yes.

“Alright. Let's begin.”

“At this time, the people would like to call Miracle Davis to the stand.”

I stood and walked slowly toward the witness stand as the eyes of the jury and everyone else in the courtroom watched me. I looked at Chris, and he gave me a smile. My stomach was doing flip flops. I was so nervous and scared, because this day has finally come. After over two years of looking and months of protective custody, I was looking my father's murderer in the face.

I really didn't want to be here, but I knew it was the only way to make sure that Goody went down for what he did. He had intimidated so many people, but the tables had turned. The very same people who had been his boys had taken deals in exchange for testimony against him, but I still didn't put anything past him. It was Goody, after all.

I walked past him, and he stared at me with a blank expression. I walked to the witness stand and raised my hand, being sworn in by the bailiff before sitting down.

"Thank you for being here today with us, Ms. Davis," Mr. Garner said.

I nodded my head in acknowledgement.

"For the record, can you state your name please… for the jury?" he asked.

"Yes… Miracle Latrice Davis," I answered.

"Thank you. Now, Ms. Davis, I'm going to get right to the point. I know that you have endured a lot over the last year or so."

I nodded my head again in agreement.

"Now, you were present the day your father was killed, correct?"

"Yes," I answered.

"And do you recall what happened?"

"Yes."

"Can you tell the jury please?" he pushed.

"Well…" I started.

"…I was having my seventeenth birthday party that day at the house. A few minutes before everything happened, my father had given me a new car, and then he disappeared. Goody was gone too, so I just figured that they were somewhere talking business or something. I know they owned a couple of restaurants together, and they had just opened up a nightclub, so I went to my dad's office, figuring that's where they were, and I didn't see them.

When I looked out the window, I saw that my dad was talking to Goody, and he looked really upset. I went downstairs and outside to go talk to him, and when I got there, it was like I knew something was wrong. Both of them got real quiet, and daddy tried to act like nothing was wrong. The next thing I know, this black van pulled up, and this guy got out with some flowers. He said that he was a delivery guy and that the flowers were for me… for my birthday. My dad said that he didn't order any flowers or something, and when he told me to go inside, the look on his face… I knew something was wrong."

I paused, because I didn't want to keep reliving this damn nightmare, but I had to tell my side.

"It… it all just happened so fast. I just remember people jumping out of the van, and… and bullets started flying everywhere. I froze, and I saw my dad running toward me, telling me to get down. I looked, and I saw Goody shooting too, but I wasn't paying attention. The next thing I know, my dad was lying there in a pool of blood, and I called 911... Everybody was screaming, and I was trying to get my daddy to hang on."

I had to stop, because I felt myself about to break.

"Do you need a minute?" Garner asked. I shook my head *no* and cleared my throat.

"No… No, I'm okay. It's just hard to talk about it sometimes, because I really loved my daddy. He was like my best friend, and Goody was too at one point, but finding out that he killed my daddy—"

"Objection!" the defense attorney interrupted.

"Line of questioning, your honor?"

"Sustained. Counsel, please inform your client to answer the question that was asked," he instructed.

"Sorry," I apologized.

"It's quite alright, Ms. Davis," he said.

"Now, I apologize that I've had to ask you to relive such a tragic day. After your father was killed, what do you remember?"

"Um, I remember the cops asking Goody and me lots of questions, and there were bodies everywhere. A few days later, I was at Goody's house when the police showed up and arrested him. They said that he was being charged with murder, money laundering, and distribution of drugs, but I didn't know that he was as involved as he let on. He was in jail for a while, and I went to foster care," I said. I thought about that bitch and cringed.

"I was with my foster mother for over a year, and right before I turned eighteen, unfortunately, her daughter was killed at school. They took us out of the home when they found out that she was not taking care of us like she was supposed to."

I was praying deep down that they wouldn't ask anything about what happened to Patricia.

"Okay now, Ms. Davis, why did you suspect your godfather's involvement in your father's murder?"

"Honestly, it was just something that stuck with me since the day my dad died. I knew that he wasn't killed by accident. I knew that somebody came to our house to kill him. I remembered asking Goody about it and him saying that he was going to find out, but it just kind of seemed like he was saying that to pacify me or to shut me up.

When I met my ex-boyfriend, Trevon, who I later found out was Goody's son, I told him that I wanted to find out who killed my father. After I was taken from the foster home, I ran away and went to live with my ex-boyfriend, and I ran into one of my foster brothers that was there in the home with me at one point. He told me that he used to sell drugs, so knowing that Goody had involvement as a drug dealer, I asked him if he would get close to him, because Trevon wasn't really interested in trying to help me. Now, I see why."

"And to clarify, your ex-boyfriend, Trevon Banks, is Marques Goodwin's son? Were you aware of that when you were dating him?" Garner asked.

"No. The entire time that we were together, he never mentioned that Goody was his father, and he had been around him a couple of times. In fact, he told me that there was something up with him and that he didn't think I should pursue it. Maybe that was his way of warning me. I don't know," I said, my mind wandering to the day he died.

"Okay," Garner nodded.

"Your foster brother is now your current boyfriend… correct?"

"Yes," I answered. Hearing it out loud sounded a little weird, but it's not like we were blood brother and sister.

"Now to speed things up a bit, at this point, you and your ex-boyfriend are still together, and your foster brother is working for Mr. Goodwin… is that correct?" he asked.

"Yes. He had been working for Goody briefly when he started gathering information, and from there, we just kind of kept digging. When he got close enough to Goody, I found out the shooter's name that pulled the trigger on him… a guy named Devon. Devon shot my father, but he was ordered to do so by Goody. We were there that night," I told the court. They were listening closely, and I had twelve pairs of eyes on me.

"And where exactly were you?"

I took a deep breath before I began my recollection of the events.

"Well, Chris had come to me and told me that he heard Goody talking on the phone with his boys quite a few times. He overheard Goody talking to JD and Cisco, telling them to keep Devon quiet, because he didn't want him going to the cops," I explained.

"We followed JD and Cisco around for a few days to see if they would eventually meet with him, and they did. I think it was the third day that we were following them, and I saw that they were going into a neighborhood that I was familiar with. They actually met up at the restaurant that both Goody and my father owned at one time. Um… we watched from across the street on top of the roof. Devon got out the car, and they started arguing. Cisco pulled out his gun and shot him. They saw us, and we took off running. We hid out at a hotel for a couple of days. One morning, I woke up, and Chris had left to go to his apartment to get some of his things, because we were planning on leaving that day, but JD and Cisco snatched him."

I paused, looking down at my feet and went on.

"At that point, I called Trevon for help when I heard that he had been taken, and I went back to Trevon's apartment with him with the understanding that he was going to help me. He had gone to get something to drink, and I heard a cell phone going off, but it was one that I had never seen. I opened the phone, and I saw texts where Trevon was messaging Goody. I saw a message where Goody had referred to Trevon as son. At that point, I knew that my life was in danger and that Trevon had been in a relationship with me because his father wanted to keep tabs on me."

I had to stop and take a breath, because I was starting to feel some anxiety, and I did not want to pass out in front of all these people.

"Take your time," Garner said.

"Um… well, I sent a text message to my foster sister who was living with me and told her to call the police. I made sure to turn the tracker on my phone just in case something happened. I tried to leave his house, but I didn't know that Goody had hit Trevon on his other cell. When I tried to leave, he snatched me and put a gun to me, taking me to a house where Goody was. JD and Cisco were there too. I tried to stall for time to see if I could find a way out, so I began to question Goody. That was when he admitted that he had my father killed, because my father wanted out of the drug game. He wanted to run everything, and my father wouldn't allow it. He admitted in front of me, his son, and two other people that he set my father up to be killed."

Garner looked at me urging me to go on and I continued.

"After that, I was brought into the basement, and that was where I saw Chris was lying on the floor unconscious and had been beaten really badly. I thought he was dead at first. I begged Trevon to let me go, and Chris woke up. He started to antagonize Trevon so that he would throw his anger toward him instead of me. The two started fighting. I heard the gun go off, and I saw that Trevon had been shot in the stomach. JD and Cisco came running downstairs, and I grabbed the gun that Chris had and aimed it toward Cisco. He threatened to kill me, so I fired a warning shot near him."

My heart was racing outside of my chest but I told everything.

"He kept coming at me, so I shot at him. Goody came from the top of the stairs, shot Cisco, and killed him. Then, he came toward me. Trevon was lying on the ground, asking him for help, and Goody ignored him like he wasn't there. I turned the gun to Trevon and told him to give me his phone, because I was going to call the cops as I saw that he was bleeding a lot. When I reached down to grab his phone, he grabbed me, and I guess I dropped the gun or something. He grabbed it and pointed it at me. Goody told him to shoot me, and I shut my eyes. I thought I was dead, but the police came bursting in, and they all had guns aimed at Goody, JD, and Trevon. Trevon still had the gun on me. There were gunshots, and JD was killed. I remembered Goody lunging toward one of the agents, and they shot him in the shoulder to disarm him. At that point, he was in police custody, and Chris, Trevon, and I were all taken to the hospital. I guess I was the one with the least amount of injuries. Chris was there for a while from his injuries, and well… you know what happened to Trevon. That was it," I finished, sighing.

"Wow… that was quite a lot that you had to go through, huh?" the prosecutor asked. I nodded my head.

"Ms. Davis, I want to ask you a question… as I'm sure the defense will ask this as well. If at any point you felt like Mr. Goodwin was behind your father's murder, why not go to the police?" he asked.

"Honestly? I thought that if I did, then I would get Chris in trouble. I mean, I asked him to basically hustle and sell drugs for him. At the time, I didn't know that Trevon was his son, so I didn't want him to be brought into it. Of course now… looking back at it, it wasn't the best decision for me to make. I should have just gone to the police, but he had gotten out of jail before on charges for murder, money laundering, drug distribution and all of that, so I didn't want to risk him being caught up in all of this. I really didn't have any proof other than that night we were on the roof, but I knew all that would happen was him denying it and getting off. I didn't want to go to the police until I knew for sure. By the time I found out, there was no time to go to the police. By the time we found out, we were running for our lives."

"Thank you, Ms. Davis… your witness."

Garner smiled. The defense attorney stood up and approached me. I knew he was about to try to do everything in his power to bring me down, but I wasn't having it. I was ready for him. I had been prepped in every possible way by Garner so nothing he could say could shake me.

That damn defense attorney asked me every question in the book and tried to make it seem like I was the one that was trying to get rid of Goody. Where they do that at? The prosecution had prepared me for it. Goody wasn't about to get away with shit else. I wanted to see that nigga fry for what he did.

"We'll take a short recess and return in a half hour," the judge ordered. Everyone stood up to go outside. I needed some fresh air. The shit was just too much. This whole damn thing was just doing the most for me.

I wanted to go back to having a normal life, or as normal as possible. I hadn't talked to any of my friends. I hadn't talked to Myesha in weeks. The last time I talked to her, I think we were on the phone all of five minutes. Ever since I found out that she and Chris smashed once, she had been acting funny, but he and I weren't together. It was when he wasn't living in the house.

I couldn't tell her everything that was going on, and I'm sure she thought that I was just withdrawing from her. I wanted to go down there and see her, but they said that they didn't think it was wise. When she came up to Dallas to visit her pops, she didn't even call me. The only reason I even knew she was in town was because of Facebook.

Every time I tried to talk to her and find out how she was, she would make a bunch of excuses not to talk. I didn't necessarily wanna involve her in any of the bullshit, but I just wanted to make sure she was good. After all the shit that she had going on with the drugs, I couldn't lose her too. I didn't even want to think about it, but this whole thing was blowing it. The more that I thought about it, the angrier that I got. It seemed like everybody in my life that I knew was somebody else.

Black had lied to me, and the person that I thought was like a father to me was the reason why my world had been turned upside down. Thinking about Black, I felt bad, slightly. Even though he was just doing what he had to do to make his daddy happy, and he had done some foul ass shit, I still felt bad. He died trying to protect me. He would never get to see his son grow up. He would never get to experience being a father, or being anything other than Goody's flunky for that matter. Because of me, he was dead. I knew I shouldn't feel guilty about it, because technically he had lied to me about so many things, but he still died trying to help me. I would be grateful for that.

I think the thing that made me feel sorry for him was knowing that he had a photo of Goody in his wallet. Seeing how he got ignored, lying on the ground and dying, really showed me that Goody didn't give a damn.

I know it was getting to Chris that I cared so much. And then, of course, to top everything off, I still had to deal with being sued from the accidental death case. Even though all of this had happened, the family was still trying to take me for everything. His wife really wanted me to suffer the most. Despite my face being plastered all over the news for almost being killed and having to hide out, I still had to deal with possibly losing everything that I'd saved up for. Even though Chris assured me that he was there for me, I was just tired of fighting over all this shit. Everything was just getting to me. Hell… at this point, if anything good happened, I would be surprised.

I'd always heard people talking about karma and how when you do bad things, bad things happen to you. Maybe this was my karma. Maybe I was going through all of this because I killed Patricia, but what other choice did I have? It was either going to be her or me. Was it karma for Kim getting my gun? It wasn't like I wanted her to get it, but what was my karma for my dad being killed? What did I do to deserve that?

I was sitting outside with Chris, trying to calm my nerves when one of the associates popped their head outside.

"Court is reconvening," he said. We both stood up and headed back toward the courtroom. The trial had been going on for so long, and after this last witness's testimony, the prosecutor and defense attorney were supposed to give their closing arguments. I was just ready for them to give the verdict, because either way, I was done. Lord knows I was tired of looking at this damn courtroom. I was tired of hiding out. I was tired of having to be escorted everywhere that I went by agents.

Chris and I would have to leave Texas, because at this rate, there was no way we were going to be able to stay in Dallas. Even though most of Goody's whole squad had been taken down, clearly there was a lot about this man that I did not know. Staying in Dallas would be risky, so I would have to leave my entire life behind, but it was probably for the best. Most of it had been snatched away anyway, so in all honesty, it was not like I was missing much. The only things that I would literally be leaving behind would be Nikki and Myesha, and it's not like we were close anymore anyway. I didn't have anything else holding me here, so a new start would be good.

I walked back inside with Chris, and we sat down and waited to see who this surprise witness was. Hopefully, it would be someone that would put Goody under the jail for good.

*****

Chapter Twenty-Three

"Alright, folks, let's get this show on the road. It's already past three. I understand that there is another witness," the judge said.

"Yes, your honor," Garner said.

"Uh, your honor, we have no knowledge of another witness. Prosecution has been claiming that they have a witness to testify against my client, however, the identity has been yet to be revealed," the defense attorney said.

"Your honor, due to the severity of the case, the identity of the witness has remained confidential for their safety."

"I'll allow it," the judge said.

"Your honor— "

"I said I'll allow it, counselor. This is my courtroom, and I will allow the witness. Prosecution, proceed," the judge barked. The doors opened, and Garner turned to the person walking in.

"At this time, I'd like to call Regina Banks to the stand."

I frowned, because I was a little confused. I thought I was supposed to be the next witness that was giving their testimony. I turned around to look at Chris who looked just as confused as me. He'd already given his testimony a few days ago. I turned back toward Mr. Garner when I saw a woman walk past that was familiar.

It took me a minute to realize it, but I had seen her before. The night I had crashed my car, she was the one that came to my hospital room. What the hell was she doing here? How was she connected to this? She took the stand and raised her right hand as the bailiff approached her with the Bible.

"Do you swear to tell the truth, the whole truth, and nothing but the truth so help you God?" he asked.

"I do," she answered. She took her seat, and the prosecutor walked toward her.

"First of all, thank you for being here today, Ms. Banks," he started.

"I know that this has been a very long and drawn-out process for you, and you've been dealing with this for many years. Is that right?"

She nodded her head.

"I'm sorry. Could you speak up so that the people of the court can hear you?"

She cleared her throat.

"Yes. It's been several years," she spoke.

"How many years would you say exactly?" he continued.

"Eighteen years," she answered.

"Wow… eighteen years… what a long time," he said.

"Now, Ms. Banks, I know that this is probably a strange question, but is Regina Banks your real name?"

She paused before she answered, looking around.

"No."

"And would you mind telling us what your real name is?"

I was sitting, looking utterly confused. Whatever was going on, I was completely lost, but I happened to notice that Goody looked shook.

"I changed my name under the advisement of the Federal Bureau of Investigations once I went into witness protection. My legal name is now Regina Banks, but at birth, it was Tiana White… then briefly Tiana Goodwin… and later, it was Tiana Davis once I married to Eddie Davis."

"Thank you, Ms. Banks," he said.

I swear to God at that exact moment my heart dropped into my stomach. I know that she did not just say what I think she said. I know this shit could not be happening right now. I couldn't deal with any more surprises.

"Ms. Banks, why did you change your name?" he asked.

"I had to, once I went into witness Protection," she answered.

"Mmhmm."

He nodded.

"Okay, let me clarify a bit. What relation were you to the defendant?"

"I was his wife for roughly five months," she whispered, squirming in her seat.

"Could you speak up a little, Ms. Banks?"

"I said I was his wife," she huffed.

"And what relationship did you have to his deceased partner, Eddie Davis?"

She sighed and looked directly at me. I took a long hard look at her and saw so much of myself.

"I was his wife… still am. I'm also the mother to Miracle Davis, my daughter that is sitting here today," she managed to choke out. God had to be playing a joke, and if he was, this was outright cruel. My mother was alive and right in front of me.

This couldn't be right. I couldn't have heard what I thought I did. My mother was alive? I looked at that witness stand, and after staring at her and really looking at her, I knew it was true. All of this time, I thought my mother was dead, and now here she was… sitting in front of me, talking to the fucking jury. I turned to look at Chris, and he was just as shocked as I was.

What the hell was going on? This shit was crazy. I open my mouth to say something, but I couldn't make a sound. The prosecutor had walked over to the table, seeing my reaction.

"Are you okay?" he whispered. I just sat there, unable to answer. I could hear him, but there was no way I could form my lips to say anything.

"Your honor, requesting a short recess. I believe Ms. Davis may need a couple of minutes to gather herself," he explained. The judge looked at me and nodded his head.

"Granted. The court will break for a ten-minute recess, at which point we will reconvene. The witness may step down," he said. I watched as she stepped down from the witness stand and walked toward me.

"Miracle," I heard Mr. Garner saying. Chris was now at my side.

"I know this is a shock. I wanted to say something to you before, but because of the severity of this case, I couldn't risk telling you and the news getting back to Goody. I'm sorry about everything, Miracle," she apologized. I still couldn't say anything.

"Baby, look at me," Chris said, pulling me toward him.

"Baby, snap out of it!"

She was standing next to me. I could feel her touching me.

"Miracle," she whispered.

"I'm so sorry."

I turned to look at her, and there were tears in her eyes.

"I'm so sorry, Miracle. I wanted to say something to you. I swear I did, but you don't understand. Goody is a dangerous man."

I could see Goody standing over at the defense table, throwing daggers at me and my mother. I guess the prosecutor noticed it too, because he stopped my mother from speaking any further.

"Why don't we go outside and continue this conversation where there are less eyes watching," he suggested. Chris took my hand and walked me outside with a few agents standing by.

"It's going to be okay, baby," he whispered. I looked at him and nodded my head. He sat me down on the bench, and my mother sat next to me.

"So you've been alive all this time?" I asked. She nodded her head and sniffed, wiping her eyes.

"Yes, and believe me, it's not something that I'm not proud of, but after what happened all of those years ago, it was better that everybody think I was dead than to risk anything happening to you," she explained.

"As crazy as it sounds, I didn't want anything to happen to you, so I had to go."

She stopped and sadly looked me in my eyes.

"I know none of this is probably making sense right now, especially with everything going on, and I promise you I will explain everything. I promise you that I will tell you whatever you want to know… just not right now, because as long as Goody is walking free, neither one of us are safe. We will never be safe until he is dead."

I was hearing her speak, but I found myself getting angry. She thought I was just supposed to listen to her and accept this shit like it was cool? I turned to her and stared at her like the stranger she was. That's what the fuck she was… a fucking stranger!

"You've been alive all of this time, and not once did you think to so much as say hello? Do you know what I've been through?" I snapped. People were looking in my direction, 'cause my ass was loud, but I didn't care.

"Do you know what the hell has happened to me?"

"Baby—" Chris stopped me.

"Not now," I hissed. He stepped in front of me, blocking my view of her.

"Look… I know you're mad, but I need you to focus right now. We got bigger shit to worry about," he fussed. He was right, but I was so fucking mad! How the hell could she just pop up and act like shit was cool?

"Miracle, I'm sorry," she apologized again.

"Whatever," I said, quickly wiping my eyes.

"Let's just get this over with."

I stood up and walked back into the courtroom. I tried to block everything out and ignored the smirk that was on Goody's face as he had walked outside in the hallway. I knew that he was getting a kick out of this. He knew all this time, and the nigga never said a thing. I swear I wished that I could put a bullet through his head right then, but I had to keep my cool. Even though my entire world had been snatched out from me, I wasn't about to let him see me sweat.

I walked back into the courtroom and sat in my seat. The judge walked back to his bench.

"Alright, let's get to this with as few interruptions as possible," he spoke.

"My apologies, your honor," Mr. Garner spoke.

"As you can see, this has been quite a stressful situation for both the witness and her daughter."

I rolled my eyes the minute that he said that. As far as I was concerned, she was still non-existent to me. I couldn't understand how a mother could know that her child is out there suffering, know that her child's father was dead, and do absolutely nothing. I couldn't understand how she didn't want to even try to connect with me. What kind of a mother would allow their daughter to go into the foster system? Why had she been hidden for so many years? And she was married to Goody… what the fuck for?

I was trying not to think about it, but it was hard. She sat at the witness stand while the prosecutor asked her all of these questions, and my mind was completely blown.

"Now, Mrs. Banks, during your marriage to Mr. Goodwin, can you tell the court what you witnessed?" he asked.

"It was a number of things. He had his business going on in the house," she answered.

"Business?" he pushed.

"He had drugs and his operations being run out of the house," she clarified.

"I told him I couldn't be around that, and he called me all kinds of names, disrespected me, and I had filed divorce papers. Shortly after, I met Eddie, and we started dating. Goody, or rather Marques, not wanting me to be happy, and wanting to torture me, did everything in his power to make my life miserable. He and I had been done for over a year, and when I got with Eddie, all of a sudden, the two were best friends. I still don't know how to this day, but Eddie wasn't as heavy in the drug game as Marques was until the two got tight. It only went downhill from there."

I looked at the jury who was listening intently, and I had to admit… I was caught in the story. I never knew how my dad got into the game, so to hear it first hand was something that I needed.

"After I had our daughter, Miracle, I just got so depressed. Goody was constantly torturing me. He knew that I had a secret that I was keeping from Eddie, and he used every opportunity that he could to blackmail me," she whispered.

"And what secret was that?" Garner pressed.

"I had a child with Marques shortly after we got together. That was the reason that we got married because of the fact that I was pregnant. Everything was fine in the beginning, but then, he started to show his true colors. When I left him, I gave the baby up," she confessed.

"I later found out that he got custody of the baby and had another woman raise him as her own. Once I married Eddie, he threatened to tell my secret. I wanted to tell Eddie, but he would tell me that he would kill him or my daughter. He saw how happy I was and did everything to stop that."

"Thank you."

He smiled.

"Now, Mrs. Banks, can you explain to the courts as to the reason for your disappearance?"

She took a deep breath and closed her eyes.

"Shortly after I had my daughter, things got bad… really bad. I won't lie… when I found out I was pregnant again, I started using. I didn't start using until late into the pregnancy, but I just couldn't stop… even after she was born. With Marques threatening me and blackmailing me all of the time, I was trying to do anything that I could to keep Eddie from finding out, and I wasn't handling it well," she admitted. This shit was just getting better and better. On top of all of that, I was a crack baby! What the fuck else did I not know?

"When I was with Marques, he would have me do runs and everything so that I wouldn't interfere with his distribution. I guess I just got weak. I started taking small amounts, and then I got strung out. One day, he found out, and he came after me. He shoved me into a trunk after punching me so hard that my eye was swollen, and he took me to an empty warehouse. He and a few others beat me within inches of my life and left me for dead. To this day, I still don't know how I was found, but I ended up in the hospital. A cop came to question me, and I told him everything. From there, it just spiraled out of control, and the next thing I know, the FBI got involved."

"And what happened after that?"

"Before I could be released from the hospital, someone dressed as a nurse tried to kill me, so the police, along with the FBI, placed me into protective custody, and later, witness protection. I don't think they planned on it being this long…" she said, half joking.

"… but as far as everyone else knew, I died of a drug overdose in that warehouse."

She had started to get choked up and was trying to pull herself together. I didn't realize that I had tears in my eyes while listening.

"It hurt like hell, but I had to leave my family. I loved Eddie, and I loved my daughter, Miracle. Even though I didn't raise him and I gave him up, I loved Trevon too," she sobbed.

"I hated that I never got to tell him that I was sorry. I hate it that all of these years that Marques has tortured my life.

All of these years, he's pretended that he cared for Eddie. He pretended that he was there for him and Miracle… and that he was his friend, but when he started to see that Eddie was getting all the recognition and doing something bigger than just drugs, trying to capitalize on his money, he got jealous. That's why he killed him. He wanted people to worship him like they did Eddie, but he was nothing like Eddie," she said with malice, looking directly at him.

"He was just a wannabe. He lived in his shadows and took pleasure in picking on people that he knew wouldn't fight back, because he couldn't get the person that he really wanted which was Eddie, so he got to everyone that Eddie loved. He destroyed my life and my daughter's life. He took my life from me."

Goody looked as if he could spit glass. I could tell that he wanted to do something, but his attorney placed his hand on the table as if to restrain him.

"I see," Garner spoke after giving her a few minutes to get herself together.

"So just to clarify, Mrs. Banks, in front of the jury… you testify that the defendant, Mr. Marques Goodwin, was the co-conspirator to the now late Eddie Davis and one of the biggest drug lords?"

"Absolutely," she confirmed.

"If it had anything to do with drugs, Goody was involved. At one point, he was trying to do things without Eddie's knowledge. Eddie found out and told him to knock it off. I heard and saw a lot that I probably shouldn't have," she admitted.

"There were a lot of times where I was around, and they didn't know it. I've seen Goody do a lot of bad things. I've seen him giving drugs to kids… seen him kill. He almost killed me on more than one occasion. He's the reason why I got strung out on drugs, abandoned my child, and everything bad that I experienced being involved with him. For over twenty years, I've been hidden and tucked away."

"So why step forward now?" he asked.

"Because he's finally been caught," she said and sighed.

"I know that sounds pathetic, but he had me brainwashed and living in fear for so long, so I wanted to testify. My daughter is braver than I am," she said, looking toward me.

I hoped she didn't think that was going to impress me, 'cause it wasn't. All she basically just told me was that she was scared.

"No further questions," the prosecutor said. The defense attorney stood up and slowly walked toward the stand.

"Well, Mrs. Banks, that's quite an interesting story there," he said and smirked.

"It's not a story… just the truth," she said.

"Truth, huh?" he asked.

"So… we're just supposed to believe that you're telling us the truth?"

"Yes," she answered, studying him.

"Well, Mrs. Banks, that's going to be hard for us to believe, considering that you have a history of sabotaging Mr. Goodwin."

"Excuse me?" she said, confused.

"Oh, I'm sorry… you don't recall the several restraining orders that Mr. Goodwin had against you after your divorce?" he questioned.

“I never did anything to him for him to file a restraining order against me! That was just his way of trying to make it look like I was crazy!” she shouted. Mr. Garner gave her a sharp look, and she calmed down quickly.

“You abandoned your son and claimed that my client took custody of him after you left him with a social worker when I actually have documentation showing that Mr. Goodwin filed for sole custody of the child. We have no records of the child ever being in the system with a social worker.”

He walked over to the table and picked up a folder.

“If it pleases your honor, I’d like to submit into evidence information from the Dallas County courts showing that Mr. Goodwin filed for sole custody of Trevon Warner after claiming that Mrs. Banks was deemed as an unfit parent and a danger to the child,” he said, handing the bailiff the papers.

“That's a lie! I was never an unfit parent. Now yes, I did leave my son, and that was wrong, but I left. I couldn't deal with anything that had to do with Goody anymore,” she stressed.

“Then if that was the case, Mrs. Banks, why begin a relationship with his best friend?” he pushed.

“Why be with someone for so many years, knowing that you would be around him? Why, if he was such a nuisance, would you put yourself in that type of situation? Because you wanted to! You wanted to be a part of his life.”

“No, I didn't!” she cried out.

“I stayed with Eddie because I loved him, and I didn't have any other choice. I couldn't go to the police and tell them what I knew. Goody would have killed me for sure!”

“Damn it,” Garner mumbled next to me. The defense was tearing her apart. Goody was practically grinning.

"You didn't want to get away from my client. In fact, you wanted to be with both of them. Didn't you?"

"Objection!" the prosecutor jumped up.

"Defense is badgering the witness."

"Sustained," the judge said.

"I'll rephrase," the defense attorney said with a smile.

"Mrs. Banks, you had several opportunities to go to the police, and you did not. You claim that you saw my client doing so many illegal things. He tortured you on multiple occasions. He was blackmailing you."

"Question, your honor," the prosecution intervened.

"Counselor, either ask a question, or move on," the judge warned.

"My apologies, your honor. Mrs. Banks, if you were so threatened and so worried and scared, why not go to the police? If he was such a danger, why leave your child with him? Why not go to the officials and have him arrested?" he asked.

"Because Goody is dangerous," she answered bluntly, staring at Goody.

"I had seen the things that he'd done. I didn't want to be a part of it anymore."

"Then why not leave? Huh? Why not just get away all together, instead of marrying his best friend and getting deeper involved in drama? You know what I think, Mrs. Banks?"

He stopped.

"I don't think you were trying to get away. I think that you were trying to be a part of it. I think that you were trying to get a piece of the pie. Now yes, my client may have participated in a few illegal activities, but he was under the orders of your husband. Isn't that correct?"

“No! Eddie did some stuff… yes… but he wasn’t a hundred percent guilty by himself. Goody had a lot to do with it. He did a lot of stuff that Eddie didn't even know about. He was under cutting Eddie.”

“And how would you know all of this? You would have to be around him to see that, right?”

“Yes,” she answered.

“Exactly... no further questions at this time, your honor,” he said, sitting back down. The way this trial was going, and the way she had just reacted, I couldn’t tell what the outcome was going to be.

“Closing arguments will commence tomorrow. We are dismissed for the day,” the judge stated. He banged his gavel, and I bolted toward the door.

This shit was beyond crazy. Like, I swear to God… this was some story book, soap opera shit that you would only see on TV. I might as well be watching *Young & the Restless*. Every damn adult in my life pretty much lied about who the hell they were from what I could see. I couldn't wait to get the hell out of here.

Chapter Twenty-Four

“Miracle, can we talk?”

I turned around, and my mother was standing there looking at me.

“I mean… I don't really know what there is left to talk about. You pretty much said all you had to say in there. So…what’s left? What did I miss? I think I pretty much got the gist of it, Tiana… or is it Regina? Let me see. You met my godfather, you married him, had a baby with this nigga who apparently was my fucking brother! Then you leave him, because you didn't want to be with a drug dealer, so you ended up with my father… another drug dealer and my godfather’s best friend… had me, basically got strung out on drugs, and decided ‘fuck my family. I'm going to do what I want to do’, and you got caught up in some bullshit.

After my father died, you knew that I ended up in the damn system. I ended up with some fucked up ass woman and her even crazier damn daughter who made it her life's mission to torture my ass,” I snapped.

“You had opportunity then, but you never said anything. You had fucking opportunity! Goody's ass was in jail, and you could have come and got me, but you didn't. On top of that, I fucked my own brother for a year and knew nothing… nothing! Do you know how fucked up that is? Do you know how sick that shit is? Do you know how nasty that is? That's some old trailer park, white folks, down south, Mississippi Damned type shit. What if I would have had a baby with this nigga? It could have come out retarded or some shit, because here I am fucking my brother and slowly but surely setting myself up to burn in hell for incest.”

I was furious at this point, and I dared somebody to stop me. They weren’t stupid.

“Oh, but no… you want to talk? You want to have a conversation? What do I need to hear? Please, enlighten me. You want me to run into your arms, hug you, and tell you how much I missed you and all of this shit, when I didn't even know that you existed? All this time I thought you were dead… is that what you want? Am I close?”

This woman actually had the nerve to come to me like I really wanted to talk to her!

“Miracle, I know you're upset, but I'm not going to just sit here and let you talk to me like I'm some dog on the street,” she said slowly.

“Oh really?” I asked.

“So you want me to treat you like my mother?” I hissed.

“Yes, because that's what I am,” she huffed. I smirked and stared at her up and down.

“Not according to the death certificate,” I sneered.

“According to the death certificate, you died eighteen years ago. Apparently, I've been visiting a fucking empty grave, so you and Goody… y'all can have this twisted shit, because as soon as this trial is over, no matter what the hell the verdict is, I'm out. As far as I'm concerned, you don't ever have to worry about me again, because guess what? I'm grown. I'm twenty years old now. The time that I actually needed you has passed. I don't need you. I don't need a relationship with you. I don't need to know you, so you can go back to wherever you came from, because no real mother would even think of letting their child endure half of what I have. From what I can see, you clearly don't know what that word means. Now… if you’ll excuse me.”

I walked past her, not even looking at her to get back inside the courthouse. Even though court was over for the day, I needed a minute. I didn’t care if I had to sit in the lobby. Anything would be better than being out here with her.

I rushed into the nearest bathroom and into the stall. Damn it! I was hurt. I was so sick of this shit! I was so tired. I cried so hard. Why couldn't I have been born to a normal family? Why couldn’t I have been born to some middle class, working three jobs between the two of them, mother and father? I had lived sixteen years in bliss, not knowing about the drama that was going on around me.

Is this what the rest of my life is going to be like? I just wanted to say fuck it and walk away from everything and everybody. I heard a knock at the door, and I already knew it was Chris. He was the only thing really keeping me sane. It had gotten to the point that he knew my every need. We were both young as hell, but we didn't have that typical high school type relationship. Maybe it was because we had been through so much, but everything was just perfect. I remember when he didn't even give me the time of day, and now, we couldn't be apart. If you wanted to be technical about it, we couldn't be apart anyway because of the situation.

I was scared that with us being together so much, we would get tired of being up under each other, but it was the exact opposite. I just hoped that it stayed like that, because if I had to deal with anything else, I might end up on an episode of Snapped. I opened the door, and sure enough, it was him. He took my hand, walking me out of the bathroom and down the hallway with the agent following.

"Look… why don't we just go back to the hotel? We've done our part. Now, it's just sit back and wait to see what happens," he suggested.

"That's fine with me," I said. At least with going back to the hotel, I could get some rest. Knowing that I had to testify, I barely got any sleep the night before, so I was all for it. The agent escorted us outside to the truck to take us back to the hotel. I was actually pretty cool with this agent, Connor. He was real nice and wasn't as tight on us as the others.

We got in the truck, and he gave me a small smile. We pulled out of the parking garage and headed toward the highway. Chris had grabbed me and was holding me when we heard the loud boom. I jumped up and tried to see what was going on, but I heard Connor yelling for us to get down.

Chris jumped on top of me, and we ducked as low as we could as gunshots were fired. One of them went through the windshield, and I screamed. Connor jumped out and began shooting, and within a few seconds, everything died down. My heart was racing, and I had squeezed my eyes shut. I was scared to look up. I did not want to see another dead body.

“Is everybody okay?” I heard. I sprung up and saw that Connor was looking at us from the front seat.

“Yeah,” I answered shakily.

“I think so.”

I was breathing heavily, and Chris was checking me to make sure I hadn't been hurt.

“Baby, I'm okay,” I told him. Connor was now on his cell phone, talking to who I assumed were other agents, and within seconds, they were pulling up. At this point, of course people were staring and watching everything, trying to see what they could talk about.

“We gotta get out of here,” he said. They hurried us into another vehicle and sped off.

“You know that Goody is behind this shit,” I said to Chris.

“Yeah… which is exactly why we need to get the fuck out of here. Like… fuck waiting for the damn trial to be over. We’ve got to get out of here, now.”

“Yeah, but how?” I questioned.

“They're not going to let us out of their sight.”

“I don't know,” he admitted.

“I'll think of something.”

“We gotta move, y’all… just a precautionary measure for when something like this happens. Don't worry. They're getting your stuff from the other hotel,” the agent said.

“I'm so sick of this shit,” I mumbled.

“I know. Me too,” Chris added.

"A nigga can't handle that type of shit… being cooped up all the time and shit. Let's just hope that they find this nigga guilty," Chris said.

"Shit, I don't see how they can't with all this shit that's turned up against him. Unless he's paying off the damn jury or got the judge on the payroll, there's no way."

"Yeah, but the question is… even if he does get locked up, for how long?" he asked.

"You know niggas now be getting shorter sentences and shit 'cause of the whole overcrowded prisons and shit."

"That's true," I agreed.

"So, how you feeling about everything else?" he asked, switching subjects.

"I'm assuming you mean the shit that I just found out?"

"Yeah," he responded.

"Honestly, I don't even know how to feel right now, Chris. Like… I'm trying to wrap my head around it," I confessed.

"I'm trying to understand why she would disappear for so long. I'm trying to understand why my father would lie to me and tell me that my mother has been dead all these years, but I've got nothing. I mean, he knows that she was with Goody, so I'm wondering did he know about Black… even if he did, I'm still trying to figure out if he would have even said anything. All of this is just so bizarre."

"I know," he said, rubbing my shoulders.

"I really wish I had something that I could say to you that would relax you with all this crazy shit, but a nigga ain't gon' lie… this here is some weird shit. Like, on the real… you handled a lot of this shit better than a lot of these broads out here," he complimented.

"Shit, I don't know many females that could hold it down like you do."

"Well, I learned from the best."

I smiled.

"You took a spoiled little brat and turned me into a beast."

"Okay, I see you," he said and laughed.

"I'm going to turn you into something else once we get to that room," he whispered in my ear. I instantly got hot. He liked to see how far he could push me before I lost it and damn near raped him.

"Now you know you gon' end up falling asleep," I teased.

"Well, I'm sure you have a way to wake me up," he growled.

"Oh, most definitely. You just better make sure that you can hang."

"We both know I can do that."

The agent was looking at us through the rearview mirror.

"What?" Chris asked. He shook his head and turned his eyes back to the road.

"You got these folks all in our business," I whispered, giggling.

"So? Let them. Think I give a damn?" he whispered. I smiled, knowing that he was about to do something that would have me wanting to rip his clothes off. Chris was the type of nigga that would fuck anywhere, no matter who was around, and I loved it. The last time he pulled some shit like that, we were in the attorney's office, and he was in there trying to make me nut, finger popping me under the table with his hand. I shuddered just thinking about it.

"Don't worry, baby. When we get to where we going, I'ma put that ass to sleep."

He grinned devilishly. I smiled and felt flushed.

"We'll see."

I liked antagonizing him, but I knew damn well he was going to back up everything that he said. I'm surprised that my pussy was still intact with the way that we fucked.

We finally pulled up to the hotel and waited for the agent to lead us inside. They got us two separate rooms like the last time. I don't know why they did that, considering we were always together. We didn't complain to them though. They were just doing their job. I would just walk down to his room, or he would come down to mine.

"Okay, we've moved all the witnesses from their locations just to be on the safe side," one of the agents told us.

"Someone should be bringing your belongings shortly."

"Okay."

He stared at Chris sitting on the bed and frowned. I didn't really like this guy. He always seemed to be judgmental. He was like that one family member that you had that was always trying to make you feel bad for wanting to enjoy life and called everything a sin. Anything we asked, he would shoot down quickly, telling us that we were going to put ourselves in danger and interfere with the investigation.

For the most part, the agents were cool. Even though they were protecting us, they didn't treat us like kids. We would talk, and they told us about their families everything, but this nigga here was a complete asshole. He finally left, and I flopped down on the bed.

"I am exhausted."

I yawned.

"I feel like I haven't slept in days."

"Oh really?" Chris asked, giving me that look. I perked up real quick.

"Well, not that tired," I said and smiled. He walked toward me and pulled my legs, making me fall backward onto the bed.

"Well damn," I laughed.

"I told you I was going to put that ass to work."

He grinned as he spread them wide.

"Well damn… can I get my skirt off at least?"

"Nope," he answered.

"Leave it on."

"You so damn nasty," I moaned as he started kissing my thighs.

"But you like it," he mumbled.

"Maybe," I teased.

"Oh maybe, huh?" he asked. He pulled my panties down and grabbed my hand, unzipping his pants and placing it on top of his now hard dick.

"You sure that's just a maybe?" he asked, pulling his pants and boxers off, exposing himself.

"Damn," I whispered, looking at it. I swear Chris had the best dick game ever… and Myesha thought I was about to give that up? Hell no! I loved my best friend and all, but there was no way I was about to just walk away from him because they had a quick little fuck once. He wasn't with me at the time anyway. Besides, Myesha had a shit load of niggas on her like always, and Chris told me what it was, so I couldn't get mad at him.

I grabbed his dick in my hands and began to stroke it. I decided to tease him, so I took my tongue and started twirling it against the tip of his dick as I continued to stroke. He groaned deeply, and I placed him in my mouth. I ain't gon' lie… giving that nigga head was a challenge, but every time I did it, I wanted to be better than the last time.

When I first started giving him head, I was scared out of my damn mind, because his dick was so damn big. I didn't have that much experience with it, because the only other person I had been with was Black, so it wasn't like I was some pro at it. I just knew I was going to gag on it or something, but he took his time with me and was patient. The more I did it, the more that I loved it. I craved his dick. I couldn't get enough of it. It was like my own personal everlasting Gobstopper lollipop or something.

There were times where he would want to fuck, and all I wanted to do is swallow his cum. A few times, I went so hard that he had to tell me to stop, because he was drained. Chris would joke and say that I gave him that kind of head that would make a nigga go into Victoria's Secret and buy everything on the shelves, but of course, he would turn around and punish me, torment me, and dick me down. He knew my body inside and out. He would always hit that spot and make me promise I would never give my pussy to anybody. You think I didn't? I damn sure meant it too!

I put all of him in my mouth and let the spit dribble out, making him go crazy. He was touching the back of my throat, tickling my tonsils as I kept my rhythm going, and I could feel his dick throbbing.

"Fuck!" he moaned.

"Gawd dammit, Miracle!"

He looked down at me, biting at his lower lip. I could tell that he was trying to hold that nut in.

"I fucking love you, girl."

I kept sucking and slurping loudly, and he lost it.

"That's it," he announced. He moved me and flipped me over so damn fast that my body bounced on the bed.

"I see you want to play games. Well, I can play that shit too," he said. He raised my skirt up and shoved his dick inside of me. My pussy grabbed him like snapper. He started to grind in me, and I threw it back at him.

"Damn, I've been wanting to do this to you all day," he told me.

"Well don't talk about it… be about it," I whispered. He grabbed my hair which was in a neat ponytail and wrapped it around his hand, pushing me forward, making me arch my back.

"You talk a lot of shit for somebody that cums in a matter of seconds."

He wasn't lying. This nigga had me turning into an all-out porn star. I started throwing it back on him and felt my body shuddering as I started cumming all over his dick. He smacked my ass so hard that I'm pretty sure he left a handprint, but I didn't give a fuck!

"Oh God!" I cried out.

"Harder, baby! Harder!"

"You sure you want that?" he asked.

"Fuck me!" I begged as I turned and looked back at him. He let go of my ponytail and grabbed my hips, pounding me harder just like I wanted.

"Yes, baby!" I moaned.

“Right there. Oh God.”

I was about to explode, and he knew it.

“That's right, baby,” he grunted.

“Cum on daddy dick.”

“I'm cummin’, baby!” I strained out.

“I'm c-c-cummin’.”

He took one of his hands off my hips and started playing with my pussy while his dick was still power driving me. I knew his ass was going to do that. That was the quickest way to get me to cum too.

“Oh shit!” I screamed and exploded my juices all over his dick.

“That's right, baby.”

He smiled as he watched me shake and held me close, now slowing his stroke. I collapsed, and he fell on top of me, grabbing my hand and holding it over my head as he kept going.

“Cum in this pussy, baby,” I said.

“Oh, you know I’ma do that,” he told me, kissing the back of my neck and quickening his pace.

“Ooo, baby. You love this pussy?” I asked.

“Hell yeah, baby,” he whispered.

“Just as much as you love this dick.”

I started to rotate my hips and squeezed my lips as tight as I could against his dick.

“Damn, girl,” he moaned.

“You gon’ fuck around and make my ass get you pregnant.”

That nigga could've told me that he had three eyeballs at that moment, and I wouldn't have given a damn. I felt my body do that familiar shake, and I knew I was on orgasm number two.

"You ready to cum again, baby?" he asked.

"Y-Y-Yes," I stammered.

"Good, 'cause I'm cumming too!"

We were both going hard, and within seconds, I exploded once again on his dick as he shot his load into me. We were lying there for several seconds as we were panting so hard, trying to catch our breath.

"Yeah, I needed that," I said, laying there, still recovering.

"I aim to please."

He smiled, pulling me closer to him, wrapping his arms around me.

"Well, that you did," I told him.

"And multiple times… might I add."

I laughed.

"That's what I'm supposed to do," he said. He placed his lips on mine and kissed me, making me want to attack him yet again.

"Look, baby… I know I'm not the type of nigga that you really saw yourself with, and I know your pops wanted you to be with one of those suit and tie niggas, but as long as you're with me, just know I'ma take care of you, aight?" Chris promised.

"Ain't shit going to happen to you as long as I'm around. You got me?"

Looking in his eyes when he said that, I believed him. He hadn't steered me wrong yet. He always made me feel safe and secure.

"I got you, baby, and you got me," I responded.

"That's right," he agreed.

"And we're going to rock the savage life 'til the wheels fall off."

"Just don't hurt me," I said in barely a whisper. Chris sat back and frowned.

"Have I ever? I'm not Black. You know I'ma always be there for you. You know I'ma always have your back. I love you. I got you. Baby, you know I ain't about to let you go through no more bullshit. I ain't the best nigga out there, and I ain't no soft mothafucka, but I ain't 'bout to have nobody I got love for getting fucked over either. When all this is said and done, we're going to be up and out. I'm going to give you the life that you're supposed to have," he said. I looked at him, confused.

"What you mean?" I asked.

"Damn, Miracle, I know I'm a street nigga and all that, but I still got consideration," he said and laughed.

"You're a pampered princess… a good girl. Your daddy wanted the best for you. He wanted you to go to college and all that, right?"

"Yea," I answered.

"That's what I'm saying. He wanted you to do something with your life, and that's what you're going to do."

"Baby, I don't want you to give me that," I argued.

"All I want you to do is be there for me and love me. Once all this mess is over, I'm going to switch from part time to full time in school. I don't need you buying me shit, because

I ain't one of these money thirsty bitches. Just because that's how I grew up, doesn't mean that's who I am. Yeah, I was a pampered princess and spoiled at one point, but look at how much I didn't know because of the way I was. Look at how much was going on around me, and I was living in a damn bubble. I don't want to live like that.

I wanna know what the fuck is going on and not be living behind a wall. I just want to be happy, because if getting everything I want means being oblivious to what the hell is going on and what the fuck people are doing, then I don't need it… just don't worry about all that."

"Alright," Chris answered after a few minutes.

"But there's one thing that you're not going to argue me down on."

"And what's that?"

"That a nigga be having you climbing the walls," he said and laughed.

"Whatever!"

I slapped him on the arm.

"Nah… whenever," he said.

"And whenever is right now!"

He grabbed me, pulling me on top of him, and I quickly got ready for round two.

*****

Chapter Twenty-Five

We had spent a week in the hotel room after the incident with the truck getting shot at. We were on our way back to the courthouse. The verdict was finally in, and we were going to find out if Goody's ass was going to prison or not. They had designated triple the amount of security as before, and we were being rushed into the courtroom by practically the Secret Service. Hell, you would have thought we were Michelle and Barack Obama, but I definitely understood why. Goody was dangerous.

They escorted us into courtroom, and we sat in the row with an agent on each end, directly behind the prosecutor. There was no point of us really being there, because I had already testified and prepared my letter for the judge for consideration of sentencing if Goody was found guilty. I wanted to see his face when they sentenced him. There was no way his ass was going to get away with it.

I looked across and saw my mother, Tiana, seated in the row across from us with agents around her. Of course the media was there, flashing pictures and trying to get us to answer questions, but I became a mute and zoned out. I didn't make eye contact with anybody. I refused to acknowledge anyone in that room other than Chris or Garner, the prosecutor.

I was just waiting on that door to open on the side and for the jury to come walking in with that little piece of paper saying that he was guilty. Aside from the media there asking questions and the random click of the cameras, the room was significantly quiet. Then again, Goody wasn't in the room yet either. If I was lucky, they would sentence his ass to life in prison or the death penalty. No matter how good of an attorney he had, even Johnny Cochran couldn't get him out of this one. There was way too much on him.

We waited for another fifteen minutes before anyone else came in. The side door opened, and the bailiff brought

Goody into the room in handcuffs. He definitely didn't look as confident as he did before. He sat down as his defense team followed and slouched with this stone-cold expression on his face. I wanted to laugh, but I had to be careful. With all the media in the room, it was better that I stayed quiet and kept my poker face. One wrong thing could be said, and I could be seen as the villain. I had seen it happen too many times.

"All rise," the bailiff announced. We all stood as the judge entered the courtroom, and a few seconds later, instructed us to sit down. The jury walked in a few seconds later and sat with the foreman continuing to stand.

"Have you reached a verdict?" he asked. My brain was screaming *what the hell you think*? Why the fuck else would we be here if they didn't have a verdict? Why was it taking them forever just to give the verdict?

The juror nodded and spoke.

"Yes, your honor, we have."

For the first time, I was glad that it was a jury of several white people. They were going to make sure that this mothafucka fried. A black man selling drugs… oh, it was over.

"On the count of murder in the first-degree, how does the jury find?"

"We, the jury, find the defendant, Marques Goodwin, guilty."

The courtroom erupted in mixed emotions, and I exhaled deeply. I didn't even realize I was holding my breath.

"On the count of conspiracy to commit murder, how does the jury find?"

"We, the jury, find the defendant, Marques Goodwin...guilty."

"On the count of possession with intent to sell, how does the jury find?"

"We, the jury, find the defendant, Marques Goodwin…guilty."

"On the count of money laundering, how does the jury find?"

"We, the jury, find the defendant, Marques Goodwin…guilty."

People began to clap and celebrate. The judge banged his gavel to try to get everyone to calm down, but people were happy. This trial was damn near as big as the OJ Simpson case. Eventually, everything calmed down, and the judge spoke.

"Marques Goodwin, you have been charged guilty on all counts brought against you by a group of your peers. Please stand up, Mr. Goodwin."

Goody stood slowly, still stone faced.

"Marques Goodwin, you are a disgrace to the community and the type of individual that I loathe. Your actions were done with no remorse, and you have shown me that you have no conscience for any of your actions. Therefore, I find you guilty of the charges brought against you. At this time, you will remain in custody until sentencing. Jury, you are free to go with the thanks of the citizens of Dallas. We will reconvene for sentencing in one month's time. Court is dismissed for the day."

He stood to exit the courtroom. Everyone was so in shock.

"It's over," I said under my breath to Chris.

"He's going to go to prison. It's finally over."

I felt like a weight had been lifted off of me. I looked over to see his wife, Tori, crying. I felt bad for her, for the fact that she had to take care of the kids by myself, but he brought this on his damn self. I couldn't feel sympathy for that. I stood up and watched as the officers walked Goody past me.

"You ain't got a clue the shit you started," he said before they yanked him away. They walked him out of the courtroom, and it was like a celebration for everyone.

"Baby, we finally got our lives back."

I smiled. My mother walked over toward our direction.

"You gonna talk to her?" he asked.

"I don't know," I answered.

"Right now, I just want to relish the fact that this mothafucka is going to jail for the rest of his life."

"Facts," he said.

"Let's get out of here," I said, wanting to leave before she could say anything.

"Can we go ahead and go?" I asked the agent.

"Sure."

He sent a text message on his cell phone which I was assuming to let other agents know that we were walking to the parking deck so that they could have the truck ready. Just as we were rushed into the courtroom, we were rushed out, but this time, I didn't have any concern. Payback was a bitch!

"So, what happens now?" I asked.

"Well basically, you're going to continue be in custody for a while," the agent explained as he drove.

"He hasn't been sentenced yet, so to be on the safe side, it's better that you stay in custody until then. Although he has no access to any communication from jail, we can't risk it.

Once that's over, you all will be able to go back to whatever it is that you were doing before you got caught up in this."

I was ecstatic. This nightmare was finally coming to an end in just one short month. We got back to the hotel close to twenty minutes later. It seemed like even the agents were happier. I'm pretty sure they were sick and tired of dealing with us. I know my ass was demanding as hell, so the sooner we got out of their hair, the better. We went back into the room, and I laid back. For the first time in a while, I relaxed.

"You know what I was thinking?" Chris asked suddenly.

"What, babe?"

"I'm thinking maybe we shouldn't move to Atlanta," he said.

"Why?" I asked.

"You wanna go to Florida instead?"

"Nah, ain't shit like that. I know you said you tryin' to get a job and all that, but all I know how to do is hustle, real talk," he admitted.

"And then plus, you know your mom just showed up and everything."

"What's that got to do with anything?" I asked.

"Her being here doesn't change nothing. Baby, at this point, I'm grown. I just turned twenty years old. Legally, she can't do anything. She can't intervene. All she can do is give me my space like I asked."

He took my hand and pulled me to him.

"Look, baby… I know you probably ain't trying to hear it, but yo… you gonna have to talk to her eventually. Shit, we all come from a fucked-up ass background, but look how we ended up. None of us got our folks, but now you do. Now, it may not be the way that you want it, but I'm gonna be real with you. If you get the opportunity to have any type of relationship with your real folks, you should take it. I mean, you ain't got to be like best friends and shit, but look at it like this. You know a lot of folks that have been through what we've been through. They don't have anybody. I mean, you got me, and I know you ain't getting rid of my ass, but now you got your mom. Just hear her out. I mean, honestly… I don't think it's a good look to really leave right now with her popping up… at least not until you and her talk."

"Now all of a sudden you want to play Dr. Phil?" I grumbled.

"Nah, ain't shit like that," he disagreed.

"You know I know how that shit feels. Shit, my mom was killed in front of me, and my daddy left my ass high and dry in a damn crack house, so I know if I had my mom here, I'd wanna at least talk to her."

I knew his ass was right, but damn. I had forgotten that he was fucked up just like I was. His mother was killed while he was in a closet hiding. She was working for a pimp, and the guy he set her up with got high and killed her over twenty dollars. She was stabbed over fifteen times, and Chris was in the closet the entire time. Then when he was with his father, he got high every chance he got and ended up taking Chris to a crack house with him where he OD'd. Somebody found Chris, dirty and dehydrated, and took him to the emergency room where he was put in foster care.

The bad thing was, Patricia's house wasn't the worst house. He had been in some pretty messed up foster homes and had endured a lot worse than Whitney. He had been abused in every way possible, so it was no wonder he snapped the way he did. I'm just glad that he was mine now.

"I just don't get how she could sit back and let that shit happen. Like… I know she dealt with some shit too. I get that.

I know she I was scared because of Goody. Am I really tripping? I mean… am I overreacting?" I asked.

"No," he answered.

"I think it's just all new right now, but look, man… you got me over here acting all feminine and shit. Just talk to her."

"I guess," I said, sitting down in the chair.

"I don't want her to be thinking that she's the reason why I'm staying. I still want to get the hell up out of here," I told him.

"Okay, I'm good with that," he responded.

"We can be out, but what about the shit with the accident and everything?"

"I don't know, but they're tryin' to take me for everything I have. That shit was an accident."

I sighed in frustration.

"Baby, I just want to have a normal life. That's it."

We couldn't have a normal life with drug money, but I wouldn't dare say it. Chris may have had an immunity deal, but my black ass didn't. I never really talked about stuff like that around the agents anyway, but if I did, I kept that shit low.

"You will, but if we're moving to Atlanta, I'ma have to do some hustling. Shit, it'll help with this immunity deal. I ain't saying I'm gonna hustle long… just enough time to stack up a little more paper for us to be straight."

"Chris… you can get a regular job, babe."

"With what?" he asked.

"Just like you, I have a GED. I don't have any work history, and it ain't like I can put drug dealer on a job application."

"Okay, well I can get a job then, but I'll put it to you like this… if you expect me to have a conversation with my mama, then you got six months of hustling. That's it," I threatened.

"Oh, word? That's how you do?" he asked.

"Yep," I answered.

"If you don't like it, oh well."

He got up and walked to the refrigerator, grabbing a bottle of water. We both sat for several minutes in silence. He may not have liked it, but oh well. It was the truth.

"You better be glad you fine," he said, turning on the TV, still not looking at me. I smiled, knowing that he had given in. Pussy was a powerful thing.

"Yeah, yeah, yeah. I'm about to go take a shower," I said.

"Oh, well let me help you."

He smirked, jumping up to chase me.

"Nah, I'm good!"

I laughed, running into the bathroom and locking the door behind me before he could catch me. I turned the water on and stripped down, getting into the water and thought about what he said. I guess he was right. He didn't have his parents. Neither did Nikki or anybody else that was in that house, and now, in a sense, I guess you could say I was getting some type of second chance or something. I just didn't know what it would be like with the two of us. How could you go your whole life not knowing you have a mother, and then all of a sudden, she's there?

I wanted to be sympathetic toward her, but at the same time, it just didn't seem like she really cared. I had to face my demons. I owed it to myself. After all, I had so many unanswered questions. A knock at the door interrupted my thoughts, and I turned the shower water off.

"You not getting in here, so go on somewhere!" I taunted through the door.

"Miracle, you need to come outside for a second. Something happened."

I could tell that he wasn't joking, so I hurried out of the water and wrapped the towel around me. I opened the door to see him standing with another agent.

"What's going on? What's wrong now?" I asked.

"It's Goody," Chris said.

"Okay… what about him?"

"He's dead," he announced.

"What?" I asked.

"Yeah. Apparently… right after he was brought in, he was walking to his cell, and I'm not one hundred percent sure what happened, but in between him being escorted back to his cell and them doing rounds, there was a riot that broke out, and they found him lying on the floor… dead," Chris informed me.

"What kind of shit… so this nigga killed himself?" I asked.

"No."

Agent Connor spoke up, cutting Chris off.

"Okay, can somebody please tell me what the fuck is going on? How the hell does he die in a jail cell where he's the only one in there?"

Chris had turned his attention back to the TV and turned the volume up.

"Y'all, look."

We both looked toward the TV and saw the caption on the screen “Convicted Murderer Killed by Guard” … shit.

*****

Chapter Twenty-Six

Everybody was sitting down, and I was trying to process everything I had seen and heard. I was not dressed, and there were about four other agents in the room with me and Chris.

“Okay…” I said slowly.

“Now what the hell happened? We just left the courtroom… what… a couple of hours ago?”

“Right,” Chris said.

“Well, they’re still doing the investigation,” one of the agents spoke up.

“From what we're told, an officer was doing rounds, and Goodwin had just been brought back. When he didn't respond, the guard called out. There was still no response, so they opened that block. The guard went inside and found him dead. When they checked the footage, it showed that a few minutes before Goodwin died, there was a guard that went in, and he took several minutes before he came out. They weren't able to see his face, but it was clear that he was a guard at the prison. Now, they're trying to figure out who it is.”

“The entire jail is on lockdown,” another guard spoke up.

“Do they know how he died?” I asked.

“There's no official word yet,” Connor answered.

“All we know is that they're suspecting foul play, and if an officer is believed to be involved in this, then it’s not going to look too good.”

“What you mean?” I asked.

“People are going to overlook the fact that he was a felon on trial, and they're going to start to make him be the victim. Then, it's going to open an investigation into the behavior and treatment of the facility and its inmates," Connor told us.

"Not to mention the fact that Dallas County Jail is ninety-eight percent white officers, and with all of that Black Lives Matter going on right now, and with all of the murders with black men that are being killed across the nation and law enforcement being under a damn microscope, it would only make Goody appear even more innocent, even though we know he's guilty. If it turns out that the guard was the one that actually killed Goody, then ain't nobody going to be even looking at the shit that he did. All they're going to be wrapped up in is the whole Black man killed by a white officer," Chris explained.

"I should have fucking killed his ass when I had a chance," I mumbled.

"Chill with all that," Chris warned, squeezing my thigh.

"You know I ain't letting your hands get dirty. If anything, I should've murked his ass. On the real, as fucked up as it sounds, the good thing is that we know he can't do shit else, and we ain't gotta worry about shit. I mean, we locked up like we in jail because of the shit that this nigga did, so now we get to get our lives back and all that."

I nodded in agreement.

"I mean… I guess that's true," I said.

"I don't know. It's just pissing me off, because I just feel like he didn't suffer. Instead of him having to rot where he belongs, somebody just killed his ass."

"Okay, well just chill," he said.

"I know you're mad, but it ain't shit we can do about it now. We don't know anything yet, so don't start tripping."

"Really?" I said in shock.

"Oh, I'm tripping? So, because this asshole that has basically fucked up my entire life, destroyed my family, snatched anything that was good in my life, and was practically the damn Devil himself, I'm not supposed to trip because he didn't suffer? Don't you think I deserve that much? Hell, he damn near killed your black ass too. Now all of a sudden, you on this nigga's dick?"

"Who the fuck you think you talking to?" Chris snapped.

"You, nigga! You can't tell me how the fuck I need to feel and what I need to think. Like, I'm sick of that shit. You don't know half of what this mothafucka did, nigga!" I yelled.

Connor and the other agents were standing around, looking uncomfortable as hell, but I didn't care at that moment. I couldn't believe Chris had lost his damn mind like that. All of a sudden, he thought he was the king on how somebody should feel.

"Okay, so we're going to go ahead and go," one of the agents said.

"Just for right now, let's just all calm down. We don't know anything yet, so until we get the official word, it's nothing we can really do anyway. At this point, all we know is that Goodwin is dead. Let's just... deal with that first. Then, we can go from there."

They left out fast, but I didn't care, because I was furious. They heard every damn thing that we talked about anyway, so it didn't matter.

"I don't know what the fuck is wrong with you, but I'm not one of these broads that you're used to dealing with. I ain't Myesha, okay?" I said in a low tone.

"Really?" he scoffed.

“Why is it that whenever a mothafucka want to tell the truth, the first thing that a female want to do is compare herself to some other bitch? I ain't say anything about what broads I was with. Ain’t nobody tryin’ to check you or no shit like that. I'm being real with you.”

“No, what you're trying to do is tell me that I'm wrong, Chris. I’m tired of having to say this shit over and over again. This nigga has put me through enough,” I spat.

“He's dead, so what does it matter? He was found guilty.”

“Yeah, but it don't mean shit if he don't deal with the consequences.”

“What the fuck you talkin’ about?” he said.

“Shit, it looks like the nigga got the ultimate consequence. Somebody murked his ass!”

“Yeah, but it wasn't me!” I said. I had to calm down, because I was losing it.

“Look, I know it sounds dumb as fuck, but it just doesn't seem like I was really given justice. I mean yeah… they found him guilty and everything, but somebody got to do what I wanted to,” I said. I could tell that Chris had finally started to understand what I meant.

“Look, baby, I feel you, but it's not like anybody can take it back right now. He's dead. Now, we just got to look at where we go from here. We don't have to look over our shoulders no more, and it's not like he going to be able to do shit from six feet under.”

“I know. Like I said, it sounds fucked up that I just wanted to see that nigga suffer, but yeah… you’re right,” I conceded.

“I know I am,” he said with a smirk.

“Why don't you just go sit your ass down somewhere… over here acting like some crazy woman.”

“Whatever,” I mumbled, flopping down onto the bed and picking up the remote to change the channel. I settled on a rerun of Scandal to keep me entertained. I loved this show. I could watch this shit all day long. Sometimes, when we were bored, and the agents wouldn’t let us go anywhere, me and Chris would order room service and literally lay in the bed and watch Scandal all day. He would do stuff like that for me whenever I was pissed off, upset, or depressed. Even though he was crazy as hell, he did have a good side. I had to remember that sometimes when I was ready to pop off on him.

He saw what was on the screen and shook his head.

“Yeah, you going to be good,” he laughed.

“Why don't you come lay down, and watch it with me?” I suggested.

“Nah, ‘cause if I come get in that bed, I’m gon’ remember how mad you made me a minute ago, and your ass ain’t gon’ be watching no damn Scandal.”

“You are such a fucking pervert.”

I laughed, turning my attention back to the TV.

“Yeah, but you love that shit.”

He smiled.

“Hmph. If you say so.”

“We interrupt your regularly scheduled program to bring you breaking news from Dallas County Metro Jail.”

My head immediately went to the television, and Chris walked over to see the breaking story as well.

“This is Melissa Anderson reporting with WGHL News 12. We're coming to you live from outside of the Dallas

County Metro Jail where we are told that the detention center is currently on lockdown. An anonymous source has called in to report that just a few short hours ago, convicted drug lord, Marques Goodwin, has been killed by a guard employed by the jail. News 12 has reached out to the spokesperson as well as the warden for the jail, however they are not issuing a comment at this time. They have confirmed that Goodwin is, in fact, deceased, but they have not reported an official cause of death of yet. An autopsy has been ordered, but there is no official information as of yet. Sources have told us that Goodwin was in an isolated area, and a guard was seen leaving his cell minutes before he was found dead. Goodwin was on trial for murder, conspiracy to commit murder, possession with intent to sell, and felony kidnapping. He was found guilty just a few hours ago and was scheduled to return next month for sentencing. Police and the Federal Bureau of Investigation are launching a full-on investigation to determine if there is foul play surrounding Goodwin's death. News 12 will keep you updated as the story progresses. I'm Melissa Anderson… News 12 reporting live from Dallas County Metro Jail."

"Shit! How the hell did that shit get leaked?" I hissed.

"I don't know."

Chris shrugged.

"Maybe an anonymous source?"

"Who the fuck was it? That's something I want to know."

He sighed.

"'Cause we just found out."

"Exactly… so who the hell was it?" he repeated.

"I don't know, but now this shit is about to be crazy," I said. This story was about to spread like wildfire.

"You think it was one of them?" he asked.

"One of who?" I questioned, completely lost.

"One of them niggas outside. I mean… it makes sense. Shit, it's only been a couple hours."

"Yeah, that's true. I mean, he did have a lot of enemies too," I added.

"Look at how many niggas rolled on his ass when he got caught. Damn near everybody that he had on the payroll flipped on his ass."

"That's facts," he agreed.

"But then it goes back to how they got to him, 'cause they said that fool was in isolation… like his access to anything was limited," Chris pointed out.

"Well, whoever it was made it a whole lot better, in a sense, by leaking it."

I smiled.

"By the time this shit is done, he's going to end up being another hashtag on one of these T-shirts. You see the way these white folks be talking about these niggas that be getting killed and shit? I mean… they damn near gave George Zimmerman's ass a metal and tried to make Treyvon Martin look like he was some thug, talking about he shouldn't have been walking with a hoodie on. Then ol' boy, Mike Brown? They ripped him apart over a Black-n-Mild. These fools ain't about to let folks forget what the hell he was doing… trust. Somebody going to bring up the whole Black Lives Matter poster or some stuff like that, and then these white folks are going to go in on his ass," I said.

"I wonder who the guard was," he murmured.

"Ain't no telling, but one thing for sure is that the shit was personal."

The news reporter popped back up on the television screen, and Chris and I watched intently.

"Welcome back to News 12, and thank you for tuning in… breaking news update. A few minutes ago, we reported that convicted drug lord, Marques Goodwin, was killed while in custody at the Dallas County Metro Jail. Not moments ago, we received news that two inmates, Montez 'Mac' Johnson and Jerrel Wilson, both inmates at Huntsville Penitentiary, have been killed in what appears to be an isolated incident. Both Johnson and Wilson were participating in cleanup duty on the prison grounds when they were stabbed numerous times by three unidentified inmates.

A third victim, Keith Thompson, was also involved in the attack, however was transferred from the prison infirmary to a local hospital where he is considered in critical condition. Johnson and Wilson were pronounced dead on the scene. Several eyewitnesses state that during the cleanup, there was an altercation between Johnson, Wilson, Thompson and the unidentified assailants when the assault happened. Johnson, Wilson, and Thompson were all convicted on felony drug charges in the Marques Goodwin case, and in agreeance to their plea for testifying against Goodwin were sentenced to seven years. We'll have more as the story unfolds."

I looked at Chris in complete shock.

"What the hell is going on?" I said.

"Yo… this shit is crazy. Mac and Jerrell were two of Goody's top runners," he recalled.

"They've been running for him for years. JD and Cisco used to tell me about it," he said.

"I mean… I remember seeing them around a few times when my pops and I would be at the restaurant and everything," I recalled.

“Yeah, and ol’ boy, Keith… he was born in the trap. That’s all that nigga ever knew… picking up money and making sure mothafuckas was handling they business. He was like the next one in line,” Chris told me.

“Wow.”

I was amazed.

“And they just conveniently got killed the same day that Goody did?” I pointed out.

“Right, which means somebody is trying to take out Goody's crew,” Chris said.

“But anybody that had to do with him was either convicted or given immunity in the trial,” I said, thinking about it.

“Wait… that means they could be coming for you too…”

“Nah, I don't think that's it,” he observed.

“I mean, I'm just saying. Every last one of them took some type of deal for rolling on Goody, so what if somebody is feeling some type of way or something?” I said.

“Miracle, come on. Don't start this shit,” he complained.

“You can't be paranoid over every little thing.”

“I'm not trying to be. I'm just saying… shit ain't adding up. It's something else that we don't know, Chris. If a nigga was going to kill somebody because they snitched, they would have done that shit months ago when the trial first started, but now? Especially with Goody about to go down, and his ass is found guilty, all of a sudden, fools start dying? Three niggas in one day and another one in the hospital?”

“Yo, you really reaching with this, huh? You gotta stop reading all them damn street lit books and shit,” he joked.

“Chris, I'm serious,” I said, rolling my eyes. He always wanted to tease me about stuff like that.

“I can see if folks was getting killed, and Goody was still alive, but think about it,” I stressed.

“Goody’s ass got murked too, and just like in those little books that you’re making fun of, in every single one of those books, if it's got to do with drugs, there's somebody always at the top. There's always some mystery nigga that's running shit and pulling the strings,” I pointed out to him.

“Whoever the hell it is that’s doing this doesn't want to be caught.”

“Which means your nosey ass is about to be tryin’ to find out, instead of leaving well enough alone.”

He sighed.

“Well, just like in those books, Miracle, the same folks tryin’ to find the truth know that there’s always somebody watching you. They gon’ dead anybody that gets close to finding out, so leave it the hell alone,” he warned. I knew he didn't want me to, but I was worried, and I was gonna have to do some investigating of my own. If anybody that had anything to do with this case was in danger, then so were we.

Chapter Twenty-Seven

“Oh shit,” I moaned. I woke up to Chris face deep in my pussy, eating me out like he missed ten damn meals.

“Really? That’s what we doing now?” I giggled, trying to maintain my breathing. He answered by flicking his tongue rapidly against clit, causing my body temperature to go through the fucking roof.

“Shiiiiiiittttt,” I murmured.

"Slow down, baby."

He grinned and kept going until I came so hard my head started hurting. He sat up, wiping his mouth, and kissed me, letting me taste my own juices as he entered me slowly, stroking me so damn good that I was in heaven.

My phone started ringing, and I groaned, looking to see that it was Nikki calling. I quickly sat up and answered the phone frustrated.

"Hello?" I answered.

"Hey, girl. You saw the news?" she asked.

"Yeah, we did. The shit is crazy," I told her.

"Are y'all okay?" she asked.

"Yeah, we good."

"Okay cool. Well, did y'all wanna come over? I was wondering if you could help me with the baby for a little bit… I mean… if you can," she drug out.

"Yeah, that shouldn't be a problem. We gotta go to the station first to have a meeting with the agents to see what we are able to do, but um… I'm gonna have to call you in a little bit, 'cause I'm a little occupied right now," I told her.

"Eww. Y'all are nasty. Go ahead and handle your business, nasty."

"Alright cool. I'll call you once we leave this station and everything, and we get an update," I rushed to say. I hung up the phone, and Chris yanked me back down on the bed no sooner than I had hit the end button.

"I love when you do it like that."

Before I knew it, we were rolling around in the sheets, and I was digging my fingernails into his back.

I woke up a few hours later and got up to get dressed. Chris and I were supposed to be going to meet with the investigators to determine if we would need to stay in protective custody. After about an hour of me showering and getting dressed, we were finally headed to the precinct.

I was hoping that they would let us go, because being surrounded by investigators and agents all the time was getting old. I wanted to get my normal life back. Granted… normality was kind of strange for us because of everything that we had known, but it would be nice.

We got to the precinct, and they had a room prepared for us. We sat down and waited for the investigators. I just knew they weren't going to let us have a normal life anymore. Something told me we were going to be in protective custody for ever.

Agent Johnson walked in the room and gave a slight smile.

“Well…” he started.

“…We've been assessing the situation, and we do believe that this is an isolated incident. Now, because of the fact that Mr. Goodwin is now deceased, it is raising questions as to if there's any concern for another party that may be involved. We want to wait it out for the next couple of days and see what happens. If everything goes well and nothing seems out of the ordinary, then you all will be law abiding citizens again.”

He paused and held up his hand.

"But that doesn't mean broadcast yourself. You'll still probably want to keep a low profile," he advised.

"Oh, don't worry. We will. Folks won't even know we're here," I said. I looked at Chris and winked. I'm pretty sure the agent caught it, but I didn't give a damn at that point. I was ready to get the hell out of Dallas, Texas!

We went back to the hotel, and I started looking at apartments and jobs that we could get in Atlanta. Although I really didn't have much experience with doing anything, taking those classes online did help.

"So we gonna go legit when we move to Atlanta, right?" I asked, reminding him of our previous conversation.

"Do you really want to?" Chris asked.

"What do you think?" I said with a smirk.

"You know it's whatever you wanna do."

He shrugged, looking in his phone. He could never make a decision when it came to things. It was either that, or he would just say "okay" and let it go. He would always tell me it was whatever I wanted to do.

My cell phone rang before I could respond, and I picked it up to see a private number.

"Oh, I don't do blocked calls," I said, putting the phone back down. Chris looked over at me, and I shrugged, dismissing it.

"I don't know who it is. It's coming up private," I told him. It rang a few more times and then eventually stopped. A few minutes later, it started to ring again.

“You think it might be one of the agents or something?” he asked.

“I don't know, but obviously you want me to answer it, so let’s see,” I said. I answered the phone with an attitude.

“Hello?” I said.

“Hi, Miracle, umm… please don't hang up. It's me.”

“Who the hell is this?” I asked.

“It's your moth— Tiana. Um… it's your mother,” she replied.

“Oh,” I answered dryly.

“What's up?”

“Listen… I'm sorry for calling you unannounced. The agent gave me your number. I guess I uh… I was wondering if maybe we could meet so that we could have a chance to talk?” she said.

“I really don't want to right now. I'm not going to lie to you. I'm not as angry as I was that day, but this is going to take some adjusting. I appreciate you for trying to reach out, but just give me some time, okay?” I huffed.

“It's enough going on, and I got enough to deal with.”

“Oh… okay. Well, I’m sorry, Miracle. I didn’t mean—”

“It’s okay. I have to go. Thanks for calling.”

I hung up the phone before she could respond. My head had been hurting for the last couple of hours, so talking to her at that time would only make things worse. I just wanted to get away from all of the damn agents and live my life.

God must have heard my prayer, because a few days later, we were actually free. I didn't know how to act. It had been so long since we were able to do anything without having an agent looking over us, but we were more than ready. Chris and I had just gotten another hotel room, because we had planned to move to Atlanta within a month and didn't want to waste money on an apartment.

The first thing we did was plan to fly to Atlanta the next day to look at apartments, but that plan failed, because no sooner had we gotten in the car to head to the airport did my ass get tremendously sick. Chris took me to the hospital, and I thought I had the flu, but don't you know that this damn nurse told me that I was pregnant?

I was about to be somebody's mother! I could not believe it. Of course, Chris was excited. When he heard the nurse say that I was pregnant, he started laughing.

"What the fuck is so funny?" I asked.

"'Cause the way we been fucking, it's about damn time!" he laughed.

"I was beginning to think that my soldiers weren't marching."

"So, you think this is a good thing?" I asked.

"You don't?" he questioned.

"I'm not saying that it's not a good thing, but I mean… we're supposed to be moving and everything," I told him.

"And we still can," he told me.

"We still will… only this time, instead of us moving into one bedroom, we just need to get something a little bit bigger."

"Yeah, but how are we going to do this?" I asked.

"I mean, you're supposed to be going legit and everything, and— "

"You just let me take care of that," he said, stopping me.

"Right now, we'll get the car packed up and just drive to Atlanta. We can look for places when we get there. If we need to stay at a hotel and do what the fuck we been doing, that's cool too. You and me both deserve to get the hell out of here, babe. Too much shit has happened since we've been here, and I wanna have a drama free life for my kid," he said and smiled.

I had to agree with him. I thought about how my life had changed since the day my father had died. Foster homes, abusive foster mother, losing Kim, dealing with Whitney's crazy ass, killing Ms. Patricia, being on the run, Nikki sleeping with Black, finding out Black was Goody's son, and then, of course, finding out Black was my damn half-brother was just so much.

"What about Nicki?" I asked suddenly.

"What about her?" he asked.

"You think we should just leave her here?" I questioned.

"I mean… babe, that's up to you," he answered.

"You know I don't care either way."

I nodded my head. I was still in shock to know that I was pregnant. I looked down at my stomach and smiled slightly. It's not necessarily the way I planned on things going, but hey… it was happening. I wondered what my dad was thinking. Was he happy for me? I was about to be someone's mother. I never even thought about kids, but I think it would be kind of interesting to see what a little one would look like between me and Chris. Black and I used to talk about stuff like that all the time… about having a family, but clearly, that was not going to happen thanks to this craziness.

"Well, I guess you're right. I'll call her. Matter of fact, if you want to, we can head over there and let her know to see if she wants to come visit or something," I told him.

"Aight, cool."

After a while, they discharged us from the hospital, and we drove to Nikki's spot. She was staying in some projects in Highland Hills, and it was tons of folks outside on the block. We parked his car and got out, heading straight to Nikki's apartment. I didn't have to worry about anybody, 'cause niggas knew Chris, so I was good.

She opened the door, holding Junior in her arms.

"Hey!" she greeted.

"Hey," I said. She stepped to the side so that we could come in.

"Hello, little man."

I smiled. She handed him straight to me.

"Here, girl," she grunted.

“He's been extra cranky today… trying to work my nerve. I don’t know why, but he's being real whiny,” she fussed. I nodded as he grabbed at my hair, wriggling, and kissed his forehead.

“Well damn, Nikki. He's probably crying because he's hot as hell! That’s why he’s whiny,” I told her, feeling how hot he was.

“Have you taken his temperature lately?”

“I took it last night. It was ninety-nine degrees,” she responded.

“Yeah… but Nikki… he’s a baby. You need to take him to the doctor or something like that,” I fussed at her.

“Girl, he will be fine,” she said.

“Nikki, he is not like me and you. You can't just assume he's going to be fine. It could be an ear infection. It could be a cold. Just take him to the doctor,” I told her.

“I can't,” she said with a sigh.

“I don't have the money,” she admitted.

“Where is his car seat?” I asked.

“It's in the back. Why?” she asked.

“‘Cause we're going to take him to the doctor. Just because you don't have any money doesn't mean that he shouldn't be looked at and treated so that he’s not so irritable. Why the hell doesn’t he have Medicaid or something, Nikki?”

“I applied, but they taking forever… talking ‘bout it’s some kind of wait list,” she explained. I got up and walked toward her bedroom with a look of disgust. The entire house was nasty as hell. Just because you had to live in Section 8 didn't mean you had to look like you lived in Section 8. I swear her room was set up like one of those memes that you see on Facebook. It's what I like to call “The Thots Room”; air mattress on the floor, clothes everywhere, and hair lying all on the floor. How could she live like this?

I grabbed the car seat and went back into the living room to strap the baby in. We walked to the car, and of course, Nikki was looking like a million bucks while the baby was barely dressed. I wanted to cuss her ass out, but he wasn't my child, and there wasn't anything I could say, but I would tell her later that she needed to do a better job of taking care of my nephew.

After getting to the doctor, of course his temperature was higher than ninety-nine, and he had an ear infection. I could tell that she was trying not to look in my direction, because she knew I was right, but I kept my mouth shut. We weren't as close as we used to be, so I wasn't as chatty and blunt as I usually was. I was trying to be considerate, but a bitch was going to be making a phone call to social services if she didn’t get her shit together. The sole reason for me still talking to Nikki was because she saved my life that day. Of course, now I had more to go off of, knowing that Junior wasn’t just her baby, but my nephew.

I didn't hate her, but it's not like I had completely forgotten what she did either. I did have a soft spot in my heart, because she did have Black’s child. Even though the two of us weren’t together, and he cheated on me with her, the baby was innocent and didn't have anything to do with it.

“What you thinking about?” Chris asked, driving back to the hotel. We had spent several hours at the doctors, then going to the pharmacy to get his meds and getting groceries for them.

"Honestly? Maybe now isn't the best time for us to move to Atlanta."

"Why not?" he asked, looking confused.

"You were all for it earlier."

"'Cause, Chris… I mean, it just seems like stuff keeps piling on… finding out that I'm pregnant, then my mother reappearing, and… and plus… you see this shit that Nikki got going on. She was just going to let the baby sit in the house sick, because she didn't have any money. She never has any damn money. It's a wonder how she's taking care of that baby just off food stamps and WIC vouchers and shit," I stressed. I sighed and looked out the window.

"I'm just saying… if we move to Atlanta, she gon' let that little boy die or something."

"Yeah, but we need to get away from here though. Too much bad shit has happened here, Miracle."

Chris shook his head.

"I'm not going to sit here and wait for more shit to happen… and you or the baby be hurt. The further that we can get away from here, the better. I ain't saying we got to move like right now, this instant, but Atlanta will be a good look," he tried to reason.

"I've already made a couple of phone calls, and I got a couple of my partners down there that said that they would look out."

"I guess."

I gave up. I just didn't feel like talking about it anymore. We had only been away from the agents for a few days, and it seemed like stuff was getting worse. I turned to look out the window. I didn't want to argue with Chris, but something just wasn't feeling right to me, and I wasn't going to tell him, 'cause all he would do is tease me and say that I was reading too many of my damn street lit books again. Maybe he was right. I read a lot of street lit books and compared our life and situation to a lot of stuff.

You know the typical street stories where the girl falls for the dope boy. She was a good girl, then she meets this bad guy, and they fall in love. She gets pregnant and has to go through a whole bunch of bull. I always said we were just like that, minus the babies, but bam! Here's the baby! That seemed to be my life right about now, but with all of the books that I read, they ended up happily ever after. As long as Chris and I made it, and my baby was healthy, I was good.

It was finally over. I found out who killed my father. He had gotten his justice. I felt like he could rest, and so could I.

*****

Chapter Twenty-Eight

The next morning when I got up, Chris was already up and dressed. He seemed like he had a lot on his mind, but I was still pissed at him from the day before.

"Good morning," he grunted.

"Morning," I mumbled. I drug myself out the bed and went into the bathroom to start getting dressed. We were supposed to go to meet with my lawyer. I was trying to take care of this lawsuit as quickly as possible. I was still being harassed by the family of the man that I accidentally killed in the car accident.

Every time I turned around, his wife was throwing the guilt trip on me, making it seem like I just killed him on purpose, talking to the media about how I was reckless and thoughtless and should have been criminally charged. She said nothing about damn near extorting me for all my coins. I was hurting that night. I did something stupid, and I already knew that I was going to have to live with that, but all the unnecessary bullshit was pissing me off. My attorney told me that they had come up with a settlement amount, and I needed to meet with them to sign the paperwork since I agreed.

I just wanted to get it over with, get the damn family paid, and be done with it. But, I had them add a clause that she could not talk to media any further once she signed the papers and got the money, because I was tired of getting attention from both the case and from her. That would be one less thing I would have to worry about on the never-ending shit list that was my life. I was definitely ready for a change. Thinking about it, I knew that Chris was right. It was better that we got out of Dallas. Now, I was going to have to apologize to his ass. Apologizing to a man is the worst thing ever… especially when it was a nigga like Chris.

“What you over there smiling about?” he asked, walking up behind me. I turned to him and gave him a small smile.

“Because I didn't want to say that you were right,” I said.

“What you talking about?” he said.

“We do need to get out of Dallas, and thinking about everything that's going down, staying here would only invite more drama into our lives, so you were right,” I admitted. He laughed and squeezed me.

“Look at you, being all cute and shit,” he teased. I don't know why, but I felt like crying. I guess Chris noticed it too, because he squeezed me tighter.

“Hey, I know your thug ass ain’t crying.”

“Shut up,” I said, shoving him lightly.

“It’s these pregnancy hormones,” I joked. He smirked and shook his head.

“Yeah, that's what it is. That's alright. Even savages have a day.”

He laughed.

“I was thinking about something though.”

“Ah hell... What?” I groaned.

“Well, it's pretty much just me and you,” he said.

“Yeah,” I responded, not knowing where he was going with it.

“I know you were saying that you were worried that Nikki was not taking care of the baby and everything,” he added.

“Okay?” I said.

“What if we just brought her to Atlanta with us? That way… you know… you can kind of keep an eye on her, and be there for the baby. Hell, maybe this is a way for y'all to get your friendship back,” he suggested.

“Have her move to Atlanta? I don't know,” I said. The thought crossed my mind of Nikki living with us. She already fucked my last boyfriend. Granted, he was my half-brother, but still... I didn't know if I could trust her around Chris.

“Now you already know she's like my sister,” he said as if he was reading my mind.

“Plus, I ain't got time to be in the bull. Hell, if you want, we can get her a spot nearby, or she just stay in a hotel or something until she gets straight. She can try to find a job out there, and hell, the further that you get along in the pregnancy, she can be there to help,” he added.

“And what the hell are you going to be doing?” I asked.

“Doing what I do best,” he said and smiled.

“I hit my boy, Markell, up. He said he knows a couple of spots that I can help out with. I mean, it’ll be low-key, but shit… that's what we need right now anyway. Then, once I get my feet wet a little bit, who knows.”

“I guess so,” I said. I was not really liking the idea of just sitting at home.

“You know I don't want you out there in the streets while you're pregnant,” he admitted.

“I know, but I just don't know what else I can do.”

“Well… I mean, baby girl, you still got school work, so that'll take up a lot of time.”

“Yeah, but I'm not trying to be one of these bitches to get all big and shit, just sitting around the house, eating and doing nothing either,” I said.

"Well, let's just see what happens," he suggested.

"Okay," I agreed. I was going to agree with whatever just to drop the subject.

"But you know what?"

"What, babe?"

"I think we should throw like a farewell party," I said.

"We could do that," he replied.

"Yeah."

I smiled, getting excited.

"We can have everybody come out, and you know… celebrate our new lives together."

"Aight, cool. I'm with it, but I'll let you handle all of that. Just let me know what you need."

Chris sighed.

"Oh, you wasn't gonna have much of a choice."

I laughed. My phone rang, and I pushed past him to go and see who it was.

"Speak of the devil."

Nikki's name was on the caller ID.

"Hey," I answered.

"How's little man?"

"He's doing better," she said.

"Cool."

"Do you think that you and Chris could help me out with some money for my light bill? They were supposed to send me my voucher, but I haven't gotten it yet, and they're talking about disconnecting my electricity by 5 o'clock," she asked. I rolled my eyes. I felt like she was using the fact that she had Black's baby against me, but I wasn't going to trip.

"Alright, cool. I'll go ahead and take care of it. I've got to get ready to head over to the attorney's office, but once I leave there, Chris and I will stop by, 'cause we got something we want to talk to you about, aight?" I told her.

"Okay," she sighed.

"Is everything okay?"

"Yeah, it's straight, but we just wanted to see about something that we wanted to holla at you about," I told her.

"Aight, cool," she responded, sounding uneasy.

"Girl, relax. Ain't nothing wrong. I'll call you when we're on the way."

I hung up the phone and rushed to finish getting ready. Chris was putting his chains on, and I caught myself waiting for the agent to come and get us before I remembered they weren't there anymore! I laughed at myself, and we walked out the door.

"Damn, this feels different," I said.

"Hell yeah, but we out," he agreed.

"That's right."

I nodded.

"Oh… before I forget, I told Nikki that we would help her pay her light bill, and I figure we can get the baby some clothes and stuff, 'cause judging by what I saw, he doesn't have much."

"That's straight, but… you know you got your own baby on the way, right?" he joked.

"Yes."

I laughed.

"I don't know. I guess in a way I feel like I've got to be responsible for him. After all, he is my nephew now. I know I was calling him that before, but clearly, he's actually my real-life nephew now," I said.

Anytime I thought about Black being my brother, it just turned my stomach. Why the hell would Goody let it get that far? He knew that we were sleeping together, but he was more concerned about his own stuff that he didn't even care that his son was sleeping with his half-sister. I guess maybe he felt like as long as he didn't create me that it wasn't a problem. I hoped that nigga was burning in hell. Thank God for whoever it was that killed his ass.

"You aight?" Chris asked, driving.

"Yeah, I'm good... just thinking about all this mess," I said.

"Well don't," he fussed.

"That's some shit that's done and over with. We're going to get back to this money and do what we do best, and that's what it is. I can't have my wife out here stressing."

My eyebrows shot up, and I damn near choked.

"Your wife?" I asked.

"Yeah, my wife," he reiterated.

"Um… where the fuck this come from?" I asked. He looked at me out the corner his eye, focusing on driving.

"So what… you not trying to get married?" he questioned. Where the fuck did this conversation come from?

"Baby, I'm twenty years old. Like… I literally just turned twenty years old a couple of days ago," I stated.

“Okay… and I'm twenty-two,” he responded.

“Well just because we're having a baby together doesn't mean that we have to get married. Plus, let's keep it real. We haven't really been together that long,” I pointed out.

“Damn, Miracle, I'm not saying that I'm trying to marry you tomorrow. It was just a joke,” he huffed.

“I'm just saying… later on down the line… we getting older. You don't think that we’ll get married?”

“I don't really know a lot of hood niggas that have wives,” I answered dryly.

“Only niggas I know like that is Nino Brown from New Jack City, and you see how that turned out.”

I was being sarcastic, but oh the hell well.

“Well, your mama was married to your daddy, and that nigga was a hood nigga,” he snapped back. He better be lucky that his ass was driving, because otherwise, I would have knocked him straight up side his head.

“Really? That's what we doing now? So you throw my mama in my face? Okay, I got you.”

“You know that's not how I meant it, but I'm just saying. You make it seem like you ain't trying to be with a nigga,” he said.

“When in the fuck did I say that, Chris?” I asked.

“When in the hell did you hear me say that I wasn't trying to be with you? All I said was I'm not trying to get married right now. You’re the one that brought that shit up, not me… bad enough we already having a baby!”

“What the fuck you mean *bad enough*?” he asked. I groaned in frustration. This shit was just too much for me right now.

“Meaning I'm twenty years old. For the last three damn years, I’ve had more fuck shit happen to me than the average bitch. We've been dealing with bullshit since we pretty much met each other. I love you… yes, but at the end of the day, Chris, it's been a lot of shit that we've had to go through. Now, we're having to alter our whole lives to bring a kid into the world. We're moving to a new city. We both have fucked up situations… like hello! We’re on the way to a damn lawyer's office to pay all of this money to a dude’s wife and kids because of some more bull that I had to deal with, and God only knows what else can happen,” I said.

“All right,” he mumbled, gripping the steering wheel. I could see his jaw clench tightly.

“Chris, I'm not saying that I don't want to be with you.”

I sighed.

“I'm just saying that I'm not trying to be in a situation where we have to be together because we got a baby. We've been together for a year. I want to finish school, and I want to be able to do something other than hustle,” I confessed.

“So what… being with me is going to stop you from doing that?” he asked.

“No, but when you said the whole wife thing, it just kind of scared me,” I answered. He nodded his head.

“I feel you. I ain't trying to mess shit up. When I said *wife*, I wasn't thinking about it being an instant thing, so my bad,” he apologized.

“At the end of the day, you got my baby, and I'm going to take care of you the best way that I can for as long as I can until they take a nigga down.”

“Don't talk like that. Baby, we've been together all this time, and for as long as I've known you, you've never gotten caught up in no mess. I mean, both of us got some blood on our hands."

I got quiet for a second, thinking about the things that we had done.

"Is that what it is? Do you think it'll ever catch up to this?" I asked.

"I mean…" he started.

"That's how life works, but if it catches up to me, I'ma go out swinging. You know I don't believe in all of that karma shit like that. The shit that I did was for a reason, same as you," he said.

"Yeah, I guess," I said. We pulled into the office and got out the car.

"Look."

He stopped me.

"I ain't trying to be fighting with you. You know I ain't trying to make you mad or nothing, but just know that I do plan on wifing you up one day?"

This shit was getting on my nerves. Like… why in the hell were we talking about this?

"Yeah… okay."

I laughed. Maybe one day I would change my mind, but today wasn't the day. I wasn't trying to be the wifey type so soon. That just wasn't me. If he didn't like it…I don't know what to tell him.

***

We spent almost two hours at the attorney's office, but it was finally done. I had to pay the family $25,000 in a wrongful death lawsuit. Of course, I had way more than that in the bank, but what twenty-year-old did you know was walking around with that kind of cash? They didn't know the real deal.

The money that I was paying them was coming out of money that had been left to me by my father when I turned eighteen. That much was true, but he definitely left me more than $25,000. I was just happy to have that over with. They had their check, and she couldn't mention it again, or she would have to forfeit all the money and risk being sued.

That was done, and now I could move on and focus on the next big thing. The minute that we left, I called TXU while we headed to Nikki's spot and paid her electricity bill. That girl was behind several months.

"I don't know what the hell this girl is doing, but if she moves with us, she's going to have to do better. Like… I don't know what the hell she's spending the money on that she gets, but it damn sure ain't her bills."

"Well, y'all can talk about that when we get there," he said.

"You know what club you want to throw this party at?" I asked, changing subject.

"Thinking of a few. One of my boys was telling me about this spot that's in Deep Ellum," Chris told me.

"Out there with the hippies?" I asked.

"It ain't that bad," he said and laughed.

"Or we can try that spot, Illume. They're popping right now. Like I said, it's whatever you wanna do."

"Well, you know any party that involves me is going to be lit."

I smiled. I was already thinking of ideas. I had a few DJ's that I knew who used to work for my pops back in the day, so it wouldn't be hard to track them down, and of course, I was going to make sure that we bought out the bar. I may not be able to drink, but everybody that was at the party was going to have a good time. People were going to know who we were.

"This is going to be a really big party. We have a lot to celebrate. We're not dealing with anymore lawyers and court or Goody's psycho ass. We are finally done with all of that, babe!" I said.

"Hell yeah."

He grinned, grabbing my hand. I leaned over to kiss his face.

"Just me and you," I cooed.

"Bonnie and Clyde."

"Sweet and Savage," he finished, referencing the nicknames that we made for each other. Normally, I was sweet, and he was savage, but every now and then, we switched roles.

I was so wrapped up in him that I didn't even notice the dark SUV barreling toward us, but it was too late. It hit us so hard that we slid into oncoming traffic and plowed into two other cars. I screamed as the impact knocked me around the front seat.

I looked over, and Chris was up against the window, unconscious.

"Chris! Baby!" I screamed, trying to shake him.

He was breathing, but I was petrified. People were running toward the car, and somebody got out of the truck, walking toward me. Something in my gut was saying that I was about to die. I looked around and grabbed the gun that was on Chris's side. Fuck that! Ain't no way in hell I was about to let some nigga murk us in the middle of the damn street.

The look in that man's eyes was something cold and vicious. He walked up to the passenger side and tried to open the door.

“Oh my God!” I heard a stranger yell out as I clutched the gun in my hand, ready to pop this fool on site.

“Are you okay?” a concerned citizen asked. They were now closer to the car, and the man, realizing there were too many witnesses, gave me one last look.

“This ain't over,” he growled before he ran off, jumping back into the SUV and speeding off. My heart was racing a mile a minute as I watched the damaged truck disappear into the distance. The car door opened on the driver’s side, and I turned, gun drawn.

“Whoa!” the man said, throwing his hands up.

“Whoa! I'm just trying to make sure you're okay.”

“Call 911! Somebody just tried to kill us!”

*****

Chapter Twenty-Nine

We had been at Baptist Hospital for what seemed like hours. Chris was breathing and came to shortly after we got there, but the impact caused him to dislocate his shoulder. They had me hooked up to machines to monitor me and make sure that the baby was okay. So far, everything seemed to be good, and they told us that we could go home, but they just wanted to make sure and run a few more tests.

Per standard procedure, as they called it, they called the police, and I lied my ass off. I was not about to have them put us back in protective custody over some shit like that. Nah… this was some shit that we handled ourselves. As soon as the police left, I looked at Chris, and he was pissed.

"So all he said was this ain't over?"

"Yeah. I don't know the nigga or nothing. Like… this shit is crazy," I said, sitting up in the hospital bed. The beeping from the machine was getting on my nerves, but it was necessary.

"Well trust and believe, when I find out who the fuck it was, I'ma make sure to put a bullet in his fucking head," he promised.

"Oh, I'm with you," I said.

"No," he told me.

"You ain't doing shit. You're pregnant."

"And? Chris, my hand still fuckin' works! It can still pull a fucking trigger. If it wasn't for me, we would both be dead right now. I grabbed the gun, and that's what scared him off," I told him.

"No… somebody else walking up to the car is what scared him off. Miracle, I'm not about to have you in the middle of this shit. This is one of the times that you just need to sit the fuck back, and let me handle things," he fussed.

"If that's the case, Chris, then I could have just told the police that shit," I hissed.

"Nah, 'cause they're not going to handle that shit, and you know it. I know you ain't trying to stay in protective custody again either. We gon' stick to the plan. We gon' do what the fuck we got to do while we're here. We gon' get the hell out of Dallas, and we gon' head to the A. If a nigga comes near me, you, or anybody that we fuck with, dead that nigga. That's it. We ain't telling the police shit."

I rolled my eyes, because he thought he was really getting me to listen.

"Goody's ass is dead. It's probably just somebody that is pissed, 'cause they ass ain't making paper no more or some dumb shit like that. We good," he said.

"All right," I agreed, but there was no way in fuck I was going to sit back and not do anything. He should have known better than that.

"How are you feeling anyway?" he asked.

"I'm fine. They said that everything was good, so we should be able to go home soon."

"Alright, cool. I'm going to go outside and holla at my homeboy about some shit," he told me. I already knew what the hell he was doing. He was calling his home boy to make sure that they were keeping an eye on shit and finding out who the nigga was that hit us.

"Okay," I said. I watched as he walked outside, and my phone rang, making me damn near jump out the bed. I read the messages from Nikki and forgot that we were supposed to go to her house. I didn't really want to tell her too much, so I just messaged her to let her know that I wouldn't be able to get to her until the next day.

Miracle: Got caught up handling business. Will stop by tomorrow and catch you up on everything. Got some stuff for the baby.

Nikki: Okay. Just call me and let me know. Thanks for paying the light bill.

Miracle: No problem.

I started wondering who the hell that could be that came after us in the car. Goody was dead, and the two dudes that he worked with the hardest were dead too. I knew a lot of niggas had lost their connects and lost paper because of the fact that he had gotten arrested and was on trial and everything, but majority of them sold their souls and ratted on him anyway. They wouldn't have to do any hard time.

I thought about Tori and the kids and wondered if she could be behind it, but last I heard, she was back living with her mom in Houston. Of course, she was there for the trial, and I remembered her face when the judge found Goody guilty, but we didn't speak. I didn't have anything against her, but anything that was associated with him… I just couldn't deal with. Everything around him had a dark cloud.

I felt bad for her though, because she was going to be left alone to take care of her kids by herself. Could she have been capable of something like this? The thought was dismissed as quickly as it came. Tori wasn't that type. Even if she was, by the way she reacted when she heard about what he'd done, I would have thought she was on my side. Who the fuck could it have been? Why was I still a target? Why was Chris still a target?

I just wanted this shit to be over. Chris was right. It was better that we didn't tell the cops, but we needed to find out who it was and soon. I wasn't going to keep hiding. If a nigga wanted me, they would get me, but they would get a whole lot more than what they bargained for.

Chris came back in after about another fifteen minutes with teddy bears and balloons. I couldn't help but to laugh.

“Baby, it was just a car accident,” I said.

“I know, but you know I was tripping earlier. I wouldn't try to pop off at you. I was just mad at the situation,” Chris apologized.

“I know you were. I mean, I would have done the same thing, so you good.”

“Cool.”

The nurse came in smiling extra happy.

“Here's our mommy to be! Well, we ran the tests, and everything looks good. The doctor said that you can go home whenever you'd like.”

“Good!” I said and sighed.

“Well, I'm going to go ahead and get your discharge papers and everything together, but he does want you to follow up with your OB in about three days,” she told me.

“Okay, no problem,” I agreed.

“Anything that she shouldn't be doing?” Chris chimed in.

“No, because she's still fairly early on in the pregnancy, she just needs to make sure that she stays as stress free as possible. Luckily, the accident didn't affect her as much, but had she been further along, then it could have been a lot worse, so she's really lucky.”

“Thank you,” I said.

"Alrighty… well, I'll be back in just a few minutes," she announced.

"Okay."

I stood up so that I could put my clothes back on, and Chris helped me get dressed.

"Just to be on the safe side, I think we need to check into a different hotel," he spoke up.

"Yeah, I was thinking the same thing," I told him.

"I figured as much. I already had my boy grab our stuff from the hotel, and he's going to meet us at the new one."

"Okay. Where we staying?" I asked.

"I got us a room at the Sheraton," he told me.

"We need to be out of here in no more than a few weeks… maybe a month," he advised.

"Well, maybe we shouldn't throw the part," I said, wondering if it would bring any attention.

"Nah, we've had enough negative shit. We need to have a little bit of fun, but I'll make sure that I got my boys in place if anything pops off. If there's anybody in there I ain't feelin', and we don't want them in the spot, or if anybody tries to start some shit, they ain't leaving up out that mothafucka without answering to me," Chris said. He may not have liked it, but they had two of us that they had to worry about. I wasn't going to argue with him. At least, not now. The nurse returned with the discharge papers, and we left. All I wanted to do was get in the bed, and go to sleep. We had checked into the hotel, and right as I got ready to lay down, my phone rang with the private number showing up on the caller ID. I already knew it was her.

"Hello?" I answered, agitated.

"Miracle, are you okay?"

"I'm fine," I answered.

"Well, agent Connor called me and told me that you and Chris were in an accident and that something happened," she said, sounding frantic.

"What happened? Are you okay?"

"I said I'm fine," I reassured her.

"We just left the hospital and got checked into the hotel and everything. The doctor said that the baby and I should be fine."

"Baby?" she whispered.

"Oh my God… you're pregnant? Oh my God!"

Fuck my life. I didn't even realize I said that shit out loud. I didn't mean to let her know that I was pregnant, but the cat was out the bag now.

"Well, baby, you gotta let the police know something. Maybe y'all should come here or something," she offered.

"No, we're good," I said, quickly cutting her off.

"I just want to lay down and go to sleep right now."

"Okay. I'm sorry. I didn't mean to push."

"It's cool," I said, calming my nerves. I knew I wanted to give her a chance, but for some reason, every time I talked to her, I couldn't help but to get angry all over again.

"Listen, I have to run some errands tomorrow. Why don't we meet up for lunch?" I said.

"Really?" she asked, surprised.

"Yeah," I answered.

"I think that would be a good idea," she responded. "Did you have any place in particular you want to go?"

"It's a couple of spots that are close by. I can check and see when they open, and then I'll call you later, but I'm going to need your phone number." I said.

"Of course!" she answered eagerly.

"I'll text it to you."

She paused, and I could hear her sniff. Was she crying?

"Miracle, you don't know how much this means to me."

"Yeah, well, we've got a lot to talk about. I have a lot of questions, and I'm pretty sure you've got some things that you want to express too," I told her.

"Yes, I do, so I guess I'll see you tomorrow," she replied, happily.

"Okay," I answered. I hung up the phone and felt a little better, honestly. I know that I would probably be really upset when we got into the meat of the conversation, but I was actually looking forward to talking to my mother. Maybe she could enlighten me on who the fuck this was that was coming after us. I just knew I couldn't say anything to Chris, because I didn't want him to worry.

"So you're finally going to meet up with your mother, huh?" he asked, bringing me out of my thoughts.

"Yeah… figured I might as well, especially if we're about to leave… go ahead and get that dreaded conversation out the way and then go from there," I told him.

"That's what's up. She said that she was going to text me, so I figured I'd meet up with her while you're handling business tomorrow."

"Okay, cool," he responded.

"Normally, I would ask if you want some company, but I think this is something you and your mom need to chop it up about one on one."

Perfect. I knew he wouldn't want to intrude, so I was good to go. A few minutes later, my phone buzzed, and I saw that my mother had sent me a text message.

214-387-1748: This is your mom, Tiana. Look forward to seeing you tomorrow.

“Well, I'm about to order something to eat. You hungry?” he asked.

“Not really. I just want to go to sleep. This day has been exhausting and crazy. I’ll just eat in the morning,” I told him.

“Aight,” he said, side eyeing me.

“You just make sure that you eat something. I don't want you going too long without having anything on your stomach.”

“Okay,” I agreed, smiling.

“I’m ‘bout to take a shower.”

I went into the bathroom and turned the water on. As soon as I stepped in, that hot water soothed my body, and I felt relaxed. I had been naturally tense and needed to feel calm. I began to wash and felt at ease. I didn't even hear the door open, but a few minutes later, Chris had pulled the shower curtain back and was standing in the shower with me, naked as the day he was born. I turned around, and my mouth fell open.

“Damn,” I murmured. Every time I looked at him, it was like seeing him for the first time. His body was amazing, and his dick was incredible. It was like a work of art… a masterpiece that you just wanted to put on display, and it was all mine.

“I have got to start locking doors when I'm taking a shower,” I said.

“Why? It’s mine,” he said.

He grabbed me and pulled me to him.

"True," I said.

"Do I need to remind you?" he growled. Before I could even part my mouth to say anything else, he shoved his tongue down my throat and began kissing me so hard. One thing that I loved about Chris was that if he was frustrated, or if he had a bad day and somebody pissed him off, his dick game was incredible! Don't get me wrong…my baby had a stroke, but it was just something about angry sex or frustrated sex that just made it all the more better.

He pinned me against the shower wall, and we both became drenched within seconds. Thank God I had braids in my hair, because otherwise, I would have been pissed later that my hair was getting wet. I placed my hands on his chest and ran my fingers down his body, grabbing his manhood and squeezing it in my grasp. It was throbbing and pulsating, and I knew it was driving him crazy.

I knelt down on my knees and placed him in my mouth as I began to taste him, slowly. I took pleasure in giving my baby head. It was like a challenge. I liked seeing how far I could place it in my mouth. Every time, I took it a little bit further. Tonight, I was going for the gold in the dick Olympics! I began a nice rhythm, and I could tell he was enjoying it, because his head leaned back, and all that could escape his lips was hissing noises.

Between the water hitting our bodies and the slurping sounds that my mouth made as I sucked his dick, he was in heaven. I couldn't get enough. I closed my eyes and devoured his dick.

"Damn, Miracle," he moaned. I opened my eyes, looked up at him, and grinned. It was time to get nasty with it. Pulling his dick out of my mouth, I spit and began to massage his dick while sucking his balls. One way to drive a man crazy was to put his balls in your mouth and give them a light squeeze. I knew he would be delirious.

"Fuck."

He tensed, grabbing me by the back of my head. Pulling me up, he turned me around and placed my leg against the shower wall, entering me from behind.

"Ssss," I hissed.

"I told you I was going to remind you that it was mine," he whispered in my ear as he held me by my waist and began to thrust in me slowly.

"Oh God, Chris, it feels so good! Baby, it feels good. Take me to the bed," I begged.

"Nah, you don't get your way tonight," he said.

"Please," I whispered.

"Begging is only gon' make me fuck you harder," he teased, pumping me harder like he said he would. I damn near exploded on his dick.

"Step out of the tub," he ordered. I did as he said, and he placed a towel on the floor so that I wouldn't slip and fall. I stood, looking at him in front of the mirror at the sink in admiration.

"Grab the sink, and arch your back," he demanded. I did, and he put his rock-hard dick back into my extremely wet pussy. So this was how he wanted to play? Okay. Game on. I started squeezing my pussy lips around his dick, clasping it, knowing that it would drive him crazy.

"You think you slick," he said as he continued to thrust. He grabbed me by my neck, pulling me back, placing gentle kisses on me as I stared up at the ceiling, and he dug deep inside my walls.

"Oh God! Chris!" I moaned.

"Say it's mine," he whispered in my ear, biting at my neck. I wasn't going to give him the satisfaction just yet. I knew if I held out, he was only going to go harder which is exactly what he did. He dug deeper, and I damn near lost my grip on reality.

“Say it's mine,” he repeated.

“Baby, you know it's yours!” I screamed. He began to pound me harder and faster until I had cum dripping down my legs. He was fucking me so good that the sound of his balls slapping against me started to sound like somebody running in flip-flops.

“Baby, I'm c-c-cummin’!” I strained out.

“Cum for me, baby. That's right… cum all over daddy's dick,” he urged. I felt my body shudder, and I gripped the sink hard. At that moment, I felt like I had super strength power. I could have ripped the damn sink out the wall! He kept going, and I felt my knees get weak.

“No not yet,” he smiled, looking at me in the mirror. He slowed his rhythm down, and I came yet again.

“Shit, I’m ‘bout to bust all in this pussy,” he grunted.

“Yes, baby,” I stuttered.

“Cum in his pussy.”

I knew when he was about to cum, but I had something for his ass. I may have told him that it was his, but I was about to remind him of who I was. Right when he got ready to cum, I pulled away and turned, dropping to my knees quickly, pulling him in my mouth and sucking his soul from his body. I could tell he was surprised by the look on his face.

“Shhhhiiiiit!” he grunted. I smirked and continued to suck, pulling every drop from his dick. I smiled, stood up, and gave him a wink. He smacked my ass.

“You play too fucking much,” he panted out.

“Sorry, but you had it coming!”

I laughed. I hopped back in the shower, and he walked over to grab a towel.

"Yeah, I definitely have to start locking doors," I said.

"Try it, and see what happens," he joked. I finished my shower and went to lay down. I slept one of the most peaceful nights ever.

*****

Chapter Thirty

I got up the next morning, and my stomach was cursing me out. Chris was already two steps ahead and had breakfast waiting on me. I devoured everything happily while he watched TV. I was feeling really good.

“Alright, so what's the game plan for the day?” he asked.

“Well, I figured I would look for some spots in the area and text my mother to see if she wants to get up for lunch around noon… maybe 1 o'clock,” I said, looking at the clock and seeing that it was already 10 a.m.

“Damn, I slept long.”

“Hell yeah. You were snoring and everything,” he joked.

“Whatever.”

I rolled my eyes, laughing and shoving more bacon in my mouth.

“My ass was tired… considering. Besides, you tried to fucking put me in a coma last night,” I joked.

“Look who's talking. You were on some Mortal Kombat shit,” he teased.

“Kiss my ass.”

I giggled.

“But no… I figured she and I could meet up at the mall or something and then grab a bite to eat… I can get her side of things.”

“Cool,” he said and nodded.

"I'm going to get some stuff set into place and go check out a couple of whips. I think we need something that's a bit more low key."

"Okay," I said.

"Do you need me to get you an Uber?"

"No, I can get it myself," I told him.

"All right. You just make sure that you're careful," he warned.

"Don't worry, Chris. I will be. Besides, I'm just going to go meet with her, and then I'll probably go to Nikki's house. Plus, she and I need to have a conversation too," I told him.

"Aight, that's what's up. Once I finish with the car and everything, I'll head over there."

"Okay."

"Alright, I'ma go ahead and break out, but I'll holler at you in a few. Keep your phone on."

"I will. You got your piece with you?" he asked.

"Yep," I said. I had a small pistol in my purse. He kissed me and left, and I jumped up to get ready. I texted Tiana to let her know where to meet me.

Miracle: Would it be okay to meet at NorthPark Mall? I've got to do some shopping for a friend of mine, so I figured I could kill two birds with one stone.

I put the phone back on the charger and got up to finish my makeup. I was doing my eyebrows when I heard the phone. I picked it up and saw that it was a response from her.

Tiana: Sure. What time?

Miracle: 1 o'clock.

Tiana: Okay. See you then.

I finished doing my makeup and called for an Uber. I was going to get there a little early, so that way, I could get in some shopping for the baby. I texted Nikki to let her know I was dropping by, since I missed her, and that's when I was going to tell her about Atlanta. I was going to see what she thought about moving with us, but first, I needed to get to Tiana. I really needed to find out everything that I could for my mother.

My Uber notified me that they were downstairs. I walked outside, cautiously, making sure that I wasn't being watched and got inside.

"Where to, ma'am?" the driver asked.

"Can you take me to NorthPark Mall please?" I said.

"Absolutely."

I sat back and played on my phone, texting Chris.

Miracle: On the way to the mall now. Wish me luck!

He responded a few minutes later**.**

Baby: Handle your business. Talk to you in a few. I got a nice surprise for you.

Miracle: □

After a twenty-minute drive and endless babble from the driver, we arrived at NorthPark Mall. I paid the driver and got out. I saw that I had twenty minutes left before Tiana was supposed to arrive.

"Might as well get some shopping done," I said to myself.

I started walking the stores, looking for baby clothes for Nikki's son. I was looking at all the little onesies and booties and was starting to get excited about my own. I couldn't wait to find out what the baby was so that I could spoil it. I would buy the whole damn store.

I must have lost track of time, because my phone ring.

“Hey, did you change your mind?” Tiana asked.

“No, no, I didn’t. My bad. I was inside one of the stores shopping, but I'm on my way to the food court now. Where exactly are you?” I asked.

“I'm standing in front of the Chick-fil-A.” she answered.

“Okay. Be there in a minute… heading to pay now.”

I went to the checkout counter to pay for the things that I had, and after a few more minutes of waiting, everything was packed up and ready to go. I walked to the escalators toward the food court, and I was looking at the older me, face to face.

“Miracle!”

She smiled, ran up to me, and grabbed me.

“I can't believe that you wanted to see me. You have no idea how happy I was to hear your voice when you called,” she rambled, squeezing me. I patted her back quickly and let go. I wasn't really sure what else to do.

“Well, I guess I'm glad,” I said.

“Well, I know I am.”

She beamed.

“I know that it was a lot to have to deal with in the court, but I really appreciate you even wanting to talk to me.”

She stood, looking at me with this weird grin on her face.

“And congratulations!”

She stepped back and sized me up.

"Thank you… so where do you want to eat?" I asked, trying to shake the nervous feeling.

"Anywhere, honey… doesn't matter. Whatever you have a taste for."

Chick-fil-A was calling my name, so I walked over to get in line, and she followed.

"So how far along are you?" she asked.

"A little over eight weeks… still kind of early in the pregnancy."

"Well, that's good. Are you wanting a boy or a girl?"

I could tell that she was a little nervous too by the way she was acting.

"Honestly, it doesn't really matter. As long as the baby is good then I'm good."

"Well, I hope that you're taking care of yourself," she advised.

"Pregnancies can be very stressful, and you don't necessarily live the average lifestyle, Miracle."

"Don't I know it… I've been doing a lot and went through a lot of bull and stuff," I said, side eyeing her.

She touched my arm and looked me in the eye.

"Miracle, I know that there's a lot that you are probably angry about, and you have every right to be. There were a lot of times when I wanted to contact you, but I couldn't. More than anything, I just don't want you to feel like you were just abandoned, because that wasn't it."

"Welcome to Chick-fil-A. Can I take your order?" the girl behind the counter asked as we stepped up.

"Yeah, can I have a number one, please, with extra pickles, large size the fries… with a Coke for the drink and some Polynesian sauce?" I asked.

"Absolutely."

She rang everything up, and I paid for my meal as well as my mother's. We got our food and walked to the table to sit down to eat.

"So," I said, opening the food.

"Now is the time for you to say whatever it is that you want to say. I'm not going to say that it's going to be easy to hear, but I really do want to know your side."

"Well like I said, it was a lot of stuff that I felt like nobody would understand. When I met your father, I was at a point where I just started using, and I was trying to get everything together, but Goody was in everything. When I left you with your father, you were happy and well taken care of. When I found out he died, it was really hard, but at that point, I knew that Goody was behind it. There was no way that I could have come forward."

"So, what did you know?" I questioned.

"I don't get what you mean, baby," she answered.

"I mean… you were with my dad, and you knew he died. What did you know about the day my daddy died? I know that you said that you loved my daddy, but at any point did y'all ever talk about you and Goody's past? Did he ever say 'hey… you know I know you used to be with my best friend?' 'Cause I know he's not a stupid person."

"We talked about it. When he and I first got together, I was nervous, because I felt like he was going to say something to him, but when I got the opportunity to tell your father, he stopped me. He told me that he already knew, but because he loved me, he could look past that. I know I hurt him like hell when he had to believe that I was dead."

"So why lie in court? You said my father didn't know."

"I had to make sure Goody couldn't have any chance of getting off," she told me. I nodded my head and focused on my food so that she could finish eating.

"When your father found out that I was using, that was one of the lowest points in my life, but he still was there and didn't give up on me. When everything happened and they put me into the witness protection program, I tried to reach out to your father to let him know that I was still alive, but at that point, the feds thought that it was better that he and everybody thought I was dead. Then, he would be able to raise you and not have to worry about some crack addict of a mother trying to take care of her daughter," she said. She dabbed at the corner of her eye and took a second to get herself together.

"There was not a day that went by that I didn't think about you. There wasn't a day that went by that I wasn't worried about you. I know that you went through a lot."

"That would be an understatement. I watched my father get killed in front of me, and I know that you weren't the one that did it, but I just really felt like had you stepped up after he died, my life could have been so much different. I went through a lot of shit and took a lot of shit because of the fact that I thought you were dead. If you had stepped up, I wouldn't have had to deal with that crazy chick, Patricia. I would have possibly had a normal life."

"But just try to look at it from my standpoint," she pleaded.

"I was in protective custody. I didn't have much choice, and as strange as it sounds, if I had stepped up as you say, you wouldn't have met your boyfriend, right?"

Was she serious?

"You don't get it, do you? My entire life, my father would tell me how my mom was just a beautiful person, but she died of a drug overdose. Yeah, it's a little shocking when I go into a courtroom over a case that's involving my godfather and found out that the woman that I thought has been dead all of these years is actually alive. Not only that, but she is the mother to my half-brother who I was sleeping with for damn near a year!" I screeched.

"Like… that is the nastiest thing I have ever heard of. My life is literally one banjo-picking, country bumpkin away from being some trailer park drama. What really irritates me is the fact that you had to have known. There's no way that you could have lived these last seventeen or eighteen years not knowing what's going on with your daughter. If you were in protective custody, I'm sure they had an eye on my father, and I'm sure that they told you what was going on. It's not a hundred percent your fault, because unfortunately, he isn't here for me to really flip the fuck out on, but that nigga, Goody, knew that I was with Black, and he didn't do anything. The thought of what I did makes me sick to my stomach!" I snapped. I was actually starting to get sick to my stomach, so I had to calm down.

"Miracle… baby, just relax," she soothed. There were a few people that were sitting around that were listening in to the conversation and staring. I had to calm down, because I remembered the nurse's warning to stay stress free.

"Like I said, I know I wasn't the best mother. I know that you are pissed the hell off of me, and baby girl, you have every right to be, but you have to understand that what I did was to keep you safe. Had I gone to the cops then and they arrested Goody on the spot or something, there's no telling what that man could have done. If he found out that I was alive, yeah… he could have easily gone after me again, but he would have went after my family too. I couldn't deal with that. I wouldn't be able to live with myself knowing something happened to you."

I could tell that she was near tears, and so was I.

"I am so sorry. I did what I felt was best to make sure that you weren't in any harm's way, and if I have to spend the rest of my life trying to prove to you that I want to be a mother that I wasn't and that I want to be involved in your life in any kind of way, then that's what I'm going to have to do."

I was crying and didn't even realize it until she put the tissue in my hand.

"It's been so hard. The last couple of years have been so hard. I've done things I'm not proud of. I was living in a foster home where we were treated like dirt. From the day that I got there, she treated me like I was a piece of shit. I watched people die in front of me. My entire life changed the day that Goody had my father killed. My whole life, I've always wondered what it would be like to have a mother. I always wondered what it would be like to have the female influence in my life. I thank God that my father was the type of person that stood up to his responsibilities, but what if he had given me up for adoption after you died?" I asked.

"I needed you. After he died, it got so hard, and I didn't have anybody. The only other mother figure that I would have even thought to consider tormented me every day for damn near two years," I told her. She dropped her head and tears fell.

"I don't know what I can say to apologize, baby girl. I don't know what I can do."

"There's nothing that can be done at this point. At this point, all I can do is move forward, and it is what it is."

"You're right. That's all we can do, but just know that now that this is all over, I'm going to do what I can to be in your life."

So you think.

“What do you remember about Goody’s operation?” I asked. She looked as if she was thinking and shrugged, picking up her food.

“Miracle, he had so many people working for him. It was hard to keep them straight. Most of them now are either dead or in jail,” she told me.

“Okay,” I said, thinking about the nigga that had walked up on my car. I don't know why I thought she would even remotely know of anyone that was still fucking with Goody after seventeen years. She had been kept a secret for so long. I was surprised that she even remembered much of anything.

We both got quiet and sat for several seconds, eating our food.

“You know I thought about your daddy a lot,” she said, breaking the silence.

“Yeah…I miss him a lot,” I mumbled.

“I know he really loves you. I just really hate that I handled things the way I did. Maybe if I had gone to the police, then stuff would be different today. I don't know.”

“Yeah, but like you said, Goody could have very well come after us. You did what you felt like you had to do. You kept yourself alive, and I can't fault you for that. I'm not saying that we are just going to be the closest, but at least now, I know I still have some family,” I told her.

“After losing Daddy, I felt like I had nobody. Goody was the only person that I had left, but then when he got arrested, all that stuff happened. Next thing I knew, I was being shoved into foster care. I had a couple of people there that I was close to, obviously, but it was not the same as having your own family,” I told her.

"I know. The last seventeen years, I haven't really had anybody. I had to find out about what was going on in your lives through surveillance," she confessed. It was kind of disturbing to know that the feds had been watching me for the last seventeen years, but it's not like I could have done anything.

"Well…"

She cleared her throat.

"Today is a new day."

She dabbed at the corner of her eyes again, wiping her tears.

"How about we just see what happens?"

"Hey, that's cool with me," I agreed.

"So tell me about Chris and Nikki."

She smiled, and I started smiling.

"Well, honestly… at first, Chris wasn't even on my radar. I don't think I was on his either. When I came into the foster home, he was there. That place was just horrible, but over time, I don't know… it just kind of happened. At first, I tried to fight it, because I felt like it would be weird, seeing as how he was my foster brother and everything. Plus, I was with Black, but low and behold, Black was the one that was actually my brother, so hey…" I said, trying to make a joke of this situation.

"So, is he excited about being a dad?" she inquired.

"That would be an understatement."

I laughed.

"He's like two different people almost. When he's with me, he's sweet and kind, and he's like one of those types of dudes that you see you on TV, but when he's in the streets, he's a completely different dude. He's like savage as hell and has no type of remorse or feelings."

"Well, it sounds like you really care about each other. Sounds like you got you a good one."

"Yeah, and then there's Nikki."

She noticed the change in my expression and gave me a look of concern.

"Well, you said that she was with you in the foster care, right?"

"Yeah. She was there when I first got there. She's a couple years younger than me. She uh… she just turned eighteen not too long ago. She's cool, I guess. I mean she and I had our little history because of Black."

"And what do you mean?" she asked, not understanding.

"Well, Black and I were helping her out when she got in some trouble, and well… she started messing with him on the low. When we were in the foster system, one day, she was there, and the next… she was gone. I know she said that somebody came and took her from Patricia's, and that's how she got into prostitution. One day, I literally just saw her in the street, and she was a mess. Long story short, Goody and I did what we had to do and took care of it, and she started living with me. Well, I guess she just decided that she was going to take it upon herself to sleep with somebody else's boyfriend, 'cause her and Black started smashing, but it's cool. Now, I got a nephew out of it. He's adorable, and he looks just like Black."

"Really?" she said.

"Yeah," I told her, pulling out my cell phone and pulling up pictures of Junior.

"Oh my God. If he isn't the chunkiest little one."

"Yeah. I nicknamed him Fatman Scoop."

I giggled.

"She's taking care of him the best that she can, but me and Chris kind of pop in every now and then and help out."

"Well, that's good."

"Yeah," I said chewing.

"I guess now, I got even more reason to make sure that he's good."

"So I have a grandson," she whispered.

"Yep… I guess you could look at it like that, and you may end up with another grandson."

I wondered if I should tell her that we were leaving Dallas. She smiled all goofy, and I was lost.

"What?"

"You're just like your daddy. You get this little crinkle in the middle of your forehead when you've got something on your mind."

"Oh."

I shrugged.

"I didn't know about that."

"Yeah."

She laughed.

"He used to do it a lot. There are a lot of things about your daddy that were cute," she murmured with a smile. I could tell she was thinking about him.

"You know he talked about you a lot. He used to tell me stories about you, and sometimes, we would go and visit your grave," I told her. Her smile disappeared, and she dropped her head.

"I didn't know that he had—"

I stopped her before she could say anything else.

"I asked him to, but he never had anything bad to say about you. I think he really missed you a lot."

"Yeah…Lord knows I miss him too. Listen, Miracle…" she sniffed.

"I'm looking for a house right now. The government is actually helping me find a place since I've been hidden for so long. Figured it's the least they could do," she joked.

"Now, it may be a couple of weeks before I can get a place, but I was thinking maybe once I get settled, you, Chris, and Nikki could come over for dinner. It will give me an opportunity to meet the people that are important to you, and of course to get to know my grandson," she suggested.

"Oh… I mean, we can, but um… Chris and I are going to be moving to Atlanta soon," I confessed. Her mouth dropped open, and she looked at me.

"What? But I just…I mean, we just…"

I knew what she wanted to say, but she was having a hard time getting it out.

"I know. It was just something that we've been talking about for a while. We were planning on leaving before Goody got arrested, but things just kind of happened. With everything that's going on here, we just felt like it would be better to get a fresh start somewhere else. Chris has a couple of friends in Atlanta that can help out, and I know there are more opportunities for me to find work after I graduate."

"You're in school?" she asked, surprised yet again.

"Yeah. I don't actually go to the campus. I'm just doing online classes, but I'm working toward getting my Bachelor's degree," I told her.

"Wow. That's amazing, baby girl. Are you going to be able to keep up with the schoolwork and still be able to be a full-time mommy?"

"I'm gonna try," I answered. She grew quiet for a minute.

"You know what? Honestly, I can't blame you. At twenty years old, yeah… you have dealt with a lot, and hey, it's not like I can't hop on a plane or whatever to come see you and my grandbaby."

She smiled.

"Yeah, that's true," she agreed. I was surprised at how well the conversation was going. I wasn't quite sure what to expect with her.

"Well, if you need anything, just let me know. I'm here to help," she offered.

"Okay."

I stood up to get ready to go.

"I gotta get ready to head out. I promised Nikki I would bring some baby clothes over to her, and I have to talk to her about this move."

"Oh, she's moving with you all too?" she asked, disappointed.

"Well… yeah, possibly. It's just so that I can make sure that the baby is taken care of… not saying she's a bad mother or anything, but I think it would be better if she had some extra help."

"Oh. Okay. Well, if it's not asking too much, maybe you can give her my number, and that way if she needs anything, she can contact me. Plus, I really would like to get to know my grandson… especially since Trevon isn't here anymore. This will be a part of him that I feel like I'll be able to make up for with not being there," she said. I nodded my head in understanding.

"I'll tell her," I said. I had a lot of stuff to fill Nikki in on.

"Can I give you a hug?" she asked. I nodded my head, and we embraced each other. I don't know if it was the pregnancy or what, but I just wanted to break down.

"You call me, okay?"

She sniffed, hugging me tightly.

"Okay," I agreed. I watched as she walked out, and I called for an Uber. I had one more stop to make, and then I could relax for a little bit. I really needed that though, and I had to admit I felt a lot better after talking to her. I didn't hate her, but I didn't know her either.

*****

Chapter Thirty-One

Once again, Chris was right, but there was no way in hell I was going to admit that. The Uber took me to Nikki's house, and I texted Chris to let him know that I was headed her way.

Miracle: On the way to Nikki's. Meeting with my mother went good.

I knew he would respond within a couple of minutes. He always had his damn phone on him.

Chris: Cool. I'm actually headed that way now. Found a spot and got news for you. See you in a few.

I wonder what he had to tell me. I looked out the window as the driver took me across town and thought about what I was going to do when we got to Atlanta. I was in school and getting my degree and everything, but I had never really worked a job before. On top of that, I was about to be a mom. I knew how to hustle, but I really wanted to do more. For a while, I guess I was going to just enjoy being in the city and seeing what was out there for me.

Chris was going to hustle 'til the day he died. I couldn't picture him working some blue-collar job.

"Okay, we're here," the driver said. I looked around and shook my head. I swear Nikki lived in the middle of the damn trap. That's exactly what the hell that was. I got out the car and tipped the Uber driver, hurrying to get inside. She opened the door, and for a minute, I thought I was in a completely different apartment. It smelled good in there, and she had food cooking.

"Damn girl. What you cooking?" I asked the smells teasing my nose.

"Girl, them food stamps finally came, so me and munchkin went to the store. I'm making some gumbo."

"Nikki, it's damn ninety degrees outside, and your ass is in here cooking gumbo like you in Louisiana."

"But I bet you that your behind will eat it," she taunted.

"Hell yeah! I ain't crazy."

"Exactly," she said and laughed.

"I see you cleaned up in here too," I mentioned.

"Yeah."

She smiled.

"I saw how you frowned up last time your ass was here, so I figured I needed to stop bullshitting and get it together."

"Cool," I said.

"Junior is back in the room taking a nap if you want to go get him," she said.

"I will, but I needed to holler at you about something first."

"Okay," she responded, walking over to the kitchen sink.

"What's up?"

"Well, it's a lot of stuff. First and foremost, me and Chris are about to have a baby," I told her.

"Biiiiiiitttttttcccccchhhh!" she squealed and ran over to hug me.

"I figured it was going to happen eventually. Congratulations! Oh my God. I'm gonna be an auntie!" she said.

"Thanks," I said, laughing at her reaction.

"Um, but the other thing is… we are moving to Atlanta," I told her.

“Oh okay, that's what's up,” she replied, her mood changing.

“Well, we figured it would be easier to move to Atlanta where we could kind of start over just get away from all the stuff that’s happened here in Dallas,” I told her.

“I guess,” she mumbled.

“Well look, I know it may be short notice, and I know our relationship ain’t really where it used to be but, what do you think about moving to Atlanta with us?” I asked her. Her eyes almost bugged out of her head.

“Like me and Junior move in with you?”

“No, no, no,” I said, stopping that idea quickly.

“Me and Chris are going to get a place, but we were going to help you out with your own spot… kind of like the situation now, only obviously, it's going to be a little bit different. Of course, it's not like we're going to be able to put you in a place the first day, but you know we could put you and the baby up with us or in a hotel for a couple of days until you find something that you like. Nikki, you're going to have to do your part too. You can't just sit around and expect the system to take care of your baby for you. I mean with the situation, I understand here, but Atlanta has a lot of opportunities,” I told her.

“I mean, I can get a job,” she answered eagerly.

“It's just that I gotta find a daycare or find somebody that can take care of the baby. I wanna work. It’s just hard to do that without any money.”

“We’ll help you. He's my nephew, so of course I'm going to look out.”

“Yeah, but Miracle… you ain't got to do for him at the end of the day. He’s my son. I had him. I knew how hard it would be after Black got killed,” she sighed.

"Yeah, um… speaking of that," I continued.

"I know I say Junior is my nephew, but he is actually my nephew."

"Miracle, what the hell you talking about?"

She looked at me confused.

"Long story short, my mother is not dead. She was in witness protection for the last seventeen years. She popped up at the trial, and I found all of this stuff out about her, my dad, and Goody. Turns out that Black was her son. Well…her and Goody's son," I rattled off.

"What?" she said in shock.

"Yeah. It was a lot of bull that happened that day… the day that Goody got killed…" I went on.

"Yeah..."

"Yeah. I found out along with everybody in the damn courtroom that I was fucking my own half-brother," I said.

"Oh my God."

She threw her hands up over her mouth.

"Yo, dead ass, that's some nasty ass shit."

"Yeah, I know."

Nikki put some gumbo in a bowl for me and seasoned it. I started eating.

"That's not too spicy is it?" she asked. This food was good as hell!

"Yo, this gumbo is banging!" I told her. She smiled.

"I appreciate it. I don't cook as much, but when I do, I just get into it," she bragged.

"Yo with food like this, you can open your own spot."

“Really?” she asked.

“Yeah,” I said.

“Maybe I could go to school for that. You think you can help?”

“I can help you apply… Like I said, Nikki, we want you to come with us, because we want to be able to help you and the baby. At the same time, we're not just going to be doing shit for you either. You’re eighteen… damn near nineteen. You’re legal and got a baby, so you can work. I'm pregnant, so it’s not like I'ma be able to be out there in the streets like before. Chris is going to kind of hold stuff down for a while. I mean, we got money stashed away and everything, but, I'm trying to be different.

I'm not trying to be living the good life one minute and then living in the projects the next, so I got to be smart with it. You know you can apply for like financial aid and stuff like that to get money,” I added.

“Okay cool. I mean, I'm with it. It's not like I really got anything here anyway other than Junior.”

“Facts. Well, this way, I can still be close to y’all and everything, and you know we can start to fix things somewhat. I know that the situation was real messed up, and I'm not saying that I’m just completely gon’ forget it, but you are like my sister at the end of the day. Now that you actually have my nephew, I have to look out. Long as you don't push it with Chris, we good.”

She laughed.

“Trust me, I learned my lesson. I'm not gon’ lie. Looking back, yeah… that was some real fucked up stuff that I did. I just got caught up in it, and I guess I got jealous. It’s just… you always had this thing about you that people gravitated to you. Like… you just always had all eyes on you, and you got whatever you wanted. I just wanted to know what it felt like. You always had people wanting you. I didn't. I know that at the end of the day, I was wrong," she confessed. I didn't know what to say. She had never told me any of this before, so I was kind of surprised.

"Well, what's done is done, and clearly, I can't date him. Otherwise, I'd be on Jerry Springer with my three-eyed baby," I joked. We both laughed. There was a knock at the door, and I jumped up.

"It's probably Chris. He's meeting me over here."

"Oh okay, cool," she nodded, focusing back on her food. I went to the door, and sure enough, Chris was standing there.

"Hey, babe," he greeted, giving me a quick peck and walking in.

"Damn, babe, what you eating?" he asked, noticing my greasy lips.

"Nikki made some gumbo."

"In the summer?" he asked.

"I don't care what time it is. My ass is hungry."

I laughed.

"I just told her about us moving to Atlanta, and she seems cool with it."

"Aight, that's what's up. Aye, when we get back to the hotel, I need to holla at you about something else."

The look on his face let me know that it was something regarding the car situation the other day.

"Okay," I said. We both walked back into the kitchen to find Nikki now holding the baby.

“Hey, fat man!” I said, picking him up out of her lap, giving him kisses.

“I guess he heard y'all and woke up,” she shrugged.

“So, we trying to be up out of here in a few weeks. How soon do you think you can be packed up?”

“I mean, I really don't have much to pack. I really don't have a lot of furniture... Just clothes and stuff,” she said, looking around.

“It shouldn’t take me too long, I don’t think. I'll have to go to Social Services and let them know that I'm moving, but other than that, it'll be straight.”

“Aight.”

“You want something to eat, big head?” she asked.

“Yeah, go ahead and hook me up,” he grunted, playing with Junior’s feet.

“I got it,” I said, getting up to fix him a bowl. We were all eating when my phone buzzed. I looked to see my mother had texted me.

Tiana: Do you think you could send me a picture of the baby that you showed me earlier?

It was then I remembered she asked me to give Nikki her phone number.

“Oh… hey, Nik… Tiana just texted me. She wanted to know if you would take her number, so that way, she could get to know Junior?”

“Okay, I guess. I mean, is that okay with you?”

“Why wouldn’t it be? That's her grandson, after all.”

“So how did that go?” Chris questioned.

"I mean, it was okay. We talked, and I kind of got to hear her side of things. I told her that we were moving to Atlanta, and she seemed cool with it. She actually encouraged it, so, I guess stuff is straight."

"So, are y'all going to talk again?" he prodded.

"I don't see why not. It's not like we're going to be going to mother daughter banquets and all of that, but I mean, I'm not going to hold anything against her either," I said.

"What's done is done, so at this point, I can just either accept it and move on, or continue to harbor resentment and be miserable."

"Aww, is my little girl growing up?" he teased. I flipped him the finger and continued to bounce Junior on my lap.

"Oh, I got some stuff for the baby too. It's in those bags that I left in the living room."

"Aww, thank you. Dang… after everything else you've already done, Miracle, you didn't have to do that," she cooed.

"It's no problem. Oh, and you need to get a sitter for Junior, because we're throwing a big ass party at Illum as a farewell thing. Everybody is coming out. I'ma call Myesha and see if she wants to come and a couple of my friends from school and everything. If you have anybody that you want to invite, let them know. It's going to be one of the biggest parties."

"Yeah, but make sure they ain't coming on no bullshit, because security will be extra tight up in there," Chris warned. He placed his hand on my back underneath the table and squeezed. I knew he'd found out something the way he was squeezing.

"Oh, I can definitely get a babysitter," she smiled.

“All right. Don’t be bringing none of them ghetto birds up in the club.”

“Whatever,” she dismissed.

“I don't really go out like that anyway, especially after I had Toodas,” she cooed, tickling Junior’s feet.

“That's fine, but I'm just saying… just don't have none of those ratchet chicks in the club.”

“I'm not,” Nikki assured me. I took her cell phone and programmed my mother's phone number into it.

“Alright, I just put her information in the phone, so just hit her up I guess.”

“Okay. Do you think I should let her see Junior?” she asked.

“I mean, I don't know why not. When I talked to her, she kinda told me that she felt like maybe by her getting close to you and Junior, it will be a way for her to connect with Black. I know it really messed her up knowing that he was dead,” I told her.

“I just can't believe that she was alive all this time, and she didn't come get you from the foster home,” she said.

“Yeah… trust me, we talked about that, but I ain’t even trying to get into that right now.”

“You ever wonder what would have happened if Patricia and Whitney hadn’t died?” she said. I looked at Chris out the corner of my eye. We tried our hardest to never bring that up, but I knew what we did.

“We would be miserable or dead. Shit worked out the way it did for a reason, so the less that you think about them, the better,” I answered bluntly.

“Yeah,” she said.

“Damn, babe, slow down,” Chris said, laughing at me, because I was scraping the bowl.

“I was hungry. Shut up. I know one thing… you have got to be cooking when we get to Atlanta, ‘cause this is soooo good.”

“The way you all the help me out, I will cook everyday if I have to.”

We all laughed and hung out for the rest of the night, laughing and joking. If every day could be like today, I would be so happy, but my mind was already preparing me to get ready for whatever it was that Chris had found out. Happiness didn’t last always.

*****

Chapter Thirty-Two

We were in the car on the way back to the hotel from Nikki's. I started grilling Chris the minute we hit the car and had pulled away from Nikki's spot. Chris had gotten a new whip, and it was nice! He got a new Charger, and I knew it wouldn't draw attention, so I was happy.

"What happened?" I asked.

"Alright… so my boy was telling me that the nigga that hit the car was paid to hit us."

"I mean I figured that much. Hell, they plowed right into us. That wasn't no damn accident, "I said.

"Yeah, but the money didn't come from any of Goody's people," he said, cutting me off.

"Okay, so some random nigga was paid to hit us?" I asked.

"From what it sounds like… so it's not Goody or any of his people—"

"But that raises a whole new question of who the hell is it?" I said, finishing his sentence.

"Exactly. Who the hell could possibly be after us?"

It was hard to determine because of the fact that both of us had done some shady ass shit. We both had bodies, and we both had done shit that we knew was wrong.

"You think it had anything to do with Patricia or Whitney?" I asked.

"Doubtful… I don't think that would go that far. If anything, they would be thanking us, 'cause they didn't have a lot of people that fucked with them."

"True."

"What about ol' boy that you hit in the car accident last year?" he asked.

"I don't think so. I made sure they got their money. I think they got their settlement check today. They knew they were getting their money, so why would they have somebody come after us like that? It would make more sense for them to come after me. You didn't have anything to do with it."

"Yeah, I guess. So then who the hell is it?"

"I don't know," I repeated.

"Well the sooner we find out, the better, because I'm off of the whole trying to be looking over their shoulder the rest of their life."

"Facts."

We made it to the hotel, and I crashed not long after my head hit the pillow.

***

I felt so sluggish getting out of the bed. We had spent the last three weeks packing and trying to get everything taken care of between us and Nikki. The day before, we had flown to Atlanta to try to find an apartment and literally flew back hours later, because I had promised Nikki I would help her with Junior. She seemed really excited about the move, but my body was just worn out.

I knew that I was going to have to get out the bed at some point, because I had promised my mother that I would meet with her before the party later on that night. Our farewell party had been promoted all over the radio and was one of the most talked about parties, so I knew I would need a lot of energy to give the people what they wanted later. Tonight, Chris and I were gonna be like Jay Z & Beyoncé before the elevator.

I hadn't heard much else about the guy that ran up on us, and neither had Chris, so we just chalked it up as somebody upset that one of us had screwed over in his past. I knew he would look out regardless, so I wasn't too worried. I was just ready to go, but my body was not wanting to get out from under those covers! I had to get up, because I had a doctor's appointment.

"Come on, baby! You don't want to be late," Chris called out.

"I don't feel good. I just want to go to sleep, Chris," I complained. I was miserable. If I wasn't tired, all I could do was throw up. This kid was draining me. Chris brought me some ginger ale and made me sit up.

"Come on now, baby. Drink this, it should help," he coaxed. My phone rang, and he handed it to me.

"Hey," I answered, knowing that it was my mother. She had found an apartment and moved in about a week ago. I was at her house every day helping her. I liked it though, because we were getting to know each other more, and she was a lot like me. We had a lot in common.

I promised her that we would go to her house to eat and then from there, we were going to go to the club. I didn't expect her to go and help us celebrate at the club, so I figured dinner would be a nice compromise that way everybody would be happy. Plus, her house wasn't that far from the club, and we could just get ready from there. My whole day was full, and I hadn't even begun to get ready yet.

"Hey, baby. I was just calling to check on you," she said.

"I'm okay, I guess. Just my stomach has really been hurting, and I can't stop throwing up," I told her.

"Oh, my poor baby. Well, have you tried some ginger ale or Sprite?"

“I'm actually drinking that right now,” I told her.

“Well, if you need to reschedule, we can do dinner another time,” she said, sounding disappointed.

“No. We'll be there. Besides, it'll give Nikki a break from cooking. I think I've been at her house every day for the past few weeks,” I joked.

It was true. Nikki was throwing down in the kitchen every chance she got, and my ass was over there every day, happily eating. I had already put on damn near ten pounds. I hoped that I was able to fit into my outfit for that night. I may have been pregnant and not able to drink, but I was damn sure going to be looking fly as hell.

“Okay, baby. Well, I'll see you guys later. I'm excited to meet Nikki and this Chris as well.”

I was happy she was excited. She had talked to Nikki on the phone a few times, and Nikki was happy to introduce Junior to his grandmother. I couldn't be happier.

I got up and rushed to the bathroom, feeling that familiar sense of nausea.

“I’m sorry, baby.”

Chris apologized, looking pitiful, ‘cause he didn’t know how to fix it for once.

“Hey, look at it like this. You're almost out of the first trimester. Morning sickness should be over soon.”

“I hope so, ‘cause I can't keep dealing with this shit. I swear it feels like I don't have anything left to throw up,” I whined.

“Don't worry. We'll talk to the doctor and see if they can suggest anything.”

“They gave me Phenergan last time, but I don't think it's really working,” I told him.

“Alright, we will see what else they suggest. Just try to get dressed,” he told me. I threw some sweats on and pulled my hair back into a ponytail. I don't even have any makeup on, but I didn't care. I was so exhausted.

“Yeah, I know your ass is sick, ‘cause the last time you wore sweats was the day you found out you were pregnant,” he observed.

“Whatever,” I mumbled.

The minute that we got to the car, I laid my ass down and closed my eyes the entire way there. If this was what being pregnant was going to be like, this would be my one and only child. I swear it felt like my entire body was working overtime all the time, and this was just the first trimester!

After about fifteen minutes, we got to the OB's office and got checked in. They drew my blood and weighed me as usual. We sat and waited for the nurse.

“Maybe you should just stay in the room today,” he spoke up.

“Hell no! I'm not about to be in the room while your ass is at the club, turning the fuck up with a bunch of hoes,” I said.

“Now you know I ain’t worried about no other chicks,” he said with a sigh.

“I know you’re not, but what I’m worried about is these other bitches being around you that don’t give a fuck that you got a girl. They see dollars, nigga,” I reminded him.

“Trust me, I will be fine. If I got to take one of them pills and it make me sleep all day, then that just means I'll be extra ready for tonight.”

He laughed, shaking his head.

“I ain't even about to argue with you,” he said.

“Good, ‘cause you’d lose.”

The nurse came back again, and I turned my attention to her.

“Well, there were a few things in the blood work that we're concerned about, so as a precaution, we sent them to the lab and should hear something back within the next twenty-four hours to specify what it is. How are you feeling?” she asked.

“Nauseous as hell. I'm always throwing up, I'm exhausted, and I have the worst pain.”

“Where is the pain?”

“Just in the side of my stomach. It's not severe or anything. It's manageable, but it's just irritating,” I told her.

“Hmmm,” she hummed, a look of concern coming across her face.

“That sounds a little different.”

“So it isn’t something that happens all the time?” Chris asked.

“Not really. Typically, if a female has pain in her side, then it’s considered cramping, and it’s a sign of a miscarriage. Have you had any spotting?” she asked.

“No… no bleeding or anything like that,” I told her.

“Okay,” she nodded, pulling up her screen.

“Well, I'm going to take another tube of blood just to be on the safe side. In the meantime, I can give you something for the pain, but just be careful about taking it. Mild to moderate activity at most because of the fact that you're pregnant. Also, try to get as much rest as possible, and maybe that will help.”

“I will. Trust me. That won't be a problem. After today, my ass isn't doing anything but laying down.”

“Okay, so what I'll do is I'll get the phlebotomist in here to take another tube, but first, I want you to go ahead and lay down so we can do an ultrasound,” she instructed. I was excited. This was the first time I was actually going to be able to see the baby. When I found out I was pregnant, it was through a urine test, but this was the first time I was going to be able to see the baby and hear the baby's heartbeat.

“Will we be able to tell what it is?” Chris asked.

“It's still a little early for that. She's just now getting out of her first trimester, so it's going to be about another four to six weeks before we can even begin to determine the sex,” she educated him.

“Okay.”

He nodded.

“Well, I'm pretty sure it's a boy.”

I rolled my eyes. It better be, because I couldn't deal with a girl.

“Well, you know what they say… the sicker you are, the more likely that it's a girl.”

“Aw hell. Well, let's just hope it's a myth,” I groaned. She turned on the monitor, and both Chris and I got quiet. I was looking at my baby. It was an amazing sight. All the sickness didn't mean a damn thing at that moment.

“You ready to hear the heartbeat?”

I nodded my head, unable to speak. She moved the object around for several minutes and eventually found it, but the look on her face had me nervous.

“What's wrong?” I asked.

“Well, the heartbeat is a little slow. Try to relax as much as possible for me.”

She continued to explore my stomach, and I couldn't help but to feel a little nervous and scared.

"Is the baby okay?" I asked. She nodded her head as she continued to listen.

"The baby is fine. At this rate in the pregnancy, we expect the heartbeat to be a little bit faster than what it is right now, but it's nothing to be alarmed about. Hopefully, the blood test will be able to shine a little bit more light as to what's going on, but you definitely need to take it easy. You're not at immediate risk or anything, but we just want to be on the safe side."

"Don't worry. She will be," Chris assured her. I looked at him a little scared and nodded my head. I guess my ass was going to be staying in. There was no way he was going to let me go to anybody's party at anybody's club with what she just told us.

"Okay, well I'm going to get you copies of the ultrasound pictures, and then you'll be good to go until your next appointment."

She smiled.

"I'll be right back."

"Okay. Thank you," I said. She handed me a towel so that I could clean up my stomach and left the room.

"You know you're not going, right?" he said.

"I know," I said, admitting defeat.

"Well, I'm not going either, 'cause I wanna make sure you're straight, so I'm gonna cancel it," he stated.

"No, don't do that. The party is in a couple hours, and we put too much money into this. Go. I can hang out at the room. Trust me. I'll be fine. Besides, one of us needs to be there, and you know you want to go."

"It don't matter. Right now, my priority is what the hell is going on inside of your stomach."

"Chris, I'm fine. Ain't shit going to happen. We've been good for the last couple of weeks. Just go. If anything happens, I can call 911 and get to the hospital, but you can't be paranoid, thinking that stuff is going to happen all the time."

The nurse came back in with the photos in her hand.

"Alright."

She smiled.

"Here you go. Now, when you get to the desk, Darlene will go ahead and schedule you for your next appointment, and we'll give you a call once we get the results back from the blood work, okay?" she said.

"Okay, thank you," we both replied. We walked to the front desk, and I scheduled my next appointment as instructed.

"Um, excuse me… I actually have a question."

"Sure, hun," she sung. She had a heavy southern drawl. I could tell that she had never been out of Texas.

"We're going to be moving to Atlanta soon. Can you recommend an OB in the area, or would you all have any partner offices there?" I asked.

"Yes, I'm sure I can help with that."

She smiled.

"It may take a minute. Our other receptionist is on lunch right now, so if you want, I can come up with a list, and I can email it to you," she said.

"Yeah, that would be good. Thank you so much."

"Not a problem. Do I have your email address on file?" she asked.

“Yeah, I believe so,” I answered.

“Okay. I'll get everything and send it to you. You two have a good day,” she told us.

“You too.”

We headed over to the car, and I sat back worried.

“You think everything is okay?” I huffed.

“It's got to be. You haven't really been doing anything extra in the last couple of days, aside from being with your mama and Nikki. If that’s it, then you’ll just have to cut back. I’m sure they will understand,” he observed.

“I know flying back and forth to Atlanta probably took a lot out of you, but once we get settled, you don't have to worry about that anymore. Just don't stress it. All I want you to do is just sit back and relax. Let me take care of you.”

He grabbed my hand and kissed it.

“I can have Nikki come by and help out if she needs to.”

“Help out with what, Chris? Everything is done,” I laughed.

“I'm talking about when we get to Atlanta, smart ass. I meant help out and help you unpack and everything, because your ass is going to be in the bed just like the nurse told you to be.”

“Oh.”

We got back to the hotel, and I was lying down, not because he wanted me to, but because my ass was tired. He had agreed that I could go to my mother’s since technically I wouldn’t really be doing anything anyway.

“Well, I'm about to go handle some business for later on, but I'ma come back and pick you up in time to go to your mom's, okay?” he said.

“Okay, babe,” I agreed.

He kissed my forehead and left. I curled up in the covers and enjoyed being by myself. I laid there for several minutes and once again got hungry. I ordered some room service. Damn, my ass was about to be eating in a couple hours at my mom's, but I still needed to put something on my stomach.

I was trying not to think about the ultrasound from earlier, but I was so scared. All those times that I kept saying that I was too young to have a baby, and now, something was wrong with the baby. I didn't know how to feel. This was one of the times that I wish I had somebody to talk to other than Chris.

I was lying there watching TV and thinking about everybody that I had lost. My entire family was dysfunctional. My father was killed by my godfather. My mother had a whole other family that I knew nothing about, and I fucked my own half-brother and my foster sister had a baby by him who was now my nephew. Maybe it was something wrong with my baby as karma for everything that had been done. I don't know, I just wanted my baby to be healthy.

A few minutes later, room service knocked at the door, bringing me my order, and I walked over to let them in with my food order. I signed the slip so that they could charge it to the room and walked them back out the door. I couldn’t wait to eat and just curl up and go to sleep.

Chris had bought me a cute little Care Bear like the one I had as a kid, so I loved to curl up with it and go to sleep. He would tease me, because a lot of times, I snuggled up with the bear more than I did him.

I had just closed the door when I heard the knock again. I probably forgot to tip them, so I grabbed some money out of my purse and headed to the door, opening it without even thinking of looking at the peephole. Who stood there damn sure wasn't room service.

"Oh shit," I whispered, backing away from the door. It was the nigga that ran up on us a few weeks back at the accident. He closed the door behind him, locking it. Fuck.

*****

Chapter Thirty-Three

"Look, man, I don't know who you are, and I don't know what's going on, but I ain't got no beef with you. I'm pregnant, and I'm just trying to take care of my child," I said.

"We have business," he said menacingly.

"No, we don't," I said.

Where the fuck was my damn gun? There was no way in hell I was going to be able to get to it without him fucking killing my ass.

"I ain't got much time," he growled.

"Sit down."

"Please... please don't do this. Look, whatever you need, I can get it. If you need money, I can get it to you," I pleaded.

"Shut up. Just sit down," he demanded. He grabbed my shoulders and forced me down onto the bed.

"Help!" I screamed. He quickly grabbed my mouth, covering it with his hand.

"Shut up! Now look, I am not trying to fucking hurt you," he said in barely a whisper.

"Like I said, I don't have much time, so you need to listen to what the fuck I got to say. I am not trying to kill you, and I am not going to hurt you, so if I move my hand and you scream, we will have problems... understand?" he asked. I nodded my head. My heart was beating a mile a minute. All I needed to do was make it to the door.

"Do not make me have to hurt you, Miracle," he warned. Shit, this nigga knew my name!

“I'm going to move my hand. Are you going to scream?” he asked. I nodded my head no so that he would understand.

“Alright,” he said. He moved his hand. I was shaking in fear. He sat directly in front of me and stared at me.

“You don't know who I am?” he whispered.

“No,” I answered meekly.

“I know who you are. I've known you since you were a little girl,” he responded. I stared, utterly confused, trying to figure out who the hell this man was. He just tried to kill us the other day, and now, he was sitting here in my hotel room, telling me not to be afraid of him? This didn't sound right.

“I know you’re probably wondering what the hell is going on. I can't tell you everything, but just know that I look out for blood.”

“Blood?” I asked, confused.

“Yeah. You may not remember me, but I'm Eddie's half-brother. The last time I saw you, I think you were about three or four years old,” he recalled.

“What?” I said. This nigga looked like he was but a few years older than me.

“Why should I believe you?”

“It's true. I know I may not look it, but I’m your father's half-brother,” he urged.

“So now all of a sudden I have an uncle too?” I asked him.

“Yeah. Like I said, the last time you saw me, you were literally a toddler, and I ended up getting locked up,” he told me.

"From what… five years old? My nigga, come on now. You gotta come better than that. You look all but twenty-five… if that," I snapped.

"Miracle, I don't have much time, okay? I'm just telling you that you need to be careful."

"Of what… people like you trying to kill me? Why the fuck did you hit us that day?" I questioned.

"I didn't think I would hit you that hard. I've been following you since the trial started to make sure everything was good, and I was trying to find out some things. When I saw that other car, I was just trying to get them away from you."

"What other car?" I asked.

"You didn't know, but you were being followed by agents," he told me.

"I was?"

What the fuck was going on? We'd been cleared from agents for days.

"There's a reason why. A couple of the agents that are in the department are crooked as shit. Before Goody was killed, he had a few of them on payroll."

That didn't surprise me. Goody was as shady as they came.

"So, you almost killed us to protect me from a car that I didn't even see?" I asked.

"Yeah, that sounds about right."

I was trying to inch my ass toward my purse so that I could grab my gun.

"I told you I'm not here to hurt you," he growled, snatching me back toward him.

“Look, whether you believe it or not, I'm your uncle. Your father was killed by Goody’s trifling ass, but Goody wasn't where the shit stops. There was somebody over him, and I'm trying to find out who it is. Whoever that person is, they're still coming after you and your little boyfriend, so I suggest that if you’re smart, you listen to me, okay? This shit is not a game. You may have gotten lucky with Goody, but whoever the fuck this other person is ain’t gon’ stop until your ass is dead. You had two agents on your ass for days and didn't know it,” he pointed out.

I looked in his eyes, and something told me that he was telling the truth, but I couldn't know for sure.

“Prove it. I need proof that you're who you say you are,” I said. He fished in his pocket and pulled out his wallet.

“See?” he said, showing me his ID. The last name was Davis, but that didn't mean shit. Davis was a common last name.

“Trust me, I have ways of proving who I am. Right now, you got one of two choices. You can either listen to what I got to say, and trust me, or you can take your chances on your own and end up dead somewhere… nobody knowing who the fuck you are by the time they find your body.”

I didn’t know what to think. I believed him, but I was still a little unsure. He hadn't killed me, so maybe he was telling the truth.

“I don't get it. Why are we being followed?” I asked.

“Because you were witnesses, and you testified against Goody. Goody wasn't just killed by accident. Whoever did this shit was under orders, and I'm trying to find out who that person is. Even though he killed Eddie, I don't think it was him that ordered it. I think it was somebody else, and he just carried it out. Whoever did that also set Goody up to die, and whoever did it is still out there. I need to find out who that person is, because I want answers. My brother may not have been a saint, but that nigga looked out for me."

He looked at me intently, and I was in a trance, listening.

"My own fucking mama left me out in the street, and Eddie looked out. He took care of me since I was a kid. I did a bid for him because of the shit that he's done for me, so when I got out, found out that he was gone, and that somebody killed my brother, I promised myself that I was going to find out who the fuck it was."

"But Goody already confessed to setting that up," I said, confused.

"I'm sure he did."

He nodded.

"But I know that there's more to it. With the shit that's going on from what I've seen, these feds are trying to protect somebody, and I'ma find out who the fuck it is."

"Damn it," I said. Why the fuck wouldn't this shit just go away?

"I need to call Chris."

"Is that your boyfriend?" he asked.

"Yeah," I said.

"Okay… but do you fully trust him? Do you know him?" he questioned.

"Yes. Chris has been there for me for the last couple of years since Daddy died."

"I'm just saying, Miracle… you've got to be careful. You can't put nothing past no nigga. I learned the hard way that these niggas are just as scandalous as a lot of these fucking bitches. They're just on some different shit," he warned.

"Well, right now, he's the only mothafucka that I can trust. The last nigga I trusted turned out to be my half-brother, so if I were you, I would just let me call him. If not, and he comes to that door, he's likely to blow your damn head off, because he knows who the hell you are… well… somewhat."

"I thought he was unconscious when I hit you though?" he asked.

"He was, but Chris got his ears to the streets and knows how to get information," I told him.

"That may come in handy. Go ahead and hit him up," he said. I reached for my phone and contemplated calling the police but quickly dismissed it. I called Chris, and after a few rings, he answered.

"Hey, you okay?"

"Yeah… Chris, I need you to get to the room now."

"Everything okay? Are you still in pain?"

"The baby is fine, and I'm fine, Chris, but I can't talk about this on the phone. You need to get here, and get here quick."

"Say no more. I'm on the way," he said. I hung up and put my phone back down.

"Congrats," he spoke.

"Thanks… so do you know who the agents were?" I asked.

"Yeah. One of them was there at the courthouse with you. Remember the day that y'all got in the car, and the shooting happened?" he asked.

"Yeah… I mean, I don't really remember everything specifically, because bullets were flying, but I do remember a few faces."

"Yeah…"

He nodded.

"He was one of the ones that started shooting. I was there. I saw it."

So was he like some ghetto guardian angel or something?

"You've been out all of this time. Why not say anything?" I inquired. It was just like my mama… there but not there.

"Because the less that I said, the better. I had to make sure that I had proof first, before I just came trying to stop a nigga. The day that you were in the car and those agents were on y'all, I knew they were going to try to kill you then, so that was the only thing I could think of was to interfere. That's why I ran up on the car the way I did. I wanted to make it look like I was gonna hurt you so that they couldn't get to you," he explained.

"Well congratulations. Mission accomplished. You could have fucking killed us," I said sarcastically.

"I know, and I'm sorry. I didn't know it was going to have such a hard impact, but right now, Miracle, shit is about to get real tight. I promise you that you got these fools watching you right now."

"See… I knew we should have just got the fuck out of Texas when that damn trial was over," I mumbled.

"Well, you can go, but I ain't leaving this bitch 'til I bury the mothafucka that's behind this."

I nodded my head. I knew exactly how he felt. That anger that I once had when my father was killed returned.

"That's if I don't get them first."

*****

Chris came bursting through the door, his gun drawn.

"Baby, put it down! I'm okay," I begged. He dropped his piece to his side and frowned.

"Troy? What the fuck are you doing here?" Chris said.

"You two know each other?" I asked as he closed the door.

"Yeah… Troy was my homeboy that told me about the nigga that ran up that day."

I looked at him confused.

"Well for one… he was the one that ran up, and second, apparently Troy is my uncle," I corrected him.

"Say what? Yo, somebody better start talking. I want to know what's going on, now."

"You ain't the only one," I said. I looked at Troy, and he took a deep breath.

"Alright. Let me start from the beginning."

My phone started ringing loudly, scaring the hell out of both me and Chris. I turned to see the doctor's office calling.

"What the hell?"

I frowned.

"Hello?"

"Ms. Davis?" the receptionist spoke.

"Yes, this is she," I answered.

"Hey, this is Anna from Dallas OB/GYN. Sorry to bother you, but we need you to go to the emergency room as soon as possible."

"For what?" I asked.

“Well, the first vial of blood that was taken before you had your ultrasound had been sent off to the lab,” she explained.

“Yeah, but I thought they said that it would take up to twenty-four hours?”

“Yes, it can. That's correct, but your test results came back, and we need you to get to the hospital,” she urged.

“What's going on? Is the baby okay?” I asked. Hearing those words, Chris turned to look at me.

“We can't make that determining factor yet. Ms. Davis, we’re not sure why, but lab results show a very large amount of Roman chamomile in your bloodstream.”

“Roman chamomile? What the hell is that?” I asked.

“Well, it's mainly used on the skin, but can be ingested as well. It is a drug that was used years ago to cause women to miscarry that did not want to complete their pregnancy. Between that and the Yohimbe that was in your bloodstream, we think it's better that you go and get checked into a hospital immediately.”

“Okay. I'll do that right now. Thank you.”

I hung up the phone and looked at Chris in shock.

“What's going on?”

“The doctor said I need to get to the hospital. How the hell did Roman chamomile get in my system?”

“What's wrong with the baby?” he asked.

“She said that they found Roman chamomile in my blood work. From what she was saying, it's some kind of herb that causes women to miscarry.”

I felt myself beginning to panic and tried to calm my nerves.

“Baby, just breathe. I don't want you to get worked up,” Chris coaxed.

“Somebody is trying to kill me. Somebody’s tryin’ to kill my baby, Chris. That’s the only way this shit happened. Somebody’s tryin’ to kill my baby.”

I started crying and hyperventilating. Both Chris and Troy tried to grab me and calm me down, but it was too late. I was already past upset.

“We got to end this shit. I'm not about to have nobody fucking with my family,” Troy said.

“Come on. Let's just get her to the hospital,” Chris said.

“All right.”

They both grabbed my hands and walked me down the stairs. I was scared as hell.

“God, please let my baby be okay,” I prayed. We got in the car and hightailed it to hospital. I prayed the entire way.

*****

Chapter Thirty-Four

I'd been held up in the hospital for hours, and they had stuck me with so many needles that I looked like a damn pincushion. Chris was there with me, and of course, Troy had come along.

He didn't say much in the room, but the look on his face was scary. The more I looked at him, I could see my father in him.

"Baby, why don't you just go ahead and go to the club. You can't really do anything sitting here."

"No! Miracle, have you lost your damn mind? Hell no. I ain't going no damn where. I want these doctors to come in here and tell me what the hell is going on, and I want to make sure that you're good," he said.

"I'm sure it's fine. I mean, we heard the heartbeat and everything at the doctor's office," I reminded him.

"Yeah, but I want to know how the fuck you got that shit in your system," he barked.

"Me too. I don't know, but I haven't done anything differently, and they said that it was an herb. Maybe it was from one of the restaurants I've eaten at or something?" I asked, thinking on it.

"I know they warned me about eating cold cuts and stuff like that because of the listeria, but they never really said anything about me having to check for Yohimbe or this damn Roman chamomile shit. Where the hell do you even get that kind of shit from anyway?"

"I don't know, but I'ma damn sure find out. Where the fuck are these doctors anyway?"

"Just relax. They base it off severity," I told him. About twenty minutes later, one of the nurses came in.

"Okay, so we ran several tests. Now, unfortunately, because of the amount that was in your bloodstream, it's going to be difficult to tell if you will be able to carry the baby to term."

"What? But, just a few hours ago, everything was fine, and we were looking at the ultrasound and listening to the baby's heartbeat," I told her.

"That may very well be true, and I'm not saying that you won't carry full term, but Ms. Davis, you had an extremely high amount in your system, honey. Do you know how you ingested it?"

"No! I didn't even know I had it in my system until they called me from the doctor's office. Is there something that I can take to flush it out? Is there a way for me to take care of it?" I asked, hopeful.

"At this point, you just have to wait and see. Typically, with this type of herb, it can cause a miscarriage or birth defects. Of course, we hope that that doesn't happen, but you just have to kind of watch for the signs."

"What signs?"

"Well, as far as the miscarriage, any spotting or bleeding that you may have, you need to get to the hospital immediately, because it could be that you miscarried."

"And you'll be able to stop the bleeding?" I asked.

"No… unfortunately not, but at least we'll be able to test here in the hospital."

"So basically… if I start bleeding, I lose my baby… fucking great."

"I understand that this is a little stressful right now, "she said, trying to soothe me and calm me down.

"Really? You understand? Are you pregnant?" I asked.

“No, ma'am, I was just—”

Chris stepped forward and stepped in between the two of us.

“I'm sorry. Do you mind giving us a few minutes?”

“No problem. I’m going to go see about finding her doctor.”

“Thank you,” he said. She left, and he turned his attention to me.

“Look, Miracle… I need you to calm down, okay?”

“Chris, you can't be fucking serious right now. You and I both know that somebody did that shit on purpose, and you really think I'ma sit here and be calm when there is a possibility of losing our baby? Do you really think that I can be calm right now? It's some mothafucka walking around here that is determined to take out my entire family! I lost my father, my mother pops the fuck out the blue, and I found out I have a half-brother-boyfriend for over a year, and nobody bothered to tell me. Then today, I found out that I have an uncle, and now, I end up here in the damn emergency room, because somebody wants to kill us!

Chris whoever the hell this is has the feds in their pocket. Do you know that they were following us? The day that Troy hit us with his car was because the feds were following us; the same feds who had us in their custody all of those months, the same feds who were at the courthouse the day that the shooting happened, the same feds who supposedly shot at us, the same fucking feds who heard us talking all the time about what the hell we were going to do when we got the fuck out of Texas and are probably in Atlanta waiting on us right now, the very same feds who could have easily gotten access to my shit and fucking poisoned me!

Fuck you, Chris. I'm not going to stay calm. I'm far from calm right now. I'm pissed because of all this bullshit that's going on… because of whoever this mysterious person is, my life is destroyed, and my baby may die!" I yelled.

"That's my baby too! You're not the only one affected by this shit, or have you forgotten? Hello! My ass is the one out here trying to fucking take care of you and make sure you're straight. You don't think that I ain't worried about our kid? You don't think I want to go fuck these mothafuckas up that caused all of this shit?"

"I don't know, but all I know is for the last two years, everything has been messed the hell up, and I can't trust nobody!" I cried out.

"Oh… so now you can't trust me?" he asked in disbelief.

"I don't know, Chris. I don't know who the fuck I can trust. All I know is since day damn one… since I met you and since I meant Black, my life ain't been nothing but drama. I swear to God… sometimes, I wish I had never started questioning who the fuck killed my daddy. Maybe it was easier for me to be oblivious and just think that it was some random act, 'cause if I did, maybe I wouldn't be dealing with all of his bull now. Maybe my brother would still be alive. Maybe I wouldn't have my friends betray me. Maybe I wouldn't have had to cover for you and what the fuck you did!" I said.

His eyes turned dark, and I knew I had taken it too far. I damn sure couldn't talk. Yeah, he killed Whitney, but I had turned around and did the same with Patricia, if not worse.

"I'm not the one that killed a five-year-old little girl, remember?" he growled. My mouth dropped open, and Troy went to close the door.

"Okay… you two need to chill the hell out before somebody hears y'all. Y'all ain't alone, and if a fed would've heard that shit, y'all would've been locked the fuck up. Now what the fuck are y'all talking about?"

"Nothing," I said turning away from them.

"Nah, go ahead… since you can't trust me. Go ahead and keep it up. Hell… for all you know, I could be the bad guy. Go ahead and tell your uncle how I killed Whitney because of the fact that she was constantly on my ass, forcing me to fuck her bird ass. Go ahead and tell him how you shot Patrician and set her and her house on fire."

He was furious as he paced back and forth.

"You can come at me all you want, Miracle. You can try to talk to me like I'm one of these random ass niggas, but we both know what the fuck I've done for both of us… not just you. I was right there in the basement with your ass when Goody's ass pulled the trigger. If it wasn't for me, your ass would be dead," he reminded me. I knew I had taken it way too far. I knew Chris was hurt by what I said, but I was trying to save face.

"Okay. Right now, you just need to calm the hell down. Now Chris, we need to go handle this while she's here. I think I know who it might be," Troy spoke.

"Who?" I asked.

"Well, I know for sure that one of the two agents that was there at the courthouse is on the payroll. When I used to run for Eddie back in the day, he told me about how he knew Goody was doing some shady shit on his own on the side, so he hired this suit named Perry to keep an eye on what was going on inside the agency. If I could go holla at him, then I can find out about this other nigga," he explained.

"I'm going with you," I said.

"No the fuck you not," Chris barked, looking at me like I was deranged.

"Miracle, for once, listen to what the fuck somebody else got to say. Sit your ass down, and stay here at the damn hospital. That's the safest thing for you to do. For once, you're gonna keep your nose out of it," he fussed. I wanted to argue with him, but I knew he was right.

"Please, don't go out there and do anything stupid," I said after a few minutes of silence.

"I'm not. I just want to get this shit handled so that we can get the hell out of here, alright? If we have to leave tomorrow, then so be it. I'ma leave my strap with you."

"No… take it. Mine is in my purse," I told him. He nodded his head.

"Look… I'ma have my phone on me, so if you need anything, or if anything happens, or if anything changes, just hit me," he ordered.

"Chris… baby, please be careful. I'm sorry," I said, whispering. He walked over, leaned close to me, and kissed me.

"Don't even worry about it. You can make it up to me later."

He half smiled. I put my lips on his, and for a few minutes, I felt at ease before he got ready to leave.

"Now look, baby girl, I know you're smart and everything, so pay attention to your surroundings. They will probably be watching from a distance, but will more than likely be in here somewhere. The minute you see some shit that don't look right, don't draw attention to yourself, but get somewhere where there's lots of people, and take your piece," Troy said.

"I got you. Y'all just be careful," I said.

"Oh, we will be," Troy responded.

"Can't say the same for these niggas," Chris spoke up. They walked out the door, and I sat there, once again, by myself. I tried to replay everything in my mind. What the hell did I miss? What was I not seeing? How was there another person involved, and I had no knowledge as to who it was?

I thought back to the conversations that Chris and I had around the agents. I couldn't think of anybody that paid any extra attention or even really spoke to us. The only one that I was cool with was Connor, and it was because he had a daughter my age, so I would give him advice on how to talk to her, but he didn't seem like he was the type that would be capable of something like this. Plus, I hadn't really said anything in front of him, but it was something that I was clearly missing.

A nurse came in and brought me some medicine to make me feel better.

"Alright, now this might make you a little sleepy," she warned.

"Is it the Phenergan stuff again?" I asked.

"Yep, but it'll stop the nauseous feeling, and it'll let you get some much-needed rest. You really do need to do that… Where did your boyfriend go?"

"Oh, he went to go handle some business, but he'll be back in a little bit."

"Okay. Well, your call button is right here, and here's the remote for the TV. If you need anything, just hit that, and we'll be right outside. I'm going to come check on you in about two to three hours just to make sure that everything is okay."

"Okay. Thank you," I said.

"Not a problem."

She walked out of the door, and I laid back, flipping through the channels. I didn't really want to take the Phenergan again, but I knew that it would help me to calm down, and it would stop me from feeling like I had to throw up.

I just wanted to make sure that anything else that was in my body was not going to hurt me or the baby. Of course, she was right when she said that it would make me tired, because my eyes got heavy, and quick. I heard my phone ringing, but I couldn't open my eyes long enough to look and see who it was. I was so damn sleepy. Within seconds, I was out like a light.

I woke up a few hours later feeling like my body had been hit by a truck. I must have slept hard. I could tell somebody else was in the room with me, but I just couldn't focus. I could hear their voice. It was my mother.

"Somebody needs to take care of it now. Why the fuck is he still alive?"

Who was she talking to? Was I dreaming this shit? There was no way that this could be a dream. No, I was dreaming. I couldn't open my eyes, therefore, I was dreaming. That's what it was. I was having a dream. I guess it was because this time when I tried to open my eyes, I saw my mother sitting in the chair, watching television.

"Hey, sweetness."

She smiled warmly.

"How are you feeling?"

I opened my mouth, but it was extremely dry.

"Oh, hold on. I'll get you some water."

She walked over to the other side of the room and poured me a cup. I drank it quickly and opened my mouth to speak.

"How'd you know I was here?" I asked.

"Well, I called your phone a couple of times, and one of the nurses answered when I called. She told me that you were here. Why didn't you call me to tell me what was going on? I know we're not close, sweetheart, but I thought maybe you would at least let me know what was going on with my grandchild. Are you okay? What happened?"

"Somehow I ingested poison," I told her. I didn't give her all of the details, because I wasn't sure what exactly was going on.

"Oh my God!"

She gasped.

"Miracle, why would you do that?"

"I didn't do it on purpose. Somebody has been trying to poison me," I said, correcting her.

"Who would do that?" she asked.

"I don't know."

It was then that I remembered the conversation that I heard earlier. I needed to know if it was a dream.

"How long have you been here?" I asked.

"Just a few minutes… maybe fifteen. Why? What's wrong?"

"Nothing… I thought I heard you talking on the phone earlier," I told her.

"No… not me. I just sat down a couple minutes ago. You've been sleep this whole time. You can ask one of the nurses if you want."

"No, that's okay."

"I'm going to go talk to one of your nurses and let her know that you're awake. She said something about wanting to look at you and check your vitals or something."

"Okay," I replied. She got up and walked out of the room, and I shook my head. I clearly was tripping. I don't know why I was imagining the shit that I was, but I wasn't about to turn completely crazy either. I looked around for my cell phone and couldn't find it. I must have left it in my purse. I would get up in a minute, but I was too tired.

My mother walked in a few minutes later with a nurse that I hadn't seen before.

"Hello, honey. My name is Yasha. I'm taking over. It's a shift change, so you'll have me for the next twelve hours," she told me when she saw my confusion.

"Oh okay, so um… you think I can get some juice or something?" I asked.

"Sure. Let me check your IV's and everything," she answered.

"Okay."

I looked at my mother.

"Do you have my cell phone?"

"Oh, yes. I'm sorry, honey. I had it in my lap earlier when I came in. I think I walked outside with it, but yes… here you go."

She handed me my phone, and I checked to see if I had any messages from Chris. I didn't see any, so I figured everything was fine. I looked over at the nurse who was changing my IV bags. I noticed that she was staring at my mother, and something in me was saying that something was wrong. My alarms started ringing, and I thought of Troy's warning.

"I have to go to the bathroom," I said, trying to get up.

"Okay, well just a second," Yasha said. She quickly changed the bags, and I saw her pull a needle out of her pocket, trying to put in the IV.

"What are you putting in there?" I asked, trying not to let her know that I was panicked.

“Nothing. It's just a little bit of saline,” she said.

“Okay… well before you do that, can we check with the doctor please?” I asked. I was trying to sit up, but now, both she and my mother were pushing me back down.

“Miracle… honey, why don't you just lay down and let her do her job?” she urged.

“Because I want to talk to the doctor!” I shouted. My mother became significantly strong and shoved me back down. I felt a needle pierce my neck. I reached out to grab her, but everything went black.

*****

Chapter Thirty-Six

I woke up on a concrete slab in what appeared to be an empty factory. I was tied to a rusty pole, and the place looked abandoned and condemned. I could tell, because the concrete slab looked like something that you would see on an episode of *The Wire*.

What happened? I tried to remember as I felt dizzy. I looked around, and I couldn't see anybody.

"Hey, sleepy head," I heard. The minute that I recognized the voice, anger flooded my body. The memories of me being in the hospital came flooding back. I began to struggle to try to break free, but I was bound and unable to move… not again. This shit couldn't be happening again. I tried to think about everything that happened right before I blacked out. That was when I remembered the nurse stuck me in my damn neck.

"Help! Somebody help me!" I screamed.

"Sorry, sweetie, but no one can hear you."

I looked up to see Tiana, the one I called my mother.

"Well, I tried to avoid this happening, Miracle," she said, walking toward me.

"But, you just don't know how to stay out of stuff. You could have moved to Atlanta and started a whole new life. I tried to tell you to just leave, and never look back, but you had to be hard headed," she chastised.

"I should have known that your ass was behind this shit. Seventeen years of you being gone, and then all of a sudden you pop up on some protective custody shit? Now it all makes sense."

I thought about everything that Troy had said about federal agents being in the pocket and how there was somebody higher up. I just never expected it to be my mother. This is why you can't trust nobody. I let this slip past me, because I let my emotions for having my mother back cloud my judgment.

"You did all of this? I don't believe this."

"It would have been a whole lot easier if you would have just minded your damn business, but you had to be playing fucking detective and shit… fucking up my money. I have plans, Miracle, and they don't involve you."

"Obviously… So, what… your plans were to kill my father and destroy my life? Was I that bad? Huh? What did I ever do to you? I went seventeen years thinking that you were dead. You could have did that shit without popping up into my life."

"I could have, but see… the little faux pas in my plan was because of you. There weren't supposed to be any witnesses left, but Goody got his feelings in the way and wanted to try to keep Black's ass alive," she explained.

"But that's your son!" I yelled. Tiana laughed hysterically.

"You are so gullible! No, it's not."

She continued to laugh.

"Please. I would never have a fucking baby with Goody. No, that was his bastard child, not mine. I just told the courts that, because I knew it was a more likely opportunity to convict. The minute that his ass got caught, he jeopardized every fucking thing that I had worked for, and you have no idea how hard it was to try to run an entire operation while in police custody."

She laughed.

"I had to be creative, but luckily for me, money is a powerful thing, and anybody will do anything for it, including police corruption."

"So, you had me thinking that Black was my brother, and he's actually not?" I said in complete disbelief.

"Nope, he's not. Had to make it believable. Don't you get that? But, it all worked in my favor," Tiana confirmed.

"So, was anything that you said to the courts true?" I pushed.

"Of course, dear. Goody did try to kill me back in the day, but not because of the fact that I was with your daddy. It was because of the fact that he tried to cross me, and I popped his ass in front of everyone. Goody was weak. He was just like your daddy. Only difference was that he had a little bit more sense to play the game. Your daddy didn't. Your daddy wanted to get out of the hustle and be legit… be on some Kumbaya shit, but I had gotten used to the lifestyle that I was living. I wasn't about to lose that for no want to be *Leave It To Beaver* mothafucka."

"So, you just walked away from me and your husband?" I said in disbelief.

"Pretty much."

She shrugged.

“But, don't take it personal. Money is money at the end of the day, and I knew your daddy would take care of you. The only reason I had you was so that he would stay hustling, but no. He wanted to all of a sudden be a law-abiding citizen, so he had to go, and Goody was going to be the one to execute that for me.

When the opportunity presented itself, I disappeared. I went to the police and concocted this whole story about how evil Goody was and how he tried to kill me. That part was true, but the only reason he tried to kill me is because I tried to kill his entire family,” she said with a smirk.

This bitch was bonafide crazy. I ain’t give a fuck if she was my mother or not. First chance I got, I was putting a bullet in her fuckin’ forehead.

“Sucks to hear the truth, huh? Like I said, love, don't take it personal. It's just a casualty.”

She paced the floor and shrugged.

“If it’s any consolation, I was actually planning on just letting you live your life, but then, you started asking so many questions and getting closer, so I had to do what I had to do. I thought that he would have been smart enough to take care of you on his own, but clearly, I was wrong. Although I have to admit… the fact that you were dating his son was rather interesting. I figured he would steer you off in the wrong direction, but once again, you returned. In the end, bang bang. Black went down anyway.”

“So you did all of this? You had me coming over to your house and talking about how you wanted a relationship with me and all of that, but the whole time, you were planning on getting rid of me."

"Not the entire time. I just had to find out what information you knew first. Now that I know, unfortunately, it doesn't look too good for you."

"And you don't think anybody is going to know? You took me from a fucking hospital. People are going to figure it out," I said.

"Not really. The nurse that came in there… Yasha? Yeah, that's somebody that has been working with me for quite a while. Matter of fact, she was a big help in getting you to the hospital. Well… her and your buddy."

I didn't understand what she was saying at first until it hit me that the girl was a nurse and had access to drugs.

"So, you're the one that drugged me?" I accused.

"Oh no… not me! I wasn't the one, but the one that did drug you… well, I'll let her talk to you. I know she's got a lot to say. Nikki!" she called out.

No! This bitch betrayed me again? Please let her be joking, but she wasn't. She walked in from a dark corner.

"You've got to be fucking kidding me!" I yelled. Nikki walked over with an expression on her face I couldn't read. I was pissed! I couldn't trust this hoe for shit!

"Go say hi to your friend," Tiana encouraged Nikki. Nikki walked toward me, and I wanted to spit on her.

"You's a bitch. After everything I fucking did for you, and you fucking drug me? You damn near killed my baby, you trifling ass, low-budget, stripping for WIC vouchers, ho ass bitch! I can't believe you. I actually thought that your ass had changed."

I wanted to cry. I was so mad.

"You better be fucking glad that I'm fucking tied up right now, hoe. Otherwise, your ass would be dead on sight."

She sniffed and tried to look tough.

"See… that's your problem, Miracle. You always want to throw it around as to what you can do and what others can't do. I'm so sick of you judging me. That's why Black was tired of fucking with you, because your ass became entitled."

"You making this about Black still? Black was my nigga… not yours! You fucked him behind my back. Hell yeah, I was entitled, hoe! You think I give a fuck about Black? Guess what? I don't. Is that why you did all of this shit… because of Black's ass?"

"No! I did this shit because you walk around here acting like you're better than everybody. You were in that fucking house with my ass too. The minute that you got the opportunity to get out, then you started acting like you were above everybody else. You didn't give a shit how I felt about Black after he died. You had moved on to Chris but still expected Black to be at your fingertips. I had to carry around his baby that I didn't even want."

"Bitch, didn't nobody tell you to have that baby! You can do whatever the fuck you wanted to. I didn't force you to do shit."

"Don't you get it? By me having his baby, that was a guaranteed check, but you fucked that up and ended up getting that nigga killed."

She sighed.

"I had a way out. If you had just left well enough alone, Black's ass would still be alive, and I would have been set, but no. You had to do shit your way. You had to be little miss nosey."

"It don't give you an excuse to fucking put drugs in my damn body! You tried to kill my baby!" I screamed.

"Come on now, Miracle. All that cooking I was doing?"

She laughed.

"You should have known something was up. Cooking every day? All I had to do was put it in each one of the meals you ate. I mean… I figured I'd kill your baby since you took mine."

"I hope you die a slow death," I growled.

"Alright… this shit is getting on my nerves," my mother spoke up.

I was pissed. I wanted to cry, but I was not about to let Nikki see me break.

"I promise you, on everything I love, if I make it out of here, I am going to fucking kill you. You have yet to know pain."

She walked up on me and smirked.

"Don't worry. When you die, I'll make sure I'm there for Chris for you."

I looked at her evil ass expression, and my heart sank.

"Ain't no way you making it up out of here alive without somebody getting suspicious," I said.

"She's right," my mother spoke up. Nikki turned around and looked at her confused.

"Huh?"

Pow!

I didn't even see the gun in my mother's hand. It was mine! She had shot Nikki square in between the eyes, and I screamed from fear as Nikki's body dropped to the floor.

"Told her… she's too damn emotional and runs her mouth too much. That's all she did was yap about that boy. But, you were right. There was no way she was going to be able to make it out of here without somebody questioning her, and to be honest, I got a feeling that if the police would have gotten to her, she would have told everything."

"So?" I said.

"So that's why you killed her," she said, waving my gun in the air.

"They're going to find you. Once Chris sees that I'm not answering my phone, he's gonna track my phone, and he's going to find you here," I told her.

"Already taken care of, honey. You're not talking to an amateur. Your uncle Troy took care of Chris's ass a long time ago. He handled him while we were at the hospital."

I knew I heard her on the phone when I was waking up.

"But, he's on the way here now. Once he gets here, I can take care of him, and then you two will be history. All I have to do is disappear, and the cops will think that Troy was behind everything… quite simple, actually… flawless, if I do say so myself. Matter of fact, let me see if I can call him and find out where he is."

She pulled out her phone and hit a button, dialing a number.

"Hey," she said after a few seconds.

"Did you take care of that for me?"

She paused and nodded her head.

"Alright, well I have the other one here. Hurry up so that we can get this taken care of and get out before anybody notices."

She hung up the phone and turned her attention back to me.

"This is going together so great! Your little baby daddy is taken care of, so all I have to do is get rid of you, and I am out."

Hearing that Chris was gone, I tried as hard as I could to hold it together, but I broke down. I didn't even get a chance to say goodbye to him. All I could think about was the last conversation we had and how I put all the blame on him.

If we were in a movie, this would be the part where I threw myself over his body and started crying hysterically, or he would come in and save the day, but neither of those was happening. A part of me wanted to feel like maybe she was lying and just playing a big trick. Maybe he was alive, but I didn't know this woman. I didn't know what to think. I just knew I didn't want to die like this, but I was tired of fighting. I had nothing left.

"You know what? Just go ahead and kill me now. I'm tired of waiting. I've lost everything… everything. Because of all of y'all wanting to rule the world, you took everything that I love. I was innocent! I was a kid… a kid born to a fucked-up family. I could never be like that. I could never give birth to a child and then just completely disregard them. I could never set my child up to be killed. That's not me. I could never choose my own life over that of my child's. So, you know what? Thank you. Thank you for walking away when you did, because you left me with someone that had human decency… someone who actually cared."

Tears were streaming down my face from anger, but I didn't want to stop.

"And I thought Goody was the bad guy."

I shook my head.

"So, if that's what you want to do, then just go ahead and do it, because what else do I have? At least then, I won't have to deal with the drama. At least then, I won't have to deal with constantly wondering who's trying to kill me or who did what to who. So what the fuck are you waiting on?"

The doors opened, and Troy walked in with somebody I had never seen.

"It took you long enough! I had to sit here and listen to this damn girl nagging, complaining, crying, and all of her melodramatic shit! What the fuck took you so long?"

"I had to get rid of the body. The lil' nigga caught on to what was going on and actually tried to fight back."

Troy looked over at me.

“I see you got her ass here.”

“Yeah, I thought she would have caught on a long time ago, but she figured it out when she woke up.”

“Damn… Nikki didn't give her enough of the drug to kill her ass like I thought,” Troy observed.

“She wanted to act like she didn't want to do it, but when she had that damn money in her hands, she was all for it… had me acting like I gave a shit about that little bastard that she gave birth to.”

Dear God, please tell me she didn't kill the baby.

“Well, what did you do with the baby?” he asked.

“I dropped his ass off at a fire station and kept going,” she said and laughed.

“I barely stopped the damn car. Shit, I didn’t even want my own fucking kid. What makes you think I want some snot nosed boy?”

Thank God she at least had the decency to drop him off with someone that could get him somewhere safe, but hearing her words, this bitch made me want to jump out this chair.

“So what you going to do with her?” he asked.

“The better question is why the fuck is he here?” she asked, motioning to the other guy.

“Perry? Because he needs to help us get rid of all of this shit and create a clean alibi. You created this big ass shit storm, so right now, you need to be thanking me for cleaning up your mess. If it wasn't for you, my ass could have stayed hidden, and they never would have known who the fuck I was."

He sneered. I looked at Troy with disgust. I forgot that he was on her side… can't trust no fucking body.

"No, your nosy ass niece is the reason for this shit. I could have been in Anguilla by now, but she got too damn close, and Goody's ass didn't do what the fuck he was supposed to do. Don't put that shit on me. You should've handle this shit years ago."

"I did what I was supposed to do, but then yo' stupid ass got caught up, and I ended up getting locked up, taking the fall."

"Look, we need to just go ahead and get this shit handled," the other guy said, speaking up.

Looking closely, I saw that it was the agent that was at the courthouse that day. I'm assuming that this was the one that Troy was talking about… Perry. I had never really had any communication with him, but he was always there. I guess somewhat of what she said was true.

"Let's just get rid of the girl, get rid of these bodies, and get the fuck out of here, because soon, the trouble will start coming my way, and the alibis will only stick in the short time frame. I'm not going to be able to cover for you all if it gets out of the time frame.

This was it. This would be my last few moments. This was how my story would end.

"Troy, grab the girl, and go put her in the trunk with ol' boy. Time is kind of winding down, so it's gonna be easier to get shit done outside of here. Take the car about a mile down, and there's a ditch already dug up. Dump the bodies, burn them shits, and ditch the car a few miles away. When you get ready to ditch the car, it's already bleach in the back seat. Make sure it burns. Tiana, you need to get out of here, and let us handle it," he said.

"Why?" she questioned, suspiciously.

"The less blood the better, right now. It's gonna support your alibi, so trust me on this. If it gives you satisfaction, ride with Troy. Let him shoot the girl and burn 'em."

This was my so-called family talking about me like I wasn't here. I wondered if they even saw me sitting on the floor. I was going to die at the hands of mothafuckas that should have been protecting me.

"Fine… whatever. Just hurry the hell up."

Troy walked toward me, and I had to think quickly. I knew there was no way I was going to be able to walk out of here with three of them armed, and the only thing I could think of was to try to get Troy's gun and turn it on my mother, but the likelihood of me overpowering him wasn't going to happen.

He pulled his knife out and began to cut at the ties that had me in the chair.

"Listen to me…" he began to whisper.

"…When I let you go, I'ma grab your arm and drag you out of here, so play along like you're being drug. The minute that we get in the car and we get out of sight, you run, and you go call the police. I'm not going to kill you. I'm going to kill her, but you need to make sure that you play along. You understand me?"

I said nothing, because Tiana was within earshot. I didn't know if I could believe him.

"What the hell is taking you so long over there, Troy?" I heard her ask.

"I'm cutting off all these fucking ties y'all put on her," he snapped back, now quickly cutting.

"Just trust me, Miracle. I'm going to get you out of here. Perry is on our side… not hers, so play along," he whispered.

He grabbed me by my arm as he said he would, and I stood up. A gun fired, and we both jumped. Perry's body fell to the ground, and blood began to pour out of his body. It was getting to the point that I had seen so many people killed, I didn't even react anymore.

"Nigga, did you think I was stupid? I already knew what the fuck was up," she said, her gun now aimed on us. Troy had his gun on her, and I stood in the middle.

"See, Troy, you forget… I know how you fucking operate. Sadly, after all these years, it's the exact same."

She shook her head.

"I know that you went to go see Miracle. I know about the conversations that you and Perry had, but I stay two steps ahead. You think I'm just going to let you come in like the hero and save the day? You think I'ma let you take everything that I worked for? Hell no. I'll get rid of you, just like I got rid of Goody, and just like I got rid of your brother," she warned.

The door burst open, and bullets began to ring out. I fell to the ground, praying that one of them didn't hit me. God must have not heard my prayers, because I felt a burning pain in my arm seconds later.

"Ahhhh!" I cried out. I couldn't run anywhere, because the warehouse was practically empty, so there was nowhere for me to hide. Tiana and Troy began to shoot at each other, and I watched Troy's body drop to the ground. He looked at me with the same hurting look in his eyes as my father did the day that he died. There was someone else in the room shooting. I just didn't know who.

The room was starting to spin, and I was getting extremely dizzy. The pain that I was feeling was taking over, and I tried to pay attention to what was going on around me. I heard Tiana scream, and looked to see her body drop. I heard another female's voice along with footsteps and began to panic.

"Dear God, save me," I prayed.

"Miracle. Come on, baby. Get up. Come on. Get up," she pleaded. I opened my eyes and saw Tori standing over me.

"Tori?" I asked, confused. I was losing it, clearly.

"Yeah, baby. I know you weren't expecting to see me, but we gon' get you out of here and get you help. Now hold on. Just stay with me," she urged. She called 911 on her phone, and that was the last thing I remembered before, once again, everything went black.

*****

Chapter Thirty-Seven

I opened my eyes to see that damn familiar ass bright light over my head. My ass is back in the damn hospital.

"Hey, nosy girl. I see you're finally awake," I heard. Tori stood over me with a look of worry and relief.

"You had us worried there for a second. You lost a lot of blood."

"What? How?"

"It's a long story," she said and smiled.

"But, you're safe now. It's over, Miracle. You're alive, and that's what matters."

"Troy, he was trying to save me. I was there, and he—" I whispered.

"I know," she said, stopping me.

"I wish I was able to get in there before then, but we had to be sure that Tiana was behind it."

"Who is we?" I asked, confused.

"They'll be back in a sec, but for now, you've got a little bit of recovery to go. The bullet hit your arm and travelled, unfortunately. The baby didn't make it, but you're young. You can have another baby."

I felt bad about losing my baby. I wish to God it would have made it, but I know it would have been hard.

"It wouldn't have felt right anyway," I said, feeling sad all over again.

"I know it would hurt having a child and not having Chris here. I can't believe they killed him," I whispered, beginning to get choked up.

"What?" she asked, frowning.

"What are you talking about, Miracle? Chris isn't dead," she stated.

"But, Troy and that Perry nigga said that he was dead," I argued.

"No, baby. Chris isn't dead. He's outside talking to the doctor."

"What!" I said, trying to sit up.

"Okay, whoa. Calm down. Relax a little bit. He'll be back in a second. Who did you think I was talking about when I said we?"

"Wait… I'm not understanding."

"Miracle, Chris contacted me a while ago and said that he was suspicious about your mom. He had a feeling that she had something to do with it, but he knew because you were emotional toward the situation that you weren't going to use your best judgment, so he had his boys keep an eye on everything. He knew what was going on. And, Goody had told me a while back that he had some agents that were blackmailing him, but he kept them paid, because he didn't want to go to jail. When Goody was killed, we put two and two together and figured out what was going on. Nobody thought that I would know anything, because they thought I left for Houston. I did, but I left and started doing some digging. Chris just didn't want to tell you, because he knew that your nosey ass was going to try to take care of it yourself," she teased.

"So, all of his time… he knew?" I asked.

"Yeah. I knew."

I turned my head to the door and saw Chris standing with flowers and balloons.

"Oh my God," I cried, tears flowing.

“Chris! I thought you were dead! They said you were dead.”

“Come on, now. You know me better than that. I’ve got to stay two steps ahead.”

“You gotta come up with a new phrase.”

I laughed, thinking about how my mother said that very same thing that night.

“Why didn't you tell me about your suspicions, Chris? I was so scared. When Perry said that they had shot you—“

“I know.”

He nodded.

“Troy filled me in on what was going on. Troy was a good dude, but he was caught up with trying to catch her in the act. He was actually helping me the whole time.”

“So, you already knew what was going down when he showed up at the hotel?” I asked.

“Yeah, I just didn't know everything, but when he came to the hotel, the reason was supposed to keep you from going to your mother's house to give me time to dig. I had gone through Nikki's neighborhood one day and saw Tiana leaving, so I knew something was up, especially seeing as how she said to you that she was excited to meet her. That's when I knew that something wasn’t right. When I questioned Nikki, she started stuttering and shit. She had been telling Nikki to do what she needed.”

“Like the whole Roman chamomile thing?” I asked.

“Yeah, she had her putting it in all the food she had been making. She was going to try to kill you and make it look like an accident. I found that out hours after Nikki got snatched.”

"Chris… baby, I'm sorry. The way that I talked to you before you left… I'm so sorry."

"I'm sorry that I wasn't there. The plan was for us to get her before she even got to the hospital. I don't know how she knew, but she figured it out. She told Troy to get rid of me, and I just laid low."

"But Perry said there was a body in the trunk," I reminded him.

"Yeah, but it wasn't mine."

"So then whose was it?" I asked.

"Don't worry about it. See, you being nosey again," Tori spoke up.

"Just know that it's over."

"Oh, I will never be nosey again! But, is it really?" I asked.

"Yes," she replied, grabbing my hand.

"It's over."

I looked at Chris.

"Everybody is gone, including the baby," I said.

"I know, babe, but it's me and you. It has always been me and you."

"I'm sorry about the shit that I said the other day," I told him.

I felt myself about to cry again.

"Hey, what I tell you about that sensitive stuff? Thugs don't cry," he teased.

"Shut up."

I laughed.

“But no, Chris, really... Everybody is gone. It just seems like everybody was out for themselves. Everybody was corrupt. Mom, Nikki, Perry... How can I trust anything that anybody says?”

“Well, I know that Goody damn sure wasn't an angel, but I know that because of Tiana. He spent many years trying to be something that he wasn't. He and your pops were tight, and she drove a wedge between them. Ultimately, he lost his life because of that bitch, so even though that’s your mother, Miracle, I'm not sorry that her ass is dead,” Tori said.

“Neither am I. Just ‘cause she was my mama, don’t mean anything. Trust me, I don't even think she gave a damn about me anyway. I'm glad she's gone. Good riddance.”

I stopped, thinking about my uncle.

“I just hate that Troy is gone. I would have liked to have gotten to know him,” I said, thinking about the look on his face as he died in front of me.

“Yeah…” Chris said, his head down.

“About that… Troy is not dead.”

“Huh?” I asked.

“He's not dead, but he's been taking care of.”

“Chris, what in the hell are you talking about? Wait, where is he?”

“Troy couldn't be caught. Perry had him on tape with some grimy shit. Tiana set it up so that if something happened, the tape would surface. If he had been caught, he would have gone back to prison, so I had him taken care of. He's going to make it. Once I get my insider to find the damn tape and destroy it, he’ll be good,” he promised.

“Oh,” I said.

"Okay. Don't worry. You'll be able to see him at some at some point, but right now, it's better that he lays low," he told me.

"I feel you," I said. I didn't know where he was, but I was just glad he was okay. At least I had one family member left that I was connected to. And even if it was an uncle that I really didn't know, it was a piece of my dad… a good piece.

"There's one more problem… Junior. I heard Tiana tell Troy that she dropped him off at a fire station."

"It's okay. I already got him. I knew that you were going to flip out if you didn't get him anyway," he joked.

"Chris, Black wasn't really my brother. Tiana lied about that. She made that whole thing up in court, knowing that Goody wasn't going to say anything about it," I blurted out.

"She had him around her finger from day one. I heard and saw more than you all thought. He knew there was no way for him to avoid going to prison," Tori admitted.

"But he didn't know that she was going to have him killed when he got there," I told him.

"Well, from now on, all we need to be worried about is our new life," he encouraged.

"That's for sure," I said.

"And as soon as you're able to be out of here, we're going home."

"So, we're still moving to Atlanta?" I asked.

"Even better... I got a surprise for you."

And, that he did.

*****

The next two weeks, I spent in the hospital, and they eventually let me go home. The day that I got discharged, I thought we were going to go back to a hotel or something, but we didn't. He picked me up, and he had Junior with him. Even though we had lost our baby and weren't planning on having any anytime soon, we were going to raise Junior as ours. He deserved to have a loving mother and father. He was going to get what we didn't. I promised myself that he would never have to go through the foster care system, have to worry about having a crackhead for a mother, or a father that could get killed at any moment.

"You ready to start our life together?" he asked as we drove to the airport.

"Where we going?" I asked, being nosey. Old habits die hard.

"Well, I was thinking maybe we could go where the snowbirds go," he replied with a grin.

"We're going to Florida?"

"Yep… got a house already waiting on us," he told me. I smiled from ear to ear. I swear I love this nigga. As savage as he was in the streets, he was a teddy bear when it came to me.

"What you over there grinning about?" he asked.

"Just thinking about how much I love my savage man," I admitted.

"Such a nerd," he laughed. We gathered all of our things and headed inside the airport to start our new lives. Everything that had happened in Dallas was being left behind. We were finally going to have what I had been wanting since the day my dad died… a family. I couldn't have been happier.

Epilogue-One Year Later

Junior was ripping and running through the backyard, and I was chasing after him, trying to wear him out. It was close to his nap time, so I wanted him as tired as possible. Chris was on his way to the airport to go pick up my uncle Troy. I hadn't seen him since the day that everything went down at the warehouse when my crazy ass mom tried to kill me, so I was more than excited to see him. I had the entire house ready, and as soon as Junior was asleep, I was going to finish cooking.

Things had been great since we moved to Florida. This last year was bliss. Chris had bought us a house, and it was gorgeous. I went back to school and was two classes from finishing my bachelor's degree. I decided that I was going to work in social services. After everything that I had been through, I could never imagine another child having to go through that.

Chris was hustling when we first got to Florida, but he kept his promise of hustling for no more than six months. He took some of the money that we had stashed to open up a night club. He was just like my father, ambitious and driven, and he had one of the hottest nightclubs in Tampa, Florida. Money definitely wasn't an issue. We had my twenty-first birthday party there, and it was the talk of the town. We had taken Junior and spent the weekend in Tampa. He surprised me with a party at the club.

At twenty-three, he wasn't doing bad for himself. We hadn't gotten married or anything like that. That was the furthest thing from my mind. I was just enjoying life and enjoying the fact that I was finally happy. I'd stopped having the nightmares about daddy dying and was sleeping peacefully. Junior was growing like a weed, and although it hurt me to think about what his mother did, I always reminded him of who she was.

They never found my mother or Perry's bodies. Nikki's body was found in the projects, but because of her record, the authorities wrote it off as prostitution and that was that. I was scared for the longest that because they couldn't find my mother's body that she would pop up, but Chris and Tori both assured me that would never happen.

After another ten minutes of running, Junior got sleepy and began to fuss.

"Alright… come on, munchkin," I said picking him up and carrying him in the house. We walked inside, and I carried him upstairs to lay him down for his nap. We had a pretty nice sized house. It was four bedrooms and three baths… nothing too big, but big enough for us. Junior had his own room, Chris had a man cave, and the spare bedroom was everything from a study room to our personal adult play room. We said that eventually it would be a nursery for a baby.

We talked about having another baby, but I just wanted to take my time with it. After all, I was still young. I had a lot of living to do, especially if I wanted to start my career as a social worker.

My phone buzzed as I walked around the kitchen, preparing lunch, and I looked to see Myesha's name on the caller ID. She and I were back talking. I found out that the reason why she became so distant was because of my mother. I thought it was because of the one little fuck that she had with Chris, but after a long drawn out conversation, I found out a lot of things that my mother was doing to her family that she never even told me about. My mother was the reason why Myesha got strung out on drugs in the first place.

Myesha had been abusing long before I knew about it, but she was doing much better. She graduated college, and she was about to move to DC to start her new job. She had surprised me at my birthday party. Myesha and I had been best friends since we were kids, so I was glad to have her back.

I heard the garage door open and hurried to straighten things up. Chris walked in, talking to Troy, and he walked over, giving me a kiss on the cheek.

"Hey, babe."

"Well hey, Ms. Nosey."

My uncle smiled.

"Y'all gon' stop calling me that."

I laughed, walking over to my uncle and giving him a big hug.

"Hey."

I grinned.

"How you been?"

"I've been doing good… Just laying low and making moves," he told me.

"Uh huh. Is it legit?" I laughed.

"Now you should know never to ask that, niece," he chuckled.

"You know what? You right," I quickly agreed. Being nosey had gotten me in too much trouble, so I was going to leave it alone.

"Oh, but I got a surprise for you," he said.

"Oh Lord."

I groaned.

"What?"

"Your uncle is getting married," he blurted out.

"What? Oh my God! Congratulations!" I said.

"Yeah, she's excited. I wasn't planning on it, but hey… when you've found the one, you've found the one."

He shrugged.

"Well, I can't wait to meet her! When are you getting married?"

"Next weekend in the Bahamas, so you know y'all got to be there."

"Next weekend!" I stammered.

"Like that soon? I mean, we'll be there of course, but wow!" I said.

"Next weekend? Okay yeah… I've got to meet this girl."

"Won't be hard. You already know her," he winked. My heart started beating. This nigga better not say my mother or no crazy shit like that. I had to keep my guard up and be prepared.

"Who?" I asked.

"She should be getting the rest of her stuff out the car," he told me.

"Oh, hell no," I said, running toward the door.

"I told you her ass was nosey," I heard Chris say.

"You damn right," I mumbled. I walked to the car, and my worry quickly disappeared. I burst out laughing when I saw Tori standing there.

"No way!"

I squealed.

"Really? You and my uncle? Oh my God!" I shrieked.

"Yeah, we wanted to surprise you."

Tori smiled.

"Well, you definitely did."

I laughed.

"Congratulations!" I said, hugging her.

"Thank you, sweet pea."

She giggled.

"I honestly wasn't expecting it, but Troy swept me off my feet. We kept in touch for obvious reasons and started dating, and then within six months, we were engaged. Me and the kids moved with him, and life has been good ever since," she filled me in.

"Wow," I said in awe. I was genuinely happy for her. She deserved it. Tori had never done anything but be good to me.

"So, where is the baby?" she asked.

"Oh, he's upstairs sleeping. I just put him down for a nap like twenty minutes ago," I told her.

"Well, the kids are going to be here in a couple of days, and we're going to do a destination wedding, so of course you know you and Chris and the baby have to be there with us. It's nothing too big, just close friends... not trying to have everybody in our business, obviously," she huffed.

"I feel you," I agreed.

"And who knows, maybe you and Chris will go ahead and tie the knot while you're there."

"That's doubtful."

I chuckled.

"I'm not trying to get married no time soon."

“You sure about that?” I heard Chris say. I turned around, and he had Junior beside him, holding a ring. I looked at Tori, and she gave me an apologetic look.

“Sorry,” she mouthed.

“Chris, what the hell are you doing?”

“Waiting on you to say yes,” he answered. I looked at him and shook my head. I couldn't believe he was putting me on the spot like that.

“Chris—“ I started.

“Miracle, just listen.”

He cut me off.

“Since I met you, I've had something for you that I haven’t had for any other female. I tried to deny it. I tried to ignore it, because we were in a messed-up situation, and we were both young and all that. I know that I kind of had a rough past, and I know we both did stuff that we not necessarily proud of, but you are the definition of a true ride or die chick. When it comes to these females these days, you the only loyal one I got on my team. You the sweet to my savage. Now, I'm not saying we got to go get married tomorrow or nothing like that. If you want to finish school and get started on your career first, I'm all for it. If you want to wait five years, then I'm all for it, but I'm not going to keep living with you as just my girlfriend. I'm going to make you my wife, so all you got to do is say yes.”

I looked at Tori and Troy who were grinning like peacocks.

“Girl, just say yes to this boy so that he can get up off his damn knees!” Tori laughed.

“Say yes, mommy,” Junior giggled. Hearing him call me that warmed my heart. This is what it was all about right here. How could I say no?

“Yes… Yes, I will marry you,” I whispered after few seconds of silence. Chris almost bounced up into the air as he swooped me up. Tori and Troy cheered. We grabbed Junior who was equally excited.

I couldn't believe it. I said yes! Miracle Davis, once a pampered princess, was in a relationship and raising a family. I had actually said yes. I was getting married. Of course it was going to be much later, but I never would have guessed this would have been my life three or four years ago. Life has a funny way of working out. I was happier than I ever imagined all because I fell for a savage.

Made in the USA
Columbia, SC
11 July 2025